NEW CITY
CHRONICLES

BOOK 1 – CATCHING A SPIDER

NEW CITY CHRONICLES

E.L. HENDRIX

New City Chronicles: Book 1—Catching a Spider

For information about this title or to order other books and/or electronic media, contact the publisher:

ISBN: 978-1-7354217-0-4 (print)
        978-1-7354217-1-1 (eBook)

To contact the author:
newcitychronicles.com

Printed in the United States of America

Cover and Interior design: 1106 Design

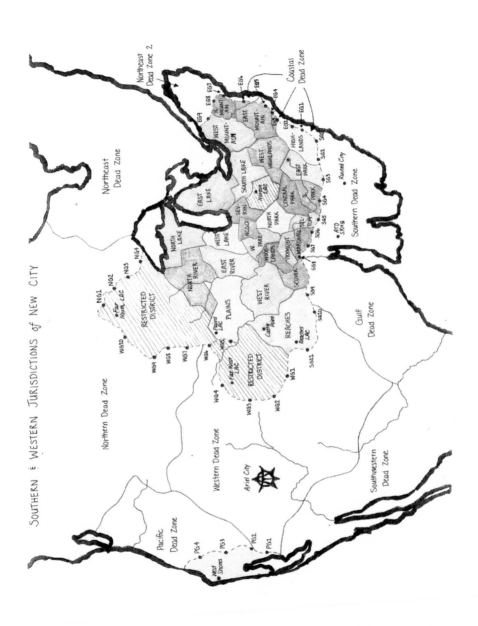

SOUTHERN & WESTERN JURISDICTIONS of NEW CITY

PROLOGUE

On October 30, 822 CE, Devan Elaniel appeared before his daughter, the witch Jennipa. At that time, he could still traverse the ethereal spheres and appear as a man, a woman, or even a beast, to anyone. It was an age of powerful magic, and Jennipa had summoned her father many times in the past to assist her.

"You were supposed to kill the girl—not try to conceive a child with her, you fool!" Jennipa sneered. "You heard Erafel's prophecy! Among her other abilities, she has the gift of sight. Now, give me the stone of fire. I have much work to do."

Elaniel handed the perfect red uncut diamond to Jennipa. He felt at his throat where the young girl Erafel had grasped him without even touching him. She was barely in her teens, but her powers were such that she could have easily crushed him.

"What is she? Tell me, Jennipa, how did this girl obtain such power on earth? Arianael killed Erafel's sister, but Erafel restored her life."

Jennipa glared at Elaniel. "I warned you she possessed miraculous abilities, but you didn't listen! Her powers don't originate from you. She has a much deeper connection to the ethereal spheres than you or I, perhaps even to the highest heaven. Why do you think I summoned you to put an end to her? I don't care how beautiful she is. The secret place where her name is hidden is a danger to you. She is no ordinary girl, and she is our enemy."

"I can't touch her again," Elaniel said. "You must send your own assassins to deal with her. Better yet, have the circle inflict a curse upon her."

"After what you have tried to do, it is not only Erafel you should be concerned with," Jennipa said. "Her descendants will destroy you. If she can't be killed, it's her prophecy about them which must be cursed. That's why I had you bring me this stone. The circle's curse can't make her barren or end her life. We have already tried; she is being protected."

"How can you curse a prophecy? And she wasn't protected. I would have sensed it," Elaniel said. "She can obviously protect herself, even from me."

"Listen carefully," Jennipa said. "This rare stone has powers that can span the generations. I will cast a curse with it tonight over this prophecy and over Erafel's descendants. Once it is done, have the stone placed in an amulet of pure gold. You must have it cut and polished with twenty-four facets. Upon each facet the name Erafel must be etched precisely. One day, you will possess Erafel and her powers. The stone will bear her name and her descendant will bear your child."

Elaniel scoffed. "What do you mean by 'one day'? Besides, a diamond can't be cut so perfectly. You've been partaking of your mushrooms again."

"There are those who now have skill with diamonds," Jennipa said, brushing off his concern. She continued, "Seven times seven generations will pass of this girl's descendants. In the last generation, one who possesses Erafel's hidden name will again appear on earth. You must find her and place the amulet with this stone around her neck. You will give her the name Erafel. She will become your queen and remain the most beautiful, powerful sorceress the world has ever seen. Her power will grow and become yours. She will restore what you will lose in the distant future, and through your firstborn male child with her you will gain even more power."

"Lose what?" Elaniel said. "And how will I know if I've found her? In so many generations her descendants could number in the thousands. There aren't enough carmelineals to keep track of them all."

"Knowledge will increase by then and you'll be able to find her," said Jennipa. "Ask Prince Pythorael what you will lose, for it is already written."

"That worrisome schemer is always triangulating events," Elaniel fumed.

"Let me remind you of what I saw on the day of Erafel's birth," Jennipa said. "Thirteen hundred years will pass until the sun and moon stand face to face with seven stars in the sky. A golden star falls, and the smallest red star will become the brightest one of all. It is a warning that if seven of them appear and find each other, one will willingly give her life for another. In this sphere, to sacrifice oneself for love is far more powerful than any magic. You should be well aware of that already and fear its potency. If they become one, they will defeat you."

"Jennipa, your prophecies are not known for their accuracy."

"Your doom is certain if you don't take the eldest one first," Jennipa continued, as if he hadn't spoken. "She is promised to you. Only in this way will you become godlike and immortal. Count forty-nine generations, beginning with her first daughter. The eldest must be a virgin and a fully mature woman, not some dainty child. She will remain perfect if she is taken at three sixes, sevens at the latest. If you fail, she'll destroy you. If she has sisters, they all must die, including everyone else in her family. If one becomes seven and seven become one Erafel's prophecy will prevail. You must carry out my instructions precisely to alter what is written against you."

"A virgin at that age? Girls marry much sooner than that."

"In the future many won't marry at all! Listen! Only when there is a convergence within her line will Erafel reappear. Be warned, Prince Pythorael will oppose you and ally himself with your enemies. He'll do this to reset the times and maintain the balance. You must also keep the carmelineals away from her. They will seek Erafel's power for themselves, and Pythorael may use them against you."

"Jennipa, *you* are a carmelineal. Should I not be concerned about you?"

She laughed. "As your daughter I will make no further transference. I will endow this stone with my own spiritual essence and power. I will be no more until we will become one. I will become Erafel when you give this stone to her descendant and consummate the bonding ritual with her. When this stone is placed around her neck Erafel's hidden name will become visible to you. You will see it with seven eyes and wings to fly. Be warned, if she escapes, she will crush us."

"May it be as you say, my daughter and my future queen." Elaniel bowed his head and disappeared into the ether.

* * * *

CENTURIES LATER...

It was now several decades since the formation of New City, which Devan Elaniel, the Archon, oversaw as the first worldwide state. New City had been established in the late twenty-first century of the old common era, several years after the Final War ended. (The New Common Era calendar was established to coincide with that event; January 1, Year 1, was the official date of the city's founding, or 01.01.01 NCE.)

The Final War and subsequent purges had reduced earth's population to less than two billion people and destroyed a third of earth's habitable lands. (They were inundated by the sea or contaminated by chemical, biological, or nuclear fallout.) Yet within decades, New City's boundaries expanded into areas that became habitable. At the time of this story, New City occupied over half of earth's remaining habitable zones. Areas outside the city walls were referred to as "Dead Zones" (DZs) and were thinly populated with small scattered settlements.

New City was divided into ten jurisdictions. The American continents comprised the Southern Jurisdiction (SJ). The SJ was concentrated in North America, where its most prosperous, productive districts were located. (South America was almost entirely restricted, and much of it remained a Dead Zone.) And although the SJ was New City's capital, Elaniel was making enormous expenditures to create a spectacular new capital in the Central Jurisdiction.

A small area of land on North America's west coast comprised the Western Jurisdiction. There was also one significant, undiscovered, place of refuge hidden within the Western DZ. There, a few million people lived outside the walls of any New City jurisdictional territory.

Europe encompassed the Northern Jurisdiction; the habitable zones of East Asia encompassed the Eastern. The Central Jurisdiction included large parts of the Middle East and North Africa. The habitable regions of Africa, Northern Asia, and the Pacific rim comprised New City's five less developed and less prosperous jurisdictions.

Each New City jurisdiction was surrounded by massive walls guarded by the military. These fortifications ostensibly kept DZ insurgents out of New City. Their real purpose, however, was to prevent New City residents from escaping to the DZs and freedom.

New City was ruled by the Archon, along with a small cabal of powerful individuals: Elaniel's inner circle and an elite group called the High Echelon. Additionally, several ultra-wealthy noble families with no governmental authority supported and collaborated with the Archon and his cabal to control New City.

Among these elite families, one held the title of Ēlantiel. By far the wealthiest and most powerful family in the world, they owned numerous luxurious palace-like homes across New City, including one in the exclusive enclave of the Government District (NCGD) in the Southern Jurisdiction.

This family developed New City's vast technology infrastructure. They also owned huge Labor Allocation Colonies; that is, slave colonies that terraformed the expansion of New City, built walls, and maintained much of New City's agricultural, energy, and transportation infrastructure.

The Ēlantiel also oversaw a massive (unpublicized) expansion of military weapons—AI-controlled UAVs (unmanned aerial vehicles) and robotic forces. It was the Archon's intention to ultimately eliminate the need for New City's human security forces (the NCSF).

The Ēlantiel's children, along with the children of the other noble families, were destined to inherit the great promise of New City. The sons of these noble families held the title of ēlar, while their daughters held the title of ēlan. These princes and princesses of New City were promised eternal life, to be forever young in a heaven on earth, which the Archon had planned for them. They were bred, raised, indoctrinated, and groomed to help guide humanity toward the goal of a perfect world, one which they would ultimately inhabit.

Even now, the ordinary people of New City lived in a seemingly pristine, comfortable world, free of crime. All public areas were beautiful and clean, and no one of any class went hungry. Medical services, ordinary virtual entertainment, and higher education were free or cost very little. Almost all human activities involving manual tasks were fully automated. What made this miraculous society possible was something most citizens of New City never imagined.

The "free" inhabitants of New City were unaware of the vast Labor Allocation Colony System. These slave colonies were kept out of sight within restricted zones and segregated areas of certain districts. Yet they provided much of the resources, energy, food, and raw materials for the remaining population.

Approximately 40 percent of the inhabitants of New City lived, worked, and died in these colonies. They were inhabited by the usual rabble of criminals, but also by those deemed to be ideologically, psychologically or physically deficient. (Most abnormalities termed genetic disorders were identified well before birth by screening techniques; such pregnancies were terminated.)

Nevertheless, many inhabitants, although not genetically deficient, were classified as genetic dissidents. These people were hunted. Once caught, they were sentenced to a life of slavery in a labor colony—or put to death.

There were three classifications of genetic dissidents. The largest group, Class 3 dissidents, exhibited traits that made them unsuitable for the Archon's Optimus Project directive; that is, they could not be controlled by the mandatory cognitive brain implants soon to be employed. The exact number of Class 3 dissidents was not known, but the Archon feared there could be millions.

Class 2 genetic dissidents were the direct descendants of enemies who had opposed the Archon before the Final War. For that reason alone, he was intent on destroying their families. However, corruption issues within New City's genetics database made it nearly impossible to identify all of them.

Class 1 genetic dissidents (the smallest group) were ruthlessly hunted by the Archon for purposes of extermination. They were not mentally deficient. On the contrary—they were a threat to his power. Class 1 dissidents possessed a remnant of an aberrant genetic trait the Archon desired to obtain; one that would give him unlimited power. He also knew these people were the descendants of his most bitter enemy before the Final War. This man was a descendant of Erafel. More than any other, his family was responsible for the loss of Elaniel's power in the ethereal realms. Elaniel had no choice but to annihilate them, except for the one girl born in the last generation who was promised to him according to Jennipa's prophecy.

Elaniel had been tracking the female descendants of Erafel for approximately 1,300 years. Erafel had been the most beautiful daughter of man Elaniel had ever encountered. Yet it was what he finally discovered within her DNA that was the key to his immortality; it would restore what he had lost just before the Final War.

Elaniel could no longer wait for blind chance that the girl he was searching for would be born naturally. His body was dying. Although he appeared to be a robust thirty-five-year-old, he had lived for nearly a century by transferring his essence to symbiont clones. Each time he transferred to another clone he became weaker; he was running out of time.

With recent remarkable advancements in genetics, the Archon's scientists identified the critical component of Erafel's genetic sequence he sought. At last, through ages of countless offspring, he had traced the secret of Erafel's alluring spiritual power. He referred to this as her hidden name. It was located on the X chromosome and referred to as the ATK15 gene, more commonly called K15.

Devan Elaniel now realized that through the scientific advancements in genetic manipulation he could create the girl's essence himself. If the prospective candidate had certain suitable traits, *he* could recreate Erafel's alluring name. With the right enhancement, he believed he could make his own Erafel to be the queen of his realm and the key to his immortality. With her he could restore the lost power that had been taken from him, and once again transcend the ethereal realms. Now he was on the brink of success.

His scientists had made him the perfect girl, and based on his calculations she would be of the forty-ninth and last generation of Erafel's descendants. This was his final chance to change his destiny. He was trapped in a spiraling labyrinth of death from which he desperately wanted to escape; this girl was his means to do so. He anxiously looked forward to the day when his new Erafel would come of age.

* * * *

Control over New City's "free" population was ultimately carried out by use of an extremely efficient and powerful worldwide computer network called LEOH. In conjunction with LEOH, security was enforced by a ruthless organization commonly referred to as "the Ministry" or the New City Ministry of Information Analysis (NCMIA). This government enforcement agency hunted down suspected enemies of the state and those deemed ideological, psychological, religious, or genetic dissidents.

Every free citizen was required by law to have either an external or implanted personal computing device (PCD). The PCD tracked their locations, everyone and everything they interacted with, and everything they said or did. This mountain of information was collected by LEOH for use by the Ministry. Most people were aware that they were continuously interacting with an interconnected global network. They didn't know or care that LEOH's AI was compiling extensive and elaborate security matrixes on them and everyone they'd ever known or associated with. They also were not aware that this included anyone they were related to.

LEOH's data matrix also included every individual's genetic code. Although the matrix had been designed for LEOH to contain the entire family tree of every free citizen of New City, flaws within the data persisted. The Ministry's Genetic Information Analysis Division (GIA) was dedicated to maintaining this massive genetic matrix. It constantly searched for traits that could result in an otherwise innocent person being identified as a genetic dissident and thus, a wanted criminal.

New City was a police state. Entire families disappeared in secret. It was as if the people had never existed. Ordinary citizens of New City received no trials; they had no rights which protected them and no system of justice. Only nobles or the elite citizens had access to justice or courts. Maintaining the perception that New City was the perfect place to live was the principal focus of the regime.

The "free" inhabitants were convinced New City was the most miraculous accomplishment humankind had ever achieved. It was a perfect society, after all. History proved it, propaganda promoted it, and persecution enforced it. It was heralded as the solution to humankind's age-old problems of being divided. New City was thus proclaimed to be the most enlightened society in history. LEOH, along with the Ministry made certain this was what everyone believed.

However, the deceptive façade of New City hid a labyrinth of horrors. Children were particularly vulnerable to this cruel, indifferent culture which devalued them. From birth, children were indoctrinated into a fantasy world, where they were taught almost everything was permissible, especially with regard to their sexuality.

Children who were institutionalized or were born in or sent to a labor allocation colony were especially at risk of being abused, experimented on, or sold into prostitution or the pornography industry. There were other forms of slavery in New City that operated apart from the Labor Allocation system, much of which was designed for the sadistic entertainment of others.

Even the noble families did not realize that their own promised paradise was a lie; that their doom was closely tied to the success of what they so diligently collaborated with the Archon to create. He ultimately had plans to remake humanity in his own image in a world where he would control every thought.

However, one girl—the Ēlantiel's daughter and his only ēlan—would eventually come to know everything. She was also Devan Elaniel's long awaited Erafel. She was believed to be the only successful outcome of the Archon's K15 initiative. To him she was perfect, the key to his immortality and to restore what he had lost.

Our story begins several decades after the establishment of New City. It tells the tale of a few brave individuals and their remarkable exploits to oppose the Archon, his henchmen, and the Ministry. It is also a story about hope and the faith of one young girl who believed she could change the world by doing one small thing: win the heart of a man.

Together they would capture a beautiful, venomous spider. In a web intended to bring New City to its knees, this cunning spider would ensnare a serpent in order to destroy the city's rulers, head to tail. What they would all accomplish would result in exposing New City for what it truly was—a deviant world of cruelty and unspeakable evil.

This is only the beginning …

GLOSSARY OF TERMS & ACRONYMS

AI – Artificial intelligence – LEOH runs on a complex array of AI algorithms based on a set of prime directives

Ariel City – Hidden city in the western Dead Zone (DZ) of North America

ATO – Ariel Tracers Organization – Assists Ministry security directive targets in escaping New City

Carmelineal – A being with the power to mimic people by taking their form and voices – They can also take possession of a person, including their memories

Cat 9 – Catenine – A short-term memory blocking serum

Citadel – The Archon refers to his numerous palaces and fortresses as citadels

CC – Computing Core – ATO version of a personal computing device—one without surveillance attributes

CCD – Central Control Division – Coordinates all NCMIA divisions across all New City Jurisdictions

CJ – Central Jurisdiction

Clarion – An adept individual specially trained in the art and science of advanced deductive analysis

Dedication Ceremony – Ēlans and ēlars go through multiple ritual dedication ceremonies for the Archon, at ages two, six, nine and twelve

DRM – Defection Recovery Ministry – Ministry division that recovers escaped fugitives in the DZs

DZ – Dead Zone – Areas outside the walls of New City

Erafel – Worn as a talisman, this rare red diamond is infused with arcane power and is a symbol of the title given to the Archon's intended mate – It was named after a girl the Archon encountered in 822 CE who had extraordinary gifts

ED – Entertainment display—a sophisticated virtual television

Final War – Worldwide conflict which took place before the establishment of New City

Formulation – An algorithm for retrieving and utilizing data stored within LEOH

FRS – Fleet Rail System – A highspeed magnetized pneumatic passenger train

Genetic Dissident – There are three classifications of genetic dissidents: Class 1 dissidents are descended from David Waters and in particular Erafel. Class 2 dissidents are directly descended from enemies who opposed the Archon before the final war – Class 3 dissidents exhibit aberrant traits which prevent them from being controlled through a direct mind implant

GIA – Genetic Information Analysis – Ministry division responsible for maintaining the genetics matrix

Gathering Storm / GS – A growing rebel faction in the southern DZ.

HE – High Echelon – Members are senior New City government officials, agency directors, governors, etc.

HES – Security service division of the High Echelon

HESF – High Echelon Special Forces – Elite security force for the High Echelon and NCIC

HESP – High Echelon Special Projects – Oversees top secret or special projects for the Archon

K15 – Genetics enhancement program sponsored by the NCIC to create the elusive ATK15 sequence

L2 – LEOH II – An updated version of LEOH being developed and deployed by NED Tech

LAC – Labor Allocation Colony – Where criminals and dissidents are permanently incarcerated into forced labor

LEOH – *name redacted* – Worldwide computer network and artificial intelligence system

Matrix – An array of data which creates an adjunct record to the database of information within LEOH

MDC – Molecular Data Compressor – A prototype miniaturized molecular storage and data collection device

NCCU/ CU – New City Currency Unit – CU is the standard monetary reference

NCDCI – New City Department of Corrections and Incarceration – Security for labor allocation colonies

NCGD – New City Government District

NCIC / IC – New City Inner Circle – High council of the Archon's most trusted senior officials and advisors

NCMIA – New City Ministry of Information and Analysis, known as the Ministry

NCSF – New City Security Forces – The general military and police force for New City

NED Tech – Norean Enterprise Development and Technology Company; it developed LEOH

NAS – New Accord Sanhedrin – religious ruling body of the Central Jurisdiction

NJ – Northern Jurisdiction

Optimus Project – The Archon's plan for reducing the world's population and fully integrating humanity with his LEOH system – and ultimately, himself

PCD – Personal computing device – All free citizens are required to carry one or be implanted with one

Phencol – A powerful truth serum used on interrogation subjects

QMC – Quantum Molecular Core – Uses DNA-based technology; the primary system platform for L2

SADEX score – Security Access Data Exchange score – determines what security credential level can access a LEOH data matrix

SCSA – Static Code Sequence Algorithm – A security feature linked to the Archon's DNA that allows him to control access to the the highest levels of the LEOH system

SD – Security Directive – Issued by LEOH or Ministry agents for the capture or arrest of individuals

SDPV – Self Driving Programmable Vehicle – Primary means of public/private transportation

SG – Sanctuary Gate – Any of the eleven southernmost gates into the DZ from the Southern Jurisdiction

SHO – Safehouse operator

SJ – Southern Jurisdiction

SRHQ – Southern Regional Headquarters – Secret ATO base in the southern DZ

Utilization – The process of compiling LEOH matrix data into a usable format, such as a security directive

VTH – Virtual terminal headset – Used to interface efficiently with LEOH through a PCD

LIST OF CHARACTERS

Baalan Arianael – aka Aros – Member of New City Inner Circle; enemy of Dalen Pythorael

Bob – Alias for the ATO guide Mark (Marcus Vincent Verigratu) meets in the DZ

Ellen Cavanaugh – Zack's physician and Jerome Haley's sister

Nick Chancery – Mercenary agent who works for the ATO

Alex Crenshaw – Executive Director of the Highlands Psychiatric Institute

Kirk Daniels – Escapee from New City

Tina Daniels – Young daughter of Kirk Daniels

Greg Duggar – ATO recruitment agent who acquired Venley

Charlotte Dylanis – Wife of Harold Dylanis

Dr. Harold Dylanis – Genetics researcher; ran the K15 project for the High Echelon

Devan Elaniel – Archon of New City

Dr. Simon Elgin – Worked with Dr. Dylanis on the K15 project; a spy for Dalen Pythorael

Erafel – A girl with extraordinary abilities who lived in 822 CE. Devan Elaniel would name a mystical stone after her and search for her descendants

Jerome Haley – Deputy Director of the CCD and former colleague and friend of Zack Waters

Jennipa – Fortune-telling witch who once foretold Devan Elaniel's future

Boris Jovanos – Kalina's colleague – Technician for the ATO

Gilliard McCaughey – Escapee from New City married to Kirk Daniel's sister

Teran Mythrael – aka Mythos – NCIC member and enemy of Dalen Pythorael

Carl Norean – Ēlantiel of New City – Father of Tabitha Norean

Kimerlin Norean – Kim – Tabitha's mother and wife of Ēlantiel Carl Norean

Stanley Norean – Norean ēlar and Tabitha's older brother

Tabitha Norean – Ēlantiel Carl Norean's daughter and his only ēlan

Talen Place – aka Tal Complaceal – Head of Special Projects for the High Echelon and NCIC member

Dalen Pythorael – aka Pythos – Director of the CCD and member of the NCIC

Nathan Prideil – Archon's security adjutant – appointed to head the NCIC – former carmelineal

Quillion – Commander in the *Gathering Storm* rebel faction

Lawrence Rogan – aka Larens Aroganceal – Head of Executive Security for the Ministry and NCIC member

Nicholas Santos – Former Deputy Director of the CCD to whom Zack Waters reported

Kalina Savadnetski – ATO technical expert in charge of exfil operations for the ATO at the SRHQ

Danette Statler – Safehouse operator for the ATO

Valen – Carmanis Valenceal – A carmineal who owes an oath of allegiance to Dalen Pythorael

Venley – Girl raised in a psychiatric institute since age five; rescued by the ATO at seventeen

Bergita and Tolar Verigratu – Mark's father Vincent's adoptive parents

Marcus Vincent Verigratu – Mark – son-in-law to Zachariah Waters

Vincent Verigratu – Mark's father – He was born Gabriel Waters and adopted by the Verigratu family

Ariel Waters – Ari – Zack Waters' great-granddaughter

Lara Waters – Ariel Waters' deceased mother

Neil Waters – Ariel Waters' deceased father

Robert Ryan Waters – Ryan – Zack Waters' brother's grandson

Zachariah Waters – Zack – Patriarch of the Waters Family and retired Deputy Director of the CCD

CHAPTER 1

A RARE JEWEL, A DISTANT PROMISE, AND A VISION IN THE NIGHT

07.01.45 NCE – CCD Headquarters – New City Government District, Southern Jurisdiction

The ill-tempered gray-haired CCD director and his smug young co-conspirator with his slick jet black hair and steel gray eyes were sitting together in the director's opulent office in the headquarters of the NCMIA's Central Control Division (the Ministry). "Lord Pythorael, everything has been accomplished according to your instructions," Lawrence Rogan informed the director.

Pythorael smirked with satisfaction. "Very good; hopefully this will put an end to this nonsense. Are you certain everything concerning this program has been completely obliterated and the child was killed, as well as the pregnant mother?"

"Given the amount of destructive force used there will be nothing left of the bodies," Rogan replied. "And no way to retrieve a genetic sample. Deputy Director Santos assured me they were all at home at the time. All that remains of this project are ashes—and its abject failures. The only loose end, of course, is the two-year-old Norean ēlan. Her twin sister is no longer a problem."

Pythorael replied angrily, "Neither would have been born in the first place had Dr. Elgin done his job. But since she has already gone through her two-year dedication ceremony, the Archon would certainly launch a major investigation into the disappearance of his most noble family's only ēlan. I'll deal with her when the time comes, should it become necessary. Besides, it will be years before she comes of age. I wouldn't doubt that the project's only successful surviving subject turns out to be another insane fraud as well. I venture this will be the end of the K15 genetic enhancement program, and we'll hear nothing more about it."

"Simon Elgin isn't trustworthy. He would betray his own mother for money," Rogan cautioned.

Pythorael grimaced. "I have corroborating sources that prove there was only one successful embryo and it belonged to the program's wealthiest benefactor. It's a mystery how such a child was produced by the Noreans. But only two other modified clones were ever created, and one clone and the control were given to Charlotte Dylanis because of Kim Norean's medical condition. Thankfully, that tot is now dead, and so is the unborn child, and the original embryo is destroyed."

"What corroborating source?" Rogan said. "Everyone who has ever been involved with Harold Dylanis is a criminal. The man made a career out of committing genetics fraud and embezzlement."

"The GIA was watching him," Pythorael assured Rogan. "The ongoing audit confirms everything."

"But somebody told him about the GIA audit. After we get rid of Elgin, what about Santos? He's a loose end and could very well talk. He knows why we had this project destroyed."

"After everything is finished, I'll deal with Santos," Pythorael said. The information about this fiasco will have to be quarantined for all future security directives. We must also keep it out of the media."

Rogan looked worried. "I would hate for the Archon to find a way to accuse the Ministry. Shouldn't we at least launch an official investigation? Two other people were killed at the lab that morning."

Pythorael winced. "Absolutely not! I want no further investigations into this. When the Archon reads the official report on these incidents, even he will forget that the two-year-old ēlan was ever born. His obsession with this poorly funded initiative has already begun to fade. It will take him decades just to complete Phase 1 of L2. We'll have plenty of time to orchestrate our coup by then."

* * * *

OVER FOURTEEN YEARS LATER...

11.21.59 NCE – Highlands Psychiatric Institute – Highlands District, Southern Jurisdiction

"Today is your birthday," said Executive Director Dr. Alex Crenshaw. The somewhat stocky, middle-aged man stared lustily at the stunning young blonde-haired girl with her bright blue eyes. He finished tucking in his shirt. "I just wanted one last time with you. You were my all-time favorite. No, not your clothes, put on the robe. There are visitors here to meet you today, and they each want to fully inspect what they've come all this way to bid on. Your career at this institution has come to an end."

Venley dropped her clothes on the floor and donned the robe as Crenshaw instructed.

"You're seventeen today and not a child anymore, Venley," Crenshaw said. "We can't keep you here any longer. I have three bids for you. One is an offer from Veritas VE; another is from Capricorn Productions. We've done business with them before. Oddly, the last is from a NED Tech research firm called Castle Point. Surprisingly, the virtual entertainment company and the research firm are interested in you for the same reason, apparently for your mental acuity, rather than your … looks." He laughed. "I guess once they realize your mental deficiencies and that you can't even speak correctly, they'll withdraw their bids. You'll end up at Capricorn where you will only have to pretend. That shouldn't be a problem for you, since you don't need to pretend to enjoy what you already like to do so frequently."

"I don't say anythling bad ablout anyone. Can't you just finalbly let me go?" Venley begged.

"I couldn't, even if I wanted to," Crenshaw said. "It's just business. When our inventory reaches your age, we must capitalize on our investment. You've been here twelve years; you know how it works. The ones who taught you moved on, but damn, you were the best. I'll miss you."

A few minutes later, Venley was led into a small lounge where a nice-looking man, perhaps in his mid-to late twenties, with light brown hair and brown eyes, was seated at a small table reviewing Venley's assessment and file history on his display.

"Hello, Venley, my name is Greg," he said, looking up. "I'm with Veritas VE."

"Hi," Venley said. She sat down with a solemn look on her face.

"Venley, I want you to know I am not really here to get you to come work in the virtual entertainment industry," Greg said.

Venley sniffed. "I'm not really here to take off my clothes. *Unless you want me* ... shut up!"

"Let me explain something, Venley," he said. "I'm looking for someone with your exact skill set and appearance. I actually work for an organization which helps people escape New City, to freedom. Don't worry," he said, when she looked fearful. "They can't pick up our conversation. I have a special device to prevent that."

"I'm not whirleed, are you here to resclue me?" asked Venley. "I don't have any skills. They say I'm stuplid ... even though I can read. I just don't undlerstand what pleople say as fast as I can hear."

"It's funny you should say that, considering your exceptional aptitude scores," Greg said. "Based on them, I know you must be able to read extremely well. But before we proceed, I have a couple of tests to administer. I'm going to show you a dossier on a young female. You have one minute to study this. Be sure to look carefully at her image." Greg handed Venley his display.

She rapidly scanned through page after page of information. After a minute he cleared the display. "Now, Venley, please enter everything about the girl you can remember. If you can't use a virtual keypad then I'll assume you really didn't complete our assessment."

"Everythling?" Venley said.

"Everything," he insisted. For the next few minutes Venley keyed in everything she could recall about what she had just read. Finally, Greg stopped her. "That's enough!"

Greg reviewed her text, then sat back. He was astonished at the amount of detail she had been able to recall—with amazing accuracy. He pulled a blank sheet of paper and pencil out of a carrying case and handed them to Venley.

"I don't know how to write," she said. "Who writes anythling anym-lore, anyway?"

"I'm not asking you to write anything. Draw the girl's face from memory," he said.

Venley looked at the pencil she held as if it was a foreign object. "You want me to draw that girl's face on this pliece of plaper, and that's it? I bet you're gloing to subterfluge me."

"Just do the best you can, from what you can recall," Greg said, ignoring her concern.

After she figured out how to hold the pencil, for the next couple of minutes Venley attempted to draw the girl's face. Once she was finished, Greg compared the image on the dossier to Venley's quickly executed hand-drawn image. The two were identical, down to the way she'd drawn the girl's loose blond curls and the exact shape of her nose and eyebrows.

"Have you ever drawn or painted anything before?" Greg said.

Venley shook her head, no.

"That girl is you, now, assuming they accept our offer," Greg said.

"See, you want to subterfluge me," Venley said. "I love you and I'll asslume her idemnity. I just don't know how to do anythling."

"We'll train you, but it will be so much more than just that ..." Greg replied.

An hour later Greg Duggar was seated in front of Alex Crenshaw. Greg couldn't get the dream his little daughter had told him out of his head. What his daughter said caused him to be inexplicably drawn to Venley; he knew he had to save her, no matter the cost.

"I'm sorry, but I've received two much higher offers," Crenshaw told him. "One tripled their original bid and withdrew the guarantee provision. It was already considerably higher than yours. What I don't understand is why you both wanted her for her mental acuity. I could understand if you wanted her for her looks; she's gorgeous. She's even kind of amusing and funny, but unbelievably dimwitted."

"Do you mind telling me who made this offer? Greg asked.

"That's confidential. But I will tell you, it's a mind integration research facility," Alex replied. "You couldn't make enough money off her on a VE platform to justify spending half of what they proposed. It's sad to think they may fry her brain by experimenting on her, but I have to accept the highest bid."

"No doubt it's owned by the Noreans or Kalitech," Greg said, with anger in his voice. "If you have any affection for this girl you won't sell her to such a place. You know what happens to children there. I'm surprised they want her, considering her age."

"Forget her age, the girl is clinically insane. She has a chronic OCD complex and a dissociative identity disorder, along with manic hebephrenic schizophrenia," Alex said callously.

"How much more did they offer?" Greg pleaded.

"It doesn't matter, the deal is done. Look somewhere else for an insane girl!"

Greg's eyes teared up. "Just tell me how much!"

"If you must know, it's over 300K," Alex said. "I'd let you have her for 400, but not a single CU less. You'd have to initiate a fund transfer right now, otherwise, she's gone in five minutes."

Greg's jaw dropped. His organization's budget was capped at 75K, and he couldn't offer a single CU higher. But he had to save this girl from a terrible fate. He had a home worth 350K, but it was heavily mortgaged. He had some savings, but not nearly enough. Suddenly, Greg heard that voice in his head again: *Five hundred, five hundred, five hundred.*

"Wait, I'll give you 500, but I need a few hours. If you let me take her now, I'll have the money tonight," Greg said. "You know I'm good for it."

Crenshaw checked his time display, then scoffed. "What's so special about this girl? She can hardly talk. She isn't worth half that, even if you could sell her as a perpetual virgin. You could buy a half dozen pretty, smarter, younger girls from here for that. Why her?"

"My reasons are my own business. We've done deals before. I'll get the money," Greg insisted.

"Take her, then. You have until 7:00 p.m. to transfer the funds. No refunds! I have the ability to track her and you know who owns this institution. He will have you hunted down and killed just for the pleasure of it, both of you."

"I know who owns this place, and others like it," Greg said bitterly. "What you people do with these children, whom you're supposed to be helping, is a crime—and someday you'll pay for it."

"Hypocrite!" Crenshaw sneered. "We train them well, so you won't have to bother or deal with their whining, because we already have. We make them into what your customers desire, along with a nice profit. It takes more than simply turning seventeen to make them … talented. And this girl is a freak and especially gifted. She's willing to do anything. You should try her; I certainly have. She's one of the best we've ever trained."

"You disgust me. I wish I could take them all. I hope and pray one day, someone will," Greg said.

"Just make certain 500K is transferred within three hours. And no returns!" Crenshaw repeated.

Greg and Venley were driving out of the remote Highlands district. He turned to her. "I'm in serious trouble. I just made a promise to pay 500K for you and I only have 75. I'm a dead man," he said.

Tears formed in Venley's eyes. "You did that for me?" She knew what money was, but she had no concept of what constituted a considerable sum.

"We're going to stop at this resort up the road. I need make some financial arrangements with my organization," he explained.

"What will happlen to me if you don't?" Venley asked.

"I couldn't let that research institute take you," Greg said. "You would die. You may think I'm crazy, but my two-year-old daughter, who can barely talk, dreamed about you. I was looking at your image and she recognized you from her dream. She said you were the most beautiful star of all, but it wasn't time for you to fall."

"I bet it's beclause you love me, and you'll marry me," Venley said, with hope in her eyes. "I've had a dream like that, but my star falls so the little red one can become the brightest star of all."

"Really, that's very interesting, since your new middle name will be Starlet. Also, I'm already married, but I guess you could say I love you like a father," Greg replied. "Seriously, I'm ten years older than you." He knew Venley was way too young, but she was the most beautiful girl he had ever seen. He knew what she was and that he could easily have his way with her.

"I don't have a dad," Venley said. "My parents died when I was two. How old is your wife?"

"Four years older," Greg said. "Like you, she had a tragic childhood. She's the reason I do what I do. I'm hoping you'll help me. I acquired you for a very important purpose, not just to save you."

"I'll beclome this other girl. I'll do anythling for you," Venley said.

Once inside the hotel, Greg bought her a soft drink and told her to wait in the bar. Venley noticed a small casino next to the bar and went inside. The roulette table fascinated her; she watched as the wheel spun until the little white ball landed on a number. Greg had given her a chip with 386CUs on it to get something to eat and drink. He expected her to spend only a little of it. She watched as the croupier released the ball; within seconds no one was allowed to place another bet. Venley decided to give it a try. Moments after the ball was released, she bet all her CUs on 17 black—and hit the jackpot.

When the croupier asked how she wanted her winnings denominated she stared at him blankly. He handed her a single casino payout chip worth 13,896CUs. Everyone around the table applauded. A small crowd started to gather. They laughed when she said, "I bet I can do it again." This time she hit on 25 black with the entire chip. Venley now had just over 500K. Within a minute, the casino manager rushed over in a panic. "Young lady, I'm going to have to ask you to leave." The other guests were outraged that the owner refused to give the lucky girl her encoded winnings token. After a few minutes, the crowd convinced the man to relent, but he insisted that Venley leave the casino and the hotel and never return.

"Okay, but I have to find my friend," she insisted. They refused and pushed her out the front door. Security was told not to allow her back inside for any reason.

After waiting for Greg for several minutes Venley started to walk away; she was freezing in the cold November air. Just as she was about to toss the chip into a pond next to the hotel, Greg yelled her name. He'd been frantically searching for her inside until someone at the bar realized he was looking for the girl who had been kicked out. He ran up to her. "Why did they throw you out? What did you do?"

"It was just a stuplid game, where you put your thling on the numbler where you know that little ball is going to land." Venley said, frustrated. "They got really mad beclause I did it twice; they mlade me leave. I'm sorry I splent your money. They finalbly gave me this, after pleople got mad. This place is crazy." She handed Greg the casino chip with her encoded winnings.

Greg took it without paying attention. He was distraught. "I begged my organization to pay and they refused. They couldn't afford it. I've got to figure out what to do with you."

"It was too much, I guess," Venley said. "It's okay. I'm glad you tried. I still love you."

"Don't be ridiculous. You don't love me," Greg said. "You don't even know me."

"I do love you. You're the only plerson who has ever done anythling for me," she replied. "Well, there was someblody who cared ablout me once, but I don't know who it was."

"Is this your winnings chip?" Greg asked, finally realizing what he was holding. He inserted the chip into his personal computing device (PCD) and gawked. "Did you bet the whole chip I gave you and let it ride?" He was incredulous.

"I'm sorry, it mlade them really mad. I just thlought it was a game. It's a terrible game, anyway. All you have to do is put it on the numbler where the tiny ball is gloing to land."

"Venley, you have just over the price I promised to pay for you," Greg said, wide-eyed. "Are you saying you can tell where the ball is going to land, before the wheel stops?"

"They have to flick the stuplid ball first, then I can, but you have to hurry," she said.

Greg looked at her with astonishment. "Assuming you let me use this money to pay them what I owe for you, all I can say is, welcome to the ATO, Venley. I promise I'll pay you back."

Venley laughed and smiled. She gave Greg a huge hug and a kiss on his lips. "No, you don't have to pay me anythling. I love you! Just don't take me back. I don't want to do that stuff with those ... pleople. *Liar!* I can't say anythling bad ablout anyone. *I would definitebly do it with you ...* shut up!"

* * * *

04.12.60 NCE – Riverpark Hotel and Casino – South Park District, Southern Jurisdiction

"How old are you?" said the older, dark-haired man who had seated himself at the bar next to the stunning young girl he'd just met in the casino. "I've never seen anyone play the roulette table quite like you. What's your secret and while I am at it, may I buy you a drink?"

"Yes, I'll have three beers and it deplends on how old I need to be," said the girl. "As to my sneakret ... well, it wouldn't be a sneakret if I told you. *Liar* ... shut up! Anyway, I have really good hearing, even thlough I can't hear very well. I heard you say somethling ablout smuggling to that uh ... *fat* guy you were with over there. Aah! That was a bad thling to say. *You have to say them.* No ... *yes* ... shut up!" She cleared her throat. "Also, I'm a really good spy and I know that large round plerson you were talkling with is a Mlinistry agent and he hunts smugglers and ... just don't talk to him. Trust me."

"I didn't say anything about ... what you just said. You talk so fast I can hardly understand you," replied the man as he ordered the girl a beer. "How do you know he is NCMIA? By the way, spies don't tell strangers they're a really good spy. That makes you a terrible spy."

"Hell merry, hell merry, hell merry ... Oh, sorry, I was saying my sacrled incanplations. Fair point, but I know I can trust you beclause I need a smuggle. I bet you're a smuggler beclause ... my brain just knows stuff. I used to have a Ouija board, but they took it away ... *beclause of the fires* ... shut up!"

"You are very odd," the man said. "But depending what you want to move and where, I might be able to hook you up," he offered, very quietly. "It's probably best if you don't say that word. Your PCD can pick up anything you say."

"Not mine; I have a two-mleeter slignals blockling radilus. What word? Do you mean smuggle?" she said, rather loudly. "What if it's differlent stuff each time? I'm also not exactbly sure where. Is that a problem? I know it's in the Dead Zone somewhere, if that helps. We can do some kid pro quote."

"Yes, that word," he gasped. "Why would a girl like you need to move something to the DZ?"

"I like to send stuff to pleople," she said, "if I love them. Actualbly, I haven't met them, but they gave me an awesome house with a huge swimming pool and all the food I clud ever want to eat, so I love them."

"I like to know who I'm dealing with and what they plan on moving," replied the man.

"Uh, my name is Starlet, and I need to smuggle stuff, I mean sneakretbly move contrabland," the girl said with a look of innocence. "It's in my room. I went grocerly shlopping today. I bought it and thlought it would be nice to smug … send it to some pleoples. It's slort of out of the way."

"You have it hidden in your room … now?" he said skeptically. "Don't use that other word, either. But show me how you hit two times on that roulette table earlier and I'll consider arranging a delivery. But it depends on how illegal, dangerous, or lethal it is," he whispered.

"If I win too much, they might kick me out … again," she said. "I was only winning a little so far. I still had to do some kid pro quote to get back in here … *oh yeah, splurt!* This is the best place to find a … shoo, that was close, I almlost said smuggler. I also won't say the word contrabland when talking ablout smuggles, which I'll never mlention again … that was slippery tongues."

"You're very strange," the man said. "But if you hit a number for me on that roulette table, I'll talk business with you."

"Okay, but don't bet any more than ten thlousand," she said. "I mlight get in trouble … again. Mlaybe they won't notice I'm near the table if I bring my sandwich. Hey, I'll just whispler to you like I'm lickling your ear." The girl whipped a huge sandwich out her bag. "Let's roll! Remlember no more than 10K."

"Are you serious? I don't have anywhere near that much, but let's do it."

"I thlought you wanted to go to the table first," she said. "Then we can *do* it. *Yes!* We have to be quick ablout it … *augh,* shut up! Not the do it plart … *Yes!*"

"What? No, I meant the table. How does it work?"

"The ball goes around and lands on a numbler, it's pretty straight florward."

"I know how roulette works. I mean, how do you win?" he asked.

"As soon as he flings that little ball and beflore he closes the bets, I'll tell you the numbler," she said. "Don't bet what you can't lose, beclause I've already had five beers, not inclubing this one and the other ones I didn't inclube. I'm also bletter with black than red or that green splace with the little ovalbly thlings."

The man asked nervously, "How sure are you that you can do this?"

"Plositive, mlaybe, sort of, but I'll give it back if you lose … if you smug … take my stuff," the girl proposed. "You can keep everythling you win. You can also have my chip and some kid pro quote, but I don't want the fat … I mean, don't bring that other round guy. He's a Mlinistry agent."

The two approached the table. Moments later, the wheel was spun and within a second or two after the ball was released, the girl said. "Eightleen red!" The astonished man was paid 35 to 1 on a 3,000CU bet. "That was close, I almlost bet on the black one next to it," the girl said, nonchalantly.

"We bletter go to my room … *o splurt!* Shut up!" she said. "It's my third time hitting this thing today … *Liar, it's numbler five!* Shut up! Not that."

Once in her room, the man, still astonished at the girl's ability, asked, "Can you do that all day long? We could make a fortune; I mean, you could. Why would you need to smuggle anything if you can make money winning at a casino like that and how do you do it?"

"I actualbly have no idea, but I don't need money. *Liar!*" she said. "It comes to me after I watch the ball. Now that you have some, will you smuggle my … stuff?"

"It depends on what it is and where to," he said, cautiously.

"Okay, give me a mlinute or five." The girl went into the bathroom, where she ran the water in the tub for few minutes. Once it was turned off, he heard something heavy splash into the tub. "Too many kids in the pool right now, so I'm just checkling to see if it doesn't float," she yelled.

She returned to the room wearing only a robe, looking wet, and drying off something heavy, large, and round with a towel. "This is excellent," she said. "I've nevler had this kind, but I had some almlost like it."

"Is that what you want to move?" he said. "Is it narcotics?"

She laughed. "Narclotics?" She tossed the heavy object on the bed.

"What *is* that?" he said.

The object appeared to have a wax-like covering, almost like a wheel of cheese would.

"It's cheese and it's awesome. It doesn't float."

"You want to smuggle cheese to the Dead Zone? Do you have an illegal device or drugs hidden in there?

"No, I also want to smuggle some slausages ... with a note. It doesn't matter if the slausage floats. I throw them in the pool sometimes to annoy my cat, Pepperoni."

The man took a deep breath, then started to laugh. "OK, where do you want it to go? Do you always take a bath with your cheese?"

"No, but it's too early to go skinny dipping in the hotel pool. I want this to go to my new friends that I work for ... at their sneakret base in the DZ. I help them get pleople out of New City and I love them," she said with a happy smile. "That's super-sneakret, so don't tell anyone, especialbly that ... large, round guy. But they can't ever know how it gets there. That's implortant, I like to be mlysterilous, *and ooblergasms!* Shut up!"

"Mysterious shouldn't be problem. You are the weirdest girl I've ever met, but I actually think I know who and where you are talking about," he said. "I mean, I don't know personally, but I have some skilled contacts in the DZ, who do. They are extremely discreet. Are you a prostitute or something? I don't pay for. ..."

"*It's free!* Shut up! Awesome!" the girl squealed. "How much does a smuggle cost?"

"Since you won me 100K at the casino, this one's on me," he said. "Just do that whenever you want another delivery, and I'll smuggle your cheese anywhere."

The girl then gave him a huge wet kiss on his lips. "I love you so much, let's do it!"

"You don't even know my name," he said. "I'm Chester, but people call me Chess."

"It's a deal, plus kid pro quote!" she said, pushing him down on her bed and letting her robe drop to the floor. "Sorry, let's shift the cheese, Chess. I don't want it slamaged."

* * * *

05.25.61 NCE – Park Central District – Southern Jurisdiction

Ari awakened in the night with sweat covering her face. She'd had the same vivid dream again, yet the last part was different this time.

Her dream always began with her standing over a wide mirror that looked like a sea of glass. She would stare at her reflection and the mirror would shatter. Her reflection had neither her dark brown hair nor her brown eyes. It was someone like her, but different and very troubled. Suddenly, she would be left standing alone in the middle of a vast desert as dark clouds gathered around seven distant mountains.

A bright light would descend from the sky from a whirlwind of dark clouds in the north. The image of a man always appeared within this bright light, like a flaming statue standing on a hot, glowing pedestal. He held a scepter and wore eight golden rings with eight stones: five were set with bright red rubies, one with a black onyx and two with sparkling yellow diamonds. On his head he wore a golden crown with a dark shimmering smoky topaz at its center. It was surrounded by four green emeralds, two on each side, and a shimmering blue diamond on each side of the emeralds. Above the center stone was another bright emerald which outshined all the other stones.

Suddenly, she had wings. She flew to a far distant mountain surrounded by enormous gates covered with thick brambles and overgrown with weeds. People struggled to enter or leave through only a single gate accessible by a raised platform. Those who managed to enter often fell into fiery pits or were caught in vicious snares. She flew to a place on the mountain where she saw a man lying underneath the cleft of a rock. A voice said, "Pick him up."

That's where the dream had always ended before. As she glimpsed the man's face and reached to pick him up, she would wake up. This time, when she reached to pick him up, she saw his face, far more clearly than ever before. She watched as scales fell from his eyes, then he kissed her gently.

A voice said: "I am sending you to this man. He is to become your husband. When he knows you, he will have wings to fly." She saw angels ascending and descending all around. They wore white robes with golden sashes. They sang a song in which they called her by a new name, and repeated, "*With love and fire, with seven eyes and wings to fly.*"

The next morning over breakfast at their apartment in the Park Central district, Ari told her great-grandfather, Zack, about the dream. He asked the usual question: "Do you think you would recognize the young man in your dream this time, if you were to meet him?"

Ari giggled. "You always ask me the same thing. Yes, this time I would, because he kissed me, and a voice said he would become my husband."

"Why are you laughing?" asked Zack.

"Because it's a ridiculous, stupid dream. The man looks so much older than me. I'm fifteen. You won't let me date boys my own age, much less *marry* someone as old as him," she said.

Zack nodded. "He's not too old. Besides, you'll be sixteen in a week. Age has nothing to do with it. Maturity has everything to do with it, along with fate. Zack pulled up a picture on his display. "Is this the man in your dreams? I've never shown you this before, because you were never certain you could recognize him. But now I will ask: Is this the man?"

Instantly, Ari knew he was. She nodded yes and stared hopefully at Zack. "How did you know? Who is he?"

Zack smiled. "Listen carefully. I need you to make the acquaintance of this young man. His name is Mark, Marcus Vincent Verigratu. He is not to know your true age or he will consider you too young. As far as he knows, you are not one day younger than eighteen, no, perhaps nineteen would be better. You are pretty, mature, and well-endowed. I can assure you that, past such a point, a young man of his age will not know the difference. He will be swept off his feet."

Ari was shocked. "You want me, your obsessively overprotected and not allowed to have a single date *ever,* great-granddaughter, to seduce an older man?"

"I said nothing of seduction!" Zack protested. "That is out of the question until marriage. I only want you to get him to fall in love with you. I have not met him. In time, I will, but you are never to bring him to me, not until I am certain the time is right. He can't know about me or your relationship to me, considering my past affiliation with the Ministry."

Ari was flabbergasted. "This is insane. I don't know him or where he lives or anything. What if he doesn't want to talk to me? Besides, I don't want to get married or have any man at all."

"*Of course* he will talk with you. In fact, he will fall in love with you," Zack insisted.

"Are you serious? What if I don't like him?"

Zack reassured her. "Why do you doubt this? You have been dreaming about him for months. Now you've seen his face. You're prepared for this. You will fall in love with him, and he with you. By the way, he is your distant cousin, very distant in fact, so it's not 'creepy,' as you would say. I would never force you to do this. You must make this decision of your own free will. Yet, I must stress how important this is. In time, when you are older, you will marry. First and foremost, you must make him fall deeply in love with you."

"What? My cousin? Distant or not, it *is* creepy. Zack, I can't believe you're pimping me off to this man you haven't met. I thought anyone who dated me would have to pass through fire. Now you're arranging for me to marry my own cousin. I'm only fifteen!"

"I'm shocked you would accuse me of such a thing," Zack said. "There is no such arrangement. Besides, I do know Mark. At least, I know about him. There can no longer be any delay. Ari, it's your dream and your vision. I'm just helping you realize it, for all our sakes."

Ari paused. "He is handsome, but I know nothing about dating boys, much less an older man. I've never had a mother to teach me these things. He must be at least twenty; he'll consider me a child. And you certainly haven't taught me how to make a man fall in love with me. In fact, you've never taught me anything about being a girl."

Zack was indignant. "I gave you a parenting book for girls."

"Zack, that worthless book was supposed to teach *you* how to raise me. At least I learned what my period was. It didn't teach me anything about relationships. Good grief!" Ari exclaimed. "The book was also so old, the pages crumbled; it was written in the early 1900s."

"New City instructional material assumes all teenage girls have sex as soon as they … anyway that's not how I raised you, and I will not encourage any such behavior," Zack protested.

"Still, you could have jumped forward a hundred years," Ari said. "Besides, I have the Net. I know what New City teaches. I'm talking about the nuance of romance with a man."

"Look, I've had only had one purpose since I left the Ministry. It is to protect you from *them.* Trust me, this young man is the answer to our prayers.

"Am I not a man?" he said. "I can assure you that you have everything any woman, even one years older than you, would need to make a man fall in love with her. I am not merely talking about your beauty, although you look so much like your lovely mother, with your dark brown eyes and brown hair. You're also remarkably mature and intelligent. Girls your age are typically vain and silly. I'm counting on your ability to read this man like a book and appeal to his heart, not just his loins. He will do anything for you."

Ari became suspicious. "You mean he will do anything for *you*, only because I want him to. What are you doing, Zack? Do you want this man to fall in love with me so you can involve him in some irrational scheme? I don't want to get married. Did you subliminally trick me into dreaming about him so I'd help you trap him into doing something crazy?"

Zack shook his head. "Don't ever deny your special gift of sight. The things you see in your dreams and visions are real. You see what no man can see. Even if you don't understand your visions, it's because it's not time for you to know what they mean. I would never encourage you seek out such a man if I didn't believe your visions are real.

"He believes the lie of New City. In part, you will help save him from it. In turn, you will both change this world. It takes only a tiny spark to set a forest ablaze. You, my child, are the spark to ignite the sun, which will pierce the black heart of this city."

Ari sulked. "Don't over-exaggerate or anything; you're being apocalyptic." She paused. "Where does this Mark live and how am I supposed to meet him?"

Zack scratched his forehead and sighed. "That's a bit of a problem. It seems the boy doesn't have a regular routine. Occasionally he hangs out with friends near the riverfront. Sometimes he visits the museum near the park not far from here."

Ari interrupted. "You're spying on him?"

"I've only arranged for a little surveillance. It's not spying. I needed to prepare for this moment. And he lives nearby."

Ari crossed her arms and stared at Zack. "It sounds like spying to me, no matter what you call it. So, I should follow him? Do I pinch him on the butt, then say, 'Hi, I'm Ari, and you're the man of my dreams?' I'll be humiliated. He's going to see I'm a teenager."

Zack chuckled. "I was hoping you might try a slightly more cerebral and artistic approach."

Ari gasped. "Don't tell me you had me trained as an artist so I could impress him?"

"No, of course not. Yet I find it interesting that you have an extraordinary ability to mimic so many artists, especially those Mark considers his favorites."

Ari knew she had a window into a vision of what would soon take place. She could hear angels all around her who sang beautifully. They sang out her name *"With love and fire with seven eyes and wings to fly."* They sang of her reflection, like the sun and moon face-to-face. Ariel Waters was a rare jewel in a shattered sea of glass who could never be whole until she found *them.* She didn't know who *they* were, but she knew they were part of her, that they were broken, and that at least one of them was shattered.

Reluctantly she knew she had to do this one small thing. She had to convince a man to fall in love with her and that he was the key to ultimately help her save them all. Maybe she would feel less uncertain about approaching this man once she turned sixteen. She was frightened, and she foresaw a terrible storm coming. Ari knew it wasn't just a dream.

For three weeks, Ari stalked Mark Verigratu, trying to get him to notice her. A couple of times she dropped comments standing near him as he viewed some of his favorite paintings while at the art museum. She also set up an easel to paint in the park, hoping he would notice her painting. She thought he might show some interest in her work, which was spectacular. She would see him walking along certain paths. Yet every time she tried to place herself in his path, he'd ignore her or walk a different way.

Nothing seemed to work. She did, however, notice that almost every day he visited the same coffee shop near his apartment building. There, he'd watch the news or read articles on his PCD for an hour.

Ari decided she would have to introduce herself. However, Zack insisted it was imperative that Mark be the one to initiate contact.

"My dear girl," Zack would say, "while I will never pretend to understand the female mind, I have at least some perception about men. Once a girl approaches a man, an entirely different chemical reaction occurs in his brain. He will objectify you. You will lose the element of vulnerability and power over him. But if he approaches you, he'll be much more inclined to fall in love with you."

"Yes, I would hate for him to think I am stalking him, which I am!" Ari exclaimed. "I could meet him over the Net much more easily. Now I'm just this stupid girl who is always lugging art junk around the park. He's had to have seen me at least once. If not, he's the most oblivious man on the planet or completely disinterested. He probably realizes I'm a child."

"Believe me, with your figure, you don't look like a child, but rather a beautiful young woman. But online contact is out of the question! Person-to-person contact is far more alluring than an image. He can get a good look at you. If you approach him electronically, he'll think you're a call girl—or worse."

"Worse?" Ari was aghast. "What's worse than that?"

"Being a tramp who throws herself at men," Zack said. "Trust me; I know how men think."

"I'm not sure your relationship advice is up to date," Ari countered. "You're ninety years old."

As she cleared the dinner table one evening, Ari said, "Zack, I am like a fly to this man ... and like fly paper to every other gross looking, ogling, stalking, pervert. It's not safe for me to be hanging around by myself with all those weirdos lurking about. The guy hasn't looked at me or noticed I'm alive. This approach is a failure. What's more, I don't think he has a job. I have better things to do than pursue an unemployed loafer. Even if I am supposed to marry him some day, he seems like a total loser and he obviously knows I'm too young."

"He doesn't need a job. He is quite well-to-do. You might just say he's more like a professional student right now," Zack said. "Be patient. I'm sure he has noticed you; perhaps he's shy. Take your painting to the park again tomorrow. Don't worry, I have people keeping an eye on you, just in case. I would never let anything happen to you."

Ari sighed. "Oh my God, those are probably some of the vile creeps I see hanging around. But if it doesn't work tomorrow, I'm not going to lug all this stuff back to the park again. In fact, I'll leave it there and never paint again. I'll be twenty before the man notices me. Zack, I'm scared, this not the right time. What if he wants me to go to bed with him on our first date? I've never even been kissed. If I refuse, he won't ask me out again because he'll think I'm a prude."

Zack said, "He won't do that. On second thought, just make sure you don't *ever* go home with him. If you do, he'll think you've given him a green light."

"So, I can't bring him here to meet you and I can't *ever* go to his place or he'll think … what is a green light?" Ari said. "How is he ever going to fall in love with me if we don't … I have no idea what I'm doing and you said he's experienced. I'll need to watch some videos just to learn how to kiss."

"Ari, remember you're always in charge of what happens." Zack instructed. "In any case, you need to get him to ask you out soon. Once you do, as soon as possible, I need you to subtly encourage him to finish his formulation analytics degree at Severyn University. He has only another year to go; he's been doddering around long enough. Promise him something … nice"

Ari stared at Zack. "Like what, a green light? What about a pretty blue one?"

Zack said, "Heavens no! Like a painting."

"Seriously? Ari complained. "You want me to date a professional loafer and give him painting to get him to finish his degree? Maybe if it's a nude … of me. You want to get him into the Ministry, don't you? That's what this is about. You want him to spy for you, like Jerome."

Zack hesitated. "Don't be silly," he said. "He's not a professional loafer. He's well educated and has already completed several degrees. He does procrastinate, however, when it comes to this one. At this rate, it could take him two years. Having him inside of the Ministry is just the beginning."

Ari huffed. "I can't believe this. I'm a fly trying to catch a spy for you."

Zack shook his head. "No! Together you are going to catch a spider, a half a world away."

CHAPTER 2

THE REVELATION OF ARIEL WATERS

Is that the same girl again? I asked myself. I watched her get out of an SDPV (self-driving programmable vehicle) carrying something. *Is she following me?* This was the fifth time I'd seen her hanging around, just this past week, but who was counting. She was extremely cute with a nice figure. I also thought she looked a little young. *Is she carrying a canvas board and easel? Maybe she's heading toward the park to paint.* I stared at her until she disappeared into the milling crowds. *Maybe I'll see what she's doing in a little while, if I can find her.* Then, I reconsidered. I didn't want her to think *I* was following her.

I decided to be nonchalant. I walked through the park pretending not to look for the pretty brunette carrying art supplies. Sure enough, within ten minutes, I spotted her setting up her easel. "Hi," I said, as I finally worked up enough courage to approach her. "Do you mind if see what you're painting?"

The girl was startled. In fact, she looked at me as if she was in shock. "No, I mean, yes, of course. It's a hobby."

I walked behind her to see the painting. Seeing it, I was amazed. "Wow, that's pretty good. In fact, it's incredible. It looks almost like a Vecellio, with all the vivid colors and the style. How long have you been working on this?"

"Not too long. It's not the right type of paint or canvas. Maybe it looks a little like a Titian," the girl said.

"I've seen you around a few times, even at the museum once or twice," I confessed. "I noticed you being dropped off by an SDPV a few minutes ago. I mean, I'm not following you or anything. It looked like you were carrying your art supplies. I thought maybe you were coming to the park to paint," I said. "That sounds like I'm following you doesn't it?"

The girl smiled at me. I noticed, for the first time, that she wasn't just cute; she was gorgeous. "My name is Mark." I started to reach out to shake her hand. I withdraw mine when I realized her hands were full.

She quickly set down her paints and brush, then held out her hand. "Hi, my name is Ariel, but everyone calls me Ari."

"Do you go to school or live around here?" I said, trying to gage her age. She looked suspiciously young.

"Nope, I've graduated from secondary school. I mean yes, I do live around here, over on Beacon. I haven't decided where I want to attend college yet," She added, "I'm pretty sure I want to study genetics formulation and profile analysis. It's what my grandfather wants me to study. I figured since I'm only *eighteen*, I can wait a little while before I decide."

That was easy enough, I thought. Eighteen was a little young, still, a respectable age, as I'd just turned twenty-one. "Would you like to have dinner with me? Maybe we can see a show or something," I said, immediately feeling pathetic. *Geez, don't waste any time, desperado.*

Ari smiled and laughed. She had a beautiful smile and her laugh was musical. "Sure, I'd love to," she said, almost too eagerly. I got her PCD contact information and promised I'd call her.

I didn't realize that I had just met the love of my life. I can still remember the first time we kissed. When I looked into her mesmerizing brown eyes, I knew in that instant, I wanted to spend the rest of my life with this girl. I think I should tell you a little about our first date. Not knowing Ari, I realize now I was a jerk, but it was also wonderful. (And later, Ari told me everything she had been thinking during our date.)

* * * *

When I picked Ari up the first time, I thought I would be introduced to her grandfather. Little did I know it would two years before that would happen. We saw a play that was somewhat risqué. She was shocked to see nudity. I hadn't realized she'd never been exposed to anything remotely racy. (And I hadn't known the play would be quite that *interesting*.)

We had a lovely dinner afterward and talked for hours, until almost midnight. She was brilliant and well educated, but was astonishingly naïve about certain things and somewhat immature. She didn't have much knowledge of current events or popular entertainment shows, especially if there was any violence, off-color humor, sex or cursing. We did watch some of the same kid's shows at one time, so we could at least talk about that or academic subjects. She was still interesting and fun to talk to. She also refused to drink anything alcoholic. This didn't bode well for my plans for a quick scoring opportunity.

"So, would you like to come back to my apartment?" I said.

Ari arched her eyebrows. "To do what?" she said. "I was supposed to be home by eleven."

"Ari, you're eighteen, what do you mean you have to be home ... by *eleven*?"

"Normally I don't, but it's a school ... I mean, I have to get up early in the morning ... to wash my hair." *That was brilliant.*

"We can get a ride back to your place early in the morning," I said.

"Are you suggesting that I spend the night with you? It's only our first date!" *I told Zack he would try to do this.*

"Have you ... I mean, haven't you ever spent the night with a guy?"

"What kind of girl do you think I am? I've never been with a man nor do I want to start now. Not until I'm married." *I'm such a nitwit!*

"I'm sorry I didn't mean to assume ..." I said. "Are you a lesbian?"

"What an insulting thing to ask a girl. Just because I don't want to go back to your apartment on our first date doesn't imply something like that."

Now I was shocked. "Are you still a virgin ... and you're eighteen years old?"

Well, for your information ... OK, I am, but what of it? I almost kissed a boy once. My grandfather is rather overprotective." *Now he is going to totally know I'm just a kid.*

"Then you'd think that he would have wanted to meet me before I took you out."

"He can't, I mean, he knows ... he wasn't feeling well, but he will ... meet you ... someday," she said. "You know that degree you were telling me you were working on at ... um ... whatever university. You should finish it, quickly ... then I'll spend the night with you ... maybe." *Did I just say that?* "What I'm saying is that guys with ... advanced formulation degrees turn me on." *I am such a freaking idiot. So much for subtle encouragement.* "Would you like me to paint something for you instead?" *Yeah, like a nude of me ... probably.*

I burst out laughing. "Well, that's a first, I'll get right on that degree. I didn't mean to pressure you to spend the night. I've never been out with someone your age who isn't experienced and certainly one who has never been kissed. Are you really eighteen? Oh, and I'd love one of your paintings ... of you"

I knew it! "Mark, I want to go out with you again, but you need to take me home now. If I flunk out on this ... I mean this ... you'd better ask me out again; it's really important." *Could I be more stupid?* "I loved the show ... except I hated it, I mean the parts where ... do you go to things like that often ... it was so ... with all of those naked girls ... yeesh."

"They were only topless girls. I didn't know there was going to be so much nudity in the play."

"They were kissing men and other girls while they were naked!" she exclaimed. "I bet none of them are even married. It's shameful." *He is so cute; I hope he kisses me! Oh no, I don't know how to kiss.*

"I think you really are a little overprotected?" I said. "Believe me there are much more explicit plays I could have taken you to. I wouldn't have taken you to a play like that. But if you come back to my apartment tonight, I would love to show you."

"Oh my God, if I told Zack you said that to me, he would have a stroke," she said. "I'm not that kind of girl, but you do need to finish that degree and do it soon!" *That does it, first and last date and I totally ruined it.*

I took Ari back to her apartment. I gave her a kiss goodnight. It wasn't a long kiss or even the most passionate of kisses, but it was our first. I will never forget looking into her beautiful brown eyes as we kissed. I fell in love with Ariel Waters at that moment. And I sure as hell was going to finish that degree.

This isn't a love story, at least not entirely. It's so much more. You must hear the rest of the story to learn the secret of Ariel Waters. Secret, perhaps, is not the right way to put it. She is more like a living revelation and the personification of a promise, one made long ago to her mother who gave her own life to make certain Ari lived. Ari is the reason everything in my life would unfold in a way which would indeed change the world. There is so much more to Ariel Waters, than she, or anyone, ever imagined.

* * * *

Two years later.

I vividly remember the evening of July 1st in 63 NCE, when my life drastically changed. I was sitting on the main patio of my penthouse apartment that overlooked the Park Central district of New City. I was thinking how wonderful the world was and how fortunate I was to have been born. Ari and I had been dating for two years, and I was hoping we would marry.

Ari had said yes to my proposal, but said I had to meet her grandfather first. Yet for some reason, this meeting had never happened, and I was becoming increasingly frustrated. So on this evening, I was more determined than ever to finally meet her grandfather. Ari and I were supposed to go out, but she canceled on me at the last moment.

I have to admit, the biggest reason I was so desperate to marry Ari is because she wouldn't sleep with me. Most of the girls I'd dated would hop into bed after a couple of drinks. Two years was beyond being patient. Ari had me in her grasp and I had no intention of losing her. I was madly in love with this beautiful girl, but she was a little prudish, most likely because she was raised by her grandfather. Even so, the girl was twenty years old, and what twenty-year-old girl doesn't go to bed with her boyfriend? This kept me unfulfilled, except in my dreams.

On this night, I found myself drawn into what would become a succession of incredibly strange events, ones which would increasingly involve ever more remarkable coincidences. I would come to realize how an old man had been orchestrating the events unfolding in my life. I can't say I was happy to learn what Zachariah Waters had done to lure me into his scheme or how he used Ari to do it.

I had been to Ari's apartment many times. I had even sat in her living room, yet never for long, since she wouldn't allow it. I had also dropped her off countless times. Even so, I thought it odd that I was never introduced to her grandfather. I decided to go over unannounced. I didn't know I was about to meet the man who would upend my world.

Strangely, when I arrived at Ari's building and asked to be let up, she said to bring something write on and write with or she wouldn't let me in. She said it was vital that I remember everything I would learn that night, and I would need to write it down.

* * * *

When Ari opened the apartment door, I grinned at her. "I may need to borrow something to write with along with something to write on. Who writes anything, anyway?"

She smiled, kissed me, and led me into the living room. "You don't really need anything to write with," she said. "Zach told me to say this to the next person who rang to come up." Ari laughed, pushed me down on the sofa, and climbed into my lap. Suddenly, her voice dropped to a near whisper. "I'm sorry we couldn't go out. Zach told me this afternoon I had to stay here because he was expecting someone important, someone I had to let in. You might think this is weird, but I'm certain this person is you."

"You don't say?" I responded. "So I finally get to meet your mysterious grandfather after two years."

Ari leapt from my lap, "C'mon, I want to introduce you. I know you don't believe me, since you have been pestering me to meet him for so long, but I've lived here with him since I was eight."

She led me down the hallway into a dimly lit study with wall-to-wall shelves full of books, real books, along three walls. There were stacks of papers on top of several small tables along the other wall. Ari's grandfather was reclining behind a large desk in the center of the room, reading a tattered book. Behind him was a lampstand topped with an odd purple-colored lampshade.

The desk was covered with odds and ends and cluttered with handwritten papers. There were no modern conveniences or electronics, not even a holographic entertainment display, anywhere in the room.

"Mark, I would like you to meet my grandfather, Zachariah Waters." I nodded my head and smiled as I held out my hand to shake his.

Ari walked to the door and said, just before she closed it behind her, "I'll just let you two get to know one another. Zack, am I correct to assume, Mark is the visitor you were anticipating?"

I thought it odd that she called her grandfather Zack.

The old man nodded with closed eyes as she left. Then he turned and stared directly at me. "Mark, I take it you have fallen in love with my Ari. I knew you would. She's perfect, isn't she, and beautiful?" I nodded. "The time is right for us to finally meet," he said matter-of-factly.

The old man had a pinched leathery face, which, at first glance, seemed fixed in a perpetual scowl. But after a while, I realized he was actually affable and spritely for his apparent age, whatever age that was. I didn't dare ask. He was funny; yet could be deadly serious.

We engaged in some initial small talk. The fact is, I was there to hear a story, one which would become a revelation about everything I'd thought to be true, until that moment. I wasn't immediately sold on what Zack was telling me. At first, I thought the information he conveyed to me was crazy.

According to Zack, everything I had been taught about New City was propaganda. His opening monologue spanned the brief history since the Final War. He explained the secret of New City, which he claimed was based on a lie that spanned all of human history. He said humankind had been continuously deceived by those who supposedly held the power over life and death. It was a fascinating recitation, and I didn't believe a word of it. I loved New City, after all, and I thought it humankind's greatest achievement.

"That's enough history for now," Zack abruptly concluded. "You're here because of a common history and destiny you and I share. Have you ever been to the southern wall, near Sanctuary Gate 3, to look out at the wasteland that lies beyond the city walls? There you will see a part of what was once a beautiful country; it was obliterated by the Final War. The beauty of the land has returned close to the walls, but it's a desolate ruin the farther south you travel."

I shook my head. "No one can go look out over the walls or into the DZ. It's impossible."

"I was born in a city about 250 kilometers south of SG3," Zack said. "That's also where your family lived. You don't realize this, but your father's grandmother's last name was Carpenter. She was the oldest child of a man who knew my father quite well. In fact, she married my brother Caleb. Samuel is your grandfather's real name. He was my brother's firstborn son."

"Are you suggesting we are related?" I asked skeptically.

Zack sighed. "Trust me, son, your real family name is the same as Ari's and my own. It's Waters. Despite the fact they are common names, having the names Carpenter and Waters are dangerous to have in your family tree in New City. Caleb had another son, Anthony, who eventually escaped to the Dead Zone with his son Ryan. Anthony had three children: Jonas, Peres, and Robert. He went by his middle name Ryan. Robert was much older than his younger siblings. Peres was a precious little girl; she would have turned thirty-four today. Tragically, the Ministry ordered her and Jonas put to death.

"I've lost most of my family in New City. My sweet Ariel is my last living legacy. You are the last legacy of my brother Caleb's, apart from your father Vincent, of course," Zack said.

I later realized I hadn't heard anything else in this exchange after learning that I was related to my girlfriend, which freaked me out. "Are you telling me I'm related to you and to the girl I am dating, and she and I are cousins? That's kind of unnerving."

"You and Ari are not too closely related," Zack said, "since she is my great-granddaughter, not simply my granddaughter. You are technically fifth cousins or something. Even so, you're not here tonight to discuss your familial relationship with Ari. I just wanted you to know where you came from and that our family lived in a city south of SG3 before the Final War."

"But why tell me all this now? We've never even met."

Zack ignored my growing discomfort. "You see, there was a moment when the world stood in the balance. At that time, your great-great-grand-father, my father, was given a gift. With this gift, he held the power to do something quite extraordinary. As a result of what he did with it, his enemies killed him for it. Mark, there are powers in this world which are not of this world. The only reason I know who you are is because we are related in more ways than through my brother Caleb."

"This is crazy. What are you talking about?"

Zack held up his hand to silence me. "Give me a few minutes to explain. It's far more complicated than the fact that we're related. By the way, my father's name was David. I think it's too soon to tell you everything. Let's just say, my father angered certain individuals in positions of power. Because of this he was murdered. Most of my family, our family, was eventually killed, including my two sisters and my younger brother, John, along with their families. My brother Caleb survived for a time, but was eventually caught, along with his son Samuel. My own son, Ari's grandfather, is among the few in our family to die of natural causes in the New Common Era. Even so, he nearly lost his life helping people escape New City."

Zack added, "They relentlessly hunt us like animals. My nephew Samuel went so far as to change his name to Terrance Fortisal. Despite this, he was captured and executed as a genetic dissident. In attempting to save his only son, Samuel managed to arrange for the adoption of his child, Gabriel, your father, to Bergita and Tolar Verigratu. The Verigratus had Gabriel's name officially changed to Vincent. They don't know your father is a genetic dissident and neither does the Ministry."

Zack continued, "In my case, I disappeared. I was never discovered, partly because so many records were destroyed. The Ministry thought I had been killed along with my brother. I was able to blend in with the dislocated masses who were being evacuated from the devastated cities. I lived for three years in a refugee camp north of here. I was eventually reinstated to citizenship. I even used my real name, because there were so many people with the last name Waters. Besides, they thought the real Zachariah Waters they were searching for was dead."

"How did you find out about this and about me? I said, growing more and more concerned.

"I was able to track you down because of your father's former last name, Fortisal," Zack said. "My wife had access to the repatriation Ministry matrix. She found the adoption records, which revealed the connection to your grandparents named Verigratu. By a process of elimination, I was able to determine my own great nephew's child is you."

I sat there, dumbfounded. "Why am I just finding out about this, after two years with Ari?"

Zack grinned. "I've known about you since you were a child. The timing had to be perfect."

"What is a genetic dissident? You knew all of this before I ever met Ari?" I felt confused.

Zack looked guilty. "You might say that. I had to be certain I could trust you before I could tell you anything. The reality is, Ari knew of you before I ever mentioned you. She's quite special. Anyway, what better way to ensure your trust than to have the two of you fall in love? Then, once you knew you were both genetic dissidents, you would never betray her. I never forced her. I only guided her to meet you and to get to know you. By the way, she only recently turned eighteen. I knew your age difference might be an issue."

My eyes went wide. "You're telling me she was only sixteen when we first...? Oh my God. No wonder she kept putting off going to college. She was still in secondary school. I swear we never ... I mean we haven't ... or anything much, yet ... I mean, not that I would expect ... well, anyway, I want to marry her. I have asked her ... wait, how did she know me before *you* told her about me? I approached *her* in the park!"

Zack shook his head. "She is more mature than most twenty-year-old young women. She is also a good girl. I had faith in knowing she was more than able to calm your horses, despite your past dalliances and considerable experience with women. Love is stronger than lust. I knew if you fell in love with Ari you wouldn't take advantage of her. Even if you tried on more than one occasion."

I was embarrassed. I added sincerely, "Ari is remarkable. She is way different than other girls ... women ... I've dated. I didn't want to lose her. I can't explain it. She has me under her control. I would never ... until we get married. Wait, how do you know about my experiences with other ... women? Never mind, I don't want to know. You've obviously been spying on me."

"I wouldn't call it spying," Zack said. He paused. "OK, maybe that was spying."

"Hold on a minute," I said. "What is a genetic dissident? Like many people I'm supposedly genetically engineered from the selected genes of my carefully screened parents. Now you're saying I'm an adopted orphan of a genetic dissident, whatever that is. Wouldn't they have discovered that in my GIA profile?"

Zack lifted his hand to cut me off. "You weren't listening. It was your father Vincent who was adopted by the Verigratu family, not you. It doesn't surprise me that you are unaware of what the Ministry you hope to work for really does. There are different classifications of genetic dissidents. Some are executed and some are enslaved. Members of our family are on the Class 1 'to be the executed' list. Ari is particularly at risk. They are hunting for her for other reasons."

"Hunting her for what other reasons? I don't understand," I said, exasperated.

"Regardless of the fact that you're engineered to be as close to perfection as humanly possible, you are still a Waters. Only the diligent efforts of many people you will never know have prevented you from being discovered. Nevertheless, the name Fortisal and its connection to Verigratu is not buried deep enough. They will find you eventually. When they do, they will make you disappear, and no one will ever hear from you again. Ari is especially vulnerable, and there are far more opportunities for them to get their hands on an updated genetic profile on her than on me. It would only take one clever formulation, at just the right moment, for LEOH to discover either of you."

"How did you know I'm trying to get a job at the NCMIA?"

Zack produced a blue disc, which he laid on the table. "I know you are trying to get a job at the Ministry for the same reason I am going to ensure you receive an offer to work there. I made certain they recruited you in the first place. Believe me, you are exactly what they are looking for. This disc identifies me as an executive officer of the Ministry, from which I am now long retired. I was the deputy director, which means I have an unrestricted license to establish a surveillance dead space within my own home. Actually, this policy has changed, but I still uphold it."

"Why would you arrange for the Ministry to recruit me?" I said, angry now.

"In time, I will tell you. Make no mistake, willingly or not, you are already an enemy of this city," Zack warned. "It's not because of what you believe or don't believe. It's because you are a descendant of my father, whom the beings who rule this city hated, because of what he did. If I told you why, you wouldn't believe me."

"Then tell me why Ari is particularly at risk," I demanded.

"That is truly an interesting question. But I can't tell you about that, either. As far as you should be concerned, right now Ariel is the only one left on my side of my father's family and must be protected at all costs. I know you two will soon marry; this is one reason I needed to meet you. She is eighteen and perfect for you, as you will eventually be for her."

"Eventually? What does that mean? It's like I don't even know who Ari is."

"I will tell you who Ari is," Zack said. "Most human beings see things only from the perspective of where they are in the world. However, some people are gifted to see things in a different dimension, a spiritual one. Ari can see things because she has a connection to God most people don't have. She has a heart for what she sees, because she knows she has an important role, as do you."

"What role? What are you talking about? I said. "There is no such thing as God. Ari has never mentioned any spiritual connections to God."

"The man who occupies the throne of this world is not really a man!" Zack declared. "Rather, he is one possessed by the ruler over the powers of darkness."

I shrugged. "I don't believe any of that or anything about God, even if Ari believes it."

Zack looked at me intently. "You will! The devil has finally gained his greatest desire, to sit on the throne of this world. He realizes his time is short and he is doomed to destruction. He is confined to the body of a man and stripped of his ethereal power. The Archon is driven by his diminished authority in the spiritual dimension. He is trying to discover how to get it back. He knows his own inescapable doom is written in the words he hatefully suppresses."

"So you expect me to believe the Archon is the devil?" I said. "Really?"

Zack responded, "I realize, at this point, I might as well tell you aliens came to earth to take over and now run things; you don't believe anything I've said."

Zack stood up and walked toward the balcony, which overlooked the city. "Tomorrow you will have your final interviews as a formulation specialist and matrix analyst for the Ministry. You will be offered a position to work for the Central Control Division or CCD. You will probably meet Dalen Pythorael. Eventually you will be given access to sensitive classified information. This will prove what I am saying about the ongoing search for members of our family, and also thousands of other families, is true."

"I don't know how to respond to this," I said, frustrated.

After a brief pause, Zack added, "I'm sure you're aware that LEOH is far more than just a centralized computer system that runs the city."

I nodded in acknowledgement.

"That's another thing which has been around since before the Final War," Zack pointed out. "Of course, it's been upgraded countless times. It's the most all-encompassing artificial intelligence and data collection system ever devised or imagined. At this very moment, your PCD is collecting information about our conversation to transmit it directly to LEOH. It would, that is, except they are blocked while you are in this room. It is specially shielded to disrupt the microburst transmissions. I can also shield conversations in other parts of my home when necessary.

"Through LEOH, the Ministry collects everything about everyone. They can discover everything about you and every citizen of New City. It is the job of the Ministry formulation specialists, and soon to be your job, to prepare utilization matrixes for the highest priority directives issued by LEOH. Just as I once was, you will be trained to hunt down people like us. If they discover who Ari is, I fear it could be far worse for her than for us."

I was horrified to hear this. "I want to know if my relationship with Ari is real?" I asked. "I love her. I want to marry her. But if all I am to her is someone you have manipulated, then I ..."

Zack held up his hand. "Mark, stop! You're here because she is in love with you. I pray you are in love with her. Your love for each other is the only reason I can trust you with her life. What I need you to do at the Ministry is only the first crucial step. Ari has given herself to you because she loves you and because you will help her fulfill her purpose."

"Ari and I can get married, then enjoy our lives away from all this," I said.

"You could do that, I suppose, provided Ari is willing," Zack replied. "But you can't run away from who you are. There is no place where the Ministry can't find you. LEOH is evolving at a frightening pace. They are also building a new LEOH, one which will be far more capable. I desperately need you to do something for me, for all of us, before this occurs. Only someone with the access you will have can do this. You will eventually be trained to accomplish what is necessary."

"What could I possibly help you do by working for the Ministry?"

"I'll tell you when you're ready. Everything must happen in the proper sequence. A hook is worthless without the bait, just as a spider won't know she has captured her prey until she feels it trapped in her web. Then you can catch the spider."

"What does that mean? And what does this have to do with Ari?"

"When Ari recognized your image from a dream, I knew it was time for her to meet you. She was fifteen when she started dreaming about you. She dreamed about you for months. I told her not to reveal her visions to you, because I wanted you to know your affection for each other is genuine. Ari is exceptionally gifted in more ways than even she realizes."

"Do you mean her artistic abilities?" I asked.

Zack laughed and nodded his head. "That's a small part of it. If I told you she picked up an artist's brush for the first time at fourteen, and within a year was able to mimic a masterpiece, you might think I was lying. She can do things with ease that others can't. Yet her grandfather wanted to have her institutionalized when she was child because he believed her to be mentally unhinged. Hard to believe, yes? Yet all these things are true about Ari."

Ari is by far the smartest person I've ever met."

"But she struggled to learn to speak clearly," Zack said. "Her brain scrambled auditory signals. And despite being told she would be severely handicapped, by the time she was eight she was able to read at a post-graduate level. Her capacity to grasp information is astonishing, but she consciously suppresses her abilities. I home schooled her for ten years, mainly to protect her from being discovered."

"She's lied to me about all of this, including her age," I said, frowning. "How can I trust her?"

Zack placed a bony hand on my shoulder. "She only lied to you about her age because I told her to do so. She doesn't know the reasons I had you recruited by the Ministry. The fewer people who know the better. You can't talk openly about any of this with her. But Ari is the key to all of this. I can't tell you everything now. Trust no one at the Ministry, except my friend Jerome. He has my old job as deputy director of the CCD. We go way back. He knows almost everything about our situation. He oversees directive assessments for the CCD and reports directly to Director Dalen Pythorael. Watch out for Pythorael; don't ever trust him."

"Now I know the real reason why she wanted me to finish my degree and it wasn't ... I already know she lied about that. What does the CCD do?"

Zack waved his hand, as if to understate its importance. "That's the Central Control Division for Ministry operations worldwide. Ostensibly, the CCD reports directly to the High Echelon, which is like a large committee of agency heads, directors, and governors. The personnel within the CCD have much greater access to the LEOH formulation matrixes than other Ministry divisions and somewhat even between jurisdictions. Dalen is also a member of the New City Inner Circle; that's the NCIC, of course."

"What about my father? Shouldn't he be told about this?"

"I think it would be best if Vincent were not informed. He's probably aware that he was adopted. There is no need to tell him he's a genetic dissident. Like you, most people have no idea what that means. The Ministry doesn't publicize their objectives. Besides, Ari has not dreamed about his generation of our family; it is you and she who will change the world."

"What if I don't want the world to change?"

"When you find out what the Ministry really does, you will," Zack said. "Why do you think everyone is oblivious to what the Ministry does and what is really going on in New City? You thought you were interviewing to work for an elite government security agency. You are about to be indoctrinated into a whole new reality about this world, my young friend. You'll be sworn to secrecy upon threat of death, and there is a whole Ministry division devoted to spying on its own spies, including you."

CHAPTER 3

SMALL BEGINNINGS

The spectacular buildings and spires of the central zone of the New City Government District (NCGD) are surrounded by enclaves of mansions and gated estates. This is where New City's titled nobility and wealthiest citizens live, as well as those mysterious members of the High Echelon and NCIC.

The Archon's colossal Southern Jurisdiction Citadel is on the fringe of the NCGD central hub. Within this realm, these privileged families live like royalty. They are unapproachable compared with my family. They run everything and live behind walls of enormous estates within the well protected NCGD. They are a breed and a class apart. No one I know associates or interacts with them. Growing up, we were taught these families are elite and honored. Even though I had money and lived in a penthouse, I was still dirt on the shoes of these people—as was everyone who was not part of their exclusive world.

* * * *

Despite the distance of hundreds of kilometers to the New City government complex, I reached the district in about thirty minutes by the Fleet Rail System. This is an underground, magnetized, pneumatic floating train, commonly referred to as the air tube, or FRS. Within about twenty kilometers of each station, the nicely appointed trains enter a high-speed underground vacuum corridor that allows them to rapidly accelerate. Trains make almost no sound as they move through a sealed tube, and are incredibly fast. Riders can hardly tell they're moving, except by noticing the scenery projections whizzing by on the electronic window displays.

The FRS is, for the most part, faster than flying. Commercial flights are typically sub-supersonic or otherwise restricted over most of New City's airspace. Few people use commercial sky ports. At this point, I had never flown anywhere, nor had I the need to do so. The ultra-rich, of course, fly in luxury in their expensive custom-made aircraft that are fitted out in opulent style and are like flying homes. Some cost hundreds of millions of currency units (CUs), which seems ludicrous. Mostly I travel via a public self-driving programmable vehicle (SDPV). In fact, so few people own cars anymore that the words "car" and "automobile" have disappeared from the vernacular of New City.

As the FRS sped through my district, I watched the eastern mountains fade into the far horizon. The government center complex is in a large area of rolling hills and thick forests on the northern boundary of the NCGD. In the southern part of the NCGD are immense expanses of mechanized farmland. These act as a buffer between the NCGD and the other New City districts. The entire NCGD is surrounded by high-tech defenses and military emplacements, along with multiple levels of high security perimeter fencing. This was briefly visible in the outside display windows as the FRS made its way into the district. The trip was relatively quick. Soon, I was standing outside the Central Control Division headquarters.

* * * *

I did meet with Dalen Pythorael and Jerome Haley during my final interviews, and I was offered a position, just as Zack anticipated. I started working for the Ministry on July 16th 63 NCE. I learned I was to be implanted again. This made me hugely uncomfortable. I'd had terrible experiences with an internal PCD implant previously, but it was part of CCD's job requirement. Besides the chronic headaches, I was also the recipient of several unsolicited services and deliveries due to integration malfunctions.

During my orientation and training, I began to realize the terrifying power of LEOH. New City operates on an open platform that uses a complex security access and credentialing module to authorize and register everyone into the system through their PCD. LEOH records every interaction a person has with any device or ID node within range. It also records and compiles every conversation of every person. Those with a Ministry security access code are granted access to the LEOH systems' immense array of formulation data matrixes, including vast amounts of signals intelligence and meta data on everybody and anything under the sun—including individuals' GIA genetic profile matrix.

The information available to a CCD operative is simply unfathomable, not to mention unsettling. LEOH is designed to assess threats across an unlimited range of human activity. Granted, no one is listening to every conversation taking place in New City. Yet, by virtue of LEOH's artificial intelligence capabilities, any conversation can trigger an alert for enhanced surveillance or a security directive if it's serious enough.

No one is immune from detection. If the Ministry wants to find you, or find out what you are doing, and with whom you are doing it, it will. This is terrifying.

Yet almost everyone in New City is oblivious to this intrusion, even though they know they are connected to everything through their PCD. It doesn't matter if your PCD is a direct implant or not.

By law everyone must be equipped with a PCD. This facilitates a security matrix profile which is created by LEOH with a link to their genetic profile. (LEOH's intelligence about targets is often enhanced by identifying genetic relationships.) The objective of a Ministry operative like myself is to create a dossier as part of an (actionable security directive). However, no one in my position is told what is ultimately done with our output, or if an operation is carried out as a result of it.

Those decisions are referred to people like the Deputy Director, Jerome Haley, or his staff.

* * * *

One afternoon I was summoned to Jerome's office. He introduced me to one of his senior executives, Merrick Taylor, who was in charge of external security.

"Merrick has asked me to recommend a junior operative from the CCD formulation team to assist with a special project," Jerome said. "This will involve updating analysis formulations for our signal intelligence facilities in the Dead Zone, where we're experiencing data corruption issues with sensor output. We suspect these anomalies may be caused by infiltration events. However, whoever is doing this is quite clever, because we can find no indications of overt tampering."

Merrick nodded in agreement. "One unlikely possibility is that someone is accessing the sensor arrays from inside these unmanned facilities. So, in addition to upgrading the formulation algorithms used in these telemetry stations, we will carry out an overall security assessment of a few sites to determine if they have been infiltrated. Though I doubt anyone could break in these secure bunkers."

Jerome added, "We need a project team to visit these sites, bring them up to date, and recalibrate and upgrade stations that require hardware and formulation enhancements that can't be handled remotely. Mark, I realize you are still in training and haven't received a permanent long-term assignment, but this is an opportunity to prove your ability to improvise, as well as gain valuable hands-on experience. In the process, you'll also learn how our overall DZ external signal intelligence works. I wouldn't give this assignment to just anyone. My decision was confirmed by our resource control application. It issued an 83 percent optimization score on this assignment for you. I hope you have no objections to a little adventure."

I was flattered. "It sounds fascinating. I've never been outside the walls to the Dead Zone."

"Oh, I forgot to mention," Jerome continued, "I know you're having an internal PCD implant mapped. This will continue, but at a much slower pace and only for rudimentary controls. Due to this assignment, I have obtained authorization to have your implant procedure postponed until after this project is complete. One reason you were chosen is because current implant technology is not integrated in the Dead Zones. Internal implants must be taken offline; we use only external PCDs outside the walls. However, this has created re-synchronization issues when implants are later brought back online. So while you're going through the mapping process your implant is indefinitely delayed, or at least the process will be significantly slowed."

He added, "Also, your extensive weapons training is a plus."

This concerned me. I said, "I did the weapons training for fun, because I was competing in a simulated combat league with friends. It would hardly qualify as real weapons training. Will this operation be dangerous?"

"Going outside the walls is always dangerous to some degree," Jerome replied. "It can be extremely dangerous in certain places, but not where your project team is headed. These are all Security Level 3 sites. They're well to the east of the high-risk zones. Everything should be fine."

* * * *

As my orientation and training progressed, and the longer I worked for the Ministry, the more I hated how intrusive it was. It pursues anyone with a contrary opinion of New City and anyone suspected of subversive activities. It was obvious they weren't focused on catching real criminals. My perspective of New City had indeed changed just as Zack said it would. We were living in a paranoid police state that spied on people to find out who was disloyal.

The most frightening aspect was the Ministry's obsession around identifying and locating genetic dissidents, of which I know I am one, at least according to Zack. The compilation of massive amounts of matrix data linked with the GIA profile system to find genetic dissidents, was clearly at the forefront of all Ministry activities.

What was odd was that the Ministry had difficulty identifying and locating dissidents. Even when it did, the security directives remained open. While my group wasn't directly involved with security actions or capture orders, I saw that the number of security directives for C1, C2, and C3 dissidents, which are not closed, always continued to increase. Managing to apprehend even a single Class 2 genetic dissident was a huge deal. All genetic dissident security directives were expedited to "high priority" and yet, for some inexplicable reason, Ministry operations initiated as a result of these directives were the least successful at capturing their intended targets. Little did I know how much Ari's great-grandfather, Zack, was in some way responsible for this.

CHAPTER 4

THE KEYS AND THE CLOAK

During the first month or so after I started working at the Ministry, my relationship with Ari remained the highlight of my life. We got married on the 21st of July 63 NCE. It was a small, private, informal affair, with a few of our friends. While I was uncomfortable with the religious nature of the ceremony, I knew this was what Ari wanted and it wasn't illegal. She was devout in her beliefs, but she knew she couldn't talk too much about it, unless we were in a dead space at Zack's apartment. In depth religious discussions were dangerous to have in New City.

The day we married was the greatest day of my life; I couldn't stop thinking about Ari while I was at work. Those first few weeks we spent together before she left for school were wonderful. Then, around the first week of September, Ari informed me that she was pregnant.

I was shocked, because we had not discussed having children. I assumed she was taking care of the birth control situation. I wasn't angry or upset. I was even happy about it, but I did think she was too young to start having children, especially since she had just started college.

When I asked why she hadn't taken precautions she said, "Mark, I was raised by my great-grandfather, someone who didn't teach me anything a girl needs to know about stuff like that. It's kind of embarrassing. The only thing he taught me is *no* boys were allowed … you know, until I got married. In fact, no boys were allowed anywhere near me."

"Ari, I'm not mad, but you know how it works—girls get pregnant without protection. It's simple biology. Also, you know what we are and New City procreation laws say we must have the fetus genetically evaluated. That could be dangerous ... for all of us."

"I know, I'm learning about that," Ari gripped. "Genetic modification is prohibited after three months and they can force me to have a chemical abortion. We have until mid-November to get a certification to have a child. They can literally destroy the child the day we are tested. They don't need our permission, and if we don't get tested, we could be heavily fined or arrested."

"I am talking about the fact that we are ... didn't Zack tell you about our family?" I said.

"Oh, that, yes of course. My God, what are we going to do?"

"Ari, LEOH will know, there is no hiding this, trust me. We have to tell Zack, and soon."

* * * *

About mid-September, Zack ushered me to his office the moment I arrived for a visit. He wanted to keep our conversations to a minimum so we didn't meet too often. He handed me a short, handwritten list of what appeared to be security access codes. "Mark, listen carefully. I wanted to wait a bit longer before giving you these. However, certain matters have come to my attention, so I must confide in you now. What I am about to ask you to do is the first reason I wanted you in the Ministry."

I stared at the list of thirty-character alpha numeric codes. Each code was followed by a long hexadecimal key.

"What are these supposed to be? Why would you actually write something like this on paper?"

Zack seemed upset. "I've received intelligence that the upgrade on the new LEOH II system is moving far faster than I'd anticipated. I knew it was years ahead of schedule, but I thought we still had a few months, at least. Not long ago, we thought we still had years."

"Jerome indicated it was moving fast. He didn't mention a specific time frame," I said.

Zack replied, "The Archon's little systems wizard has managed to speed up development considerably in her short tenure as the L2 project lead. Being a technologist yourself, you may have heard of her. You've certainly heard of her family if you listen to the NC News Service. She is the Norean ēlan and she's renowned in academic circles for several remarkable accomplishments. Anyway, Jerome says he heard yesterday she's returning to the Southern Jurisdiction permanently. We don't have an exact timeline. If she is returning to the Citadel server complex, it could only mean she's completed Phase 1 of L2, and it may be a matter of weeks before it is fully implemented."

"Jerome was making a big deal of this new platform to our division. It's going to vastly reduce the need for human intelligence operatives. So, what's the issue?" I asked. "Didn't you say they're always upgrading LEOH, and it even upgrades itself?"

Zack shook his head. "L2 is no mere upgrade. It is vitally important we act now, or we may lose our critical window of opportunity. I've been developing this plan for well over a decade, since I retired from the Ministry. There are a great number of people depending upon you at this very moment, even though they don't realize it."

I raised my eyebrows questioningly.

Zack continued, "What I just handed you are ghosted security access codes, along with their passkeys. I created them when I worked for former Deputy Director Nicholas Santos under Dalen Pythorael. Memorize them! They are unrestricted and untraceable in the system. They are also illegal.

"Using these codes must be done from inside the Ministry operations at a CCD access node. Those nodes are specifically designed to handle the necessary bandwidth for the data I need you to obtain. They are also inside the classified SADEX firewall. You will need to use several storage cubes for each formulation that I will give you to run. The data could be quite extensive. It will have to be done over several days or weeks to prevent triggering a bandwidth utilization alert. There is another way I am considering. It could collect the data much faster. It's also far riskier. Once L2 goes live, we may not be able to use these codes. It is probable she developed safeguards to stop them."

"Hold on a minute," I said. "What do you mean by the data you need *me* to obtain? Are you asking me to steal classified data?" I was stunned. "Is this why you wanted me inside the Ministry? Am I an expendable patsy? I never agreed to become a spy, and I don't think this is what Ari would want me to do."

Zack said soothingly, "I can see how you might think this. All I need you to do is to initiate the interface. It shouldn't be too dangerous. Let me finish explaining why this is so important. Then you can ask questions."

I shook my head, as if already refusing. "No, I won't use these codes inside the Ministry. They watch everything we do, all the time. Are you trying to get me killed? How did you manage to create these? What you are asking me to do is criminal!"

Zack looked disappointed. "Mark, *they* are the criminals; this will prove it!"

"Zack, they track everything, including if I don't breathe normally or if my heartrate increases. If I sweat too much or get nervous it could trigger an alert."

"I think you're overreacting," Zack said. "Pythorael used to control T-Alpha access to LEOH. Under the direction of his former deputy, Nicholas Santos, I was given the responsibility, using his credentials, to create some special access codes. Dalen wanted access to the system no one could trace. To do this he used these special codes to create a series of spybots. A protocol was designed to ghost the activity of these codes to remove evidence that their activity was indexed. These codes cannot be deleted, or their access changed. Their security profile is invisible even to *her*. At least they are in the current version of LEOH"

"I don't care if they are hidden from God; I am not using any illegal access codes," I insisted. "How do you even know they are still invisible?"

"It's a complex process to create one of these," Zack said. "It was only intended to be temporary. Yet Dalen had created a monster he could not put back in the box, or rather, something that could not be removed from it, so to speak. In the process, I secretly created these additional codes. Pythorael never knew about these. Even if they could be detected, there would be no evidence they had anything to do with the original codes. Most likely, the Ministry would perceive this as a new threat. But I have every reason to believe they are still valid in this current version of LEOH, but not L2."

"So, I can use these codes at any access node and my data formulation and utilization activities would be untraceable? This is insane. There is no way I am doing this inside the Ministry."

Zack was unmoved. "This is, in effect, the key to the safe where they keep their informational jewels. It's also an invisibility cloak, and I am giving it to you."

"Why didn't you use these codes yourself when you were at the Ministry? Why now, and why me? What about Jerome?" I said.

"I have put a few of them to good use over the intervening years," Zack countered. "I couldn't use them myself inside the Ministry. Pythorael had Santos removed shortly after they were created. I was then appointed deputy director. I think Pythorael was trying to cover his tracks for something, possibly even this, or some other conspiracy. Once I was a high-level executive, it was impossible for me to use them for this purpose. Besides, my system activities were being scrutinized more so than a lower level operative. Even so, Pythorael never knew Santos allowed me to use his credentials to create these additional codes. The man was sloppy and lazy. That's probably what got him killed, although I think he was framed.

"Mark, while I was at the Ministry, I did things that went against my conscience. Yet I also created the opportunity to help you and others permanently weaken and undermine the Archon. If the Archon is indeed about to flip the switch on L2, it could prevent us from accomplishing anything. At some point, we are going to have to deal with *her*. That will come later, once you obtain this information."

"What do you mean, *deal with her*?" I said. "Is this the ēlan you mentioned before?"

"Yes, the L2 developer! She is a venomous spider and LEOH II is her web,"

"You must really hate her."

Zack shook his head. "On the contrary, I love spiders. They are quite clever and adept at catching all sorts of harmful prey. I just happen to know that this one can even catch serpents."

I was incredulous. "Whatever. I've never heard of a spider catching a snake. Anyway, how are using these codes going to undermine the Archon? I believe you're exaggerating the impact of stealing classified information. This is way too risky and I don't feel comfortable even talking about it."

Zack looked at me and smoothed his beard. "There is still much you need to learn about this world, Mark. You also have much to learn about those you work for, especially the Archon, as well as Dalen Pythorael. I have tried to tell you these things slowly, over time. I had hoped you would have been farther along in your understanding, but we are running out of time. By the way, how are things going with you and Ari?"

"Thing are wonderful," I said. "However, given our dissident status, we are terrified because she is pregnant. We will eventually have to go through fetal genetic screening. She was apparently ignorant about how to prevent it. I foolishly thought she was handling this particular marital department."

"Already? Congratulations!" Zack laughed enthusiastically. "I'm thrilled for both of you. It's all the more reason why you must do this now. Verigratu or not, your child is another Waters the Ministry will try to find. L2 may ultimately uncover what has been done in the past to protect you and Ari. Your child will be extremely vulnerable. That will make you vulnerable, and especially Ari. If they discover Ari, the consequences for her could be dire. You must do this for her sake."

"How will my stealing classified data protect Ari?" I said, confused.

Zack handed me a data cube. "It won't, right away. Mark, this contains the formulations I have created thus far to obtain the information we need to expose the Archon's most monstrous plans. With these codes you can grab anything within LEOH with a maximum SADEX score. I assume you know about the Security Access Data Exchange score. It determines what credential level can access a particular record matrix. The higher the score, the more security clearance you need, up to T-Alpha-Prime."

"Yes, I know what a SADEX score is," I sighed.

Zack was clearly growing weary. He sat down and bowed his head. He looked up at me. "What I have given to you is the backdoor into LEOH and the black heart of this city. These codes are both the key to allow you in and a cloak to keep you hidden. What I've told you before is mainly about the past. It's the present and future that needs to be exposed, so the whole world will know the truth."

Zack continued, "Mark, the impact of this could be far reaching. They will stop at nothing to prevent this information from getting out once they discover it has been stolen. In time, I will make certain they find out. By then, they'll have no way to know who actually stole it. Once it is out, it will be too late for them.

"When he does find out, the Archon will send his most rabid dogs looking for whomever took the data. Undoubtedly, the CCD will be given primary responsibility to investigate this. It is my hope—and certainty— that the Archon will involve this spider, or she will get involved herself. Then you'll have a chance to help me catch her. Jerome will appoint you as the CCD liaison to deal with her. I can't tell you why yet. This will change everything. Do you love Ari?" Zack asked. "If you truly love her, you will do this. She has dreamed about this for years."

I had no idea why Zack kept referring to this supposed spider. I clearly didn't have the whole story. "What do you mean, everything could change? Who is this ēlan spider you keep mentioning? Why would Ari dream about this?"

Zack replied, "She's someone you would otherwise never have an opportunity to meet. She can be extremely … dangerous. You've probably heard her name before, or seen her image. I'm certain, if you had, you would remember her. Her name is Tabitha Kimerlin Norean. She's extraordinarily beautiful, with blond hair and blue eyes, and exceptionally intelligent."

"I might have heard of her," I said "Maybe I've seen an image of her, but I've never been interested in their world. I don't keep track of what some aloof ēlan is up to, even if it involves technology. Everyone else in the world are mere peons to those people."

Zack laughed. "To be acknowledged as a peon means they would actually have to consider you at all. Most of them would be content if they were the only people left in this world. However, my illustrious little spider is of particular interest to me. I can guarantee she will be interested in finding you, once you steal payloads of classified data out of the Noreans' precious LEOH system. Their company, NED Tech, developed every version of it for New City. She will doubtless take it personally if it's breached. That's my hope, anyway. I would also like to have at least one last chance to personally meet her, even if her venomous bite results in my death."

"You just said you like spiders; now you think she will kill you?"

"Mark, you must understand, everything I am asking you to do is coming from Ari. It is perhaps my interpretation of her visions and dreams, nonetheless, it is still from her. Moreover, it is coming from the spiritual realm. I have faith it is God who is speaking through her."

"God tells Ari to dream about a spider? Why hasn't she talked to me about any of this? She has never mentioned her dreams, and certainly no visions about ēlans or spiders."

"In time, she will," Zack said confidently. "When she does, I advise you to listen very carefully. What she sees could be a warning that could save your life."

CHAPTER 5

THE LAIR OF THE SERPENT

Apart from his Citadel in the Southern Jurisdiction, the next primary residence of the Archon was a remote bastion, hidden away and largely underground, in the central Alpine regions of the Northern Jurisdiction. Here, he had carried out many of his plans since well before the Final War. It was more than a mountain fortress or a military installation. It was also a magnificent palace and a clandestine research facility. The Archon had many such "Citadels," as he referred to them, all over the world.

This Citadel, at Interlochen, was perhaps his most prized stronghold, built upon the backbone of the old world. It was concealed in what was once considered the most staunchly neutral of all independent states. The Swiss had remained neutral throughout the Final War. As a concession, the entirety of Switzerland was still considered a special district within the Northern Jurisdiction of New City. They were thus allowed to maintain at least a pretense of sovereignty.

It was to this Citadel that the Archon summoned his director of the NCMIA CCD and his NCIC director of internal security.

* * * *

The Archon paced behind his massive, ornate desk in the cavernous throne room of the palace Citadel, which was now his private office.

"Thank you for making the trip here on such short notice," he began sarcastically. Rogan and Pythorael had been waiting an entire day for an audience. "Allow me to get to the point. The thing that should have been your highest priority has somehow become virtually impossible for you two misfits to accomplish. So I have undertaken to ferret out the problems myself, while waiting to hear of any progress from a hapless Ministry, which is apparently unable to track down the enemies of this city, *MY* city." He slammed his fist down on the desk as he glowered at Pythorael and Rogan, who sat before him fidgeting.

The Archon continued, still enraged, "As a result of this twenty-year-old corruption issue within the GIA profile matrix for the Southern Jurisdiction, we still don't have a complete list of targets. The ones we do identify, or attempt to apprehend, manage to escape into the DZ with astonishing ease. Not only that, we still have no idea of the location of this 'hidden' city. It doesn't take a genius to realize there is a sophisticated organization behind this. Over the last twenty years, they have gained access into our security directive matrix and also corrupted the GIA profile compiler. As a result, nearly seventy years after we activated LEOH, matters are worse. Instead of improving our ability to identify and locate these dissidents the Ministry cannot account for the ones we have identified. We don't even know if they are still within the confines of the city walls. This condition is about to change!"

The Archon stared at his two hapless ministers with contempt. "Some months ago, on my orders, I had the last version LEOH, including the genetic profile matrix, fully restored through the last upgrade on a separate quantum network. The technical division also reintegrated all the old matrixes, which pre-dated the war. Would you like to know what we discovered?"

"I am certain you intend to tell me, Devan, so you can stop the theatrics," Pythorael replied.

The Archon glared at him. "What we discovered is, someone has managed to penetrate the LEOH system with astonishing regularity over the years. This infiltration is far worse than we anticipated. I am greatly concerned that this could impact our new LEOH II implementation. You should also be concerned about what we discovered about how this came about."

A double door opened from a side room. A man wearing gaudy robes walked into the chamber. Dalen immediately recognized the shifty looking man with his bulging squinty eyes. "Prideil? How, did you manage to get released?" Pythorael walked over to Prideil. The two embraced, then clasped hands.

The Archon bellowed, "Sit down, all of you! Nathan is no longer subordinate to you. He reports only to me. I kept his release secret so he could oversee my investigation of the Ministry."

Nathan Prideil sat down in the last of three chairs in front of the Archon's desk. The Archon continued, "Lord Prideil and his staff have run comparison analyses between the current version of LEOH in use today within the Southern Jurisdiction and the previous version that we restored. This also happens to coincide with a point in time, in which you, Lord Pythorael, controlled full T-Alpha credential authority. He has discovered some interesting anomalies, which are quite troubling. I will let Nathan explain." The Archon nodded to Prideil.

"Before you begin," Rogan interrupted, "It is urgent I return to the Southern Jurisdiction at once. LEOH has generated a series NCIC directives against the CCD deputy director in the Southern Jurisdiction. Jerome Haley has been detained for questioning. There is also a time sensitivity to these directives as they involve the possible illegal transit of Class 2 genetic dissidents and their families. We have only a small window of time to act on this intelligence."

The Archon waved his hand. "Certainly, you have my permission to leave at once. I'm anxious to find out if there is a rogue executive at the highest levels of the CCD." The Archon stared at Pythorael. "It is a shame that you won't be present to hear more about our upcoming plans. No doubt you have heard rumors. By the way, this will be your last official duty for the NCIC. I am reassigning you back as head of Executive Security over the CCD. Both of you will report to Nathan until this mess at the Ministry is sorted out." He gestured for Prideil to continue.

Prideil turned to face Pythorael. "In my recent investigation we have discovered systemic intrusions into several areas of LEOH," he said. "This spans a time period of over eighteen years. This is far beyond the deliberate downgrading of security directives to prevent enforcement actions. There are an enormous number of breaches into the security directive matrix as well as the GIA profile compiler. We are still in the process of reconstructing these corrupted indexes and the accompanying records."

Pythorael cut him off. "I am well aware of all of these anomalies." Pythorael was clearly nervous, but he remained calm. "Are you suggesting I had something to do with this?"

Prideil was unperturbed. "Our findings raise concerns about the possible use of certain unrestricted access codes we discovered. Evidence clearly shows that someone with ghosted credentials is infiltrating LEOH on a regular basis. They are accessing active SD matrix data on dissidents and other subversives. They are taking advantage of the lag in our procedures. The implications for the exposure of classified information could be catastrophic. If someone inside the Ministry were to have one of these codes and the necessary formulation skills they could access everything."

Pythorael said emphatically, "This has nothing to do with the use of rogue access codes."

"These are not mere anomalies," Prideil said. "Your attempts to cover up evidence of this was obvious. Your former deputy director may have had his name on this, but your hand was clearly behind it."

Pythorael acted indignant; he had prepared for this eventuality. "As the T-Alpha system controller at the time, I did what was necessary to complete the upgrade. I could not do my job without the temporary activation of a handful of unrestricted access codes. If Nicholas Santos were still alive, he could verify what I am telling you. The man was hardly a technical genius. He was a bureaucrat. He didn't possess the technical skills to steal these codes or create additional ones. I can no longer control these events, given my diminished system authority."

"So, you claim you had them disabled a short time after you created them?" Prideil said. "Is this your defense? We are seeing evidence that these codes, or similar ones, are still active."

Pythorael nodded. "Essentially, they have all been quarantined. I can assure you, LEOH can confirm that none of the codes I authorized to be created were utilized again. Don't you think I'd have been aware of this issue if they had?" Pythorael turned to the Archon. "I would have uncovered this security threat years ago had I been allowed to retain my T-Alpha controller credentials. Since the last upgrade, you handed authority for this system over to your L2 development team. Even the High Echelon administration is subordinate to NED Tech R&D protocols."

"Lord Archon, speaking of the L2 development, don't you think it is wise if we relayed these findings to your project lead." Prideil recommended."

"Absolutely not! Tabitha will go off on a costly hunting expedition and try to delay the L2 implementation. I can't risk her knowing about these findings."

The Archon turned to Pythorael, "I will find out what malfunction has occurred within the Ministry to thwart our efforts to capture every genetic dissident and subversive target. If you are involved in this, or if these codes you created are, my systems genius will discover it. LEOH II won't need to rely on the frail limitations of human formulation specialists within the Ministry. It will ultimately become a far more powerful, self-upgrading system once every phase is fully implemented." The Archon laughed. "I won't even need the Ministry, once she completes development of what is outlined for Phase 2."

Pythorael scoffed. "Speaking of frail limitations and human intervention, you have made my point precisely. Regardless of Carl Norean's nobility, not only have you given his company authority over our systems, you've allowed him to put his own daughter in charge of developing the latest version."

"I own the house of Norean, and especially Carl's ēlan. Come, I would like to show you what we have accomplished," the Archon said. He gestured for Prideil and Pythorael to follow him.

The Archon led them out of his office, down several halls and through a maze of passages. They boarded a lift that descended much deeper underground. As they emerged from the lift, they entered a cavernous chamber filled with an abundance of system consoles and cables that fed directly into a central core. A massive machine towered several stories above their heads. The two stared at it in amazement.

"I want to introduce you to someone," the Archon said. They followed him into a control room filled with technicians working furiously at virtual screens. Each one had a PCD implant slightly protruding from the side of their heads, allowing them to directly interface with the system. A beautiful, elegantly dressed blond-haired young woman entered the room from a glass enclosed office. The Archon put his arm around her.

"This is ēlan Dr. Tabitha Norean. She, of course, is our project lead for the development of LEOH II. All these people plugged into this massive quantum molecular system via sensory implants are now her assistants. You obviously know her father, Ēlantiel Carl Norean, CEO of NED Tech. You probably know Kim, her mother. She used to be in charge of this project. Ēlan, I would like to introduce you to two of my associates, Dalen Pythorael and Nathan Prideil."

Tabitha nodded to the two men. "I am not actually a doctor," she said. "But if it gives you more confidence, by all means, make it so."

Pythorael responded, "It's a pleasure to finally meet you ēlan. I heard you are returning to the Southern Jurisdiction. I assume you are planning to hand over this project to someone else, so you can work on the R&D for the next phase?"

Tabitha seemed surprised. "I thought you, of all people, would be aware I'm returning the SJ to complete the rollout. L2 is going live at the end of this week despite my recommendations to rebuild the SCP to Darth Scrooge here."

"Ēlan, the IC committee has evaluated your SCP recommendations and concluded the security risk to be low versus the delay and costs," The Archon said.

"The SCP?" Pythorael said. "L2 is going live this week?"

"The security and credentialing platform," Tabitha fumed. "It's a rat's nest. Devan your committee is nothing more than a bunch of groveling toadies. I wouldn't trust them to evaluate the specifications on a coffee maker."

"Nevertheless, we are proceeding. You have surpassed everyone's expectations. You've certainly surprised the esteemed director of the CCD."

Pythorael was practically speechless. "I am indeed surprised. I would have hoped to have more time to prepare my staff for the eventual changes which will necessarily follow."

The Archon placed his hand on Pythorael's back. "You can give them a preparatory talk the day before. It will take some time before staff reductions will begin to be implemented. We are going to have a grand affair at the Citadel in the Southern Jurisdiction to celebrate this success."

Tabitha rolled her eyes. "Devan, please don't expect me to attend some obnoxious event in celebration of your megalomania and for pushing humanity toward an inescapable abyss."

"Nonsense!" the Archon said. "You deserve to be recognized for this achievement. Do you have any idea the billions of CUs you will ultimately have saved New City by completing this project so far ahead of schedule? Then there are the ongoing operational savings we will realize."

Tabitha yawned. "No, Devan, and I really don't care. If all I had was a billion for each time I cared about how much money I saved you and this city, I would be destitute."

"It certainly matters to me. For this, I am grateful," the Archon said. "You're only twenty years old and look at what you've accomplished. It was a virtual impossibility, yet you did it."

"Don't remind me of what I've accomplished," Tabitha said bitterly. "And I don't wish to be publicly acknowledged for building this system for you. It is tantamount to being celebrated for discovering the plague and creating the means to make certain everyone is instantly exposed to it."

The Archon laughed. "I do adore your sense of humor, ēlan."

"Yes, I'm living proof that people can adeptly accomplish what they oppose. Don't worry, Devan, I'm sure it will be even more horrific than you ever dreamed it could be."

"That's what I love about you, ēlan." The Archon smiled. "You never forget you're a Norean."

"Don't remind me. I live every day trying to forget that inescapable fact."

"You're adorable. I will miss having you here every day and watching you ... work." He smiled.

"Don't say things like that to a clarion, especially with a pregnant pause," Tabitha retorted.

* * * *

"She is an impertinent, disrespectful child. I mean, she's impressive, but she's so young," Pythorael complained as they headed back to the Archon's council chamber. "I had no idea you were this close to rolling out your implementation for LEOH II. I was aware you were making remarkable progress. Yet two years ago, the L2 Phase 1 was still a decade away."

The Archon said, "I thought you would have been more aware of our progress, since we keep the CCD technical services group up to date. Perhaps your deputy director isn't keeping you as well informed as he should. It's my intention to convert every jurisdiction to the Phase 1 platform by the first of the new year. Phase 2 should be completed by this time next year."

Pythorael sighed as the three of them exited the lift. "Devan, need I remind you of my concerns about these overly ambitious plans? I realize you have been working diligently on the Optimus Project, in tandem with this new version of LEOH, for as many years. I am fairly certain that humanity is not prepared to accept what you have in mind for Phase 2."

The Archon seemed unconcerned. "Let me worry about compliance problems. I'm far more interested in accomplishing my goals with ēlan Tabitha. She has extraordinary potential for power in the ethereal realms. You are aware, she was the only successful subject from the K15 initiative?"

Pythorael scoffed. "I am, but I seriously doubt that discredited, fraudulent quack, Harold Dylanis, had anything to do with enhancing her abilities, or if she even has the sequence. As far as her connection to the ethereal realms, I believe you are still living with the delusion that that hag, Jennipa, was a credible seer."

The Archon said, "Do I detect some measure of doubt that I have finally discovered my long-awaited vessel, who will soon be at the age of three sevens?"

"Your obsession to produce an offspring is disturbing," Pythorael said, scorn in his voice. "If you attempt to complete the ritual with her, you may press matters beyond any point of return. To raise such a pow-erful sorceress, as you desire, is only a foolish fantasy. I strongly advise against this. Besides, she is not even likely to be a maiden, given her attractiveness and her age. She's also Ēlantiel Carl Norean's daughter. Is he fully aware of your intentions for his only ēlan?"

"She is still a virgin, although not untouched," the Archon insisted. "She has been living here for the last three years. I have been keeping a close watch on her. Apart from an occasional short trip to return home to the Southern Jurisdiction, she never leaves this Citadel. She is not involved with any man. She only engages in her own self-gratification, which I carefully monitor and initiate as needed, for research purposes. Besides, her disdain for men is well known, due to certain incidents in her past."

"Are you telling me you spy on the girl in her own chambers and induce her ... to do that?" Pythorael asked, indignantly. "She is not a lab rat. She is an ēlan of New City."

"You know full well she must give herself to me voluntarily. Her sensual response must be highly susceptible, accentuated, and cultivated to perfection. In her case, let's just say, her response would be difficult without these measures, with a man anyway. A sensual climax is precisely where the most intimate details of a female's hidden name is revealed," the Archon said.

Pythorael grimaced with revulsion. "Carmelineals don't need to do it this way, only you do."

The Archon ignored Pythorael. "Her eighteenth year would have been preferable. At the time, I considered it more important for her to continue her lead role on the L2 project, rather than have her waddling around with child. First things first. Once Phase 1 is finalized in the SJ I intend to complete the rite with her at the precise opportune moment."

Pythorael was shocked. "I can't believe she was only eighteen when you put her in charge of L2."

The Archon nodded approvingly. "She has unmatched cognitive abilities. We have never come close to replicating this in any of our Optimus subjects. Her K15 genetic sequence is perfect. Therefore, so is her ability to pass it on to her offspring. If such an offspring is sired by my own host, I will readily be able to possess her and the child without diminishing my essence. I fully expect to become more powerful than ever, and she'll become the mother of a new race."

This was exactly what Pythorael had been trying to avoid. He glowered at the Archon. "You are utterly mad. Leave the girl alone. Use one of your Optimus project females to do this with."

The Archon snapped, "Those children are for producing symbiont hosts for others of our kind, as you well know. While the desired attributes are the same, none have rivaled ēlan Tabitha." He became giddy with excitement. "You do realize she is a highly advanced, natural clarion. Only those with an optimal K15 sequence inherently have this ability."

Pythorael laughed. "Well, this changes everything, especially if she attended the Clarion Academy. It is notorious for exploiting young girls. They don't typically graduate as virgins."

"She's still a maiden," the Archon replied. "She may actually be a lesbian, which hardly matters. She definitely engaged in that sort of thing at the academy, but she graduated early, at age fifteen."

Pythorael had no idea the Archon had been so obsessed with her. "You spied on her when she was a young girl? I noticed she was utilizing an external PCD. Is she not fully integrated?"

"No, she's quite extraordinary. She utilizes a specially designed external PCD more efficiently than anyone who is fully integrated. She is able to communicate directly with this external PCD with the slightest sensory input with eye and finger movements. She has incredibly fast optical responses. We always knew we had to significantly improve our current implant technology to accommodate the Optimus candidates. She is living proof of the necessity for advanced dynamic synaptic integration, but it's been difficult to keep the test subjects alive long enough to fully perfect the technology."

"Your obsession with this ēlan will be your undoing. It will inevitably hasten the destruction of us all," Pythorael said.

"Unlike you and your allies within the inner circle, I have no consideration of your blind understanding of how to navigate what is written to avoid the supposed inevitable consequences. I refuse to accept that there is no means of escaping this labyrinth we have been trapped in since before the Final War!"

"You cannot manufacture spiritual power," Pythorael responded. "I don't know how Dylanis managed to create this ēlan or if she truly is what you think she is, but you are facing a dangerous paradox if Tabitha Norean is a direct descendant of that infamous little miracle worker."

"She's not merely a descendant, but her hidden name is a perfectly created replica and she is mine. Jennipa foresaw I would discover the essence of Erafel and I would possess her descendant who would restore what I lost. It's coming true."

"Devan, this girl is a clone," Pythorael warned. "You are fortunate Dylanis was murdered and his project destroyed. Had he produced seven or more, the girl Erafel's prophecy could have been fulfilled by your own foolishness. Not that I ever gave the girl's prophecy or Jennipa's any credence."

"This is the only way and I will not be dissuaded," Devan said.

Pythorael thought, *Not if I can persuade your little ēlan to turn against you.*

CHAPTER 6

LEOH AND THE RABBIT HOLE

A few days after my last meeting with Zack I was starting to feel more confident that my DZ project work with Merrick was progressing well. That's when I heard Jerome had been arrested. I didn't know why this had happened, but it concerned me. If Jerome was compromised, this could lead to Zack and Ari, and, of course, to me. I had decided to help Zack with the insane idea of stealing classified data from LEOH. I primarily agreed because he convinced me it was for Ari's sake and that of our unborn child.

While I wasn't sure what Jerome's arrest might mean, there was yet another announcement I would hear this day. It would upend our plans and distress Zack.

The LEOH system would be taken offline at the end of day Friday for a major upgrade. As such, all non-implanted employees would be asked to surrender their PCD devices for upgrade or replacement on Monday. I was concerned, but not yet alarmed. However, when I told Zack the news Wednesday night, he became extremely troubled.

* * * *

"I told Jerome the rumor of her returning to the Citadel was a sign the L2 implementation was imminent," Zack said. Zack and I were sitting in his office at his apartment, discussing my news. "Jerome assured me the CCD technical services division insisted it was still several weeks away. Pythorael hadn't mentioned anything to him about this."

"I assume you're talking about your spider again?" I said.

"Of course, it's her! I was hoping to have more time to figure out a way to deal with her. Mark, there was so much I needed to tell you about. This is happening faster than I thought possible. I feel like I've wasted the last couple of months while you were being trained. Fortunately, Jerome has no idea of my plans to have you infiltrate the system. Even so, it is disturbing he was arrested at this particular time."

He pondered the situation and he finally said, "I think it's best we cease communications until you return from your assignment in the DZ. I fear the next couple of days may be your first, and perhaps last, chance to use these codes with any degree of success."

"Do you still want me to try to get what I can over the next two days?"

"If the Archon kept the timing of this implementation secret," Zack said, "he may be suspicious that something is going on at the Ministry. He may intend to start reducing CCD staff immediately. If this shutdown takes place Friday, you won't have enough time to use the data cubes to get what we need."

Zack stood up, retrieved a box from his safe room, and set in front of me.

"How familiar are you with molecular core computers?" he said.

I shrugged. "They are unreliable as a basis for long term utilization and storage."

"That's partially true. Yet even back in my R&D days there were some incredible advancements in creating temporarily stable matrix platforms for data, as well as accompanying utilization components. Frankly, the advancements on this device concerned the Archon and Director Pythorael so much that the entire R&D project was scrapped. All the prototype devices were ordered to be destroyed. But as you can see, not all of them made it to the incinerator."

Zack paused. "This was developed before I was reassigned to the CCD. It was a few years before the creation of the access codes. There is another component to this device, which is the basis for Pythorael's spybots. It's what allowed him to authorize the creation of the ghosted access codes in the first place. That was of course, before the last upgrade, which added the static code sequence algorithm to the security access and credentialing module."

"You do realize I don't understand anything you're saying," I said in frustration.

Zack handed me what appeared to be a small external PCD drive device less than three centimeters long and about two centimeters wide. "Take it. This is a matrix download compressor (MDC). I hesitated to give you this because I thought it would be too risky. I was hoping you would have time to take things more slowly and cautiously. This device will allow you to transfer nearly a million halobytes (HBs) of data, along with their encryption keys. With compression, this number can more than triple. It mimics the way DNA stores information at the molecular level. But MDCs are unstable over long periods."

"So, I'm supposed to use this device instead of data cubes? Why didn't you give it to me in the first place if it's more efficient for storage? And how is it riskier?"

"I'll explain," Zack said. "This little MDC is a marvel of engineering. This technology was developed for high-end PCD devices for the High Echelon and the ultra-rich. I smuggled it out after Pythorael ordered them destroyed. The Archon didn't want this technology to proliferate so he ordered the R&D moved to a more secure NED Tech lab. It must remain powered up to retain the formulations and data captured on it. If it's turned off, the molecules realign and the data is lost."

"I'm getting really uncomfortable about doing this," I protested.

"Don't worry," Zack said. "Grab whatever information you can. We can analyze it later. I pre-loaded it with my formulations. Once turned on, it will literally harvest LEOH. Take it slowly. Initiate only a single formulation at a time so it doesn't overwhelm the bandwidth and trigger a usage alert. If you start tomorrow, by the end of the day Friday you can pilfer a substantial amount of compressed, highly classified matrix data. This way, they'll never know anything was taken.

"There is one other problem you need to know about," Zack said. He looked at me with concern, which worried me. "This device emits a low frequency electromagnetic field. It can be detected by any standard LEOH sensor node. It will show up as an unregistered electronic device with an unusual hex code. If you go through a security checkpoint with it once it is activated, they could find it. So when you exit the government district, you need to swallow it. This will suppress the signal."

I stared at the device in horror. "Swallow it? How am I supposed to swallow it?"

Zack continued as if I hadn't spoken. "Also, once you've used it, you must place it within a meter of the formulation module within thirty-six to forty-eight hours." Zack handed me another device, one slightly larger than the compressor. "This is the formulation and utilization module. I just call it the formulation module. It's used to program the MDC. It will allow you to analyze the information loaded on to the data compressor and extract it. It maintains the long-term stability of the MDC." Zack showed me how the MDC fit neatly inside the other module.

This was starting to sound way more complicated than I'd imagined. "I'm afraid to ask: How I am supposed to retrieve this thing once I swallow it? Also, if we aren't supposed to contact one another, how do I get it back to you?"

"You need only worry about getting it through the security checkpoint. Just keep the MDC close to the other unit to keep it stable," Zack said. He showed me a small compartment on the end of the device and pulled out an ultra-thin filament attached to the MDC. "This is a little modification I added. Leave this in your mouth, so you can pull it up," he said, as if this were no problem. "The device is "solid state" so it won't be damaged once you swallow it. You could alternatively insert it into your. ..."

I sputtered, "Nope! I get it, no need to explain the other option. I would rather swallow it."

Zack demonstrated how to use the formulation module. "Remember, you can't actually utilize data on this until you're in a dead space." He handed me another small device the size of a walnut. With its crinkly surface, it looked like one. "This is called a walnut, for obvious reasons," Zack said. "If you hold it tightly in your hand for five seconds it will beep three times. This is a portable dead space, completely illegal, of course. It will block any burst transmissions within about a two-meter radius for a few minutes at a time. You probably won't need it. It's just in case you see a surveillance UAV outside your window."

"Wait, why would I have a surveillance drone outside my window?" Zack looked at me like I was an idiot

"Zack, this is starting to sound like a horrible idea," I said. "What if I'm caught with this walnut thing?"

Zack was indignant at the suggestion. "It's only for emergencies while you're in your apartment. Just follow my instructions. Everything will be fine. This sounds riskier than it is because of the extra precautions; honestly, even swallowing the device is probably unnecessary. Yes, they can detect it, but thousands of people go through the FRS tube station every hour of every day. It's really only a precaution to cover your tracks, in case there is an after-the-fact investigation, which there will be eventually, but not for a couple of weeks."

"I'm afraid I might die if I try to do this," I said, feeling unnerved. "What does 'taking it slow' mean?"

"It will harvest data at a maximum volume as fast as your node connection can transmit it," Zack replied. "That's why you need to be careful. The nodes within the CCD complex have incredible bandwidth speeds. They're all hardwired directly into the LEOH server complex. Remember, just one formulation at a time. Small spikes won't be an issue inside the CCD.

"Oh, yes, before I forget," he said excitedly. He handed me a curious package filled with what appeared to be tiny syringe cartridges. "I need to tell you how to use these dangerous little things in case you are interrogated. Be extremely careful with these. This stuff could kill you."

I stared at Zack with growing apprehension. "Interrogated? What do you mean, it could kill me?"

Zack said, "In the unlikely event you are detained for interrogation, you may need one."

CHAPTER 7

NERVES

I was a bundle of nerves the next morning when I arrived at the Ministry. I occupied a cubicle workspace in one small section of the third floor of the fifty-story CCD tower, with about two dozen other formulation specialists who were almost all senior to me. As soon as I arrived, per Zack's instructions, I walked around with the activated MDC device so it would be picked up by several node relays.

When I returned to my station, I initiated an interface formulation for my DZ project. I left it running while I switched my PCD over to interface with the MDC. All I had to do now was locate another virtual terminal headset (VTH) and log in to LEOH using a ghosted access code.

If Zack was correct about these codes, the only activity that would register in the system would be the bandwidth utilization on the nearby access node—and not the ghosted activity on my PCD. I decided to make an ad-hoc request for a dual interface VTH, which were generally only provided to implanted senior operations managers and directors. I accessed the technology quarter master (TQM) application. Within a few minutes, a top-of-the-line multi-interface VTH was hand delivered to me by a very pretty and friendly TQM staff technician.

"Hi, I'm Briana," she said, handing me the VTH. "Will you need any assistance operating this? When I saw your profile picture, and how cute you are, I wanted to deliver this personally. This baby is one of the newer triple interface VTH devices, and it's super-fast at compiling.

Merrick's assistant told us to bring you one, even though you are just a noob. No disrespect intended; Tech was about to deny your request. But Merrick can be a real shit if we are stingy with anyone assigned to his projects. So, here you go. I doubt you'll need a tri-con, unless you want to listen to music or watch porn while you utilize two streams. This is only useful for people with direct cognitive integrations who still perform manual procedures while they are direct brain interfacing. I got mine done recently. It's a blast with virtual sex."

Briana started to show me. "Here let me show you what you can do with it. ..."

I stopped her. "I don't need this for ... that. I'm just trying to get up to speed on a project. While I appreciate the offer, I know how a tri-con VTH works."

Briana stepped back. "Hey, that's cool. I'm just saying, you can still triple load compiled data while it is only in single interface mode. It's not like you get a single processor running with a tri-splitter. It has three separate registry signatures. It will allow you to compile three times faster. It's good for porn, if you don't have the patience. All of us secret cyberbationists use one and nobody knows. It has a connection overlay for us girls which ..."

I cut her off again. "It's not a secret anymore! Thanks for the tip. I'll call you if I need further assistance. I'll put in a good word with Merrick Taylor about how ... forthcoming you've been." *Gee, what kind of women do they hire over there in TQM?*

"Okay, see you around. You are so cute," she said. Briana stood there looking at me for a moment. When I remained silent, she decided it was time to mosey off. While not for the reasons Briana liked it, I was thrilled to get this, although I didn't dare show it. I had just received a profound gift, exactly what I needed to download to the MDC in record time. Since this was perhaps my last and only chance to use these codes, I wanted to make quick work of it.

I was anxious to get started and extremely nervous. I inserted the MDC in my new VTH and immediately saw the virtual login display for

LEOH that I normally viewed each day. After logging in a second time, I switched to the secondary display. I tried the first access code and it failed—twice. About to panic, I attempted a second access code. It was successful on the first try. Apparently the first code had been disabled, or perhaps it was incorrect. I was able to login with two more codes before I filled the connections. I began running separate formulations on each of those codes.

It wasn't long before the MDC began registering the data captures. I kept thinking about Briana, which is why it didn't occur to me that I might be overloading the nearby access node. Nor did I realize that I was doing precisely what Zack warned me not to do—grabbing way too many payloads, way too fast. I soon realized the MDC was sifting and tearing through halobytes of data every minute or so as it prepared the matrixes for capture. By the time it occurred to me to slow it down, it was already too late. *Dammit, if that Briana girl hadn't talked to me about her covert ... digitizing.* I'd forgotten to initiate only one formulation algorithm at a time. I wanted to be quick, but not this quick. Before I knew it, I had dozens running simultaneously on three different streams. No alarms were going off, so I foolishly decided everything was fine, or perhaps nobody would notice.

I worked through lunch. By mid-afternoon I was astonished that the MDC had compiled and compressed enough data to fill over a third of its capacity. On a hunch, I decided to see if what I was doing had created a bandwidth utilization alert. After all, I could search anywhere within LEOH with these codes with a quick formulation. To my horror, there weren't just alerts, there were multiple high-level security directive matrixes being compiled by LEOH for classified data breaches.

A Level 4 priority security directive had gone out to notify the head of internal security, Lawrence Rogan, about an unauthorized security access penetration. Another one notified a shielded access group under the name HESPD. I formulated this name and nothing came up. I was more successful in accessing the security directive routed to Rogan and was able to download this matrix. A Level 4 directive was high priority *and* time sensitive. Both these SDs bypassed the Ministry executive security apparatus, which included both Jerome Haley and Director Pythorael. Whatever I had done was going directly to the NCIC and the High Echelon SPD, whatever that was. I started to panic, although everything still appeared calm.

I crashed out of the access code sessions and switched over to my own active logins. I began to utilize and create formulation queries on the official project data I had been compiling on my PCD. The directives were time stamped less than an hour before I spotted them. I thought I should probably hide the MDC as quickly as possible. I removed the device from the VTH, then swallowed it. It took me three tries and half a bottle of water before I finally managed to do so. I secured the attached filament and made certain it was well hidden in my mouth. Even if a whole troop of security forces burst in to take me away, all they would find would be a multi-channel VTH running on a dual port accessing officially authorized project records I needed. I thought I was safe for now.

But soon, pandemonium erupted on the third floor of CCD headquarters.

CHAPTER 8

THE HIDDEN AGENDA

Lawrence Rogan's assistant entered his lavish offices on the 35th floor of New City's Southern Jurisdiction main administration building. He bowed. "Director Rogan, a Level 4 security directive has been issued for suspicious bandwidth activity at the CCD operations headquarters. You are requested to contact the Archon's security adjutant, Nathan Prideil, at the Northern Jurisdiction Citadel in five minutes."

Rogan grimaced. "Give me a moment to review it, then connect the Citadel in my conference room."

Rogan's mind was patched into to the SD report. The voice of LEOH in his head gave him detailed information and instructions about the directive. Hearing this, Rogan snapped at his assistant, "Have the entire CCD building locked down. I want every VTH and external PCD of all personnel confiscated for inspection. Everyone assigned to the third floor is to be taken to the sublevel 2 detention center. Have the entire NCGD quarantined. Close the FRS stations and every sky port and security post in and out of the district, until we account for everyone working on the third floor between 9:00 a.m. and 1:00 p.m. today."

"Thousands of people work at the CCD on any given day, including all the NCMIA executives. Does this include Director Pythorael?" Rogan's assistant replied, stunned.

Rogan barked, "No one is to leave until I receive instructions from the Citadel. Summon the High Echelon Special Projects director, Talen

Place, to my conference room. I intend to catch this culprit, even if it means holding the entire Ministry in custody."

Three minutes later, Rogan entered his richly adorned private conference room accompanied by Talen Place. Only among his compatriots in the leadership of New City was Place known by his true name of Tal Complaceal. Moments later, the image of Nathan Prideil appeared on the large screen.

Rogan said, "So, should you begin, or should I?"

Prideil looked stone faced. "I assume you have activated the necessary security measures? The Archon has been briefed. This is to be handled with the utmost diligence and highest priority."

Rogan rolled his eyes. "Naturally, yet I fail to see why this isn't a matter for the CCD. After all, it was a breach inside the Ministry. It was their bandwidth anomaly protocol that notified us to the possibility of the data theft. Without the CCD technology group, we would not have been warned of the possibility that the stolen data payloads were highly classified."

"The Archon has reason to believe the Ministry has been severely compromised under Pythorael's leadership," Prideil said. "He doesn't want anything to prevent the L2 implementation from moving forward as scheduled. In any case, NED Tech will have to be informed about this, especially the Norean ēlan. The Archon has given me full authority to speak for him on this matter. I want no stone left unturned under the provisions of this directive. This is perhaps our best opportunity to discover who is behind these system breaches. Are there any questions so far?"

Rogan shook his head. He said, "So far, you have been about as helpful as a steaming pile of turds. I rather think the Archon doesn't want to risk having the plans for his little ēlan's birthday delayed. The perverted freak! Rest assured, no one is being allowed to leave the government district. As soon as we disconnect, I am going to the detention center to start interrogating everyone from the third floor, which could take half the night. If this thief is among them, I will find him or her."

Prideil bristled at this comment, but kept his face neutral. "We don't know specifically what was downloaded since the activity was shielded. We only know it has a high SADEX score. Whoever is responsible used a registered node on the third floor of the CCD HQ. Since all of the activity indexes are missing, we have not yet made a determination as to the specific interface device used or how the data was formulated. LEOH can elaborate further on the risk profile associated with this event. LEOH are you online with us now?"

Rogan erupted, "I know all this! I just read the directive."

After a brief pause, a smooth and almost human robotic voice emerged over the audio inputs of the participants. "Shall I advance to the strategic analysis outlined for this briefing?"

Prideil responded, "Give us an overview, not the event specifics."

With no delay, LEOH proceeded. "Central to the Archon's prime objective is the identification and interdiction of all active and potential enemies of the New City state. The existence of veiled or 'ghosted' access coded entities is a potential threat to the successful outcome of this objective. The activities of these entities are of paramount concern. They are detected only when anomalies trigger a response to events where combinations of sensitivity thresholds are met. High security access protocols are vulnerable to these entities. This is due to systemic inabilities to prepare a matrix on their activity, while they are formulating data ..."

"Shut the hell up, LEOH! This is useless!" Rogan growled. "Wait! How do you know there are multiple entities involved? Otherwise, what you said was a complete waste of my time."

LEOH proceeded. "Since 12.16.44 NCE, to date there have been 51,264 previously downgraded or quarantined directives involving suspected activities of these entities, as well as the possibility of an unknown number which could have occurred without detection."

"I'm confused," interrupted Rogan. "Are we talking about SDL4.17150.63 or another directive?"

"Please Rogan! Allow LEOH to finish the briefing," Prideil said.

LEOH continued, "The anomaly that generated SDL4.17150.63 was due to the volume of data captured. The access point is within the NCGD, specifically within the CCD Ministry operations headquarters. All previous breaches occurred outside of the NCGD access grid."

Rogan clapped. "Finally, I heard something that I was not aware of. You could have mentioned this, without saying anything else, useless contraption."

LEOH briefly recalibrated. "I will quote from director Pythorael's approved downgrade conditions, which are still in effect, as prepared by, then deputy director Zachariah Waters. *'Due to the insufficiency of evidence in addition to the lack of resources available to investigate these anomalies, such events are to be catalogued and submitted to the office of infrastructure security. These events could be explained by legacy index glitches. LEOH is instructed to continue to track these events. They will be elevated only under certain conditions...'* "

LEOH continued, "I have isolated only three such conditions, given the exhaustive length of the list. Number one would be a significant change in the volume. Number two, the sensitivity of the data transfer; number three is an irregular origin or source location of the intrusion event. At such time, normal protocols in place will prevail. SDL4.17150.63 satisfies eleven of the conditions to elevate this matter to the office of the HES and NCIC internal security. Primarily, the breach has been isolated to a third-floor node within the CCD headquarters facility. The volume of data transferred is estimated to exceed 300,000 compressed halobytes. Further, the data suspected to have been stolen is highly classified and requires a maximum level SADEX score to compile into a matrix assembly. There is one other addendum which was added to this protocol."

Rogan retorted, "I understood that last part at least. Are you kidding me? That could be over a million HBs of classified data! Did the son of a bitch get everything?"

LEOH replied, "Please be more specific as to the term 'everything.' No information is available on the user to determine the gender or familial relations. Under the addendum protocol, a directive which meets the three conditions I indicated, or which exceeds such criteria, is required to be exclusively referred to Director Pythorael's attention. This has resulted in an unresolved routing conflict for this matter. Protocols direct me to route conflicts of this nature to the attention of the Archon and the NCIC security directorate."

Rogan looked at Complaceal. "What in shit's hell is he saying?"

Complaceal shrugged. "It sounds like LEOH has just indicated Lord Pythorael may be involved in this somehow, or at least his ghosted access codes are."

"LEOH, continue with the strategic assessment," Prideil said.

LEOH paused briefly to compile strategic considerations. "I have added a listing of specific types of devices that could have been utilized in this event. I have also included several possible methods for conceal-ment to consider in your investigation. I further recommend the LEOH II implementation be postponed until certain previously unidentified vulnerabilities are assessed. Item of note: There was a ping on one access code and at least one re-login attempt was made. I was only able to flag this attempt, not the origin. This access code was identified in a previous event involving a current detainee, Jerome Haley, SAC T-EPSJH4578. The code was issued to him by Director Pythorael for purposes of altering tracking configurations. All such references to this access code were officially stricken from the SD matrix. Director Pythorael established a protocol to transmit a false login failure if there was an attempt made to use this or certain other listed access codes in the future."

Prideil spoke up. "LEOH, terminate the briefing. That's more than enough for now. Rogan, we have no choice except to continue the quarantine lockdown until this person is identified and the device used to store the stolen data is recovered. Go, catch this ghost! When you are satisfied you have the right man, bring him to me. Also, I strongly suggest you question Mr. Haley again, as directed. He is under your jurisdiction, so make him talk. I also want to know with whom he's been associating."

LEOH interjected, "Shall I re-issue all security directives involving Jerome Haley, his former associates and past acquaintances he may still be in contact with? There is a matrix pattern developing involving certain former executives of the NCMIA. I would not rule out the possibility he could be conspiring with them. I have narrowed the search down to ..."

Prideil cut LEOH off. "That's enough for now! Rogan, you're dismissed. I am counting on you two to deliver some good news on this to me quickly. I want this resolved immediately."

"I don't need your dumb ass to tell me I'm dismissed or what I have to do," Rogan said angrily.

Rogan got up to leave as Pythorael entered the conference room, clearly angry. "Wait, before you leave. We need to clear up a few matters." Looking sternly at Prideil on the screen, Pythorael said, "Did you really think I wouldn't be alerted about this little meeting? I'm not sure why you decided I was not relevant to this conversation. I'm still head of the Ministry and the Ministry is head over security in this city. This authority entitles me to have jurisdiction over any LEOH system breaches. LEOH, offline this zone." The green light on the console display for LEOH darkened.

Prideil refused to be conciliatory. "This breach is now a matter which falls under the jurisdiction of High Echelon Security. It even supersedes the NED Tech development protocols. HES has special project directive jurisdiction over all infiltrations and suspected subversions related to senior executive investigations. As you well know, all matters relating to the ongoing use of these rogue security access codes you authorized now falls under *my* authority. Your Ministry, NCIC Internal security, and by extension, the HE special projects division, report to me."

Pythorael stared menacingly at the image of Prideil. "When you lock down and detain the entire staff of the CCD operations headquarters it damn well falls under *my* jurisdiction. Bypassing me with this directive has far exceeded the scope of your investigative authority. I am still privy to all LEOH security directives. I am just as concerned about catching those who are responsible for this as you are. This is far more than a mere data breach."

Prideil said, "What about the attempted login today, with a code which was included on your flag list? According to LEOH, it was once used by Jerome Haley."

Pythorael was suddenly attentive. "It certainly wasn't the deputy director, considering he has been in detention. Let me see that code." Pythorael looked at the information on Rogan's display. "It looks out of sequence with the others. This may have been the same code I allowed Jerome Haley to use only once, for a particular purpose. It's all in the historical SD matrix and the matter was cleared. If LEOH says it's the same code, then it probably is. I don't see how it could have anything to do with this data breach. All the codes I authorized Santos to create are fully quarantined."

"Then why would our data thief attempt to use it?" Prideil said. "It's not a coincidence that login attempt was tracked to the same node this morning where this took place."

"I don't know," Pythorael said. "These codes are tracked, because I made it possible to track them by removing their shielding routines. I can also prove none of the codes I authorized had the ability to create additional access codes." Pythorael turned to Rogan and Complaceal. "You can both leave. Let my staff go as soon as you catch this thief. Nathan and I need to discuss something privately. Both of you, go!" Rogan and Complaceal left for the detention facility. Rogan gave Pythorael a quizzical look as he departed.

"I can assure you, every access code on my quarantine list is accounted for," Pythorael told Prideil. "There is something else going on here, which brings up the question of a decades old R&D project, along with the piece of equipment I used to create these codes in the first place. I am going to confide in you something you need to know about the Archon's plans for the Inner Circle. It involves a girl, and to be precise, she's a prominent, dangerous, and annoying ēlan. Arianael and Mythrael may be in on this conspiracy with the Archon, and you will need to soon decide where your loyalties lie."

CHAPTER 9

SUSPICIONS

After being asked to turn over all our devices, the personnel on my floor were led across the large courtyard outside to another building. A number of armed guards surrounded us. The building to which we were led was the New City central intelligence bureau, or the NCIB.

None of us were aware that underneath this building was a detention center housing over a thousand government personnel who had been arrested and detained for various reasons. Like so many aspects of New City, especially in the government district, the façade of well-landscaped tranquility and beautiful architecture masked the harsh reality of a brutal police state.

Everything on our person was removed. We were forced to undergo a humiliating strip search while several guards conducted a thorough search of our clothing. A cavity search was also conducted in front of everyone, male and female alike. Fortunately, the oral cavity search was hastily done. The thin thread filament in my mouth attached to the MDC went unnoticed.

Hiding the MDC in this manner was supposed to prevent it from being picked up by the security scanners at the district exits. It would not hide it from a probe or body scan. To think this was all my fault made me ill; I felt guilty for causing my colleagues to endure this.

Fortunately, due to the amount of clothing to be examined, none of the guards discovered the small thin syringe hidden in the armpit of my shirt. Zack gave this to me in the unlikely event I would be detained. *Right.* The drug would suppress an allergic reaction to the highly potent truth serum, Phencol, used on interrogation subjects. It was also effective at allowing a person to control their responses more coherently. He warned me, however, it was fast acting, with a short-lived potency. It would also greatly increase my heart rate. In a worst case, it could cause cardiac arrest if I injected it without being exposed to Phencol within a few minutes.

After this humiliation, we were told to put on our clothes. We were then called by name to enter a large room where we would await our turn to be interrogated. I realized I must have seriously screwed the pooch to trigger this kind of paranoid reaction. I decided I had to get rid of the MDC device. The risk was too great they would medically examine me. I didn't care if Zack's plans were ruined. My life was at stake if I didn't flush the thing.

I waited and waited, hoping we would be allowed a bathroom break. After a few hours, the room was still half full. Since we were seated alphabetically, I knew I would be one of the last people to be interrogated. At this point I needed to go quite badly.

I finally asked a guard if I could use the restroom. Several other people immediately demanded to use it as well. We were led there in groups of six, along with a guard. Fortunately, there were stalls. This was outside the incarceration area and I saw no surveillance equipment in the stall. I quickly extracted the device, while desperately trying to keep myself from gagging out loud. I stared at the slimy device in my hand. I was about drop it in and flush it. Then, a huge wave of guilt hit me.

Zack had waited for so long and sacrificed so much for this. He'd even sent his great-granddaughter to pursue me. I loved her and believed she loved me. He risked himself and his friend Jerome to get me into the CCD. I was the one who'd screwed up. It was my fault I was about to be interrogated. What would Ari think of me if I failed to get this supposed vital classified information to Zack? Was I literally about to flush all this effort and sacrifice? My final thought was whether Ari would be willing to take the risk. I shoved the device inside my sock and pushed it down as far as I could into my shoe.

After another hour of waiting, I heard my name and was ushered into a smaller room, where I sat down. Moments later, a man entered and introduced himself as Lawrence Rogan, CCD Executive Security Director. We'd never met before, but his name was on the security directive for the bandwidth alert. He held a display screen in his hand and obviously had an implanted audio device in his ear. He looked fatigued and frustrated at his inability to find the suspect he sought.

I answered a few questions about my position, my work assignments, and what I'd been doing all day. He pulled my PCD and the two VTH devices I had relinquished earlier out of an envelope to examine them. While there were some gaps in my PCD integration and utilization activity, there was nothing out of the ordinary. He then focused his attention on my VTH devices, which likewise indicated normal activity for my ID code. "Why were you assigned a multi-channel VTH? Isn't this unusual for a new recruit without an implant? Who issued this device to you?"

I told him I had requested only a dual interface this morning from TQM and explained the reasons why. I told him I was likewise curious as to why I was assigned a tri-con device, when I clearly had no need for it. "Do you mind telling me what is happening?" I asked as I fidgeted.

Rogan eyed me suspiciously as he glanced up from the PCD display. "Your personnel file indicates you graduated with top honors from Severyn University with a degree in formulation analytics. It says you were recruited by Jerome Haley. How did you know Mr. Haley?"

I froze for a moment. "I didn't know him before I came to work at the NCMIA. I met him for the first time during my final interviews. I received several form recruitment coms from the NCMIA. Maybe they were e-signed by him. I wasn't recruited by any specific person. I'd never met anyone from the Ministry before I started interviewing at the local branch in Park Central."

This answer seemed to satisfy him. I wasn't sure how much I should voluntarily disclose if I was asked about Ari or Zack. As far as the Ministry was concerned, Zack was a reclusive retired former executive and a sick old man. The director pressed me, "Your latest profile says you are married. Your application doesn't have this in the disclosures and there are no links to her profile."

I was petrified, but tried to remain calm, "We got married a week after I started working for the Ministry."

Rogan seemed puzzled. He undoubtedly wondered why this information was not highlighted and why there was no link to my wife's profile. Thankfully, I don't think I was the type of person for which he was looking. I was just an inexperienced new operative, but he had to go through the motions.

Rogan asked me a few more rather simple questions. He flicked the report off of his hand-held display, then stood up. "I am sorry you have been detained. However, I must insist you endure one last indignity before we can release you to go home. You will be subjected to medical probe to see if you have either ingested or inserted any foreign objects or hidden devices into your body."

While I didn't let on, I was in a state of panic. What if they discovered the MDC, now irritatingly hidden in my sock? As I was thinking, Rogan was studying his display again, while listening to a hidden audio device. Suddenly, his expression changed. He looked up at me, then paced around the room slowly, looking intently at his display screen.

Director Rogan glared at me with penetrating grey eyes and rubbed his fingers through his jet-black hair. "Why didn't you mention who your wife's great grandfather is? It says here, your wife has been living with Zachariah Waters since she was eight years old. That was around the time he retired from an executive position at the CCD. In fact, Jerome Haley used to report to him."

While I was afraid of this line of questioning, I was also glad to have an opportunity to explain without being under the effects of Phencol. "You didn't ask. He had nothing to do with why I came to work here, or why I was hired. I only met him the day before my final interviews began. By then, I had already had two interviews at a local Ministry office."

Rogan looked at me skeptically. "How long had you been seeing your wife before then?"

"We had been going out for two years," I replied. "You can run a full spectrum analysis on my matrix. It will show you that I never spoke with the man before then. I never even saw his face. I was the one who finally asked Ari if I could meet him for the first time. Every conversation I had with Ari will prove she rarely mentioned him, if at all. She never even told me what he used to do. I never discussed my position at the NCMIA with him, ever. He is ninety years old. His previous role at the Ministry is coincidental and irrelevant."

"According to your wife's profile, she would have only been sixteen at the time," Rogan pointed out. "That's a little disturbing, for someone your age to be dating a sixteen-year-old."

"She told me she was eighteen when we started dating. She certainly looked eighteen. LEOH probably has a record of that too," I said angrily. "What does my wife's age or when we started going out have to do with this? Everything in my matrix will prove I first met Zack Waters the day before my final interviews. I also didn't meet Jerome Haley until my final interviews."

Rogan was thinking again, still staring at his display. Finally, he looked up and said, "I believe you. However, I would be derelict in my duties if I we didn't examine you further. I hope you understand. We've had a serious security breach. As you have probably heard in the rumor mill, Deputy Director Haley has been detained for questioning. Due to your connection to his former superior at the Ministry, and for reasons I cannot disclose, we have reason to believe this association may have a direct bearing on our investigation. I am going to ask you to go with Dr. Maskell."

I acted confused. "I have no idea what investigation you're referring too. You said there is a security breach, but I still don't know what you are searching for."

"It won't take long," Rogan assured me. "If your testimony checks out, you'll be free to go."

He again looked at his display. He was probably running an active utilization against all my responses. He left the room and I was summoned to follow another man through a different door from the one I'd entered. I was certain I was about to be doped with Phencol. As I walked a few paces behind him, I located the syringe cartridge in the armpit of my shirt and administered the antidote. Fortunately, or perhaps unfortunately, my assumption about the Phencol was correct.

We entered a room that appeared to be more clinical in nature. In less than five minutes, a nurse injected Phencol into my shoulder. I was asked to lie back in the examination chair in the center of the room to wait. I began to feel a strange sensation all over my body, as if I were unable to move. I faded in and out of consciousness. At the same time, I could also feel periodic rushes of adrenalin, which would momentarily clear my head from the onslaught of delirium overtaking my mind.

I heard the nurse and a doctor discussing completing the probes before director Rogan returned. The nurse commanded me to stand up, remove my shoes, and all my clothes. I groggily looked at her and laughed. That was the wrong thing to do. The woman was mean and strong. Her hair was pulled back so tight into a bun, it was as if she was wearing a thin black helmet. She jerked me up to restrain me herself as another man stripped off my shirt and pulled my pants down to my ankles. It seemed Zack's advice to act drunk wasn't necessary. I was saying pretty much whatever popped into my mind, like a wasted teenager under arrest at a music festival. I cursed at them and accused them of all manner of foul intentions during this indignity.

After my clothes were removed yet again, this fiendishly strong woman forced me to lay flat on my stomach, as she put restraints on me. Moments later, a probe was slithered down my throat. I gagged, and snot poured out of my nose. I gasped in pain as another probe was inserted in my nether regions. I could see the nurse reviewing the scans out of the corner of my eye. She said, "It is likely by now that if he'd swallowed a device, it would be in his small intestinal tract. A detailed body scan would be more revealing."

The doctor, who had been watching this, grunted. "Proceed with a full spectrum axial scan using the hand-held resonator." The probes were removed, and I was turned over on my back. The nurse ran a hand-held device up and down over my stomach and my intestinal region, trying to pick up any sign of a device. I was turned over a couple of times as she swept the device over my midsection. Little did they know that what they sought was still in my left sock. After a few minutes, I was told to pull my pants up, then ordered to sit in a chair to wait.

I don't know how much time passed before Director Rogan reappeared. He sat down across from me and asked me my name again. I told him, then I asked, woozily, "What in the hell was that mean ass, helmet-headed, bitch looking for?" I cursed a few more times.

Rogan grinned malevolently. "Fortunately for you, they didn't find it, or you and I would be having a very different conversation."

There was no question I appeared to Rogan to be fully under the influence of Phencol. Within about a minute, thanks to the counter agent, my mind started becoming more coherent as he asked me a series of questions about my relationship with Zack Waters and Jerome Haley. He even asked whether I had used any access codes not assigned to me by the Ministry. For at least half an hour, he continued to question me. I was able to reply in a way consistent with my previous answers, despite my speech, which was tainted with slightly slurred, involuntary curses.

Finally, Rogan stood up. He called the doctor back into the room. "Give him a release injection to make him sleep this off. Bring him out of it in a few minutes with a stimulant."

I was injected with something and started to fade into sleep. However, the counter agent kept me from complete unconsciousness. My eyes were closed as I tried to regain my senses. I heard Rogan and a new man, who had apparently entered the room with the doctor, whispering about my interrogation. The other man said, "Is he conscious?"

I heard the doctor reply, "He can't hear you. He's under anesthesia. It will keep him out for a while. It keeps them from being overstimulated once we give them something to bring them out of a session. It has a normalizing effect, unless you want him placed in a cell to have it wear off on its own. That can take several hours."

"Fine," I heard the man say. "You and your assistant can step out for a moment, if you please."

Believing I was unconscious, the two men began speaking in low whispers. I heard Rogan say, "If by some chance he is our culprit, I'd like someone to explain to me how a new operative, with zero experience, could have infiltrated our systems with a rogue access code? And how did he have the know-how to run the kind of formulation algorithms we suspect were necessary to access highly classified data? He's clean under a chemical interrogation with no device. I am tempted to detain him for twenty-four hours because of his association with Zack Waters. Yet Waters has never been the subject of a single security directive and I verified that he is a near-death invalid."

The other man replied, "Lord Rogan, you know full well that the most obvious stratagem any good spy aptly makes use of is a seemingly impenetrable vail of undeniable innocence."

I recognized the voice of the other man as that of Dalen Pythorael. Pythorael added, "Put a trace on him and his PCD with drone surveillance. Meanwhile, I want an updated utilization matrix on his past processed before the system is taken down. I also want Zack Waters re-matrixed and correlated. The only way Verigratu could have carried out the data theft is with expert help with inside knowledge of our systems. Waters is the only tangible link to this. When Verigratu wakes up, reassure him that he's free to go. I have a strong feeling this kid is involved. He must have stashed the device somewhere. I want the entire CCD complex thoroughly scanned for any sign of it."

I sat in the chair with my eyes closed for another few minutes, when I felt my arm being pricked with another needle. I must have drifted off. When I opened my eyes I looked around, shaking my head slightly. Rogan said, "Mr. Verigratu, I regret having to put you through this. This kind of investigation is rarely necessary. I hope you realize how much we appreciate your cooperation. We have kept the commissary facilities opened late for those who would like to grab something to eat before returning home for the long weekend."

He added, "The Ministry offices will be closed tomorrow. The LEOH upgrade will begin ten hours earlier. You and your colleagues will be able to take tomorrow off to recuperate from your experience. Also, don't worry about completing your final preparations for the Dead Zone mission with Merrick Taylor. Everything has been pushed forward two days. You should have plenty of time Monday or Tuesday to finish your mission formulations."

It seemed my ordeal was almost over. I still had to get out of the government district with the MDC. This meant swallowing it again. I tried to process what I'd overheard Rogan and Pythorael whispering.

I said to the nurse, "I'm not feeling well. I'd like to use the bathroom."

The nurse who strong armed me a short while ago now looked at me sympathetically. "I'll show you where it is. After that, I will escort you to the commissary so you can have something to eat before you head home. The next tube will depart in about thirty-five minutes. Let's get you up."

CHAPTER 10

A LABYRINTH OF DEATH

I arrived home just before midnight. Ari was away at university, so the place was empty. I was lonely without her. We'd had only a few weeks together after we married, and before she left for school. She wouldn't be back for at least two weeks. While this was probably best, considering the circumstances, I desperately needed her company and advice.

All I wanted to do was sleep off the grueling terror of the day's experience. I didn't know what it meant to be traced, or what they might discover by correlating my matrix with Zack's. I imagined a team of operatives pouring over data to connect me to his past. It dawned on me: They wouldn't have the tools or resources they needed for a few days because LEOH was going off-line in the morning for the weekend. Also, the Ministry wouldn't reopen until Monday due to the system implementation.

The next morning, it was raining heavily. It wasn't a good day to venture out.

During the upgrade, redundancies in the LEOH system would allow commercial transactions and interactions to continue. Each module would be taken down, one at a time, as they were backed up to the new system and resynchronized. The core Ministry access and security modules would need to be taken off-line, later to be brought up together as one integrated platform. I wasn't sure how long this would take, but I decided it wasn't safe to use the MDC. Despite my overwhelming curiosity, I would have to wait until I could utilize the data in the secure confines of Zack's dead space.

I knew I needed to transfer the information on the MDC to a more permanent storage device as soon as possible. I was still uncertain of Zack's specific plans and how he intended to get this information out to the public. I had achieved Zack's objective. I held in my hand the reason he'd used his great-granddaughter to lure me to him. I had a flash of anger at him for manipulating us.

While I didn't know what I had captured on the MDC, I had some idea as to the general nature of the data. I thought about this as I stood on my balcony drinking coffee and watching the rain come down. The rain would keep roamers grounded. These surveillance drones could pick up voices inside targeted dwellings, as well as any number of other, unconnected signals from devices not linked directly to LEOH. They were primarily used to detect artificially created dead spaces, such as the one Zack could establish in his home.

How he had avoided suspicion over the years was a mystery. The man had access to all kinds of tech from his days in the Ministry. This probably enabled him to do many things he'd not revealed to me. As far as dead spaces went, his walnut was useless. What was I supposed to do with a dead space that lasted only a couple of minutes? Zack probably didn't have room for it in his trinket drawer.

Then, I remembered my penthouse had a walk-in safe. I was told the original owner had it installed when the apartment was built. It was a relic of the past. In the four years I'd lived in the apartment, I had never used it or opened it. With no valuables worthy of being kept in a safe, I had no need for one. Yet there was one hidden behind the shelves in my library.

The library was another relic. Few people had real books anymore since everything was now electronic. Most old books were considered contraband; it was dangerous to own them. The only person I knew with a significant number of real books was Zack, and all of his were probably illegal.

My library was a joke. The shelves held useless trophies from my college years and a couple of marksmen awards from my weapons training competitions. There were a few decorative sculptures and some old hardback "legal" pre-war books, most left by the previous owner. A few inexpensive paintings hung along one wall. Ari and I had discussed renovating the room, which I wanted to fill with her artwork. We also intended to put a piano in the library, to turn it into a combination art and music studio. Yet during our conversations about the library, the safe never occurred to me. Even so, I remembered where the combination to the old-fashioned keypad lock was hidden. The existence of the safe was obviously not a major consideration when I bought the place.

Any respectable bachelor would have tossed the books. I kept them to provide neighbors for the one book that contained the combination. I went to the library and grabbed it off the shelf. I laughed at how appropriate the title was. The combination was on a sticker pasted to the inside back cover of this pre-war hardcover called "Bad Prodigies." Its subtitle read, "How those who exceed their measure inevitably leave destruction in their wake." *No shit!*

I committed the combination to memory. To access the safe, I had only to pull a lever hidden by a piece of trim with a spring flap. The back wall of the shelves was hinged, like a door. I unlatched the shelf. The bookcase released and swung outward on its hinges.

Behind the shelf stood an enormous metal door about three meters high from floor to ceiling, framed by several centimeters of steel. The safe probably weighed several metric tons. It had been built into the penthouse before the building was refurbished about forty years earlier, at the height of redevelopment in this upscale section of New City. Rather than requiring special reinforcement of the floors below, it was constructed into the massive reinforced concrete pillars that held up the structure. Happily, it wouldn't show up as a void space on any floor plan.

The electrical keypad entry released the lock mechanism once the correct combination was entered. This allowed the large handle to be rotated counterclockwise. The handle was rotated twice clockwise to reset the locking mechanism.

The safe could be used as a short-term safe room. It was ventilated by a small shaft with a fan, which blew air outside to the rooftop above. It also had several small round intake vents. Four bright LED ceiling lights turned on when the door was opened. The room was about 2 square meters. I could fit a chair and a small table inside the room to work. I'd been told I could close the safe and open it from the inside with the installed manual controls.

But could I utilize the MDC in this room without detection? I decided I had to try, if only to back up the device to more stable data cubes. I intended to store everything Zack had given me in there. I put his walnut in one of the drawers and provisioned the safe with some water and food, just in case. I brought in a chair from my dining room and a small end table from the den. Now I had to test whether I could get out once I locked myself in. I was nervous about this. But once I worked up my courage it worked like a charm. I felt claustrophobic with the door closed, but I was confident I could use the MDC safely when I saw that my PCD had no signal inside the safe.

I connected the MDC with several storage cubes and began unpacking the massive amounts of stored compressed data. It took just a couple of minutes for each cube to fill up; I realized I needed many more data cubes. Only now did I understand how much data I had stolen.

* * * *

I can't relate everything I would ultimately learn from the data I'd extracted from LEOH. I knew it would take quite a while to make a dent in it. Zack had waited years to carry out this plan. Despite my near disastrous failure and the near hasty decision to throw the MDC away, I was glad I had retrieved it. I only hoped it was secure in my safe, at least temporarily.

Most of data I retrieved went well beyond what I'd imagined. I found it fascinating that the Archon and his confederates were certain LEOH was secure. They must have felt it was important to store everything on an interconnected system, never imagining someone could steal it. LEOH had countless partitions and held mostly raw, unformulated matrix data. It also held top secret archives, statistics, histories, reports, and dossiers about every aspect of New City and the plans of its ostensibly benevolent rulers.

The Archon should be well over a hundred years old, yet appeared to be in his mid to late thirties. Director Pythorael likewise, should have been long dead. Contrary to what Zack believed about them being the devil and his angels, I was still trying to figure out how so many top leaders in the New City government were immune to the effects of aging. But these facts were meaningless compared with the labyrinth of horrors that had been created to control people.

There were details about making clones, or symbionts, of people. There were files about transferences to these symbionts involving bizarre arcane rituals with sacred oaths. Most made no sense. They were experimenting with people, especially children, on a frightening scale for mind integration research. They were attempting to find something hidden within individuals' brains and DNA. It was extremely technical.

Zack was a masterful formulation expert. I began to respect his intellect more and more, because his formulations had captured and compressed this damning information about the Archon's plans. I didn't understand half of it, but I knew it was revolting.

One matrix discussed degrees of cognitive immolation, re-assimilation, bonding, and fertility assessments. This fell under a broad matrix heading for something called the Optimus Project, and a secondary matrix called the K15 Advanced Clarion and Cognitive Genetic Enhancement Program.

I noticed an oddly referenced submatrix in this K15 directory called "preparatory response assessment—subject one." I clicked inside the submatrix. It was filled with video files arranged in ascending chronological order. When I accessed the first one, I was amused to see poorly produced voyeur porn of some girl. After clicking on couple of videos at the top of the list, I realized the entire catalogue was of the same blond-haired girl.

I thought: *This girl is a wild freak... and loud.* Then I noticed clinical reference notations. Each video indicated whether the event was chemically induced, hypnotic, involuntary, or self-initiated. The images covered a three-year period beginning when the subject was seventeen. *Someone is seriously obsessed with this girl. Why in hell would this stuff be highly classified?*

I could tell the young woman in the videos was pretty, although I didn't look at a closeup of her face. Okay, maybe I was not looking at her face. I confess I looked at five before stopping. Besides, I was married to the most beautiful girl in the world. She would have to be gone a long time for me to resort to porn. I couldn't imagine why anyone would want a catalogue of two thousand videos of the same girl, doing virtually the same thing. *I wouldn't mind having a few of Ari*, I thought as my mind wondered.

I snipped the catalogue to put it on a separate cube, then deleted the submatrix from the MDC. *I have to keep a copy for academic purposes*, I reasoned. Besides, it could be important since it was classified. If Zack planned to disseminate this data, I didn't want two thousand voyeur cam videos of the unfortunate "subject one" to be publicly distributed. It was the noble thing to do, right? I congratulated myself for my concern. This random girl was somebody's daughter, after all. She didn't deserve what was being done to her. Nevertheless, I moved on after an inappropriate length of time.

In other matrixes containing the LEOH II Gateway project, I learned that this weekend's upgrade would be the first in a multi-phase reimplementation of LEOH. This new version would be radically different from anything the citizens of New City had previously faced. New implant technology was going to be mandated for everyone. *This is thought control*, I realized with horror. There were also plans to eliminate most of the Ministry staff. Human resource needs would be reduced to a bare minimum over the next few years. *I guess you don't need the Ministry if you can control everyone's thoughts.*

I was shocked to learn there were slaves in New City and the number of them was astonishing. They toiled away in vast infrastructure projects and immense mining and drilling operations, as well as huge resource procurement and processing complexes across New City. Output statistics and records tracked what the slaves produced, extracted, constructed, processed, or assembled. I also found projections, quotas, and performance measurements, even for the most mundane and seemingly irrelevant metrics about these labor allocation colonies. This data spanned several decades.

LEOH meticulously kept track of everything, except for the people themselves, once they were incarcerated in the so called "labor allocation" system. Names were replaced with numbers and numbers were summarized into statistics and body counts with consumption and production measurements. Even more deeply troubling were references to the number of children in labor allocation colonies. LEOH tracked how many were sent there, how many were born there, and how many died there, as well as the number "reassigned" for institutional research purposes or sold into the "entertainment" industry. This included children who were lost to theft or "slippage" almost like they were inventory."

New City's labor allocation organization had its own separate monetary system for those who lived out their bleak lives in its cruel clutches. The intent was to extract as much productive capacity as possible from these people, while using as few resources as possible to provide for them. Everything was closely monitored. It was shocking how clinically they garnered statistics on the use, disposition, and incarceration of people, especially children.

The revelation that millions of people were held in bondage throughout New City was nothing compared to what I discovered about humanity's fate. Apparently, the new version of LEOH was just the first step to allow the Archon to carry out his most odious plans. The most highly classified reports referred to something ominously called the Optimus Directive, or the OD protocols.

The OD was the Archon's ultimate vision for New City. On the surface it sounded like a new heaven on earth. It would be a spectacular Garden of Eden for the select few who would remain in the world. Yet the details of the OD's numerous connected projects revealed a terrifying holocaust for the vast majority of New City's population. But even those who remained would be controlled by the Archon by virtue of their direct integration with him through LEOH.

Addendums to various reports stipulated that another 90 percent of the earth's population would ultimately be removed in order to create the optimal world. The goal was to reduce the population of New City to two hundred million inhabitants from its current population of nearly two billion within thirty years.

This was expected to be achieved via various milestones. First and foremost, all remaining genetic dissidents would be eliminated, as well as any remaining pockets of human inhabitants in the DZ. There were goals for expanding the boundaries of New City by stages into areas of the DZ now deemed suitable for habitation. There was also a reference to an as yet undiscovered stronghold, where it was estimated that up to three million persons who had escaped New City lived. At least 75 percent of these people were estimated to be genetic dissidents or criminal insurgents, all formerly targeted by Ministry security directives.

There were detailed estimates on the number of both human and mechanized combat forces required to eliminate these threats. During this extermination process, the city would begin to retract areas for human habitation within the boundaries of New City. The city would gradually be destroyed, district by district. The plan was to re-terraform it into vast estates and gardens for those considered worthy enough to live in this new heaven on earth forever.

* * * *

There was one inescapable conclusion about what would enable the Archon to succeed: LEOH. It had to destroyed before we could hope to survive. Yet even if everyone in New City became cognizant of the ultimate doom which awaited them, would they know how to fight back?

What good would it do to disseminate this information far and wide? Even if everyone in New City knew the truth, it would be useless if the system that controlled and imperiled them still existed. Some people might resist. Even so, the Archon and his kind had been using people to control and oppress their fellow humans for decades. Humankind had lost the will to govern itself. I was dismayed at how humanity had been duped by these megalomaniacs.

LEOH calculated a carefully laid out spiral of death. It would make certain there were just enough people left to destroy ourselves. Was Zack a fool to think stealing this classified material would change the inevitable outcome? If he didn't have a plan to deal with LEOH, it would all be for nothing.

I began to wonder about Zack's spider. How did he intend to capture her? She had helped create this new version of LEOH. This meant *she* was one of the few people who could help destroy it. She was also an ēlan—*one of them*—an untouchable collaborator. She was an enemy, and I wanted nothing to do with her. No one could reason with the likes of those people, especially an ēlan from a family like the Noreans. Zack was delusional if he thought he could influence her or change her. I had never met her, but I already hated her.

CHAPTER 11

TABITHA

Elan Tabitha Norean arrived at her parent's luxurious estate on the fringes of the New City government district of the Southern Jurisdiction just after 2:00 p.m. Sunday. This was sixteen hours before the L2 system was scheduled to go live the next morning. Incredibly, she had taken over as project lead three years before from her mother, at age seventeen. She was officially appointed project lead just after she turned eighteen. By then, she had been running the project and personally reengineering the AI algorithms for months. She didn't impress her colleagues because of her family or title; she impressed them because of her innate abilities.

Tabitha traveled in one her parents' supersonic luxury aircraft, capable of extreme high-altitude flight. It took just a few hours flight time from their private sky port at their Interlochen estate in the NJ. The exorbitantly high cost for such high-class travel was, of course, reimbursed by the government.

Despite traveling in the lap of luxury, Tabitha dutifully worked during the flight, just as she had the whole night and day before. She was checking the immense volume of last-minute details for the cutover to the first phase of L2.

She slept only about three or four hours a day, just as she had most of her life. When she needed a break, she would watch her comprehensive library of pre-war classic cartoons. This was her favorite pastime apart from her embarrassingly disturbing tendency to compulsively and frequently gratify herself.

The Noreans, through their company NED Tech, were well compensated by New City. NED Tech had been called Norean Enterprise Development and Technology Company before it went to a public share offering. The Norean extended family collectively owned over 60 percent of the stock. Ēlantiel Carl Norean controlled 90 percent of all Norean family holdings, including the shares held in Tabitha's well-endowed trust fund.

The Noreans were the wealthiest family in New City and Carl was the senior and most titled noble among the elite families. In addition to his holdings in NED Tech, he owned other conglomerates all over New City, including several very profitable labor allocation colonies. At one time, his wealth was estimated to be over 500 billion NCCUs. Tabitha was thus the heiress to the greatest fortune in the world. She was essentially royalty, not only because she was Carl Norean's daughter, but by design in beauty and intelligence. Even so, Tabitha Norean hated herself.

She had an older brother who had been recently disinherited. Ēlar Stanley, six years her senior, constantly flaunted his status and abused his powerful connections to get what he wanted. One thing he had wanted: Tabitha. He had once been infatuated with Tabitha, who eventually proved she was no helpless maiden when it came to self-protection.

Unlike her brother, Tabitha cared little for money, nor did she care about being a Norean. She wanted out of her family and had tried to extricate herself from them when she'd turned eighteen. All she needed to do now was wait until her twenty-first birthday on October 31. On that date her trust would mature, and she could leave them behind.

Tabitha was acclaimed as a marvel of genetic engineering. Her IQ would have been off the charts—if it could be measured. She was profoundly talented in so many ways, it seemed miraculous. She was a proficient speed reader of even the most complex technical literature. She had a near perfect photographic memory. With her ability to multi-task she was not unlike a high-powered computer.

She intimidated brilliant colleagues and her parents. She could speak and read fluently in almost every remaining functional language—and some that were nearly extinct. She could paint faces and landscapes with uncanny accuracy and unrivaled skill and played several musical instruments expertly. Her greatest skill was her technical prowess and ability to design artificial intelligence algorithms, which mirrored her mind's eye and thus her incredible intuition. For this reason, ēlan Tabitha was the quintessential human collaborator for the Archon. She designed a system for him that could capture, not only his enemies, but everyone in her web.

Tabitha could remember the slightest details of the face of anyone she ever met and effortlessly recall almost every conversation she'd ever had, word for word. Beyond her stunning beauty and intelligence Tabitha was a natural clarion—someone trained in deductive reasoning and supposition.

A clarion could deduce virtually all possible outcomes along multiple strings of possibilities, then conclude which were the most likely ones based on a given set of circumstances. A skilled clarion could also deduce the most likely causation of any event. Tabitha deftly engineered this same cognitive ability into L2. This expanded its self-formulation and AI competence far beyond its already terrifying capability.

Tabitha could be abrasive and unyielding. She knew what people were going to say before they did. She annoyingly deduced the answers to questions before they were asked. On the surface, she appeared dispassionate. Yet underneath her stiff, intelligent façade she was far more sensitive than she allowed anyone to know. She was an expert at masking her emotions.

Tabitha had been neglected, abused, and molested throughout her life, especially by her brother. But the older she grew, the liberties other people attempted to inflict upon her were met with scathing verbal retribution and calculated enmity—or self-defense moves. Tabitha became skilled at physically hurting people, and she was deathly quick.

Humble was not an apt description of Tabitha, yet neither was she self-absorbed or narcissistic. She could be quite generous. At the Clarion Academy she was known for giving money to people and causes. She wasn't trying to be superior, but she didn't realize other girls used her and resented her generosity. She never boasted about her accomplishments. It didn't occur to her to care what other people thought. She had no desire or need to impress anyone. Should it come down to it, Tabitha would sacrifice everything to do what she thought was right.

She could also viciously insult others who were wrong. Even the Archon did not escape her blistering contempt. She called him Devan, not Lord Archon, never bowed, and she routinely insulted him to his face.

Tabitha had felt guilty about helping develop LEOH II since the time she crossed a threshold of understanding about its purpose. But it never occurred to her that she had no choice. Once Tabitha reached a conclusion, even if it altered her previous reasons for doing something, she would undo it if necessary, even if it took time and meticulous planning to do so. L2 was her biggest mistake and it was going to take all of her abilities to stop it.

She was privy to far more than just LEOH's technical specifications, protocols, mountains of formulation code, and complex algorithms. She knew the Archon and his retainers of lordly followers were not the benevolent rulers her mother and father idolized.

She hid in her heart many questions about what she was doing. Her desire to achieve perfection clashed with her sense of morality and weighed heavily on her conscience. Her moral convictions were not based on any religious beliefs, but rather on her own sense of what was right and wrong.

Perhaps Tabitha's biggest flaw was her lack of diplomacy. While she could be sophisticated and erudite, she was also spoiled, immature and even childish at times. She never socially matured as most adults do. Second to her father, the Archon was the most frequently on the receiving end of her juvenile and disrespectful tirades. She refused to tolerate blatant ignorance, especially when others were condescending toward her. When they were, Tabitha rarely held back her contempt and she had a sensitive threshold for what she considered ignorance.

Tabitha clearly recalled the strange and terrifying ritual her parents had forced her to undergo. She was only six when she was presented to the Archon in front of a host of New City elites. She had been under the influence of a drug that dulled her senses so she wouldn't feel pain as a sharp knife was drawn across her small left palm. She didn't understand the words spoken, but she did understand the context. It was a mock sacrifice, as she and several other young ēlans and ēlars stood before the Archon. He tasted their blood and placed his hands on them. She remembered him staring into her eyes as if he were looking into her soul.

This event traumatized Tabitha and was just another reason for her to hate her life growing up as a Norean. Her childhood memories were not happy ones. As a small child Tabitha was exceptionally difficult. Her parents thought she may never learn to talk. As a result, they isolated her and kept her away from other children because she was an embarrassment. They even contemplated sending her away to an institution if she didn't improve.

After expensive therapy and several special tutors, once she turned six years old, it was like the lights were turned on. She was mostly educated at home and she never learned how to make friends with other children. When she was finally around them, she kept to herself.

For those caught in the path of her relentless recollections, she could be devastatingly vicious. She vividly recalled how Stanley had molested (but not raped) her over the years. It grew progressively worse until she turned twelve, then for two years, she managed to avoid him, while they were away attending different schools.

When Tabitha was fourteen, Stanley attempted to rape her. Thanks to one older boy who had befriended her and who taught her to fight, she was now able to defend herself with deftness and skill. Despite Stanley being much bigger and stronger, she quickly disabled him. She shook her fist in his face and threatened that if he touched her again, she would murder him. She wanted her brother arrested, yet her father did nothing.

She hated her father for his neglect and disregard of how she was treated. Her aloof mother ignored Tabitha. She had no close familial relationships and virtually no friends, except for that one older boy at the academy. He did his best to protect her, at least from other boys, and sometimes teachers. She was not abused by boys. It was older girls who targeted and despised her, primarily because she was the Norean ēlan.

Tabitha spent three years away from home at the Clarion Academy from age twelve until she was fifteen. But once her only friend graduated, she was terrified. It was then that she discovered a humiliating truth about what was being said about her behind her back. She only experimented sexually with other older girls, at first, but eventually this became more frequent.

The girls made fun of her and over time they created a cruel name game. They watched her, participated with her and then they shamed her. She was called Tabithscream, Tabithskank, slut, squeal, threesome, spurt, trout, slurp and worse. The demeaning variations on her name were endless. By the time she found out, grossly exaggerated explicit details of what she did had spread all over the school. Her small breasts were also a cause for further mockery with the name Tabiteeny being a favorite of her hateful tormentors.

At one point, she contemplated suicide and she didn't have any friends to help her through this. After some embarrassing therapy, where she had to talk about her escapades, she finally put it behind her, but not out of her steel-trap mind. She never forgot the slightest insults or scandalous details of her experiences in which, for over two years, she shamefully participated. She wasn't gay, but her reputation said otherwise and most boys avoided her like the plague. Tabitha had become an isolated emotional wreck and she would remain that way for years.

Within New City's wealthiest noble families, teenage ēlans were considered available at an early age. It was not unusual for ēlans as young as thirteen or fourteen to be "given" to older men. They weren't "given" for marriage; it was more like formal training and considered respectable. These weren't ritualistic events but more like short-term arrangements, where nobles traded their daughters to each other or between their sons. Fortunately, for Tabitha she wasn't compelled to do this. Her father had reserved Tabitha exclusively for the Archon.

The older Tabitha got, the more she was propositioned, often by other nobles or close colleagues of her father's. Even her teachers propositioned her. By now Tabitha disliked both genders, except for her friend from the academy. He was now a man, and yet he continued to treat her like the helpless twelve-year-old girl he first met at school.

Tabitha decided to take her revenge at one of her parents' lavish dinner parties, one held just before her sixteenth birthday. She stood up as the main course was being cleared. She pointed out her molesters in front of their spouses, the other guests, and her parents. She named names and dates and exposed their vulgar propositions and attempts to seduce her, fondle her, or worse.

She ended with a blistering tirade: *"I am not a sex object! My body is not now nor will it ever again be a plaything for any of you. Nor for you, my incestuous pedophile brother, nor for any of your friends. I am sick of having to fend off your unwelcome, undesired, and frankly, disgusting attentions and intentions toward me. You may be able to get away with this sort of behavior with other girls, but not with me. There is no one in this room I will not kill if you touch me again. As for you ladies who like to swing that way, I don't! I have no interest in you, either. Now, since we all understand each other, including you, mommy and daddy, and by the way, thanks for bringing these child molesting predators into our home, let's have desert."*

No one in that room bothered Tabitha again. Tabitha's parents were so shocked and embarrassed, it was two years before they held another dinner party; and never one with Tabitha present.

* * * *

After this event Tabitha's life changed dramatically. Her father made a pathetic effort to confront her about her accusations, partly to make excuses or amends for his friends. He told her that what she had done was socially unacceptable.

Tabitha looked at him with contempt. "Dad, when does a daughter have to defend her virtue because her father won't? I'm not anyone's plaything. I will not become a whore because of your neglect or lack of concern. Did you hear any denials tonight? You didn't, because I revealed the truth about each of those lecherous toads. When I am ready for sex, I will do so with a man I love. I don't know what my purpose is, but I was not born to be sex object for your noble friends and certainly not for Stanley or his disgusting friends … or girls, either!"

Carl squinted his eyes in discomfort. "Of course not. I promise you, if anyone …"

"Stop! Don't promise me anything. Tell them your daughter is off limits, not because you say so, but because I will kill them if they try, and this includes Stanley. I told you he molested me and tried to rape me. You made excuses for him. You will pay for that one day."

Indeed, her father would pay dearly for his son's indiscretions, not so much with Tabitha, but for other crimes Stanley committed.

Despite Tabitha's blistering tirade that evening, Carl was proud of his daughter. At one time, it was his hope, that she would make up for his own failures and weaknesses and improve his standing with the Archon. After all, she was promised to him. That's why he paid so much to Harold Dylanis to engineer her. Even though for years he thought his investment in Tabitha had been a failure and a waste of money.

Despite her early learning difficulties, over the years, it had not taken long for her to surpass all her teachers and mentors in knowledge and understanding. Carl wanted to take advantage of her skills before the Archon took her for himself. He started to dread that day, not for her, but for himself. He dreaded it because he knew Tabitha would refuse. In fact, he knew if she was pushed too far, his little ēlan could be very dangerous. She was like a powerful gathering storm.

Carl Norean had something he wanted to offer Tabitha. After some additional discussion about her outburst, he broached the subject of her career. "Tabitha, I need to ask you something. As you know, NED Tech has overseen several R&D projects for the Archon for the last two decades. I think it is time for you to be introduced to him."

Tabitha lashed out, "I've met him, and I'll never forget it. If you think I am ever going to give myself to that alien Archon ... don't try to deny it. I can fill in the blanks. Good god, you can't put a bow on me for him. I'm not even sixteen. He is at least a century old. I don't care if he looks thirty-five. I won't sleep with him so you can get more lucrative contracts for NED Tech. How many billions do you need to justify selling your own daughter? You disgust me!"

Carl objected. "That's not it at all! I am talking about a professional career. We have been working on an important project—to develop the next version of LEOH for the Archon. You would be perfect as an entry level formulation specialist and systems protocol developer. With your intelligence and technical knowledge of molecular platforms, after your next degree is completed, I think it will be time for you to work for NED Tech. You can assist us in rolling out the next version of New City's operating system. It is what we have educated you to do."

"Then why do I need to meet the Archon, if I'm just supposed to be an entry level developer," Tabitha said. "Didn't I just say, I met the Archon already, and I will never forget it?" Tabitha held out her left palm to Carl. She mimed it being cut. She made a fist to indicate how the cut made blood flow from her hand. She pretended to mark the symbol the Archon drew on her chest in her own blood. She held a pretend cup in her hand, acting like she was drinking from it. "Our first meeting went something like that, if you recall. You were there."

Carl was taken aback. He knew exactly to what she was referring. All the parents of the children from New City's elite families had been assured that none of the children would remember the experience of the sacred three twos ritual they underwent that evening. Carl was silent a moment. "That was only a token ceremony of our commitment to raise our children to be loyal to New City and the Archon. You weren't even supposed to remember it. You were given catenine."

"You're a liar! Since when do children have to be stripped naked, stand in a circle, and have their hands cut so the Archon can drink their blood as a token of their parents' commitment to raise them to be loyal? No thanks for reminding me I've met the Archon before. If that prick wanted to perform a ritual like that with my child, any loyalty I had would vanish. As one who can speak for the children who were there ten years ago, what happened engendered no loyalty from me, in fact, quite the opposite. They may not remember it, but I will never forget. What else do you want from me, Dad?"

Carl was nervous. "What else? Tabitha, L2 is the most complex molecular data compression and formulation system ever conceived. This is the most ambitious upgrade ever attempted, to convert everything to a quantum molecular platform. The successful development of this system will keep our family fortunes intact for perpetuity. This is the purpose for which you have been educated. I didn't think you would be ready for a few years. Yet I can see you are more than ready. In time, you will oversee this project. It will probably take another ten years. You are perfectly suited for this."

Tabitha contemplated this. "I'll meet the Archon again. The question is whether or not he is ready to meet me again," she said with contempt. "I won't give myself to him, even though you gave me to him. You don't own me, and neither does he. I don't care who he is. He's a disgusting alien pervert who drinks the blood of children. What normal person does that? What normal parent stands there and watches? They aren't real people, Dad! I'm not stupid."

Carl knew his daughter had been chosen by the Archon for a special purpose when she turned eighteen. He believed the Archon wanted to marry Tabitha, even though it would likely involve some bizarre, arcane ritual. Mostly he remembered the Archon's promise to him: For the price of his genetically perfect daughter, Tabitha, he was promised even more wealth and power—and eternal life.

The following weekend Tabitha met the Archon for the first time since she was six. He was very impressed with her, so much so, he was more than willing to have her join her parents on the L2 project in the coming year. In fact, even though the Noreans had a palatial home only minutes away from the Interlochen Citadel by shuttle, he insisted she live in the Citadel when the time came. Carl knew the reasons for this and approved of them.

Little did Tabitha know the Archon wanted her at Interlochen to keep her away from anyone else and to keep a close, admiring eye on her. He spied on everything she did, in the supposed privacy of her rooms. He would have liked her to be filled out a bit more. Yet, he was entranced by her beauty. He especially enjoyed watching her when she bathed or was being dressed by her private valet. He meticulously kept track of her cycles, especially how she was progressing when she was hypnotically or chemically induced to pleasure herself.

Beyond all this, the Archon was most interested in her ATK15 sequence. He desired what would ultimately be revealed to him of her hidden name when he bonded with her when she turned eighteen. The power of her hidden name would once again give him access to the ethereal realms and so much more.

The Archon's desire for ēlan Tabitha consumed him to point of distraction. Yet for the sake of the rapid progress being made on L2, he decided to forgo the bonding ritual at three-sixes. Now, less than three years later, the Archon's dream of a quantum molecular core system was about to be realized, years ahead of schedule. He diligently worked out the dates. Her cycles were perfect for consummation of the rite, precisely at three sevens on October 31st 63 NCE. Ēlan Tabitha was his, and thanks to her, so was his most insidious tool of oppression, L2. It was an inescapable web for humanity and his little spider had done well.

* * * *

It was far too late to consider whether she had done the right thing. Tabitha wept as she contemplated this on the eve of the first phase rollout of L2. She faced herself in the gilded mirror of her bathroom at her parents' estate in the NCGD of the SJ. *Well, you can't quit now, since you're about to unleash a beast on this city. Your only choice is to somehow stop it before it destroys them all.* As she stared at her reflection, the house shook and the mirror broke into pieces. Tabitha could swear she heard thunder, or a distant explosion that sounded like a roar. She gaped at her shattered reflection and cried uncontrollably.

The tremor had lasted seconds. Tabitha realized that nothing else in the house was broken, except the gilded mirror. It didn't shatter or fall to the floor in a thousand tiny pieces. Rather, it fractured from the center, like a pie, with seven relatively even spaced cracks. It spread from between her eyes in the reflection of her face to the edge of the mirror, forming equal wedge shapes between each crack.

She studied the mirror, trying to understand the physics behind this odd phenomenon. After a minute, she shrugged it off. She filed it away in the tiny virtual folder in her mind where the few things she didn't fully comprehend were kept.

One such incomprehensible issue was herself. At times, she felt that she lost control of her mind and was overcome with intense sexual desires. She worried something was wrong with her. She had never experienced anything like this before she came to Interlochen, not to this degree. At the academy, she was usually with other girls. She was convinced she was going insane.

Tabitha was constantly undergoing counseling for something but she was too embarrassed tell her therapist everything about this, or to seek medical help. She knew she was a freak with an excitable libido, and her mind didn't function normally. She hoped her condition would improve over time. Instead, her disorder was getting worse. She knew she should address it. Instead, she ordered more things to facilitate her activities. *God, if Julian finds my "things" she would melt with scandal,*

Tabitha admitted to herself. She ultimately blamed her self-obsession on those older gay girls from the academy who first enticed her.

She recalled her prudish valet, Julian, catching her at a young age. She'd scolded Tabitha, "Shame on you child! Ēlans are never to touch themselves like that!" Later, at the Clarion Academy, Tabitha was encouraged to do so. No wonder she was losing her mind. She was a mess and the weird thing was, she fantasized about being watched, like those girls had done with her at the academy.

Tabitha often imagined being with her protector, the boy with whom she had fallen in love. She visited him and practically threw herself at him, but he wasn't romantically interested. She was in love with him and desperately wanted to marry him now that she was twenty and he was twenty-three. But she was an ēlan and he was a nobody from a backwater, hick district. She was frustrated that she was still a virgin and her only consensual experiences had been with those awful, jealous girls who made her the object of their cruel jokes. She felt worthless, and she often cried herself to sleep. She was lonely and desperately wanted to be loved.

Tabitha returned to thinking about how to correct the biggest mistake she'd ever made: her decision to work for her father and the Archon in developing L2. Meanwhile, she was being applauded for it by the "alien" she hated. This made her hate herself even more for being such a fool. She determined that the only way to make things right was to destroy her family and LEOH—or at least try to steal L2 from them. She knew if she headed down this path it could ultimately result in her own death.

She recalled her last meeting with the Archon, the day before she returned to the Southern Jurisdiction. Something was going on within the old LEOH system and she was determined to learn who was behind it. She didn't need notes, since she remembered everything precisely.

* * * *

The previous day in the Archon's office at his Interlochen Citadel.

"Élan Norean," the Archon said, "you of course remember Nathan Prideil. He has been working with me on several investigations of lapses in our system security in the Southern Jurisdiction. Nathan, if you will, please proceed with the briefing."

Prideil cleared his throat. "Of course, Lord Archon. This past Thursday, we discovered a major security breach in the SJ initiated by someone with inside knowledge of the Ministry. We believe the perpetrator may have been using one or more unrestricted and ghosted security access codes to steal classified data. These are similar to codes we suspect were created approximately eighteen years ago. We were unaware of the potential for such an intrusion until this event occurred. According to NED Tech protocols, I have been asked to bring it to your attention, to address the likelihood if this could have implications on the current L2 implementation."

"What codes are you referring to? Tabitha asked, irritated. "I was never informed."

The Archon said, "These are all recent findings."

"How recent? What event?"

"These codes, in particular, were created ..." the Archon said.

Tabitha said, "You just said these 'ghosted' codes were created eighteen years ago. That doesn't sound recent!"

Prideil said, "We are not certain if these exact access codes were utilized in this breach, or merely similar ones. Director Pythorael has a list of codes he claims were created around this time. He says he removed their ability to shield their index activity. However, LEOH has indicated the signature of this recent breach appears to have the same elements of fifty thousand similar quarantined intrusion events which have occurred over the years."

Tabitha remained calm, despite her irritation. "If you were unaware of the possibility of such an event, how have over fifty thousand similar intrusions been logged by LEOH? This was never disclosed during our risk assessment reviews. I meticulously checked for possible threats based on these assessments. I also recommended a complete redevelopment of the security and credentialing platform and all related subsystems, regardless of how long it would take. It could take longer to contain this than it would be to do what I first suggested."

Prideil seemed flustered. "I don't know the answer to your question."

"Then why are you in this meeting? I can read a security directive faster than you can talk about one. Send me the SD that alerted you to the breach!"

"This event occurred two days ago within the confines of the CCD HQ in the SJ and apparently involved a large quantity of highly classified matrix data," Prideil said, his tone conciliatory. "The information was illegally downloaded to what we believe may be a contraband device. A security directive was issued, primarily due to the bandwidth utilization alert. LEOH then connected it to the other intrusion events. But we don't know if they are actually connected."

"What's the SADEX score on the data?" Tabitha said. "This was two days ago?"

Prideil shrugged. "I can't specify the SADEX level. We don't know exactly what was stolen. There is an indication from the CCD technical services group that it was highly classified information. We think ..."

"*I can't specify, we don't know, we think*! Devan, why am I even talking to this know nothing dingtard? I should have been informed on Thursday about this, before we pulled the trigger on the system migration Friday! If fifty thousand intrusions didn't trigger a security directive, you have a much bigger problem than you realize. This is a single integrated system. Every PCD has at least a minimal level of access. If someone can get to data with a max SADEX score with these codes, there's not much they can't do. This latest breach is not a new threat because the access codes could not have been introduced prior to the last upgrade. Not unless someone has direct access to your implant, Devan."

* * * *

Late afternoon Sunday Tabitha was still thinking about the theft. She reviewed the updated security directive on the incident. She had no idea how the ghosted codes were created or where they were embedded in the system. She hit upon the idea of designing a negative formulation algorithm. She could trace the codes and learn where they were stored in the old LEOH system. For this she needed a known incident when the codes were used to either utilize, transfer, or compress data. She had it with this recent intrusion event.

Tabitha realized that the user of an untraceable ghosted access code would never utilize a matrix while in the system; that would create an orphan index record. Yet a raw data compression and file transfer would only appear as a bandwidth spike. To use such an access code, the user would need an authorized credential. This would launch a hidden procedure to erase its own tracks. How this index suppression routine functioned was something she still had to figure out.

The more Tabitha thought about this, the more it puzzled her, given her knowledge of how LEOH operated. The problem with attempting a negative trace on LEOH was its daunting size and scope. By a process of elimination she knew that, given time, she could find out how, when, and ultimately, who the user was. Tabitha searched the old LEOH logs until she found the bandwidth spike of three days earlier.

Tabitha knew the systems had been shut down and locked out later that evening, after the incident. This meant the deleted access indexes were probably still pristinely written on the storage sectors. It was like an undisturbed crime scene. If she worked quickly enough she could learn everything she needed to know about this security breach and the access codes used to accomplish it.

Despite being exhausted, Tabitha worked diligently. Within hours she had succeeded. At first she thought there must be some mistake, due to the huge amount of information transferred over the node. After cross referencing her findings with the security directive's log reports, she realized her findings were correct. The breach had been carried out so rapidly that it must have been done with a highly advanced molecular data compression device. The security directive suggested it could have been one of three advanced prototypes developed by the Ministry R&D division years earlier.

She soon knew exactly whose port address and device had been used. Tabitha now had proof of who the culprit was, the access codes he used, and the contents of the classified matrix data that had been stolen. She accomplished what LEOH itself, the NCIC internal security division, and the HES had been unable to over the last several days.

Good grief, this guy stole almost every classified matrix in the system. Devan will freak out when he realizes the magnitude of the theft, Tabitha thought admiringly. *At least he won't have to worry about anything else being stolen. He got almost all of it. Way to go!*

Tabitha wondered how a new Ministry hire could have come into possession of a decades-old prototype MDC. To their credit, the Ministry's security forces suspected Mark Verigratu of having such a device. While the Ministry had its suspicions and she had proof, nonetheless, the man had extricated himself from their clutches, at least temporarily. This was after a strip search, a lengthy interrogation with the administration of Phencol, a body cavity search, and an abdominal scan. *Yikes, poor guy.*

Tabitha memorized Mark's profile matrix. He was well educated and genetically enhanced, from a well-to-do family. She wondered how on earth he'd obtained old ghosted access codes that must have been created prior to the last major upgrade. The more she contemplated this, the more the man intrigued her. *What was he up to? What could he possibly hope to accomplish?*

He must be part of some larger conspiracy, Tabitha mused. *Perhaps I can meet him.* She looked at his image on her display again. *He's not bad looking, although he's married.* She sighed, disappointed. *I wonder what his wife looks like?* She accessed Ari's profile and displayed several images. Tabitha cocked her head with interest. *That's curious. Eighteen?*

He obviously likes younger women. She's very pretty, with a nice, athletic body. Of course, she has a much better figure than me, but who doesn't? The girl probably had bigger breasts than I do now when she was ten. Wait, why am I even looking at this?

CHAPTER 12

THE INVITATION

I returned to work Monday morning knowing full well suspicion still hung over my head. When I arrived, many of the CCD operatives and formulation specialists were notified to report to the main floor conference theatre, which seated about four hundred people. At the meeting, people were shocked to hear that many of our subordinate divisions would be slowly phased out over the coming months as the new LEOH system became fully operational.

CCD Director Pythorael spoke. During his talk, I received a high priority notification on my PCD to report to the top floor executive suite in a half an hour. I was to be accompanied by Talen Place and Lawrence Rogan for a meeting with Pythorael in his office. Rogan was not someone with whom I wanted any more dealings. I had never met Place. I knew who he was from my data analysis activities over the weekend. I was nervous at the prospect of meeting with all three of them. I confirmed the invitation, as if I had an option.

As I left the conference theatre I was met by two CCD security guards and a third man. He introduced himself as Talen Place. "Mr. Verigratu, I need you to come with me," he said.

"I accepted the invite and I know where the lift is to the executive floor. I don't think an armed escort is necessary."

Place nodded toward the two guards. "Of course, please, follow me."

He escorted me to Pythorael's private conference room that over-looked the central government district. The room's floor-to-ceiling glass windows framed its opulent structures. After ten minutes, Pythorael's private secretary led me down a hall, through a pair of ornate doors into his office suite. I hadn't been to Pythorael's office since the day of my final interviews. Seated with him were Place and Rogan.

Pythorael welcomed me pleasantly. "Please be seated, agent Verigratu. This won't take long. We are all busy, especially with this ongoing implementation. I hope you understand why we had to interrogate you so extensively last Thursday. It was an unprecedented situation."

I sat in stunned silence wondering if they still believed I was guilty or were playing with me. "No one explained exactly what they were looking for."

Pythorael laughed. Then he turned serious. "We can all speak freely. But since we are all friends here, I want you to tell me how you did it, who helped you, and what your intentions are with the data you stole."

I sat back and crossed my hands on my chest. I casually felt for my syringe. Thankfully, I'd remembered to replace it. "I don't know what you're talking about."

Pythorael said, "We are having your apartment searched. If we find a shred of evidence you have an illegal storage device or a dead space, I can assure you there will be no way for you to confess later. You should do so now, while I am being lenient with you."

I could tell Pythorael was bluffing. They were hoping I'd confess. "I've already told Mr. Rogan everything I know. I have no illegal storage device and there is nothing in my apartment to prove otherwise."

Pythorael winced. "I have never been one to ignore coincidences, especially extraordinary ones. The root of these coincidences are likely the reason for your actions. Please don't make this difficult on yourself. Please tell me everything."

I began to speak, and Pythorael held up his hand to stop me. "You misunderstand my intentions. If you would let me explain, you might change your mind about confessing. I'm not trying to entrap you. I'm sympathetic to your cause, as are my associates." The director nodded at his two companions. "As you heard this morning, the Ministry is about to undergo significant changes. We are not exactly pleased with them. Secretly, we wish to enlist your help. We are looking for creative and capable operatives with the right skills to aid us in our cause. You can trust us."

I wasn't buying it. "Look, if you are trying to get me to confess to some conspiracy, you can forget it. I don't give a damn about whatever extraordinary coincidence you think you've uncovered, or whether or not you tear my apartment to pieces. I have been stripped searched, my mind altered, and my body probed. If you have proof against me, then arrest me. If you think I would be of some help to your own conspiracy, you can forget it." I started to get up, but Rogan forcefully pushed me back in my chair.

"I will have you arrested if you so much as flinch," Pythorael said. "I must say, I am impressed." Glancing over to Rogan he added, "He is as good as they get. This man can sit here, guilty as sin, yet deny it with a straight face in the presence of the highest-ranking security officials of the Ministry and the NCIC. It's truly amazing!"

Pythorael leaned forward. He glared at me with eyes like daggers. "I don't know how you pulled this off, or how you got out of the district with the device carrying the classified information you stole. Yet I intend to find out how and who helped you. With a word, I could have you killed or imprisoned in a labor allocation colony—and your pretty young wife as well.

"I am offering you your only chance to live. If the Archon finds out about you, or believes you're a threat, your life will be cut pathetically short. I am offering you a chance for us to help protect you. You can make a difference. I am offering you a great opportunity to help me and my associates set things right." I remembered Zack's warning to never trust Dalen Pythorael.

Somehow, I knew I was about to be dosed with Phencol and needed to inject myself with the counter agent. I folded my hand under my arm, as if to scratch, then deftly injected myself. After I did, my heart started to race and two people entered the director's office from behind me. Before I could turn around, someone held me down.

The massive dose of Phencol I received quickly overloaded my ability to comprehend what was being said. I tried to open my eyes, but my eyelids felt too heavy. I felt sick to my stomach and my head was buzzing loudly. After about ten seconds, my head gradually began to clear. I heard the director repeat his questions. "Who provided you with the access codes? Who else is involved in this? Where did you get the device you used to smuggle the data out of the district?"

I felt bleary, even though I was able to form words, interspersed with curses. I told Pythorael: "I don't know what you are talking about. I didn't steal any data. I don't have a device." For the next ten minutes the director peppered me with questions, and I answered the same way. I could feel the two drug cocktails battling for control of my brain. At one terrifying moment I felt myself lose control of the words spilling out of my mouth. I cursed at Pythorael and told him that I quit. Then I vomited on his desk. I felt like I was going to die.

I couldn't believe I'd thrown up on the director's desk or told the director of NCMIA to go F himself. I saw Pythorael snap his fingers and felt another injection being administered into my arm, just below my shoulder. I slumped back in the chair. Moments later I retched again, then passed out. I'm not sure how long I was out, but when I woke up I was dripping with sweat and a female doctor was attending to me. She injected me with yet another concoction, then I passed out again.

When I opened my eyes, the director was seated on the corner of his desk leaning over me, his left hand gently shaking my right shoulder. I was still seated in the same chair. "I am sorry we had to do this again. I had to be certain you were telling the truth. We can't be too careful. Once your head clears, I'm certain you'll reconsider your intoxicated decision to leave the Ministry. I know I can trust you and so can the Archon. I promise it will be much more pleasant going forward." The director handed me a tall glass of water. He watched as I drank it thirstily.

I rubbed my eyes and my forehead. I was still feeling ill and was mad as hell. "That crap made me sick all weekend. Just when I was feeling better, you dosed me again? I need to lie down."

Pythorael stared at me intently. Then he smiled and turned to the window. "Let me see if I can make it up to you. After you get back from your project mission on Friday, I would like you to accompany me to the Citadel for the weekend. You will have a chance to meet the Archon. The LEOH implementation team will be there, along with most of the executives of the Ministry. I promise it will be all play and no work. There will be splendid food and entertainment. Invite your wife. Afterward, you can take the next three days off. I know the two of you never had a chance to get away together following your nuptials."

I didn't want Ari around this nest of vipers. I said, "Let me give it some thought. I'm not going to easily forgive this. I hope my home has not been utterly destroyed."

Pythorael looked at me with an expression of insincere remorse. "All I can do is offer my apologies, a few perks, and my sincere sympathy for what you have had to endure."

* * * *

Rogan and Pythorael waited for Complaceal (Talen Place) to return from escorting me to the third floor. The director paced impatiently. "Let's hear it. Did the search turn up anything in his apartment?"

"Nothing!" Rogan said. "There is no evidence of a dead space or a safe room. Every meter of his apartment was scanned for evidence of an unregistered compression device. It was clean."

Pythorael smirked and pursed his lips. "I don't know how he could have avoided answering truthfully this time. He had no opportunity to administer an anecdote to such a heavy dose. Keep the trace on him. Have his apartment thoroughly probed and searched again while he is in the DZ with Merrick. If the Archon didn't want to meet him, I'd have him imprisoned. He's our culprit, despite his ability to deny it."

"Do you think this could be a spiritual intrusion?" Rogan asked.

"No, I didn't sense he was being spiritually assisted, at least not directly," Pythorael said. "What about Zachariah Waters? What have you found out about the old man?"

Rogan pulled out his display. "He's attended periodically by a private physician, a Dr. Ellen Cavanaugh. She prescribes him drugs for dementia, arthritis pain, and various other ailments. I checked the records to compile a detailed medical matrix. Her prognosis for his recovery is somewhat vague, but not optimistic. A home health nurse attends to him each day. There are various individuals at different times who visit. Compilations on their backgrounds are pending. There is nothing out of the ordinary. He has ..."

"I don't give a damn who is coming in to change the old man's diapers, if he's so feeble," Pythorael said. "I want to know if you suspect if he is involved in this conspiracy with Verigratu."

Rogan held up is hand in a mock apology. "No, there's nothing obvious, but look at this—there's a plethora of additional coincidences you should know about. Zack's only son, Aaron, was wounded in a military exercise in the DZ under questionable circumstances. And an old downgraded security directive hinted at his involvement in the trafficking of dissidents around that time. You're going to be more suspicious about this family once you hear what else I discovered."

Pythorael glared at Rogan. "All right. What is it?"

Rogan smiled. "Aaron's son Neil is Ariel Waters' father. Neil and his wife Lara were killed in the K15 genetics research lab explosion. Lara worked for Dylanis! Neil worked for the Ministry's GIA division around the same time. This was when the widespread genetic matrix corruption occurred, along with the GIA audit on the K15 program."

"That explosion took place in the early morning hours," Pythorael said. "No one should have been there. Why would Dylanis' research assistant be on the premises? Are you saying their deaths were never investigated?"

Rogan shrugged. "I assume information about their deaths was in the security matrix at one time. Yet everything about the lab incident and the assault on the doctor's home was quarantined or obliterated. This information was discovered in the obituary matrix. Why they were in the lab at the time of the explosion was never investigated. We need to run an extensive correlation."

"I agree," Pythorael said. "Put our most experienced formulation experts on this as soon as LEOH is back online. If L2 is as intuitive as it is promised to be, perhaps it will figure out everything we need to know. It seems odd that the specter of the K15 project has come back to haunt me—in more ways than one. But I have a plan that might accomplish our objectives."

Rogan said, "What about ēlan Tabitha Norean?"

"What about her?" Pythorael snapped.

Rogan shrugged. "As a formulation expert, I mean. I realize she has no investigative experience. Yet she's perhaps the most knowledgeable person available on the new L2 AI platform, since she designed it. You've said you want to align yourself with her. You've also pointed out the necessity to alienate her from the Archon, given his 'other' interest in her."

"I am well aware of the threat the Norean ēlan poses to us, not the least of which is the Archon's obsession with her," Pythorael said. "But the last thing I want is that spoiled, rich, know-it-all, pompous ēlan snooping around this issue. If she gets involved, she may well discover my own little secret for the codes' original purpose. Leave her to me. The Archon should then leave the rest to us."

CHAPTER 13

THE HOUSE OF NOREAN

The Archon invited Ēlantiel Carl Norean into his luxurious office at his palace Citadel in the high security zone of the New City government district in the SJ.

Carl was seated in front of the large desk and offered a glass of high-quality Scotch. "My lord, I am humbled by the honor you have bestowed on my family over the years. How may I be of service?"

The Archon smiled. "You have a fine daughter, Ēlantiel. I have never worked with such a ..." he stuttered ... "a more highly qualified and exceptionally gifted professional. That she is only twenty years of age is astonishing. Her achievements have far exceeded my greatest expectations, especially given the glacial progress of the previous decade on L2."

"I'm gratified to know that NED Tech has satisfied your desires for this system," Carl replied. "Her mother and I are very proud of Tabitha. Perhaps NED Tech should have charged New City more for her unauthorized scope expansions, given how pleased you are."

"I indeed factored this into my intention to richly reward her," the Archon said. "She will receive a large bonus, a new title, and an estate across the river from the Citadel. Do you think she will be pleased by such rewards?"

Carl nodded appreciatively. "Lord, I know you are aware of her contempt of her maiden title of ēlan. Whether she would be pleased by a new title is doubtful. It would also be highly irregular, and not in keeping with the City's financial practices to compensate anyone directly who is engaged under a government contract—a contract which employs hundreds of people from NED Tech who are also worthy of a reward for this effort, not to mention the company itself."

The Archon frowned. "NED Tech will receive all it is entitled to receive. Don't forget your place, Carl. If I wish to reward someone by virtue of my own generosity, you have no say whatsoever. How much are *you* paying her, if I may ask?"

Carl stuttered, "Perhaps 150,000 NCCUs per year, plus bonus, benefits, and perks."

"You are a miser when it comes to your own children."

Carl said, "Trust me, Tabitha wants for nothing. Everything we have is hers. I meant no disrespect to her as far as her compensation is concerned. I don't believe she is even aware of how much she makes. She has her own trust fund, in addition to what we provide for her. I am simply concerned about the optics. NED Tech is no longer a closely held entity. My board of directors has been less than forgiving about such matters since the Castle Point debacle. Even my title and position in the company can't insulate me from their oftentimes overbearing scrutiny."

"Yes, that was an unfortunate situation. It's a pity you decided to put your company on the public exchange in the first place, even though you made billions on the offering. Nevertheless, if your board has any concerns about it, I will be glad to draft a memo absolving you of any conflict of interest. Your son may have been a catastrophe, but your daughter has more than redeemed my confidence in your family. Besides, once the board sees the amount of bonus money the city will be paying the company, they will have no reason to complain about anything."

"I'm looking forward to seeing the Phase 1 project settlement proposal," Carl responded.

The Archon said, "I would like to discuss your beautiful ēlan; I need her help with a delicate matter that concerns a threat to the security of New City, which is why I called you here today. I have every confidence in her. In my opinion, she could run your entire company or even this city, if she put her mind to it."

Carl shifted in his chair, betraying his nervous energy as he sipped his Scotch. "Of course, my lord, whatever you ask. I had always intended for my son to follow in my footsteps into the executive ranks and for my daughter to follow her mother's career in the more technical aspects of what we do. Yet she is difficult sometimes, and …"

The Archon said, "I am not suggesting you make her a senior VP, Carl; I am simply pointing out that her talent destines her for much greater things than running NED Tech. Tabitha is privy to a great many state secrets, and she is the only one I can trust to undertake this security operation. I need her to play a role akin to a covert agent."

"You want Tabitha to be a spy?" Carl said, almost choking. "She isn't known for subtlety."

The Archon confided the news about the data theft and the suspected thief to Carl and the possible consequences. "My difficulty is, I have doubts as to the loyalty and ability of my security minister to ferret this out. He may be compromised. At the very least, he has a conflict of interest. This requires a swift resolution. I believe your élan will help us infiltrate the organization behind the conspiracy. The ministry was unable to obtain a confession or discover any incriminating evidence on the man we are certain is involved."

"Tabitha would be a horrible spy."

The Archon sipped his own glass of Scotch. "I disagree. She easily grasped the gravity of the situation when it was disclosed to her and quickly and insightfully understood the risk and potential exposure we have to such a threat. Revelations of this highly classified data to the public could be catastrophic."

"Threat assessment is one thing, acting as a covert agent is not …" Carl started to say.

The Archon waved him off. "I want her to get close to this young man and gather intelligence on him. She is quite alluring. I am certain she will captivate him. I also believe the organization behind this theft would consider her quite a prize if they thought she could be turned to support them. If there is a web with which to catch our prey, your lovely ēlan possesses all the necessary attributes, skills, and entanglements to ensnare them. I'm confident your beautiful little spider will utterly expose them, simply and quickly."

Carl argued, "She may be quick. Even so, Tabitha does nothing simply."

The Archon said, "I am not asking for your permission. I promise, I will not allow her to be put in any real danger. She is far too valuable for that. When she has discovered what we need we will intervene. I realize she is not trained in spy craft. It is her insight as a clarion which will be valuable. She may very well uncover everything in a day. Even so, I know Tabatha can be volatile. Because it may require her to be manipulative her tendency to be brutally honest, even with me, concerns me. This will require her to act a part in which she will have to be deceptive and even lie. What are your thoughts?"

Carl finished off the glass before setting it down. "Her trademark is telling people the truth, even when she shouldn't. She is unsociable toward her peers, especially the opposite sex. She doesn't make friends easily, and she tends to be an annoying know-it-all. She talks so fast most people can hardly keep up. It's probable this young man will despise her. She can be horribly undiplomatic. What you are expecting of her is not well suited to her overbearing personality."

The Archon laughed. He said, "Yet when she puts her mind to something, she can accomplish it remarkably quickly. As far as this data breach issue is concerned, we have little time. I believe these same people are responsible for the escape of a great many dissidents. Your daughter may even help us discover the location of their hidden city in the DZ. This is of extreme importance to me as well."

"We are talking about Tabitha," Carl said. "She thinks more like a machine than a person. She is also a disaster in unscripted social situations. If there is a mental equivalent to a manic, compulsively organized hoarder, it's her. Her goal in life is to know everything. Bring her into this investigation and she will treat it like a mandate to run the Ministry. To most people, going down rabbit holes is a distraction. I assure you she will explore them all. Then she will create a map with their dimensions, along with a census. She masters every detail, yet never wallows in them. She never stops until she's mastered all of them. Frankly, sometimes I think she's insane."

"That is precisely why I need her on this," the Archon replied. "I will keep her focused on this particular existential threat so she doesn't explore too many tangents."

Carl said, "You can't manage her. Believe me, I've tried. It will be her way or no way."

"Nevertheless, I have every confidence in her," the Archon said calmly.

He rose from his chair, walked around his desk, and stood a couple of feet from Carl. "If certain factions got their hands on this stolen data, they would fail to understand its true beneficent purpose. Many would violently oppose these objectives and the means by which we intend to accomplish them. I need your daughter to recover this data and I need her to do it quickly!"

"I'm not sure she is right person for this—or for you, either!" Carl exclaimed. "Tabitha can be a bitch. If you cross her, it's difficult to get back on her good side, which is a rare microscopic sliver of this dimension. I haven't been there in over ten years and I don't expect to ever return."

The Archon laughed. "I didn't think she had a good side. Nevertheless ..."

"I think you're making a huge mistake. Even so, shall I speak to Tabitha on your behalf or tell her to come to you? I warn you she will make demands you have never contemplated. She will make herself equal to you."

The Archon remained unperturbed. "Yes, of course, speak to her. Then have her appear before me in the morning. You can tell her generally why I want to see her. You know how she always annoyingly fills in the details herself. She's worse than any textual conversation enabling device."

Carl laughed. "She is well known for that, even when the blanks are the entire conversation." He added timidly, "I would, however, caution you not to mention your plans for her upcoming birthday. You should rather try to endear yourself to her or better yet, pick a different girl entirely."

The Archon nodded and smiled wickedly. "Don't concern yourself, Carl. I have no intention of mentioning it. She has been conditioned to freely give herself to me. Her cycles are perfect. Once it is done, she will be delighted. She won't even care that her own father sanctioned it and was a witness to the event. I don't need to court your ēlan."

* * * *

The man has no idea who he is dealing with, Carl thought on his way home. He dreaded the outcome. *I hope he has a new clone prepared. Tabitha will likely kill him.* Once home, he poured himself another large drink and then two more.

CHAPTER 14

WASTELAND

I spent the next couple of days finalizing my work for my trip to the DZ surveillance station with Merrick Taylor. After the Final War, satellites became a relic. The enormous amounts of space debris (wreckage and trash from the destruction of countless satellites) and active anti-satellite weapons in space made orbital surveillance and communication nearly impossible. The cost of trying to clean up space and disable orbital weapons systems meant that for now, New City had to rely on ground-based telemetry stations for its DZ surveillance.

While I was not a field agent, it was not uncommon to send formulation specialists along on such trips to the DZ. Each station upgrade had to be individually customized to recalibrate their sensor arrays. The type of upgrade I was working on could not be installed directly from the city grid, due to com limitations and security features that prevented external hacking of the stations.

Teams of maintenance engineers were constantly sent out to replace, repair, and upgrade the detection equipment strategically hidden across the DZ coverage zones. This first facility we were visiting was well known for its consistent detection of DZ insurgent forces. It was also plagued with equipment failures and the need for sensor recalibrations. As one of the more strategically valuable sites, it was also one of the highest priorities, in terms of external security. New City was planning to expand into this zone.

* * * *

I packed for two days. I was supposed to rendezvous with the project team at 6:00 a.m. at the battalion station just inside Sanctuary Gate 3, leading into the Dead Zone. However, around 5:30 that morning, Ari contacted me as I was heading out.

She sounded panicked. "Mark, I had a dream you need to hear about," she said. "Something terrible is going to happen during this trip. An angel in my dream said to tell you these exact words: *'The battle you run from in fear, you'll find. You will have a choice, which will change your destiny and mine. If you choose to be a coward, all will be lost. The battle must take place and you must do this at all cost. A child will lead you to be brave to rescue those you must save.'*"

"Thanks for the pep poem, Ari," I said, irritated. "What are you talking about? Look, I have to go, NOW! I love you, but I don't have time to hear about your dream ... or angels. I'm running late and I have a lot of work to finish on the way."

"Mark!" Ari shouted as I cut off the com. I didn't answer her afterward, when she tried to contact me again. I love Ari, but she can catastrophize. This was the first time she'd mentioned a dream to me, yet I blew it off. At the time, I didn't appreciate how accurate Ari's visions could be and ignored Zack's advice about paying close attention to them.

At the battalion station we were issued a small, but highly advanced firearm and special protective gear against radiation. The weapon shot fatal bolts of energy up to about thirty meters, and its ballistic mode fired a 9.37-millimeter round from a twenty-round magazine. Our protective gear didn't offer much ballistic protection. We were told it could prevent a small arms round from penetrating it and could provide some protection against a knife attack.

In the unlikely event of an attack we were advised to take cover. Excursions like ours had been attacked in the past; Dead Zone bandits were keen to steal anything they could get their hands on. A twenty unit patrol in two vehicles would escort us. In addition to NCSF personnel, armed drones would provide reconnaissance and security. Our three-ve-hicle convoy exited Sanctuary Gate 3 just before 7:00 a.m.

Our team rode in the small, lightly armored NCG CCD marked shut-tle. The NCSF team flanked us front and aft in more heavily armored troop transport vehicles arrayed with quite a bit of weaponry, as well as communications and threat detection capability. On the way down, Taylor briefed us on updated project parameters. Our five-person team included Taylor, me, two engineers, and a senior analyst in the CCD DZ monitoring division. I wanted to watch the passing scenery but was obligated to focus on the briefing. It was the first time in two years Taylor himself had accompanied such an expedition.

He began by pointing out we would be traveling south southeast for about 250 kilometers and the roads would be rough in spots. I remem-bered what Zack had said at our first meeting, about where our family once lived. But my interest in seeing the old, devastated city was purely academic, rather than nostalgic.

After the backup had been completed Friday, there had been over 1,100 engineers hooking up all the data feeds. However, when the engi-neering team tried to reacquire the microwave signals from 4UB6 and 4XT5, both of those facilities had gone offline, for no apparent reason. It was speculated a storm could have caused a cascade failure in the power system for the primary antennae array, or, in a worst-case scenario, the stations had been compromised. Taylor assured us reconnaissance indicated no hostile activity around 4UB6.

A coded entry was required to gain access to the station, through thick, solid steel doors, into to a highly secured bunker. Merrick seemed concerned that something had taken the 4UB6 facility offline. We had to bring it back online before we could upgrade the systems.

* * * *

We were delayed at the checkpoint station due to another power failure. The NCSF commander decided to call in extra patrols to secure the area. We were a couple of hours behind schedule when we arrived at our destination. It was a bumpy, hour-long drive from the checkpoint, which we planned to return to that night to sleep.

We drove about fifty kilometers into the DZO9SL3 zone. The farther south we traveled, the sparser the vegetation became, but surprisingly, there were quite a few trees. I was amazed at the desolation of the abandoned urban landscape We exited our transports, walked a short distance through the ruins, then entered a building through the debris-strewn lobby of what appeared to be an old hotel. We proceeded down a stairwell to the subfloors where the facility bunker was hidden.

Most of the security team was deployed to cover the surrounding zone and look for or engage any hostiles. Half a dozen men accompanied our CCD team to the bunker.

Taylor activated a switch and lights hidden in the recesses of the stairwell came on, lighting our way to the lower levels. We exited the stairwell through the still clearly marked B4 doorway into a large open basement area. We saw a set of door frames to our far right with glass shards embedded in them. As we carefully walked through the frames, mindful of the shattered glass, I saw a small sign plastered on the back wall behind a counter. It read: "Horizon Hotel Security Services." The security office was strewn with broken glass and rubble. In the back of the room was a heavy metal door. A tiny blinking red light was located on a small panel beside it.

Taylor tried to activate the commands on his display, then paused. I heard fear in his voice. "OK, even if a facility is offline it should have no impact on the access security. When I activated the entrance code this red light should have turned green, and I should have been prompted to touch the pad so it could ID me."

The sergeant with us said, "Should I try to force the door?"

Taylor looked at him like he was an idiot. "Yeah, like that's going to do any good." The light started blinking rapidly for a few seconds. It turned yellow, then began blinking more slowly.

Taylor looked puzzled. "No way this is possible. Someone could be inside. The light should turn yellow once the facility is accessed. The door is sealed and it's ten centimeters of thick steel. It requires a synchronized random password key and a genetic confirmation ID to open it. Fewer than ten people in the CCD are able to access these bunkers."

The sergeant said nervously, "I'll go up a couple of levels and tell the commander he needs to come down here."

"Shut up and listen," Taylor said. "I'm going to run the sequence again. Maybe this has a connection to the facility going offline. It could be a built-in security reset feature." Taylor started reentering the code into his PCD display. Still, nothing happened. The light continued to blink yellow. "Dammit, what the hell is going on?"

Just then, we heard an electronic voice coming from a speaker in the dark area near the door. "You are attempting to access a secure NCMIA bunker facility. Protective countermeasures are active ... ten, nine, eight ..." Taylor looked at the sergeant. "What the hell. Back away to the stairwell entrance. Hurry!"

We grabbed our gear and hustled out of the security office. Suddenly, the lights went out. I stumbled forward, striking my head hard against something solid in front me. Disoriented, I sat down to clear my head.

I could still hear the countdown coming from the bunker door on the back wall of the office: "three, two ..." The voice went silent. I heard everyone moving in the general direction of the door to the stairwell. I unhooked my vest light to turn it on, but dropped it. As I groped around in the dark, I banged my head again against what turned out to be a concrete pillar. In those few seconds, no one had had time to activate their lights. We could hear each other, even though we couldn't see anything. Taylor called out, "Everyone, stop moving! Activate your vest lights! I think I know what's happened."

I felt blood dripping down my face from my head. I held my sleeve up to wipe my face.

"Someone tried to breach the facility," I heard Merrick say. "It has gone into an automated defensive mode ... I think." He switched on the

NEW CITY CHRONICLES - CATCHING A SPIDER

light attached to his vest. The soldiers who had been standing sentry outside the security office activated their weapons lights. Now we could see to make our way back through the huge open area of the sublevel floor. Taylor said, "We need to head back upstairs. I need to review the protocols. I've never heard of a surveillance facility bunker denying entry to an authorized code input."

Gordon, one of the engineers, spoke up. "I don't know anything about the countermeasure alarm, but the yellow light only flashes when the bunker is occupied and the lock mechanism is set to manual control. It's so we can let team members come and go without having to re-enter the access code. This begs the question: Why was the light red initially? Did someone in the bunker just now switch it to manual lockdown?"

Taylor said, "Why didn't you say something before?"

Meanwhile, I was kneeling on the ground behind the pillar, trying to stop the bleeding on my forehead. Just then, blinding spotlights lit up the rest of my team. I didn't move. The soldiers with weapons at the ready instinctively dropped to the ground. Two of them started firing toward the bright lights. They were instantly killed by blistering gunfire.

Everyone else froze and raised their hands in surrender. I pulled out my weapon and glanced around the corner of the pillar. My team was being approached by a group of six men and one woman, each carrying heavy ballistic weapons. I froze, hidden by the thick shadows cast by the spotlights of the advancing hostiles. I knew my CCD-issued weapon was no match for these well-armed hostiles.

A loud voice said, "Hold your fire!" A tall, skinny man and the woman walked closer to my companions. The other four men held back. They were silhouetted by the bright lights, so I couldn't make out their faces. "Drop your weapons!" the man shouted. The three remaining soldiers looked tentatively at their sergeant. When they saw he was complying with the order, they followed suit. "Who is in charge here?" the man demanded.

Taylor said, "I am." I could now see the man was a wiry black man who looked to be in his late forties. The woman was younger, perhaps in her early thirties.

The man approached Taylor to within a couple of meters. He said, "Your military escort have all been killed or captured. We have also destroyed your armed reconnaissance drones." He commanded his men to search my team and the remaining military units. I remained hidden and silent. I glanced back through the gloom into the abandoned security office. I could barely make out the tiny light on the entrance control pad glowing red again.

So much for the unlikely event of our being attacked. I briefly considered surrendering, but decided it wasn't a good idea. As I peered around the pillar again, I could see my team being searched. I heard someone refer to the man in charge as Quillion. He was whispering to his female comrade.

Just then, two more hostiles came into view through the far end of the basement sublevel. One of them said additional patrols were forty minutes out. This meant our military escort must have alerted the New City security force battalion station.

There was more whispered conversation. Quillion said, in a distinctively gruff voice, "You'll be coming with us; zip-tie their hands." I slumped behind the pillar as I heard them shuffling around securing my colleagues and start to lead them away.

I heard Taylor say, "Where are you taking us?"

No one answered. Someone said, "Quiet! You might have a chance to live."

I waited about ten minutes in the pitch dark before venturing out with my weapon drawn. I turned on my lamp, then put my weapon in ballistic mode, thinking I might need the range. It was a silenced weapon, so even in ballistic mode the noise from the explosion would be suppressed within the firing chamber.

My sophisticated weapon, with its digital displays, was nothing like the crude archaic guns the insurgents were using. Yet it was far less powerful. I'd started walking slowly back toward the stairway when I heard a noise from the direction where my team had been taken. I switched off my light with my thumb. Pitch black enveloped me. I turned to look in the direction where the sound originated. I could now see two lights, probably about sixty meters away, heading in my direction. The lights were bobbing up and down, coinciding with the motion of steps.

I slowly felt my way, as silently as I could, back toward the pillar. I kept one hand out in front of me to keep from smashing my head again. I reached the pillar and slid around to the back side, away from the oncoming lights. Just before they reached my position, they shifted to their left, heading into the abandoned hotel security office, toward the facility bunker.

I knew I was being a coward. I had allowed my colleagues to be captured and hadn't lifted lift a finger to intervene. Now I was scurrying around in the dark like a rat, hiding from a couple of bouncing lights. If they gave out medals for valor for these types of excursions I wouldn't qualify for my actions so far. What was I supposed to do, apart from surrendering myself or die trying to stop whomever these hostiles were? I felt nothing but fear and I was trembling.

CHAPTER 15

ENEMY OF MY ENEMY

I watched the men approach the bunker. There were three altogether; two were nonmilitary. They were dressed like technicians, carrying equipment. The third man was armed. He was probably there to either provide protection or to guard them. Within a minute, I heard the massive door click and slide back into its hidden recess pocket. The three silently entered the bunker. I waited a minute as the lights disappeared into the facility. Once again, I was left in complete darkness.

I had a reasonably good idea of the size and layout of the bunker. I knew it had been designed to house a three-person team for extended stays. Facilities inside included food and water. If I could get into the bunker and access the COM array, I could send a distress message to alert someone at the Ministry or NCSF battalion. However, if what they said was true about additional patrols coming, the NCSF was already aware our security detail had been attacked.

But to enter the facility I would have to take on at least one man with a gun, and possibly three, if the technicians were armed. Based on my fear at that moment I decided to do nothing. Maybe I could link up with the NCSF once they arrived.

I thought my best option was to try to make my way across the underground basement to the stairway and then outside. But I could still picture the two bodies of our armed escort lying on the ground a dozen or so meters away. I didn't want to end up like them. Then there was the rest of our military escort who were reportedly already dead outside.

I decided my best chance was to attempt to get the drop on the three now inside the bunker. Since I had a weapon, I might be able to take out the one who was armed. Then I could lock myself inside the facility until the NCSF rescued me. But if they could open the bunker once, they could likely open it again. I reasoned these guys wouldn't stick around long. They wouldn't risk facing an NCSF counterattack.

I wondered what these people were doing in the bunker. Why would a group of ragtag Dead Zone bandits access a remote CCD surveillance facility? As I contemplated this, I heard a noise from inside the security office. I saw the armed man exit the bunker. His weapon hung from his shoulder on a strap. He was carrying a small lamp that he attached to the wall next to the entrance behind him.

He lit a cigarette. I could smell the smoke as it wafted out of the busted opening to the old security office. I waited as he continued to linger around the door. The light wasn't bright enough to illuminate my position, about twenty meters away. My position was just in front of him and slightly to his left.

My mind was racing. I knew I could take him out from where I was. I checked my weapon. It was still on ballistic mode, which would have more range than an energy discharge. The guy had made himself a sitting duck by lighting up his position from behind. I slipped on my display goggles, which were linked to the weapon's sight. Its automatic targeting mechanism revealed the man was right in the crosshairs. I aimed, then locked the targeting on his head. Now I could fire the weapon in his general direction and the guided round would find its target.

Then I changed my mind. I didn't want to kill someone in cold blood, even though I knew he would kill me if he could. I stepped forward with my weapon drawn and told the man to put his hands up. He looked at me with a curious gaze. Instead of raising his hands to surrender, he started to reach for the weapon dangling from his shoulder strap. I held my breath as I squeezed the trigger. The weapon made a barely audible muffled sound. The auto targeting was still aimed at his head. It exploded against the wall, and his body dropped to the ground.

I cringed at the grotesque stain of blood and brains on the wall. *You idiot!* I gagged and spat. I rushed into the security office, then glanced through the door into the bunker.

A short hallway headed three meters into the facility. At the end of the hall a stairwell descended to the control room. I quietly entered and began working my way down the hallway to the stairway. I winced as the floor panels creaked. I reasoned I could take the two other men by surprise, but hoped the techs would surrender quietly, unlike their guard.

Our briefing had indicated the control room was small; up to four or five people could work inside comfortably. At the bottom of the stairs there should be a central, open area containing some lockers, with two doors on either side and a third door on the far side. One door would lead to a small commissary and living space. The opposite door would lead into the ballistic proof glass enclosed control room. A third door would lead to a small bathroom and shower.

I needed to catch the two technicians by surprise, but any effort would be useless if they were locked inside the control room. I could see light coming from the central common area at the bottom of the stairs. I slowly made my way down, pausing at the first landing. At the bottom, there was another short, two-meter hall leading to the common area. I moved forward, glancing around the corner to my right.

I saw only one technician in the control room; it turned out to be a woman. Then I heard what sounded like an air compression flush. I snuck back up the stairs a few steps to remain hidden from the person exiting the bathroom. I heard the bathroom door open, then close automatically. After a few seconds, I heard the control room door open.

Quietly, I stepped back down. Looking around the corner I saw the glass door slide back into place. The door was supposed to slide open when a security key was scanned. The scanner was apparently disabled; the two could get in and out by pressing a key on a pad just below the card scanner. The facility was over fifty years old, so the key card functionality had probably been disabled long ago. The technicians didn't appear to be armed.

Through the glass I saw an array of screens on the far wall of the room. The technicians were working at the central terminal; the woman was keying in commands while the man looked over her shoulder. I couldn't hear their conversation through the soundproof glass.

Since their backs were toward me, I knew I could enter the room before they could react and hold them at gunpoint. I hoped I wouldn't have to shoot them, since they weren't military personnel. I wanted them to tell me how they broke into this facility. I moved slowly across the common area, then pressed the access key below the card reader. The door to the control room slid open quietly. I entered, pointing my weapon toward the technicians. They turned to look at me, reacting to the change in the light entering the room.

"Whoa, don't shoot," the man said nervously, raising his arms. The woman, who was at the terminal, stood up. She crossed her arms, calmly; she didn't look frightened.

"Keep your hands where I can see them. Don't move!" I barked. "Do you know how to automatically close the door to this bunker from here?"

I had a moment to study them. The woman was young and pretty, maybe in her late twenties. She had beautiful gray eyes, with dark hair tucked beneath a cap. The man was even younger, thin faced, with light brown hair and a scruffy beard.

"Who are you and what are you doing here?" I demanded. "How did you gain access to this facility?"

The woman stepped forward. She said coolly, "It hardly matters who we are. You will be dead in five minutes if you don't leave. Consider that free advice."

I glared at her. "Is that right? Answer my questions. But first, close the bunker door and lock down this facility." I hoped she knew how, because I had no idea how to do it.

The woman activated a control switch on the console in front of her. "The door is closed and locked," she said. "*They* call themselves the Gathering Storm, or GS. I suppose you took out their man upstairs? We're not with them. We are only here to remove some of our equipment; then we'll be on our way. Since you didn't materialize through a wall, you must have gained access the same way we did—from the door up those stairs."

"Don't be a smartass! Who are you and what are you doing here? How did you break into this bunker?"

"Are you planning to retake this facility on your own?" The woman said sarcastically. "The GS are going to destroy this facility. They're returning to the subfloor above us in a few minutes to trigger the detonation timer and they don't have to be inside the bunker to do it." She pointed to a series of small packages wired together across the length of the control room's ceiling. Obviously, someone had been inside earlier to rig this up.

As I tightened the grip on my weapon she realized I wasn't satisfied. She said, "Look, we agreed to take the facility offline and give the GS access to this bunker in exchange for a few favors. That's how it works out here. Oh, and they wanted your vehicles, your weapons, and all your equipment, including your PCDs, even the implanted ones. They want everything."

"You haven't answered my questions," I said.

"What difference does it make if I tell you anything?" the woman replied. "Do you think it's going to give you any insight into who we are and what we do? We've been breaking into your worthless technology for years. We can easily penetrate the pitiful security of these surveillance stations. Believe me, it's far easier to get into them than to get to them."

"If you're not GS, then I want your names and the name of your organization."

The woman chuckled, "We don't have any ID and we aren't in your LEOH system. For what it's worth, you can call me Kalina. This is my colleague Boris. Our organization is called the ATO."

I saw Boris step back, as if he were waiting for something to happen.

"If you happened to have dispatched our friend upstairs, I will give you fair warning," she said. "Leave, now! You will have at least a head start. If you wait they *will* catch you and you'll die, just like your friends, who are as good as dead. There's only one of you. There are hundreds of GS surrounding this area. They plan to draw in and ambush as many NCSF as they can."

Boris said, "Kalina, don't risk it." She turned on him with an aggravated look, then turned back and moved toward me.

"Don't take another step," I warned.

I shot a glance toward the console where Kalina had been working and was shocked to see an MDC device hooked up to an adaptor plugged into the console. It looked identical to the one Zack had given me.

I decided to change tactics. "I know what that device is," I said, pointing to the MDC. "It's a molecular data compressor and it's stolen technology. You must be using a ghosted access code to upload formulations or you're downloading matrix data through this surveillance station. I know the old man who gave it to you or to someone in your organization. I'm married to his great-granddaughter. I used one exactly like it to steal hundreds of thousands of halobytes of classified data from LEOH. It's hidden in a safe room in my apartment in New City." I holstered my weapon and backed away from Kalina. "I'll give it to your organization if you're interested. Just help me get out of here."

Boris said, "Do it, now!"

Kalina held up her hand to silence him.

"Don't trust him. He's bullshitting you," Boris spat out. "He doesn't know anything. He's just trying to get information."

"How much time do we really have?" I said softly. "Look, I'll take your advice and leave, regardless, just help me."

Kalina glanced at the time display. "We have about five minutes."

Boris was furious. "You can't trust these assholes ... do it!"

Kalina said peremptorily, "Boris, gather water and provisions from the commissary stores. Two days rations; no, make it three. Now!"

Boris hissed, "This is a mistake."

"Where did you get that device? I said. "That's decades-old prototype technology. Seriously, I know the man who stole it from a Ministry R&D project over two decades ago."

"I can't tell you anything about it," Kalina said. "You are *seriously* running out of time."

"If you are working against New City, maybe we can help each other. I'm not lying to you. I'm the prime suspect in the largest classified data theft in New City history. I work behind the SADEX firewall in the CCD. That's why I went to work for them—to infiltrate LEOH and steal their classified data."

Kalina shook her head. "You have no idea what you are asking or getting yourself into. Besides, we don't need help from anyone, especially from a CCD operative. If you really are a spy working against the Ministry, you're terrible at it. A real spy wouldn't admit to that."

"I'm not a spy," I said. "I just stole a huge amount of highly classified NCIC data, actually, most of it. If what's in it is true the whole world is going to run out of time. The old man told me that MDC device you have is going to be useless as soon as the new version of LEOH becomes fully operational."

Kalina walked over to a small touch screen console. She pressed a couple of virtual buttons on the display, then turned back to me. "Just in case," she muttered. A once-darkened screen lit up. It displayed a wide-angle view of the dimly lit abandoned hotel security office upstairs. "I just locked the station door; no one can get in now, at least none of those GS pinheads. There is another way out of this bunker. If you can make it the sensor array on the 17th floor, from there you can get back down, once the coast is clear. It's a long climb. I'm not sure exactly where the access door to the array is located. But it has to be somewhere inside this facility."

"How do I know I can trust you? You could just turn me over to the GS."

"You really are a terrible spy," Kalina said. "You shouldn't trust anyone. Once you reach the top, don't activate your locater beacon, because the GS will find you. Get as high as possible as soon as you can. When that K-EMP goes off, it will disable everything within a fifty-meter radius. Wait until you're into the SL2 zone before you activate your beacon. Don't head toward your checkpoint. They'll expect you to go that way. Head north by northeast, then circle back to the checkpoint or keep going toward SG2. It's a couple of hundred kilometers to the east of SG3."

Boris reentered the room with a small sack of rations and some water. "This is all I could get, enough for two days. It's should last you until you reach your checkpoint."

I took the sack from Boris, thanked him, and stuffed it all in my pack.

"Tell me your real name," Kalina said.

"It's Mark, Mark Verigratu. But my real last name would have been Waters had my father not been adopted." I knew this organization was connected somehow to Zack and his name would mean something to them. I was also certain they were the enemy of my enemy. "I am related to the man who helped me steal that classified data and who gave your organization the MDC device. He wants to get the data out to the public, and I'm certain he would want you to have a copy of it. You know the man I am talking about, don't you? How can we contact you?"

Kalina was slow to react. "Look, Mark Verigratu, or Waters, or whatever your name is, you can't contact us. You talk too much. Out here it's dangerous to tell your secrets to anyone, especially that one."

Then she jumped back, startled. "They're here! Boris, get on the console to finish up!" We stared at the display screen. It showed the visual of the security office upstairs. "It's Gravitz. There are five or six of them. They've discovered their dead man upstairs. The door is sealed, but if I don't open it in a minute, they'll assume the worst. You need find the access to the sensor array!"

I jumped on the console next to Boris and located a schematic of the facility. "How do I get into this room?" I pointed to a utility closet on the display that appeared to be adjacent to the control room. I looked around but couldn't see any other door in the control room, apart from the glass door which lead to the common area. "It should be behind that bank of server racks over there."

Although most of the computer servers looked old and inactive they were still powered up. Several newer servers were also running. "Help me move these racks out of the way," I demanded. I ran over and squatted down to look behind the racks. I saw a two-meter square metal panel with a latch. "I think the access to the sensor array is behind that panel. If nothing else, I can hide in there."

Kalina shook her head. "Not likely; as soon as we're done here the GS really will destroy this facility. You'll be killed if you stay there. Start climbing. You can worry about how to get down later. I've got to open the outer door or they'll blow us all up while we are still in here. Honestly, these people don't care what happens to us. I told you they can detonate this K-EMP from outside the bunker."

We started shifting the racks, which were lighter than they looked and slid easily. The panel led to a small utility room that was more of a maintenance space for conduits and cables. It apparently had not been accessed in years. Once inside, I turned on my lamp as Kalina and Boris shut the panel behind me.

A thin metal ladder ran up the back of the utility closet, leading to a small circular hatch on the ceiling of the room. I could hear them sliding the server cabinets back in place. I climbed up to open the circular hatch which opened downward. A pile of dust and debris landed in my face. I spat as I shone my light up the tube. Hopefully this would lead to a way out.

I had no idea if I could find any way down from the upper floors of this bombed out pre-war structure. My recollection from when we approached was that the upper part of this structure appeared to be an unstable mangled mesh of steel and concrete. Without other options, I started to climb up the ladder through the dark, narrow tube.

* * * *

Kalina and Boris stared wide-eyed at each other briefly once they slid the racks back in place. Kalina shifted the dust on the floor around with her feet to disguise any marks. She said, "Release the door to let them in. Let me do the talking. Don't say a word about the man who was here. Understand?"

Boris nodded. "Why didn't you kill him when you had the chance? Do you really believe he was telling the truth?"

"Boris, he knew we have an MDC. He claims to know the man who stole the technology and gave it to the ATO. Do you know what this means? The old man is active again. I realized that even before he said he was a Waters. Besides, you destroyed any element of surprise."

Boris shrugged. "I was afraid you were going to try to kill him before he was vulnerable."

Kalina grinned. "I would have waited for the right moment. He certainly gave me the opportunity once he holstered his weapon. I can handle myself. I don't need you to tell me how and when to do my job."

Boris activated the door mechanism, walked over to open the glass door from the common area, and sat down at the console to work, as if nothing had happened. Kalina spoke in a barely audible voice, "Keep your mouth shut!"

Boris growled, "I can't believe you told him our first names and didn't kill him. I also can't believe you didn't kill him because he knew we have an MDC. That was seriously stupid."

Kalina picked up the device. "How would he know this is an MDC? Also, when I'm in New City, which is practically never, I'm someone completely different. Why would I give a damn if he knows my first name out here? I don't need an alias. They would have to catch me. If they catch me out here, my real name is about as useless to them as how many moles are on my butt."

Boris quipped, "You have moles on your butt?"

Kalina smacked him. "Shut up! I'm just pointing out that it's an irrelevant data point."

"I don't want some CCD asshole to know my name," Boris retorted. "You could have taken him out. Now we have to lie."

"No!" Kalina insisted. "I'm going to lie. You are going to keep your pie hole shut!"

Commander Gravitz of the GS militia and two soldiers rushed down the stairs to the control room. "What the hell happened upstairs? Why is one of my men dead? Somebody practically blew his head off. Why didn't you answer when I hit the com?"

Kalina glanced at him contemptuously. Then she turned back and continued to work. "Are you talking about the guy who came down here with us?"

"Who the hell do you think I'm talking about?"

"How are we supposed to know what happened to your man?" Kalina said calmly. "He has a nicotine habit. It must have killed him; probably made his brain explode or something. I've heard cigarettes can do that, especially when you're really stupid."

Gravitz glared at her.

"Gravitz, we don't have weapons. We didn't shoot him, or know he was shot. He said he was just going up there to smoke. We weren't watching him. He was supposed to be watching us. Maybe he got sick of life and killed himself."

"Tell me what happened," Gravitz demanded.

"What do you think could possibility have happened, Captain Feckless? Could it be, one or more soldiers with the NCSF managed to evade Quillion? Could it be, they are probably still out there? I guess it's a good thing we reactivated the door lock, once he stepped out. I told Mr. 'I need a smoke,' we would come back up when we were done. We'll be finished here in five more minutes. The more you distract us the longer this is going to take."

Gravitz was pissed. "Is there a video feed showing the entrance to the bunker?"

"Maybe, but what's the point? It's completely dark up there," Kalina replied. "You couldn't make out anything if there was."

"I don't care, I want to see a playback of the last fifteen minutes," Gravitz insisted.

"I need time to finish up what we came here to do," Kalina said. "I'm not going to stop what I'm doing to locate a security cam replay which won't show you anything valuable. Here's a hint: It's probably someone armed and dressed in an NCSF or CCD uniform, or both. If I fail to obtain my exchange relay data, our deal with the GS is off. You're own your own getting inside 4XT5. My guess is, the shooter is long gone. What good will it do to see a shot in the dark, anyway?"

"He had a light mounted. We might at least know how many there are," Gravitz grumbled.

"Really? Do a body count," Kalina snapped. "You guys were watching when their team arrived. We also gave you the intel on how many there were, including the exact number of regular NCSF verses Ministry operatives. Do a little math and leave us alone so we can complete our work. Oh, and we would greatly appreciate a sufficient escort back above ground, so don't leave us only one man this time ... and no smokers!"

Gravitz turned to one of his lieutenants. "Send two men back outside immediately to find Quillion. Inform him there's at least one man from the CCD bunker group at large. And tell him the guard who escorted the ATO personnel was killed. Also, have them do a body count. Kalina and Boris are five minutes behind you. Now, go!" Gravitz turned to walk back upstairs. "Five minutes!"

* * * *

"Do you think this guy has a snowball's chance of getting out of the DZ alive, considering what's coming?" Boris said. "And if he's a Waters, do you think he really married his own cousin?"

Kalina shrugged. "That would be creepy. If he *is* a Waters, maybe I should have done more. If he stays put for a while, and he's smart, he might have a decent chance. When we get back to the SRHQ I'll send someone to New City to look in on our old friend. I need to check out this guy's story, and I'd like to know if he makes it back alive. Even if he does, he may not live long, if he really did carry out the largest classified data theft in New City history. There should be several high-level security directives on Mr. Mark Verigratu if he was telling the truth."

"Are you planning to send Nick?" Boris asked. "You know he just went back inside the walls and you know why." Boris clicked off his screen. "I'm done here. The relay change algorithm transmission is complete. Let's leave." The two started to gather up their equipment.

"I saw the briefing, and yes, I know Nick's inside the city," Kalina said, frowning. "I also know exactly who he's there to see. That crazy little nympho knows it's against the rules to be cavorting with a mercenary like Nick. I swear, I'd have her pulled if she wasn't so damn good at what she does. It's hard to believe she has a perfect operational record, with multiple commendations. For three years she's busted more counter-surveillance traps than anyone. Even so, her reports are ridiculous. They make her sound like a blithering idiot. Seriously, there should be a rule against food analogies or conversations with your pet cat in official briefings. Then there's the other crazy stuff she does. ..."

Boris laughed. "You're one to talk. I mean, the part about cavorting with a mercenary."

"I don't operate a multi-million CU safehouse in East Park and Danette does," Kalina complained. "It's not the first time that bimbo has broken the rules. She probably uses her house to throw lavish pool parties. Her food budget is three times higher than any other safehouse operator. I can't keep shuffling ATO personnel around to keep them away from her. Now she's lured Nick, of all people, into her seductive web."

Boris said, "I hear she's gorgeous, sweet, and very smart." I would ..."

Kalina glared at Boris. "Don't remind me that 'sweet' girl stole my boyfriend! She may be smart but she's also a promiscuous, inebriated mooncalf. She requests enough beer in her house budget to keep an entire fraternity of hardcore party animals boozed up. That drives Jared crazy."

"Terminate her then, if she's such a problem," Boris said. "But Greg will quit if you do. You know he adores her and she has the highest intelligence and reflex combat scores ever for an ATO operative. Almost everyone who works with her loves her."

"Yeah, I *know* they do, that relationship wrecking weirdo. Here's another thing: She's never once been to the SRHQ. Apart from a few names, she doesn't personally know anyone. It's a clandestine top-secret base, for crying out loud! How is she constantly having ridiculous stuff smuggled out there with those crazy notes like we're her best friends. I'll uncover her ring of useless contraband smugglers if it's the last thing I do. It's been going on for almost three years."

"I enjoyed that toffee and the gummy worms," Boris said. "You can't get those in the DZ. Oh man, and the cheese is usually to die for."

"We could actually benefit from her secret pipeline of worthless crap for something useful. You know, like PCDs, weapons, ammo, other devices; stuff a covert organization can use. Instead, we get breakroom goodies. It must cost her a fortune to smuggle one package worth 50 CUs. Her entire snack smuggling connection network must be boinking her. We know everyone who comes in and out of that base and no one will admit to being involved with it."

Boris laughed as he and Kalina left the 4UB6 bunker for the last time.

CHAPTER 16

THE FORMULATION OF A PLAN

Tabitha closed her display and considered the situation. At breakfast, her father had pleaded with her to be respectful toward the Archon, who had requested a private meeting with her this morning at the Citadel.

"So he wants to get me involved in an investigation?" Tabitha grumbled. "I'm not interested in doing operative work for him, of all people. He has an entire Ministry with specialized agents who do that every day. I assume this has to do with the ghosted access code issue they told me about the day *after* the migration to L2 began."

"Well, as I said, he needs someone personally loyal to him to take charge of this matter," Carl said. "He believes his own Ministry may be compromised. This classified data theft is a serious matter and could also be an embarrassment to NED Tech."

Tabitha rolled her eyes. "If he's looking for someone personally loyal, that rules me out. I can't stand that alien. Who knows how many backdoors there are in that ancient bastardized Frankenstein monstrosity? LEOH security is a mess. You ought to be embarrassed. We should roll back the cutover and reverse the implementation until we rebuild the security access and credentials platform—from scratch, as I recommended from the start!"

Carl looked at her with concern. "You have a good point, but please be respectful, and don't antagonize him. This special assignment involves more than formulation work. The honor and future of our family is at stake. NED Tech built this system and it's our responsibility."

Tabitha huffed, "Yes, and there will be more at stake when a far more devastating breach occurs. Whom do you think he will blame then—his own stupid decisions?"

Carl pleaded, "Tabitha, my darling, you cannot sit before the Archon and blame him for anything. He wants you not just for your technical skills but for your clarion insight. He also has someone he'd like you to befriend. He wants to discover who else is involved in the breach and if there's an organization behind it."

Tabitha knew her father was referring to Mark Verigratu. Only the day before she had been wondering how to reach out to Mark to help him. Now it seemed the Archon himself was about to make it possible, albeit for the purpose of entrapping or spying on Mark.

Tabitha did not believe in coincidences or fate. Yet she couldn't argue with the possibility of blind chance. "You don't need to plead. I'll meet with him and be polite. Unlike you, I don't equate politeness with being a groveling, shoe licking, ring kissing, sycophant. Besides, I need a break from the mind-numbing tedium of this project. The project team doesn't need me to babysit them, and I get more work done than most of them do in a day before my first cup of coffee."

Carl sighed. "Well, most people don't start their day at 4:00 a.m. after only three hours of sleep. Just be nice to him. No, be respectful. He's showered our family with everything we have."

Tabitha glared at her father. "I guess it's a good thing his rain doesn't fall all at once; otherwise you'd drown in all that money you love so much. You sell your own daughter for it; that's how much you love it."

"Everything I have is yours, Tabitha, and you know it," Carl said. "The Archon demanded I make you the sole heir to our family fortune and to our title. You will be the next Ēlantiel."

Tabitha rolled her eyes, "They're not human, Dad! Who cares about Devan's stupid titles?"

* * * *

Tabitha was led into the Archon's grand office in the Southern Jurisdiction by one of his numerous attendants. Nathan Prideil was standing in front of the Archon's desk. The Archon rose to greet her. She was politely asked if she wanted anything to drink, then seated in a comfortable chair in front of the Archon's desk. Prideil sat down in the chair beside her.

The Archon said, "As you know, ēlan, I am extremely pleased with your work. I look forward to the celebration this weekend in honor of your successful completion of Phase 1 of the L2 project. Yet as much as I hate to blemish the upcoming celebration with a serious matter, I am afraid I must. I assume your father provided you with some background on it?"

Tabitha nodded compliantly. "He said it involves an investigation with which you would like me to assist. I assume this has to do with the data breach."

The Archon stared at her lustfully, which made Tabitha uncomfortable. "There are some within the NCIC hierarchy who might use this as an opportunity to impugn my objectives and other matters of importance to me. This data theft is a potential public relations nightmare."

Tabitha nodded. "Devan, I'm not concerned with your objectives being impugned or your public relations issues. I spent my only day off looking into this matter. I've read all the security directives. Would you like to know what I've already discovered?"

The Archon seemed surprised. "Yes, I would."

Tabitha sighed with mock frustration. "I suppose my briefing notes aren't part of your regular reading regimen. Sunday, I sent you an outline of my opinions about whether breaches could be prevented in the future. The short answer is no, unless we unwind the implementation and rebuild the security platform. Since my report, I have investigated this matter further. You might be interested in what else I've uncovered about your prime suspect, Mr. Marcus Vincent Verigratu."

Tabitha paused briefly as the Archon looked at her in astonishment. She continued, "I already know this man is the suspected thief.

Precisely how he did it, and who is the mastermind behind this, is a different question. Given the negative results of his interrogations, it's possible he is unaware that he was being used to carry out the theft. In any case, it's highly unlikely he acted alone. I conclude you want me to get to know this man. Perhaps you want me to make myself available to him to infiltrate his organization?"

The Archon said, "You are quite perceptive. What makes you certain he did this?"

Tabitha tilted her head. "Blackholes exist by virtue of their signature and the evidence of their activity. I was able to identify him despite the lack of direct evidence. The indexes of his file captures and transfers are still in the LEOH backup. You just can't see them. My analysis confirmed what your Ministry suspected for different reasons. Yet I understand his interrogations and the lack of substantial evidence proves he is otherwise innocent, which is curious."

Both the Archon and Prideil looked confused. Tabitha continued, "It was irresponsible to continue with the full migration on Friday, given the breach that occurred Thursday. Even LEOH recommended the implementation be postponed. Yet no one bothered to accept its advice, just as you didn't accept mine. I would have stopped it had I been made aware of this incident. Given the nature of these codes, I can't give you any assurance they weren't replicated into L2 during the migration. It is likely they were. I will discover who is behind this, but again, Mark Verigratu may be unaware that he was involved. He may have just been carrying the virus, so to speak."

"How would he not be aware given his proximity to the event?" the Archon said.

Tabitha raised her eyebrows. "Perhaps they used a digital worm or a hidden device. Perhaps he was forced to steal the data via a hypnotic suggestion. How else could he have denied it twice under chemical interrogation?"

The mention of hypnotic suggestion made the Archon uncomfortable, since he had done the same to Tabitha.

Nathan Prideil said, "Ēlan Norean, I realize that as head of development for L2 you have extraordinary access. This does not give you permission to formulate new security matrix information yourself without authorization, even on the L1 backup. It's disturbing that you believe this was somehow within your scope of responsibility or prerogative."

Tabitha glared at Prideil. She said, "Any matter which has direct implications on the integrity and security of this system, *is* within the scope of my prerogative to discover. Since no one in the High Echelon or Ministry felt it was necessary beforehand to keep me informed of such a critical risk profile, I will investigate this in whatever manner I deem appropriate! This includes formulating security matrix data. I don't work for you. I work for Devan. I have his authority. I don't need your permission to do anything, Mr. Magoo. Why are you even here? You are useless."

Tabitha turned back to the Archon. "In my view, this was a substantial oversight on the part of Ministry higher ups, who thought this security matter was not critical enough to consider in the L2 development."

"I understand your concerns, but we can't roll back the implementation," the Archon said.

"Didn't you say there were over fifty thousand suspicious access code intrusions which were quarantined without a directive?" Tabitha reminded them. "Not once was this disclosed in the L2 security briefings. Pardon me for having a rational sense of deduction. Wouldn't someone high up in the Ministry, who just happened to want this festering security flaw to persist, intentionally fail to mention it? Do either of you consider such a deliberate oversight as cause for suspicion? Even if you don't, I do. I guarantee you that L2 will generate a security directive on that question for investigation."

Prideil stared at Tabitha.

"Stop looking at me like a squeezed cat!" she said.

The Archon tried to quell the conflict between Prideil and Tabitha. "You make a good point, ēlan. Nathan has only recently been appointed to his executive role in my cabinet. I hereby direct him to provide you with whatever you need to assist you *without* limitation. I also authorize you to formulate and utilize whatever security matrix data you deem necessary. This includes investigating the quarantined intrusions. You have my full support, as well as the full support of Mr. Prideil, along with his resources. I stress the importance of quickly containing this data breach.

"And I would like to discuss the matter of befriending our suspect to gain his confidence. He will be attending this weekend's celebrations. Use your best judgment on how to convince him you are a potential ally or a possible love interest. This could lead to the apprehension and identification of key members of a subversive organization who have evaded capture for years."

"This is a terrible plan," Tabitha said. "Coming on to this Mark guy or trying to get to know him at the event will make him suspicious. If he is knowingly involved in a conspiracy, he won't trust me. I'm the L2 developer and a Norean, with a ridiculous title of ēlan. You do realize that the average person despises people like me."

"Please, do not disparage your title. It's unbecoming of a noble," the Archon said.

"I'm glad to know everything else I said had merit," Tabitha replied. "As long as I don't disparage my title, this terrible plan will be a stunning success. I'll likely infiltrate this conspiracy over breakfast while wearing the tiara that I'm obligated to wear in public. That way, everyone can be certain I'm a pompous bitch with a useless title. Normal people don't wear diadems."

"There is no need for sarcasm," the Archon said. "What are your further insights?"

"You *are* a pompous bitch. No diadem necessary," Prideil said under his breath.

"Don't screw with me you frog-faced troll," Tabitha hissed. "Look, whoever put Mark up to this must have been aware the implementation would begin the following day. It's clear they were in a rush to get as much classified data out of the system as quickly as possible, regardless of the risk of triggering a bandwidth alert. This was done in under three hours. The man was expendable. No one with any real experience at espionage would have done what he did. He exposed himself. Maybe someone high up in the Ministry did this to stop the implementation."

The Archon was astonished at what Tabitha was intimating. "Are you implying the CCD director is involved in this?"

"That remains to be seen. I am simply saying everything points to someone who would not have knowingly done this, if he was smart. You don't get a position in the CCD unless you are intelligent. Maybe the interrogations and the search of his apartment yielded nothing because he had an antidote to the truth serum. Also, how did he get the device out of the NCGD?"

"Ēlan, let's just stick to the plan of trying to see what this man knows," Devan insisted.

"OK, how deep do you want to go with this? How much latitude do I have? This is not an investigation. It is a covert infiltration. If Mark is innocent, it will be a waste of time if I don't involve myself with his associates who put him up to this. They are the ones I need to infiltrate. Even if he is involved, he's not the one who created the ghosted access codes, nor the one who engineered the technology he used. He wouldn't have the opportunity, knowledge, or experience to do this himself. At best, he is an ignorant tool. If he's being framed, this goes much higher up in the Ministry."

"So, what are you proposing?"

"I'm going to need free reign to do this without any interference from the Ministry. If this Zachariah Waters mentioned in the LEOH cross directive is the real culprit, he is probably aware Mark is compromised, and needs to believe Mark got away with it. The Ministry must distance themselves. It must appear that Mark's been cleared. I'm not even a spy and I have sense enough to know this. Even if I seduce Mark for his secrets, it won't get you past the people who put him up to it. Keep in mind, Zachariah Waters would also be a convenient fall guy for an inside conspiracy, given his history of working for Dalen Pythorael.

It's all a little too convenient. This may be a pretense for something more sinister."

The Archon was impressed with Tabitha's insight. "All your activities will of course have to be monitored. They will be quarantined. Only Mr. Prideil and I will be privy to the security directives formulated by LEOH on this. I will also make certain that this investigation is independent of the Ministry. However, I must insist you not give yourself to this man sexually, even if you are inclined to do so. You are too valuable to me."

Tabitha brushed off the insincere compliment. She stood up and stared into his steely eyes. "*You* insist I don't give myself to him? Who do you think you are? You don't own me or have the right to insist either way. If I hump him on your desk, it will be on my terms and in accordance with whatever reasons I dictate. Do you think just because my daddy allowed you to have your little ritual with me when I was a child, I belong to you? Yes, I remember that perverted freakshow you put me and those other children through."

"Every ēlan and ēlar goes through that rite. I am surprised you even remember it. It was harmless. I will not have you denigrate its arcane beauty," the Archon said.

"Arcane beauty? You will never drink my child's blood!" Tabitha retorted. "I don't need the arcane beauty of a perverse ritual or a title to be loyal. I certainly didn't need a naked child bloodletting ceremony in my memory for the rest of my life."

"I promise, no child of yours will go through that," the Archon said.

"*I* didn't need to! What I do with anyone is my business. Let's keep our relationship professional and entirely out of the question of my sex life ... or persistent lack thereof."

"My apologies, ēlan, I wasn't trying to ..." the Archon started to explain.

"Look, I must convince Mark or his associates that I'll become a willing participant in their scheme," Tabitha said. "They must be convinced I despise you and this government and am able to help them at the highest level. I must convince their organization I would be a powerful and indispensable ally, even if their plans rise to the overthrow of your government. This won't be accomplished by meeting the man one time over the weekend. And if I learn they had nothing to do with this, I will discover who did, including whether or not Mark is being framed for this."

"Élan, I am uncomfortable with you involving yourself in something which could endanger your life," the Archon said.

"Augh, how sweet," Tabitha said. "Your concern for me is so reassuring."

"I only need you to discover who is behind this data theft so we can recover it and, more importantly, prevent it from being disseminated," Devan insisted. "Even if you should uncover a conspiracy within the Ministry, it doesn't change the fact that an organization is infiltrating our systems. The scope of your investigation should not go beyond discovering the source of these existential threats. I would hate for some rogue organization to attempt to kidnap you should you become too deeply involved with them."

Tabitha countered, "Do you want to know who took this data and who has also been hacking LEOH with ghosted access codes for two decades or not? Here are my conditions. Take them or leave them. I will access the full matrix dossiers on Mr. Verigratu and Zachariah Waters as well as every intelligence matrix concerning these ghosted access codes and anyone ever involved with them. This will include every utilization and security directive on every matrix going back to the source of how these access codes were created, including any suspected conspiracy around their origins. I will report to you alone. Who knows even if Mr. Magoo here may somehow be compromised or involved in a conspiracy or not? I don't trust him."

"Mr. Prideil has my confidence to oversee ..." the Archon started to say.

"He doesn't have mine! I require a special security clearance in case I'm accosted by Ministry agents. I will have free reign to move about anywhere within the system or the SJ. All my system activities, conversations, and actions will be off lined. I will be a walking dead space. There will be no possibility my activities can be traced or tracked by the Ministry, the CCD, the High Echelon, or the NCIC. If you don't trust me, we should end this now. You can terminate this investigation at any time. I will report only to you, not your useless Mad Cat sidekick. If we can agree on these terms, I will set to work. Otherwise, find someone else."

The Archon threw back his head and laughed. "Very impressive. Apart from your childish insults, you already sound like a well-trained field operative. If Dalen Pythorael retires, I should put you in charge of the Ministry." He glanced over at Prideil. "Only Mr. Prideil will have access to your reports. Send me the protocol authorization."

Tabitha responded, "Since when has anyone in the NCIC ever retired from anything? You don't grow old." Prideil snickered at Tabitha's comment.

She glowered at Prideil. "Devan, if I discover anything that implicates your snickering Muttley dog here or anyone in the Ministry, including from the executive security division, I must have the ability to conceal such a discovery from them. This data theft may be an orchestrated ruse. Perhaps these codes were generated as part of an effort to create an elaborate spybot infiltration."

At those words, the Archon became visibly uncomfortable. "What is a spybot infiltration? And what does it have to do with the access codes?"

Tabitha raised an eyebrow. "These codes were created for a specific purpose and it was not to facilitate anything above board. Whatever the bot is programmed to do or obtain could be accessed through any number of covert means. If there is a spybot infestation within the security framework, I will discover it—or L2 will."

The Archon was taken aback by this suggestion. "We will have to discuss this possibility more in depth later. For now, I need you to concentrate on this data theft and these external threats."

Tabitha said, "A spybot could be formulated to spy on *you* without leaving any trace. Once it has entered your private security perimeter, it could get to your implant through any device connected to the system. The SD AI for L1 and L2 are automated bots which navigate the system to carry out formulations. They have no registry, so they remain undetected. This is not something you should dismiss. Pythorael created them for some reason, and it wasn't so he could do his job. I bet he used them to create bots to scry out your secrets, Devan."

"Ēlan please, you talk so fast you give me a headache," the Archon complained.

Just then, the Archon's private secretary entered the office. She walked over to the Archon and whispered in his ear. After a few seconds, he dismissed her, then pulled up information on his display. He looked up at Tabitha and Prideil. "Reports have come in from the NCSF battalion station at Sanctuary Gate 3. The CCD operations team sent in to upgrade the 4UB6 node and their military escort were attacked by insurgents. Unfortunately, Mark Verigratu was among the CCD operatives on the mission."

Tabitha suddenly felt sick, but she tried to sound unconcerned. "Well, I guess that's the end of that. By the way, the security for those facilities is ridiculously antiquated. I bet they've all been infiltrated to blind you out there. Their com transmissions could easily be piggybacked. Whoever could do this is technically skilled enough to make the Ministry think it's a recurring equipment failure or a recalibration issue. I've studied the matrix data on those dinosaurs. It's fragmented and practically useless. It's impossible to tell if the connected equipment has been compromised or whether they're sending out corrupted telemetry signals. The physical access controls are also weak."

The Archon shook his head, "Ēlan, let's deal with the issue at hand, and please talk slower. It is possible Verigratu survived and will be returned safely. Should he return from the DZ by the weekend, you will make his acquaintance, then bring him before me. Compared with you, he is a mere peasant. I am confident that, even in your most casual attire, he will consider you the most graceful creature he has ever seen. You forget sometimes that being who you are naturally intimidates anyone, so don't overdo it. Even at work, you overdress. These people you will infiltrate are quite common. You will need to learn to fit in with them. I do, however, expect you to be dressed appropriately this weekend.

I am simply pointing out that you will need to look like a normal person when you are in their world and not like the Norean ēlan."

"I think I already made that point," Tabitha observed. "I'll have to give blending in with 'normal' people additional thought. I certainly will not be wearing an ēlan tiara! Although Julian will give me endless grief if I don't wear my hair up."

"Tabitha, I want a quick resolution to this," the Archon insisted. "I know with your clarion skills you will unravel this conspiracy quickly. I look forward to your first report." He then dismissed her and she was escorted out.

Tabitha had always dressed elegantly, even in childhood when she was away at the prestigious Clarion Academy, during the day, at least. Her private female valet, Julian, made certain Tabitha always looked perfect. To this day, Julian dressed her and did her hair and makeup. The prim woman had even bathed her, until Tabitha put a stop to it. She was present each time Tabitha emerged from her bath to dress her. Maybe it was time to cut this ridiculous pampering out her life.

Tabitha thought, *I need to shop for some regular clothes.* Perhaps the way she dressed was the problem she was having with the love of her life. He was always saying he wasn't good enough for her. She needed to look like any New City girl! She'd have to research how to pull that off. Tabitha didn't know how to fix her own hair, without at least some jewels in it, especially if it wasn't up.

CHAPTER 17

A NERVOUS CONSPIRACY

I am telling you, Dalen," said Prideil, "the Archon's decision to use the Norean ēlan is ominous for us. You wanted a talented formulation specialist to assist us on this investigation. Well, the Ministry no longer has an investigation. She made him stipulate that the Ministry, NCIC, and the HESF be prevented from utilizing any data or analytics from her activities. She is exceptionally intuitive. Even my own access is going to be tightly restricted and limited to her reports prepared for him. He is her handler, if you can even say she has a handler."

"Calm down," Pythorael said.

"She suspects the reason for the creation of the ghosted access codes was so you could create spybots," Prideil said. "She even told him they could be used to spy on him. She was briefed just once on the origin of these codes and is already implicating you. The Archon trusts her more than he trusts me, even though I am supposed to be surveilling you, Talen, and Rogan. She's called me a dingtard, Magoo, Muttley dog and a Mad Cat sidekick, whatever any of that means. She's an insufferable, insulting smartass, little brat."

Pythorael affected nonchalance. "It may be a moot point, anyway. Verigratu is probably dead. Our latest reconnaissance reports confirm at least nineteen killed in the vicinity of the 4UB6 station. The chances of him making it back alive on his own from an SL3 zone crawling with hostiles is extremely remote."

Prideil was insistent. "Maybe you didn't hear me. She is investigating the origin of the ghosted codes and can expand the scope to whatever she deems necessary. She's had her own activities shielded. She is now a walking dead space with an unrestricted T-Alpha clearance. She has to be stopped before she discovers everything."

Pythorael grimaced. "I can discover what she is up to. Even if she suspects I created them; she can't hide from *my* spybots. I would have her assassinated, but she is more than just a nuisance. If something bad were to befall her, Devan would stop at nothing to take revenge. Yet, I am confident I can secure her loyalty. Most likely, she doesn't know what he has planned for her."

Complaceal replied, scathingly, "What does it matter? Human loyalty is like holding sand in a wave. This girl could potentially blind us by destroying the mechanism we depend on to control this city. She is a perfect example of why we should never allow humans to have this much power."

Rogan, who had been silent, said, "You said you would deal with her, if necessary, when the time came. You said every one of the K15 girls who survived are insane. Yet how many of them, at age seventeen, could complete a project like L2 in under three years after it was floundering in R&D. You said not to worry about her. I think it is time for you worry about her and deal with her, permanently!"

Pythorael growled at Rogan, "You know very well she was different than the others. We are potentially dealing with an inherit ability to be connected with a higher sphere, for good or evil. He may even have actually created what he was seeking. I don't necessarily believe all of that mystical Erafel bullshit, but he certainly does. He even thinks the essence of that witch Jennipa is embodied in his sacred Erafel stone. If she returns, she will attempt to kill him as soon as she discovers how weak he is. But I know his plans don't include resurrecting that carmelineal bitch. He wants all power for himself again, including ours."

Rogan said, "Then for the sake of all of us, including the Archon, kill her!"

Pythorael turned on Rogan. "Why do you think I wanted her turned to dust before she was born? The last thing I want is for her to have a permanent connection to Elaniel so he can increase his power through her. Such a trait can potentially transcend the spheres. We also cannot simply have her eliminated. I don't know how such a child descended from a Norean, but she did. That's something else which confounds me. The ideal ATK15 sequence is a derivative of a pernicious Class 1 genetic dissident trait. Such a trait should never be in the Norean bloodline."

"Will you please shut up!" growled Complaceal. "This angst about how dangerous this girl is gives me a headache. Once the little bitch is dead, what can the Archon do about it, anyway?"

Pythorael responded, "He'll turn us to ashes if we touch her. Prideil can tell you what is hidden in the secret place of such a mind. He was stripped of carmelineal powers by one of them. Elaniel is after her hidden name. Am I going to have to bring a carmelineal out of confinement to convince you of this? They don't need a sex ritual to connect with a creature like her. If she is what the Archon believes she is, a carmelineal would be a powerful ally against her."

"Don't even think about releasing one of them," Rogan said, glancing up from his PCD display, "Did you see the last update on the recovery operation on the 4UB6 expedition? It looks bad."

"Anything on the fate of Mr. Verigratu?" Pythorael said.

"He hasn't been identified yet. Our forces are still securing the area."

"Let me know if you receive any word about him. It's time for me to pay a social visit to ēlan Tabitha. I've only met her once, but I want to confront her to see how clever she really is. I also think I can persuade her to see things my way. She seems to have the three of you quite convinced she is our doom. LEOH, open a personnel location inquiry construct."

LEOH responded, "Open, previous credentials accepted."

"Is Tabitha Norean currently at her residence or at the L2 server complex?"

"T Norean, sec code classified, inquiry denied. Parameters are accessible only by SL primary 1-3 and T-ALPHA-X or above security access designation. The presence of specific personnel operating within the LEOH server complex facility is classified ..."

Pythorael snapped, "Terminate! Inform me when Tabitha Norean arrives home in the evening."

LEOH responded, "Request denied. SL primary 1-3 T-Alpha personnel location services are only accessible by SL primary 1-3 T-Alpha clearance privileges."

Pyhorael hissed, "Terminate inquiry."

LEOH responded, "Construct terminated, security directive log compilation in progress ..."

"Stop talking, you irritating machine! Can someone tell me why the chief executive officer of the NCMIA cannot get a location ping on someone? I don't care if she is an ēlan or the L2 project lead. Imagine me having to use a spybot to discover the location of this girl or her personal PCD code."

Rogan held up his hand. "I just received an urgent update from the DZ09. The GS have launched a counterattack and our forces are now taking heavy casualties. They have made an urgent request for additional reinforcements. A full-scale battle is underway between several hundred NCSF units and an unknown number of heavily armed GS militia guerillas who have encircled their perimeter at 4UB6. This is a disaster. I am guessing the Battalion station will have to send in a fleet of heavy bomber drones to intervene."

CHAPTER 18

THE BATTLE OF 4UB6

Unfortunately, I hadn't climbed high enough to prevent my light and other electronics from being instantaneously fried by the EM surge from the explosion meant to destroy the facility. Moments after the explosion, I was engulfed in choking dust surging through the access tube. This told me the tube wasn't airtight, and there had to be ventilation somewhere above me. Who knows what I would find back in the facility if I had no means of escape at the end of this long climb?

I thought about waiting out the impending clash between the GS and NCSF but knew I couldn't do it at the top of this sensor array. I had to get out of this structure as soon as possible, given the likelihood it might soon be in the epicenter of a battle. This might result in the collapse of what remained of the crumbling ruins of this building. Then, of course, there were the flying combat drones that might even more easily detect me if I was exposed up there without a PCD ping.

The climb up the now pitch-black dust-filled tube became even slower, as I had to keep my mouth covered to keep from choking. Eventually, the air began to clear somewhat. When I reached the top, I was confronted by another hatch. It opened outward and thankfully, easily. What I'd climbed into was a small control room, which at first glance had no exit.

The hexagonal room was twice as large as the safe room at my apartment. There was a small window on each of four of the six sides, each one barely wider than my head. All the electronic displays and monitors were dark, either from disuse or the detonation. I searched for a door or hatch to the outside. Not finding either, my heart sank. The windows were so small that even if I could break the thick glass, I couldn't hope to squeeze through them to escape. And they were so grimy I could barely see out of them.

Peering out of one dirty window I glimpsed the components of the sensor array equipment mounted on the outside of the building. It was several meters away from the control room and connected by round metal conduit tubes that obviously led to a junction below the room. From the opposite window I couldn't see much at all, due to dried gunk on the outside of the glass. It must have faced the building's mostly darkened interior side. Only a tiny bit of light came through it. The other two windows were too dirty to see anything out of them.

I reasoned there had to be a door or hatch from this room to the sensor equipment mounted on the outside of the building. Even though maintenance on the array was now handled by specialized robotic drones, this was not always the case when this facility had permanent staff.

I collapsed on the floor against a wall. The room was devoid of furnishings. The small number of controls and monitors were old. They probably hadn't been functional for decades. This room was likely used to monitor visual adjustments to the connected equipment. *Why would there be no external access?* I pondered.

The metal walls were thick and well insulated. The thought of having to climb back down the tube in the pitch black almost made me puke. Besides, there would be no guarantee of an exit that way, or if anything would be left of the bunker. I drank a few sips of water as I tried to think. The room was dim, so I felt around carefully to see if I could find a way out.

Finally, I noticed a small access panel near the base of one of the control consoles. I pushed, then pulled, at the small, nearly invisible latch on it, and the panel door opened. I sighed with relief when I saw a manual pull lever clearly labeled "emergency maintenance hatch release."

I pulled it and heard a click underneath the floor a few centimeters away from the tube hatchway. Underneath the floor panel was another small hatch. I had apparently released the locking bolt.

I grasped the handle to open the hatch. To my dismay, it opened into the air. Where there had once been a ladder similar to the one I'd just climbed, there was now a mangled wreck of a ladder precariously hanging seven or eight meters below me. It had once led to a lower catwalk beneath the array. I could see several intersecting catwalks and additional ladders, which likely led to the platforms where various components of the array were mounted. The only way to get down to the catwalk would be by using a rope—and I didn't have one.

I thought about my new problem as I stared around the room. Using my heavy boots, I kicked one of the panels off the wall to get to the wiring behind the controls. I pulled out several meters of electrical conduit and was able to cut the wire easily with my utility knife. With considerable difficulty, I tied off one end through the locking bolt mechanism for the hatch. My only chance would be to lower myself down to the catwalk or swing out so I could get a foothold on the adjoining structure.

It's practically impossible to tie a secure knot with heavy electrical conduit. I wasn't confident it would hold if I tried to swing toward the building. I reasoned it would be far easier to drop to the rusty catwalk below and hope it didn't collapse. I slithered down my makeshift wire rope as far as I could. I was still a couple of meters above the catwalk and the twisted remains of the old ladder. Fortunately, as I let go, it held up, and I avoided impaling myself. Then I found a way into the adjoining structure.

I rested on a crumbling ledge looking down into what appeared to be a minefield of potentially dangerous ways through the labyrinth of ruins of the abandoned building. Before I started down, I surveyed the area to try to make out anything going on at the street level. I also wanted to visualize a route to navigate through the maze of derelict buildings and crumbled streets far below. Beyond a couple of blocks, this effort wasn't helpful. As I looked out over the ruins of the old city,

I could see off in the distance what appeared to be military vehicles to the west, east, and north. Based on their configuration, I could tell they weren't NCSF.

The climb down from seventeen floors was a perilous, bruising struggle. It took at least an hour to make my way through the dark, crumbled central stairwell. A few times, I had to scale debris or jump down to what I hoped would be a surface solid enough to hold me. Finally, I reached the building lobby, where I could see the shattered glass façade of the front of the building to my left, where our team had entered that morning. At the far end, to my right, was the door which led to the stairway leading down to the facility bunker.

My sense of time was sketchy, but I guessed it was at least 2:00 p.m. I inspected my weapon. It was still set on ballistic mode, which meant it would still fire even though the gun's electronics and targeting mechanism no longer functioned due to the EMP. I hurried through the lobby as quietly as I could, toward the broken-out windows next to the entrance. There were no visible signs of the GS anywhere. I cautiously started to make my way out of the old city as I zigzagged my way through the maze of streets.

* * * *

I had gotten several streets away from the bunker without encountering anyone. The GS intended to make it easy for the NCSF to reoccupy the area around the facility. I had no way to warn them about what was coming. Even so, I wasn't planning to wait around. I knew the NCSF was capable of unleashing devastating force. If they were certain the facility was destroyed, they might flatten a ten-block radius or more with bomber drones. New City had lethal military capabilities. This was an unpredictable conflict, and I was in the middle of it.

I heard an engine that sounded like a gasoline powered transport. It was much louder than the familiar buzzing sound of an electrical engine. I ducked into the closest building, the ruins of an old restaurant. The place was filled with wrecked tables. I hid back behind the crumbling, termite-infested ruins of the bar.

Within minutes, a heavy military vehicle moved slowly down the street, and stopped about twenty meters away. There were at least sixty men walking behind it. As it came to a halt, they clustered around the back of the vehicle in a half-semicircle. At least two men had dogs on leashes. Most likely the dogs were used to detect the faint hum of aerial UAVs.

I froze. The commander, or whoever was in charge, climbed out of the vehicle's hatch. I could hear him clearly as his voice echoed off the nearby canyon of surrounding structures. "OK, I want all three squads to fan out. Take positions on the first and second floors of these two buildings." He gestured to the buildings to his right and left.

These were clearly GS militia soldiers, as their insignia and roughly similar shabby uniforms indicated. "The NCSF counterattack should begin shortly," the commander said. "We expect they'll be outfitted with small arms, armored transports, and drone support. Keep your heads down until we're given the order to close in. I want every drone rocket sniper we have as high up as we can get them, in these two buildings. I want the canine units to reconnoiter every street between here and one block from the target zone. We are still looking for at least one NCSF, who may be communicating our movements to the enemy. I want him found and taken out if possible."

With my weapon in hand, I crept to the back of the building, through what must have been the kitchen. The way was dark and enclosed, but I could clearly see a crevice of light through a back door at the far end of a hall once I reached the back of the kitchen. Just before I reached the back door, I knocked over something large and metal, which made a loud crash. I was convinced, even at this distance, that the men gathered in the street had heard this; I was certain the dogs did.

I ran for the door, hoping it wasn't locked. I push downward on the levered handle. It practically crumbled, but held enough for me to pull the door open. I rushed through the door and emerged behind two armed men, three meters away.

The men jumped around to face me in the close quarters of the alley. Without thinking, I pointed my weapon. I shot one man in the chest before he could take aim. His body dropped to the ground. As the other man drew his weapon, I dove and rolled over. I shot three times in quick succession, hitting him once in the neck and again in the side; my third shot went wide. The man stood momentarily. Then, as blood started gushing from his neck, he fell beside his partner. I had done this dozens of times for fun in simulated combat, knowing full well it wasn't real. I was shocked at how I instinctively did what I did, without pissing my pants in fear.

My weapon was suppressed, so the noise of the shots was nothing compared to the noise I had made in the in the kitchen. I grabbed the first man's weapon and managed to find his ammunition and a few extra magazines. I heard another man shouting from far down the nearby street, in the opposite direction toward which I needed to flee. I didn't wait to see if anyone else or the dogs were following me. I ran as fast as I could down the alley, my newly acquired weapon in hand. A shot rang out behind me as I turned down another short side street, only a few meters away. After two more turns, I was getting turned around in the tangle of streets. I realized I was no longer certain which direction I was heading.

Moments later, there was an eruption of weapons fire and explosive munitions in the distance, back toward the station. I also heard the distinctive humming of low flying heavy combat drones. They sounded like a swarm of bees. As I rounded the next corner, onto a wider street, I stopped dead, then ducked into another doorway. There were hundreds more GS militia troops massing in the distance, a few streets away from from the facility. Apparently this was part of the counterattack force. I was in the middle of exactly what I had hoped to avoid, with no way out.

I decided my best bet was to find a place to hunker down and hide. Hopefully, the NCSF had sent enough fire power to be victorious. Yet from what I had witnessed, it looked like the GS militia might be closing in on them from all sides.

I backtracked, then made my way down another side street and ducked into a large ruined structure. Inside, I located what looked like an ancient vault. Its door was ripped off its hinges. It now lay on the crumbled tile and concrete floor. If nothing else, in the event of a missile or bomb assault, I could hope to be reasonably protected by the thick reinforced walls, even without the door. I sat in the dark against a wall and rummaged in my pack for some food. From inside, I could barely hear the sound of battle. It was beginning to intensify a few blocks to the south and the east. I decided I had no choice but to wait it out.

As I sat in the dark, I thought about the dream Ari had hastily told me about that morning. *How did she know these things?* She had said I'd be in a battle and would run away ... and that I would face a choice that would change our destiny. She also said if I chose to be a coward everything would be lost. I certainly felt like a coward hiding in the dark, thinking about the dream that I didn't understand. I kicked myself for cutting her off and not answering her coms when she called me back. *A child will lead me? What did she mean by that?*

CHAPTER 19

ESCAPE FROM SL3DZO9

I would learn much later that the GS had killed or captured nearly four hundred NCSF troops that afternoon, while suffering fewer than one hundred casualties. They also captured hundreds of high-tech weapons, tons of equipment, and numerous heavily armored transport vehicles. They had, of course, defeated our small escort squad, along with another, larger, battalion force sent to retake the facility and the reinforcements that arrived later. They had achieved their objectives, along with taking out a critical surveillance facility in the heart of the DZO9. It remained to be seen if the GS was prepared for the consequences of escalating a war with the NCSF.

As battles go, it wasn't much of one. It was a rout and didn't last very long. The GS executed their plan well. With a few minor skirmishes, they drew the NCSF forces sent to recover the facility into a confined area. They fainted a retreat, sacrificing a few men in the process. Once the bulk of the NCSF forces was concentrated within their perimeter they sprung their counterattack. It was over in under two hours. Prior to this battle the GS had been a largely unknown insurgent faction. Recent consolidations and alliances with other rebel outfits in the DZ had started to get them noticed. News of their victory today would most certainly do so.

I was nervous about being a warm body without a PCD ping or locater beacon in a combat region that might soon be swarming with drones. I didn't realize at the time that the NCSF drone forces were so depleted after this battle that there was little drone coverage in the DZ09. Due to the extensive GS surface-to-air missile weapons, virtually the entire UAV contingent from both the SG3 and 2 gates had been decimated during the brief engagement.

I waited until it was almost dark and silent, then cautiously walked north, out of the ruins of the old city. The GS militia apparently had no intention of staying in the area long. Streets that had been crawling with hundreds of GS militia soldiers were now deserted.

On the outskirts of the city I came across what looked like a small missile launching platform, with a few dead GS militia soldiers lying beside it. It appeared to have been hit by a drone attack. The platform had a sophisticated detection and tracking array. It must have been taken out by a low flying ballistic drone unit capable of firing a rapid burst of high caliber rounds. It was a grisly scene. I was able to pilfer some additional water rations, a combat knife, and a flashlight off one of the less mangled corpses.

I followed the overgrown remains of an old highway north. It was becoming an increasingly cold night, lit by a bright three-quarter moon, in a clear sky. The farther north I walked, the thicker the vegetation in the surrounding forest.

I knew the DZ was mostly uninhabited, and kept my ears attuned to the potential faint humming sound of an approaching drone. This was probably useless, as there were high-flying reconnaissance drones that would be impossible to hear. For now, I needed to find shelter for the night. I reasoned it was best to continue along this crumbled road until I came across an abandoned house or building where I could take shelter.

Almost everything in this sector had been obliterated during the Final War. What the war had not demolished, the ravages of time had. I walked for another hour or so in the dark. The terrain was getting hilly, with ever steepening grades.

I reached a point where the road ended abruptly. I approached the edge, where it seemed to fall off into oblivion. I realized I was at either a dry riverbed or a lake. The bridge that once spanned the gap was long gone. I hated the idea of climbing down this steep embankment in the dark. I made my way underneath the jutting remains of the bridge and stopped there for the night.

* * * *

Arising early the next morning I saw that the riverbed below appeared to have a creek's worth of water flowing through it. I could easily refill my water supplies. Then I decided I shouldn't trust anything flowing through this wasteland.

The sun confirmed I was heading north; I would eventually reach the walls of New City. But I had no way to tell how far east and north I needed to travel to reach Sanctuary Gate 2. I imagined the reception I'd receive once I arrived, knowing full well how bedraggled I looked and lacking a functioning PCD or locator beacon. I would be immediately targeted by a drone or automated defensive weapon, so I couldn't just walk right up to the gate.

The sanctuary gates, contrary to their name, were not inviting. They were essentially solid metal walls that opened onto tracks that led into an inner tunnel through ten-meter-thick reinforced concrete. The far side opened into a military compound before you were even inside the city. The imposing forty-meter-high walls were fitted with sentry towers every seventy-five meters; the sentries were armed with automated weapons.

There was no procedure to reenter the city. The New City gates were not like border crossings, where people routinely pass in or out. This fortified barrier allowed only armed patrols to enter or leave. My best option would probably be to flag down a patrol that was approaching the gate and hopefully avoid getting shot. While I knew there must be other ways in and out of the city, I was unaware of where they were or how to gain access to them.

The road continued up to a ridge on the other side of the dry riverbed. I hoped it would provide a wider view of the terrain beyond.

I gathered my weapons and supplies, then cautiously climbed down the treacherous embankment. I saw little from the top of the ridge; just another, even higher ridge beyond the one I was on. The only certainty was the terrain would become more mountainous as I headed north. I knew SG2 was in a mountainous region. I also knew these mountains extended northeast into New City and farther east to SG1.

I eventually emerged at the top of a ridge, overlooking a somewhat level stretch of land which extended for leagues in all directions. The once sparse vegetation of the lower SL3DZ09 had given way to a thick blanket of pine and hardwood trees whose leaves were starting to transform with the season. The land appeared lush and was surprisingly beautiful, with the tinges of early autumn.

The road was slowly disappearing into the more heavily wooded and ever steeper terrain. Gradually, it became more of a trail until it was barely a path. I had attempted to maintain the most northerly trajectory along the various trails, which split off occasionally. I was considering turning back, to try to find a more obvious trail, but decided to rest for a few minutes to eat. Then, I heard gunfire in the distance.

At least four or five shots were fired in quick succession; but they weren't the sounds of modern weapons. I grabbed my gear and ran toward the sounds. This was probably not the smartest thing to do. As I drew closer, I heard angry voices, a woman screaming, and children crying. I crept forward until I saw a clearing with a cluster of four concrete brick buildings with the largest one in the center of the compound.

Four rough-looking men were pointing guns at a group of nine people: two men, three women, a teenage boy, a girl of about ten or eleven, and two small children. The bodies of two men lay on the ground, one near one of the women, another just outside the door of the largest building. I checked the weapon I'd stolen and switched the safety off. It was far superior to the hunting rifles and pistols these men were carrying. They were obviously planning to rob these people—or worse.

I told myself to walk away. There were four bandits and nothing I could do to help. Once again, my courage deserted me. My desire for self-preservation convinced me I really was a coward.

The children continued to cry, and I heard soft pleas from one of the women. This was answered by raucous cursing and lewd comments from the roughnecks. I was about to slink away when it dawned on me these people would die if my sorry, cowardly ass didn't do something to help them. I looked again at the tearful face of the young girl and the terrified children.

Dammit! I cursed at myself. I couldn't leave these people to the mercy of these men.

One of the four, who was wearing a full-length trench coat, said, "Shut those damn kids up. Tie them up together! Tie the girl up separate. We heard from Calin McCrae over in Silver that some of you New City exiles had trekked down here and might have some gold money. He said there were pretty young women in the group and he weren't lying. I didn't know we was gonna strike gold with so many kids, not to mention the bounty we'll get for you grown-ups." He glared at the group of women. One of his group, who was wearing shiny metal-tipped boots, grabbed a woman by the arm and roughly dragged her toward the speaker. The front of her shirt was ripped, exposing her underclothes.

"Dammit, Gibble! Tie the men up first. Blow their brains out if they resist." The man wearing the coat walked over to the young girl. He stroked her hair and laughed. "You sure are a pretty one. I know you New City girls start young. You're going to make us a fine profit along with these other little kiddies, even if we do sample the merchandise first."

The young girl said, "I don't care what you do to me. Please, don't hurt my mother."

The man laughed raucously. "You're about to find out what will happen to you—over and over."

His comment infuriated me, and the girl's brave stand made me ashamed of myself. *Not if I have anything to say about it,* I said under my breath, as a movie hero might say. I knew I wasn't a hero. But I wasn't going to let these people die or allow that little girl to be harmed if I could help it.

I raised my weapon and looked through the scope from about twenty meters away. Two men were fumbling for rope to tie up the children. I had a clear shot at them and at the man who had grabbed the woman. In fact, I had a decent angle to shoot all of them, without too much risk of hitting anyone else. I fired a short burst that dropped the first two in the dirt where they stood. The third man, with the fancy boots, raised his weapon and looked around, uncertain where the shots came from.

I stepped out into the clearing. As he started to point his gun in my direction, I shot him in the face; his head exploded. The last man, in the coat, took off running in the direction of their old truck. I put a three-round burst in his back. I walked toward the group. "Are there any more of them?" No one answered. I shouted, "I'm not here to hurt you, just tell me if there are more of them." No one made a sound or moved a muscle. As I approached, I shouldered the large caliber gun alongside my NCSF weapon.

The people I'd rescued looked stunned. I realized they were probably terrified of me.

One of the men stepped forward. "That's all of them … for now. They would have killed us for a bounty or worse for the women and children, so thank you!" His expression changed as he caught sight of my uniform insignia.

"I'm surprised you're not with them, seeing is how those men are paid by the Ministry." The man gestured to my CCD insignia. "Who are you? Why would a CCD agent be in the DZ?"

I joked, "Well, obviously, I am here to assist fugitives. The Ministry doesn't like people they relentlessly hunt to be mistreated." The man's face showed little expression. I smiled. "Seriously, I'm just lost. I came across you and you looked like you could use help. I'm trying to find my way to SG2."

When no one said anything, I said, "I am hoping you can help me. If nothing else, at least give me directions, maybe a little food and water. Who were those men?" Still no response. "My name is Mark. I'm not going to hurt anyone. It's a long story as to why I am here, and I'm only trying to get home."

The man who first spoke looked at me skeptically. "Why should we help anyone from the CCD, even if you did save us? Those men were bounty hunters who work for the Defection Recovery Ministry. The DRM are just another part of the Ministry."

I looked at him sympathetically. "I don't have much love for the Ministry, despite my uniform insignia."

I held out my hand for him to shake. He said, guardedly, "I'm Kirk. Our guide warned us there could be bounty hunters or bandits out here. I'm not sure what we'll do now, since he's dead. We shouldn't wait around here long." He gestured toward a body.

He added, "These bounty hunters get paid whether they bring us back dead or alive. They would have done what they wanted with the women and my daughter and probably would have sold the children. So, for that, you have my gratitude."

I walked over to the dead guide. He was lying face down, with a bullet wound in his back below his right shoulder. As I rolled him over, I heard him groan. "Hey, he's still alive!"

Two of the women rushed over. One took charge and yelled for the older boy to run inside to find a medical kit. "Kirk, you and Gil get something we can use to carry him inside."

The guide had a second wound in his chest. I assumed a bullet had gone clean through him. He was barely conscious, with his eyes closed. He wore a jacket similar to those worn by Kalina and Boris. He also had the same small distinctive insignia on the collar, an odd rounded shape with pointed tips. He also had on coveralls, which were more like military fatigues. The two men came back with a thin, worn, reasonably clean mattress. They placed the injured man on it and carried him inside the building.

I walked around and picked up the weapons the men I had killed were carrying, then searched their bodies. The one with the boots, Gibble, had the keys to the rundown pickup truck in his pants pocket. "We should probably drag these bodies out of here and hide their vehicle," I said.

Back inside, I walked over to Kirk, who was watching one of the women treat their guide. "I know the insignia on his collar. I saw one just like it yesterday." I gestured to my own collar. "What does it stand for?"

Kirk shrugged. I persisted. "What can you tell me about this man? Two people from his organization helped me escape from the GS militia yesterday. They said they were with the ATO. My team was attacked while working at a surveillance facility in the old city. I wouldn't be here if it weren't for their assistance."

Kirk was impassive. "I can't tell you anything about those people. Look, I don't know why you helped us, but you are a CCD agent heading back to New City. We shouldn't discuss anything about what we know or who we are with you."

I held up my hands, as if in mock surrender, then turned to look at the man on the table. "What's your guide's name?" Kirk started to walk away. I grabbed him by the arm. "I want to get out of New City as much as you do, but my wife is still in the city. I need to get out; I'm suspected of committing espionage."

Kirk looked at me suspiciously. "All the more reason I shouldn't tell you anything. They will question you. If we are caught, they will question us. You of all people should know what that involves. It's probably best if you don't tell us anything and we shouldn't say anything to you, either."

I nodded. "Unfortunately, I know firsthand about being questioned by the Ministry. You could at least be friendly."

Kirk sighed. "When he wakes up, *if* he wakes up, talk to him. His said his name is Bob."

I was frustrated. "What's your wife and kid's names? Look, Kirk, they're not going to ask or know I encountered any people out here. You don't have to give me your last names. I just saved your family from these rogues. Believe it or not my wife saw this happen in a dream and she even said a child would lead me. The way I see it, I had to help you because of the bravery of that little girl."

Kirk sighed. "No last names and don't ask why we are on the run. My wife is Caroline; the little boy is Maxwell. We call him Max. The older girl is my daughter, Tina. She's twelve. That's my sister Sandra and her husband is Gil. Their kids are Theo and Karal. The man with us who was killed was Vance. He was supposed to be our security. He and Bob were the only ones armed. They joined up with us after we left New City. The young woman helping my wife is Samantha, or Sam. She was brought out with us."

"Do you and Gil know how to handle a gun?" I pointed to the weapons I'd brought in.

Kirk nodded. "I spent some time in the security service and so did Caroline."

I handed my NCSF weapon to Kirk. "The electronics are fried, but the ballistic mode works."

Kirk grinned as he looked the weapon over. He checked the ammo. "Thanks. I guess it's hard not to trust someone who hands you a loaded weapon."

"Look, I'm sorry for what happened," I said. "I'm going down the road to get their truck. We need to move the bodies away from the front of the building. If more of them show up we don't want to advertise what happened to their buddies, I suggest we all get in their truck and leave. They mentioned a place called Silver. Did you come through a town on the way here?"

Kirk shook his head. "We stopped at a trading outpost to pick up supplies. It was a cluster of a few rundown buildings about ten kilometers back. But we can't leave Bob until he is able to move or he dies. He's our only link to wherever it is we're headed."

I nodded in agreement. "Were there roads most of the way?"

"We traversed some mountainous ground in the last two days. Part of the time we were walking at night on foot paths."

"Is there a back entrance to this building?" Kirk nodded yes.

With my assault weapon strapped on my back, I stepped toward the door. "I'll get their truck so we can load up the bodies. Then I'll take it around the back so it's not visible from the road. Ask the older boy to let me in the back door once I bring the truck around."

Kirk said, "There is a garage in the back with two bays. The one on the left has enough room inside."

I cautiously walked down the road, past the dead man who had been shot while running away. It was strange to hear so many birds, and the mountain air smelled fresh. As I reached the truck, I stopped to listen. I was satisfied I couldn't hear any noise of approaching vehicles. But as I opened the truck door I heard the faint hum of a motorized engine in the distance. I jumped in.

I hoped I could figure out how to drive the ancient jalopy. I found the key ignition and it started up. As it lurched into gear, I felt the tires spinning out. I took my foot off the gas and gradually eased forward. I realized there was no time to pick up the bodies. It was obvious I'd never driven a vehicle before. I understood the basic process, but was clearly terrible at it.

Within a minute, I was circling the main building. I jumped out to open the garage door. The truck barely fit, nearly scraping the concrete supporting pillars on either side. After closing the garage, I hurried to the front of the main building to see if anyone was coming. I heard at least two vehicles drive up. Then I heard the clamor of men getting out.

I dashed to the back of the building. Theo opened the back door and waved me inside. I ran toward the large front room. I checked my weapon. I had no idea how many hostiles were out there, but there was little doubt we were about to be under attack.

CHAPTER 20

THE BATTLE OF NORTHRIDGE TRANSIT CAMP

As I entered the large front room, Kirk and Gil were holding their guns. Caroline, Sandra, and Sam each grabbed one of the old guns we recovered off the bounty hunters. Theo protested he was old enough to fight. Kirk told him be quiet and go with Sam. She took the other three kids to a side room down the central hall leading to the rear of the structure.

I was kicking myself for not dealing with the bodies sooner. Breathing heavily, I looked out one of the large front windows, and saw two men starting to head toward the main building. I asked Kirk, "How many did you see?"

He shot a glance out the window. "At least ten or maybe a dozen. They've spread out. A couple are behind their vehicles. Four, maybe five, are in the woods surrounding the building." He yelled back to the kids to get down on the floor. "I saw one of them head around the right side of the building carrying what looks like a rocket launcher."

Gil was struggling with his gun, but Caroline was helping him. One of the men outside was yelling at us. I unlatched the horizontal panel on one side of the middle window and eased it open a crack.

Two men were walking toward the front of the building, out in the open. That was foolish. I guessed they figured they had us surrounded and we wouldn't put up much of a fight. They'd clearly seen the body on the road and the others near the front entrance. One of them shouted, "Listen up, I don't know how y'all managed to kill Sawblade, Nachodip and Weasel. I'm tellin' you, you might as well come out with your hands up. There ain't no escape; you're surrounded."

The man with him said, "They got Gibble too; his head's 'bout blowed clean off. I can tell it's him by his boots. I told them stupid horny sons-a-bitches to wait until we got our tanks filled. But you cain't tell Weasel or Gibble nothin'. They had to drive up here quick to get the first slice, armed with nothin' but pistols and huntin' rifles." After seeing the devastation inflicted on Gibble's head the two backed away and took cover behind a small masonry wall.

I went to a window on the far left front of the building. A man was crouched in the tree line, barely concealed, about thirty meters away. Another one was about six meters to his right, lying prone. The window was stubborn, but I managed to open it enough to place the barrel of my GS weapon through the narrow horizontal opening. My gun's scope with a marginal zoom allowed me to get a perfect bead on them. They must have thought they were sufficiently concealed in the trees.

I squeezed off a three-round burst, taking out the first man. I shifted my position, then squeezed off another volley and nailed the second one. There was no point trying to negotiate with these guys. They wouldn't let us go for any amount of money, nor would they try to take us alive.

A barrage of heavy gunfire pelted the walls, windows, and the door. The bullets did not penetrate the thick concrete. They left small indentions on the inside of the heavy metal door and snowflake-like scatter cracks on the reinforced window glass. Someone had done a decent job of fortifying and securing this place. I checked my ammunition. My magazine was nearly depleted with only a half dozen more rounds, but I had four more full magazines. I changed it out for a full one. It was time to make these guys sorry they'd parked so close.

I went back to the center window, which I'd already opened a crack. I clicked over to full auto. The moment there was a lull in the shooting from outside, I unloaded an entire magazine into the two vehicles. One of the trucks exploded in a tremendous fireball as my heavy rounds penetrated the fuel tank, or possibly hit something explosive inside the vehicle. The two men who were near the vehicles staggered out into the open. One rolled on the ground in agonizing pain from the fire which had engulfed them, and the other soon fell forward on his face.

Within a few seconds, the other vehicle also exploded in a huge fireball of flaming debris. Apparently they were carrying something highly explosive, as both trucks were obliterated. I changed out another magazine, then moved to the right window. The first two men had taken cover out of sight on my right. I saw a knee barely protruding from the low retaining wall, a few meters to the left of a small outbuilding twenty-five meters away. I fired at the wall near the knee. The heavy rounds easily penetrated the masonry wall. A bullet-riddled body collapsed forward on the ground.

I saw another man running for better cover. I heard them yelling and cursing at us as another hail of bullets started pelting the building, door, and windows. A man shouted now, much more distantly, "God damn it! You kilt Snakeskull and Beartrap! None of yuz are gonna get outta that building alive. You'll wish you'd never been born; when I get my hands on y'all, I'm gonna carve you up and feed you to my dogs, Harlot and Redsnow."

I shouted back, "If you leave now, we won't have to kill the rest of you." More shots splattered the windows, and I ducked down. Fortunately, even though this group seemed better armed than the last one, nothing penetrated the reinforced glass. But it was starting to shatter and break away in places.

"Last chance! Come out with your hands up or we're blowen' this building to smithereens." A barely audible voice shouted in the distance, "Where's Corky with them damn missiles?"

"The guy with the launcher—was it a rocket launcher or was it more like an RPG?" I asked Kirk.

He shrugged. "How should I know? It was on his back. It was some kind of launcher."

I motioned to Kirk to indicate I was going to the back to see if I could spot anything from the small windows in the side or rear rooms.

I headed down the hallway toward the back room, where the rear exit was. I was about to enter the room on the left, opposite where the kids and Samantha were hiding, when a tremendous explosion shook the building.

The concussion wave from the blast knocked me to the ground. Fortunately, no heavy debris struck me. My ears were ringing, yet I could hear the children screaming. Smoke and dust billowed through the hallway. Heavy automatic gunfire blasted through the breach where the back door had been. I went prone, pointing my gun toward the back of the building. I waited for the dust and smoke to clear, so I could see if anyone was coming in through the breach.

Hearing a thud on the floor and something heavy and metallic rolling around, I scrambled to my knees and dove through the door on my left. The blast ripped through the structure's back room, covering me with debris and making a huge hole in the wall of the adjacent room I dove into. The metal beds and other furniture in the room shielded me from the direct impact of the blast.

I heard Samantha in the room across the hall, trying to calm the kids. One of the men outside said, "Throw out your guns. Come out with your hands up." I tried to see through the hole in the back wall, but the veil of smoke and dust was too thick. I yelled, "There are children in here. Hold your fire and we'll come out! Give us a minute!"

I had no intention of holding my fire. I crawled out of the room, knowing that if they threw another grenade I was probably going to die, and Sam and the children, too. They were here to take corpses, not prisoners. One of the men out back yelled, "You have ten seconds or we come in blasting." Then one of them said, "I'm negotiaten, stupid shit. Hold it! You fucking moron, why did you toss the pin. Hold the lever."

Seconds later, another metal object hit the floor. From where I was peering out through the huge hole in the room's back wall, I saw another explosive rolling around, less than a meter away. Without thinking, I lunged for it. I snagged it in my right hand and backhanded it through the gaping hole where the rear door had been. As I did, one of the men said, "I had to throw it ..." The other one: "Dammit, Roadkil, you could have ..."

They had no time to react. The grenade blew up in front of a stack of rotten lumber and roofing materials the men had been taking cover behind. The sound was deafening. The lumber may have given them some protection from bullets. But the explosion created a cascade of shrapnel that detonated their grenade supply and killed them instantly.

A third man, who was crouched in the trees farther back, was unharmed. As I moved toward the back of the building, I glimpsed him taking aim at my movement. I ducked as automatic gunfire ricocheted all around me. I felt a searing pain, as a bullet or shrapnel grazed my left shoulder. I rolled over, away from the opening. I glanced at my injured shoulder. I heard gunfire erupting from the front of the building again. I was in terrific pain, but I wasn't seriously injured.

Erratic bursts of gunfire from the man behind the trees continued to shower the back room. There was a pause, and I realized he must be reloading. I scooched back toward the opening, remembering exactly where I had seen him. I readied my gun, then popped my head up. I saw him bring his weapon up to fire again. I squeezed off a few rounds into his chest, which killed him instantly. I waited for a minute. I wasn't sure if there was anyone else in the back. I also knew if Kirk was right, there was one these men, somewhere, armed with a rocket launcher or RPG. I looked into the room where the kids and Samantha were, to check on them. Apparently, she had fled, taking them back to the front room of the building.

Once my ears stopped ringing, I slipped out of the space the back door once occupied and ran to the tree line behind the building. I glanced at the mangled corpses of the grenadier and his buddy. I then swiftly moved toward the corpse of the man who had just been shooting at me. There was no evidence of an RPG. Fortunately, no one else seemed to be in the back. I could still hear plenty of gunfire being exchanged from the front of the building. Even so, I knew at least five hostiles out front were either dead or seriously injured by gunfire or the exploding vehicles.

My heart was pounding as I moved as quietly as I could though the trees. Dried, crunchy leaves covered the forest floor. With every step, it seemed like I was trumpeting my position to anyone nearby. I paused momentarily, scanning the back again for the presence of more hostiles.

As I slowly circled around the structure, I smelled the acrid smoke from the burning vehicles from the front of the building. My goal was to circle behind the remaining men who were still assaulting the front of the building. I could barely see anything beyond ten meters of the front of the building, due to all the smoke.

I managed to climb up a small ridge that overlooked the compound. That was when I spotted a man just below me. He had what looked like a shoulder fired rocket launcher. He was apparently having difficulties figuring out to use it, struggling with the trigger mechanism. He would lift it up to aim, then bring it back down to inspect it, trying to see why it didn't fire.

A man yelled from the distance, "Dammit, Corky! Shoot the damn rockets!"

I pulled out my knife, then took off running down the wooded slope. I was on him before he realized what was happening. I stabbed him in the gut, pushed him down and plunged the knife again into his upper chest, just below his throat. Blood spurted everywhere, as he gasped and gurgled. Then he breathed his last, even as his dead eyes seemed to glare at me in surprise.

From this vantage point, I could see two assailants taking cover on the flat roof of the closest outbuilding, away from the main structure. Shouldering my weapon, I picked up the launcher to examine it. The man had released the safety, but he'd left a latch pin on the back end of the weapon, which kept it from firing. I pulled out the pin, then took aim at the small outbuilding.

I wasn't certain how accurate the weapon would be at more than thirty meters. I raised the trajectory a little, to make sure it wouldn't fall short. To my surprise, it fired straight and true and over the heads of the men on top of the small one-story building. I'm not sure they noticed the rocket whizzing by a couple of meters over their heads. I wasn't going to give them a chance to consider why something had just exploded in the trees beyond them. There was a case of six more rockets. I reloaded the launcher and lowered my aim for a second attempt.

Before the men could think to scramble off the roof, the building under them exploded in a huge fireball, flinging debris across the surrounding compound. If the man I'd stabbed had been able to get off even one shot from this launcher, it would have killed everyone inside our building. Fortunately, I was able to use it to take out the last two assailants. Everything was quiet. I counted eleven dead within the space of about five minutes.

I waited a few minutes before emerging from the trees, to be certain there were no more hostiles alive. One badly burned man didn't die until a few minutes after the battle. When I tried to question him, he was unable to speak. Once back inside, Kirk stared at me in disbelief. "We thought for certain you were dead when you didn't return after the explosion in the rear."

Fortunately, Bob was alert now and talking to Caroline. When he saw me he looked surprised; I was covered with dust and a considerable amount of blood, both from my wound and from the man I'd stabbed.

I guess Bob wasn't expecting a CCD agent to save his party of refugees. I went to the sink in the small kitchen to wash my arms, face, and hands. I removed my bloody vest and filthy jacket. My injury wasn't too serious, although I would need stitches. I grabbed a rag to compress the wound to stop the bleeding, then went over to the wounded man to introduce myself.

"I guess we have you to thank for getting us out of this situation," he said.

I tried to make light of it. "All in a day's work, to protect and serve people the Ministry is trying to eradicate. We are also trying to keep bounty payments to a minimum." I smiled.

Bob held his chest in pain as he tried to suppress his laughter. "It's rare for a CCD agent to help people trying to escape the Ministry's clutches. I'd very much like to hear how your timely arrival to rescue us from these Carnivore bounty hunters came about. This outfit has been a pain in our side in this sector for a long time."

Sandra did a decent job stitching me up. Soon, Bob and I were sitting down face to face. I was about to ask him some questions, when he said, "I hate to break up this talk before it gets started, but we need to move to a safer location—right now. I'm certain these guys had radios. I am not sure how far we can get on foot today, considering my condition ..."

Kirk interrupted. "We have a truck from the first group who attacked us. It's in the garage."

Bob nodded appreciatively. "Then we'd better get moving. That road is the only one in or out of this transit camp. The main road is about four kilometers away. If more of them are coming, that's the way they will come. We need to reach the turnoff on the main road to another camp before they converge on Northridge again."

After leaving the Northridge camp, we soon reached the "main" road. We traveled along it for a few kilometers. From my perspective, these weren't roads. They were made of dirt or loose gravel. If they had been paved roads in the distant past, there was no evidence of it. A short time later we made another turn. Then we made several more, one after another. I quickly realized, I would need a map to find my way out of this mountainous wilderness, crisscrossed with trails and washed out excuses for roads.

The last road we turned on, if you could call it a road, became increasingly narrow and was overgrown with small trees and shrubs. The brush scraped the sides and undercarriage of the truck as we bumped and rumbled down the narrow trail.

The transit outpost where we eventually arrived was much smaller than Northridge. It appeared to have been unoccupied for quite some time. It was in a thickly overgrown, densely wooded area. The main structure was not as well built as Northridge and didn't have reinforced glass windows. Its metal shutters were visibly rusted. Though not as comfortable or well equipped, it was nonetheless dry. We were just glad to be far away from the carnage.

I reflected on what Ari had said about having to choose to be brave and that a child would lead me. When I remembered how brave Tina had been in the face what could have been a horrible fate, I started to weep. I knew that somehow, the fates of the people I'd helped were connected to my fate because of what Ari had told me.

That evening, under the dim glow of a chemical lamp, Bob and I had a few minutes to talk alone. "Kirk tells me you're in some kind of trouble with the Ministry," Bob said.

I nodded. "Kirk didn't want us to tell each other much of anything. I mean, I get it. Anything we reveal could become information the Ministry could use."

"You are quite a curiosity given that you're a CCD operative," Bob said. "Kirk told me you encountered someone with an insignia like mine, who helped you get away from the GS in the old city."

"I met two techs in the bunker of our surveillance station. They advised me to climb up to the sensor array to escape the GS, and gave me advice and supplies. Beyond that, they didn't turn me over to the GS."

Bob looked concerned. "They wouldn't have helped a CCD operative unless you told them something vital enough to make them trust you. Otherwise they would have killed or captured you."

I shrugged. "I threatened to kill them unless they helped me."

Bob said, "It doesn't matter. Kalina wouldn't have helped you if she knew you were CCD. You must have said something rather convincing."

"How do you know her name?"

"Everybody in the ATO knows Kalina. And I know how talented she is at breaking into New City security and especially those surveillance stations. She is also a deadly killer."

"She wasn't armed and she didn't have much choice. Bob, if I told you my wife foresaw what would happen today, you probably wouldn't believe me. She also said I would escape from a battle and I did. Somehow, she knows we have a connection. I think I know why; I know what you people do."

Bob looked intensely at me. "Information can be dangerous, even on this side of the wall. I admit I'm intrigued to know what you could have possibly said to Kalina. You were a dead man the moment you encountered her, even if you had a gun pointed at her. I can assure you; she was armed and very dangerous. She may have seemed like a technician, but she could have killed you, even before you thought she gained your trust."

"I told her I know someone who is connected to your organization. I also recognized the tech she was using. I know the old man who gave the ATO the molecular data compressor she was utilizing. He's the one who stole it over twenty years ago. He also created the ghosted access codes used to operate it."

Bob's guarded expression intensified. "You should know, whatever ends up in my head could be extracted by the Ministry if I'm ever captured. You talk too much."

I breathed deeply. "I know your organization must use MDCs to get information about security directives on targets out of LEOH. That connection assures me that I can trust you and that's why I trusted Kalina."

Bob nodded his head and snorted. "Did you tell Kalina all this?"

"Yes. That's why she trusted me. Everything the Ministry accused me of doing, I did because of the old man. He gave me the ghosted access codes and the MDC device I used to steal classified matrix data. It's a miracle I wasn't caught. Now I'm afraid for my wife and I'm afraid for ..." I stopped before I mentioned the name Zack Waters. I sat back, then took a deep breath.

Bob stared at me in disbelief. "What else did you tell her?"

I sighed. "I told her who I really am. I told her I married that old man's great-granddaughter. I'm apparently his brother's great-grandson and some kind of genetic dissident and I'm distantly related to my own wife. That's what you do, isn't it? You get people like me out of New City and find them a new home if the Ministry identifies them. I'm not worried about trusting you."

"Do you see this insignia?" Bob said. "It identifies me as a Tracer, or ATO. That's what we call ourselves. This also means I will lay down my life. Underneath this patch is a lethal dose of poison. If I'm ever captured and fail to inject this to take my own life, I'd be putting a lot of people at risk. The Ministry would love to find out what is in my head, including my knowledge of Zachariah Waters and what he has done for our organization over the years. He's practically a legend. I can only surmise that I'm talking to a man who has married one of his three great-granddaughters. That geezer hooked you up with your own cousin. The oldest two are what, seventeen? What year is it? Anyway, it sounds like something creepy he would do."

"It's not creepy, she's eighteen and my fifth cousin. Wait, how do you know Zack Waters? And Ari doesn't have a sister and she's never mentioned any close cousins. Who told you this?"

Bob stared at me in shock. "You married Ariel Waters? She's like fourteen or fifteen, isn't she? Wait, you're right it's 63 NCE. I lose track of years out here. But did Zack never tell you who, or rather what, Ariel is or where she came from? Fascinating! Zack insisted no one *ever* mention them, even within the ATO. He wanted them left alone for their own protection. He said he had plans for them. Yet here I am with a man who is not only related to them, he married one of them. This is a very odd coincidence."

I laughed. "Zack told me she was special. But I'm pretty sure I would know if my wife had a sister or a cousin. She has never mentioned having either in the two years I've known her. Neither has Zack. In fact, Zack told me Ari is the last surviving member on his side of the family. He said she needed to be protected at all costs. He also said, practically all the members of his family have been killed. If he had any other great-granddaughters, they are probably dead by now."

Bob shrugged. "It's 63 NCE that means, let's see … I've had no contact with Zack for … wow, over eighteen years. But I can assure you they aren't your wife's cousins. All three are identical sisters and two of them ... Mark, they are clones; exceptional, rare, modified clones. He should have told you this before you married her. I can't say more or it could be dangerous for her and even more so for her sisters. I can't tell you who they are."

"That's crazy," I replied. "Zack would have told me that ... or Ari would have. But I would love for you to tell me about his involvement with your organization."

"I think it's best if we don't discuss anything else about Zack Waters, Ariel, or your relationship with him," Bob said. "You've gotten involved with an extremely dangerous man. He has obviously lied to you and is using you. He has put your life in peril to help him in some sort of scheme. He is up to something."

"I did it because I love my wife," I said. "He says everything I've done for him comes from her dreams and visions. After what she told me I would encounter on this trip, I'm starting to believe him."

"I can assure you, that if you told Kalina any of this, you have stirred up a hornet's nest within the ATO," Bob said. "They've been wanting to get him out for decades, but he's refused. When you see him, tell him Jonas Peres sends his regards. It's an old alias of mine. He'll remember me."

CHAPTER 21

THE PYTHORAEL CONSPIRACY

Tabitha had a private personal contact link, as did most in her position and social class. No one, not even the Archon, had her personal access code, which she changed frequently. She gave it only to her closest friends, that is to say, one person. The Archon, her parents, and her work associates were always able to message her through her official PCD contact link, to which she rarely responded.

As she was getting ready for her usual short night of sleep, she was messaged through her private contact link by the CCD Director, Dalen Pythorael. He asked to visit her the next morning. Tabitha was more than a little perturbed. She assumed he was trying to send her a not so subtle message that nothing was hidden from him.

Despite her new assignment, she had been planning to go in early the next morning to oversee the completion of several simulations for Phase 2. She knew she could easily refuse to meet with Pythorael, since he had no authority over her. Nevertheless, he was a powerful man. She assumed, of course, word had gotten back to him about her suspicions about Ministry higher ups. This confirmed to her that the slithery Nathan Prideil was no more than one of Pythorael's stooges. Tabitha confirmed the invitation, and thought, *If he thinks he can capture me in his orbit, he's sadly mistaken.*

* * * *

The knock on the door of Tabitha's private suite of rooms in her parent's palatial home was a throwback to a time when servants personally informed the master of the house that a guest had arrived. Tabitha winced. "Enter, Julian! You know you don't need to personally come to my rooms." Julian curtsied respectfully. "Ēlan, Director Pythorael has arrived. He is waiting in the east lounge, as you directed. Allow me to finish dressing you and to put your hair up."

Tabitha waved off the suggestion. "No need, I am trying to do it myself."

"Ēlan, please, I can see that you need help," Julian said, looking critically at Tabitha.

"I'm trying to learn to take care of myself," Tabitha insisted. "I love you Julian, but I don't want to be constantly pampered anymore by having you do *everything* for me."

Julian nodded and curtsied. "As you wish, ēlan." She picked a piece of lint off of Tabitha's blouse.

Tabitha rolled her eyes. "You know I hate titles! Call me Tabitha. You've known me since I was in diapers; stop all this bowing and curtsying!"

Julian replied, "Of course, ēlan." She reached up to tuck in a loose curl of Tabitha's hair.

Tabitha cringed with irritation. It was useless to tell Julian to cease her formalities, as the woman repeatedly ignored her requests. "All right, help me finish my hair. I'm thinking of wearing it down from now on. I need to acquire a much more casual wardrobe, like regular people."

"Gracious no," Julian objected. "Unmarried ēlans should always wear their hair up with jeweled lace, accompanied by a diadem, at least in the evening. It signifies your maiden title and availability."

"I work in an enclosed office with computers. I feel ridiculous," Tabitha protested. "You know that's why I've never had friends. Nobody wanted to be around me, except for those horrible … never mind. I'm tired of looking like a doll. I want to be me—a regular girl."

"The Ēlantiel's daughter and heiress doesn't need friends; everyone serves you," Julian said as she worked on Tabitha's less than perfect efforts. "I suppose this will have to do."

"I'll finish up," Tabitha said. "Please inform Dalen I will join him shortly."

Tabitha entered the spacious lounge where Pythorael was enjoying a cup of coffee provided by one of the servants. Tabitha greeted him curtly, on a first name basis, just to annoy him. "Dalen, if you don't mind, we need to keep this meeting brief. I have a tight schedule today."

Pythorael started to stand. Tabitha stopped him. "Please, don't get up." She sat down opposite him. "Let's get right to the point. Why are you here?"

Pythorael was not surprised at her directness. "Of course, ēlan."

"Just call me Tabitha or Ms. Norean."

Pythorael nodded and smiled. "I won't call you Ms. Norean to your face, ēlan. Even for someone in my position, formalities must be observed."

Tabitha glared at him, but was silent.

"At any rate, thank you for agreeing to see me on such short notice. I will endeavor to get directly to the point."

Tabitha stopped him. "By the way, *never* contact me again on my private contact link, for any reason. You are neither a friend nor someone whose name I ever want to see in my private coms. Even so, I can assure you, today will be the last time you will ever have such an opportunity. There is no better way to annoy me than by demonstrating a capability I am now obliged to take away. Don't think for a second I don't know how you got it. I can track your bots."

Pythorael ignored Tabitha's threat. "I understand from the Archon's executive security adjutant, Nathan Prideil, you have been tasked by the Archon himself to undertake a security operation involving one my newest CCD operatives, Mr. Mark Verigratu. Since you've been made privy to all the security directives and utilization matrixes on this matter, I'm sure you understand the sensitive nature of this investigation. We should coordinate a strategy to deal with him. I'm offering you an opportunity for us to help each other."

Tabitha tilted her head. "Deal with Mark Verigratu—or the Archon? The last thing I need is help from you, and I have no intention of helping you, in any capacity."

Pythorael clarified. "Mr. Verigratu, of course. I'm not sure if you have heard about the attack on the 4UB6 facility in the DZ09 sector. We have reason to believe the CCD operations team and their entire military escort were likely killed. Our ability to discover whom he may have been working with may have perished with him."

Tabitha nodded her acceptance of this news. "I would have thought Mr. Prideil had told you I was aware of the 4UB6 incident, since he was there when the Archon informed me. Why are you really here, Dalen? You can speak freely, as I certainly will."

Pythorael was furious at this impertinence, but suppressed his anger. "You are playing a dangerous game. The Archon is not someone with whom you can trifle. I am trying to save you from a fate worse than death. You know you are his singular obsession, and he treats you like his pet."

Tabitha was not about to allow herself to be intimidated. "'Dangerous game,' and 'a fate worse than death'? Your clichéd threats don't frighten me. I did not get to this position because I'm his pet. You're mistaken if you think I don't know what you're up to."

Tabitha stood up, prepared to leave. "I know exactly why you created those ghosted access codes and why you've been so careful to conceal the reason for doing so. The entire security edifice of New City has been infiltrated; this data breach is the tip of the iceberg. Once your classified data gets out, this city will erupt in rebellion. You and the Archon have this fear in common, besides the fact that people will discover you are not human."

Dalen was stunned Tabitha would reveal this knowledge to him. "You assume too much. You are privy to information for which he might have you killed, if he knew you were aware of it. You are obviously a smart girl. He doesn't keep you close to him because of your beauty, skills, or intelligence. If he cannot possess all of you, he will destroy you, along with your obsequious family. It would be better for you to know nothing than fail to comprehend so little about what you do know."

Now Pythorael stood to leave. "If you interfere with me it will not end well for you, or this world. I promise you this: You will ultimately have no choice other than to help me oppose him. Foolish girl, you have mistaken your soul for your intellect. He will soon take what is hidden in you for himself. You need to get away from him, not join with him."

Tabitha said, "There will be no place for either of you. I promise *you*: I do have a choice and it includes not helping either of you. I am not joining him, nor can he take anything from me or make me do anything. I see little difference between you and Devan Elaniel. Stay out of my way. Leave me to my own designs or I will expose your conspiracy against him."

"Clarions are useful, yet there is one thing they are not very good at," Pythorael said. "They have difficulty imagining what they cannot possibly know, since they don't imagine they cannot eventually know everything. You have no idea what is at stake. You are an ēlan of New City and you belong to Devan Elaniel. You are being led to your own scaffold."

"I belong to no one but myself!"

Pythorael continued, unperturbed. "I've been at this game much longer than you. I'm fighting to prevent the fulfillment of what is written in an inescapable paradox, one as old as the foundation of this world. Run that through your clarion mind to see what emerges. As for the Archon, he is far more dangerous than I am. He has only one weakness—his relentless pursuit of everything. He will not stop until he has achieved his heart's desire. Let me warn you, part of his heart's desire is to become intimately bonded with you, little ēlan. Once he does, there will be nothing left of you."

Tabitha followed Pythorael toward the Norean's enormous foyer. "What is that supposed to mean? I know how weak all of you are. Your groveling presence here proves this!"

Pythorael waited in silence as the ornate double doors at the front entrance of the house opened automatically. He turned to Tabitha. "Unfortunately, you have chosen to be an adversary to me rather than an ally, at present. Perhaps you will reconsider before it is too late. You are a rude and impudent child. I don't know why the Archon puts up with you. If you truly want answers, you know where to find me." He flashed her a wicked grin. "I will tell you this. He is convinced that what is contained in your DNA is evidence you possess the key to his immortal life. He intends to take it from you and make it his own, in the most intimate of ways that only he can do. It doesn't matter if you really have what he wants, or if it's only a myth. He believes it to be true. You will give yourself to him and it will be your choice. He can be very persuasive. In your case, I can assure you; his persuasion can be exceptionally effective."

Pythorael turned and left.

What a prick! What was he talking about? She would have to play back his words. *The Archon is not going to be intimate with me. I'm not having sex with an alien!*

Her thoughts turned to this so-called celebration in honor of her achievements the following day. *This is going to suck!* She felt alone, with no one to trust. Mark Verigratu had most likely been killed. Tabitha checked her probe. Unfortunately, nothing on Mark had pinged. *Yep, he's probably dead.*

* * * *

Pythorael grinned as he climbed into his vehicle. *The ēlan will soon be in the palm of my hand. If not, I will have to do away with her once and for all.* He considered the carmelineals in the fortress of Rome. *Perhaps I should have her name read, to see if it's as alluring as Elaniel believes it is. If she is truly as dangerous as that little miracle worker who nearly crushed his neck thirteen centuries ago, she must be stopped. Humans are such intricate and precarious creatures, especially their females.*

CHAPTER 22

WHAT THEY ALREADY KNOW

Everyone at the small transit camp awoke early Friday morning. Bob had indicated the night before that as soon as he was able, the group would be traveling on foot. He was expecting a replacement guide to arrive to take his charges through the next leg of their journey. Bob seemed remarkably fit for someone who had taken a bullet. According to Samantha, nothing vital had been hit and she expected him to heal quickly, as long as he rested.

With some reluctance, I was obliged to take the truck north on my own. After some last-minute thanks, hugs, and goodbyes, Bob advised me to get back on the main road and head northeast about thirty kilometers. I was then to head north when I reached a certain crossroads. He gave me a small handheld map device. He said I should abandon the truck before I reached the next "town," once I'd made it north about twenty kilometers past the crossroads. I would have to travel around it on foot, since there would likely be more "Carnivore" bounty hunters there. I didn't want to be seen in a vehicle that belonged to them. Bob explained that the markings on the top of the truck indicated to the DRM it was "friendly."

We had scavenged quite an arsenal of weapons from the second wave of attackers at Northridge. I had enough ammunition to replace my spent magazines, plus add a few additional ones. I even had a loaded rocket launcher in the back of the cab, along with a box of grenades and two side arms. I had no intention of carrying all this weaponry once I headed out on foot. I tried to convince Bob to stash at least some of the weapons at the transit station, but he refused. His reasoning made some sense. He didn't want to create an escalating conflict between the ATO and other DZ gangs, even bounty hunters.

* * * *

In under two hours I reached the designated crossroads without encountering anyone. I turned left, heading north. Soon, the road started to climb steeply. It turned into a winding mountain road. I had gone only about fifteen kilometers, when I started heading down the other side of the mountain.

I took it slowly because the road was dangerously narrow. I rounded a sharp curve and was startled to see a gate across the road, about fifteen meters ahead of me. Three armed men stood beside it. They didn't look like the same type of bounty hunters we had fought the day before, but I was still alarmed.

There was no way to turn around or reverse without plunging off the side of mountain. I could drive up to them or try to bail out of the vehicle. But the road was so narrow I could barely open the door without hitting the side of the steep, rocky embankment; not unless I drove forward another ten meters. I decided my only option was to talk my way out of this situation.

I pulled up to the gate. One of the men, who was armed, approached the vehicle. On Bob's advice, I had removed my CCD insignia. I casually rolled down the window. The man strode up to it and glowered at me. "You one of Seldane's bunch?"

I replied curtly, having no idea who Seldane was. "Who wants to know?"

The man studied me. "This transport has his signet on it. We hear you fellas are looking for a group of defectors who were heading south, via the old river route. You wouldn't happen to know anything about that?"

I was nervous, yet tried to remain calm and assertive. I adopted the kind of good ole boy twang I'd heard the others use. "We found 'em, and they kicked our ass at a transit camp yesterday. I've been runnin' these roads for the last sixteen hours looking for them. There's nothing back that way so I'm heading in. I figgerd I'd stop in Catch Fork for a bite." Catch Fork was the town I was supposed to avoid; it was a few more kilometers up the road.

The man looked at me. He could see my GS weapon on the front seat beside me. "You out here all alone? I never knew any of you to travel without a pack of men."

I said, "I usually do, but I lost three of my best men yesterday in that fight. Weasiltooth, Sawblade, and Nachodip are dead. I'm pissed off. That's why I'm out here looking for those bastards loaded up. I'd appreciate it if you'd let me pass." Fortunately, my scruffy whiskers and disheveled looks must have convinced him I was just another Carnivore ruffian.

"What's your call name? We gotta have it for the gate log," he demanded.

"My call name is Gibble and this is my truck," I said, confidently. *Geeze, I hope that's a real call name.*

The man studied me a second. "I thought this piece of shit truck looked familiar. I know that sadistic bastard personally. Gib is my cousin and you ain't him. Get out with your hands up! Did you kill my cousin you son of a bitch?"

I should have known all these bastards were cousins, I thought.

Suddenly, a burst of high caliber ballistic gunfire sprayed the area. The men at the gate were mowed down in an instant. The man who was questioning me was killed moments later. I looked up to see a low flying NCSF combat drone just above the tree line, about twenty meters away. It was bearing down on my vehicle. I scrunched down in the front seat as the old truck was riddled with bullets and the reinforced windshield was shredded with impact craters. I needed to get out fast, in case a bullet hit one of the grenades or rockets in the truck.

Yet I remained motionless for a few seconds. When the firing ceased, I heard the faint rumble of vehicles approaching. They had the hum of electrically powered NCSF military transports. I jumped out of the vehicle. I raised my hands in surrender, hoping the automated drones would recognize I was no longer a threat. As three NCSF transports advanced up the road directly in front of me, the drones backed off. Now I had to figure out how to explain who I was to the approaching NCSF.

Several men emerged from the first NCSF military transport, which stopped just on the other side of the gate, about five meters in front of my bullet-riddled truck. Still holding my hands up, I approached the officer in charge as several men surrounded me with pointed weapons. I spoke clearly and loudly: "I am with the NCMIA CCD. You can verify this with your battalion command. My name is Mark Verigratu. I escaped from the 4UB6 facility in the SL3DZ09 two days ago, after it was attacked. I would be grateful for an escort back to New City. I have critical intelligence to relay to my superiors."

The officer gestured for his men to lower their weapons as he eyed me suspiciously. "My electronics were disabled," I said. "A retinal scan will verify my identity." I reached into my jacket and held out my inoperable PCD. The soldier glanced at my disabled vehicle. He waved a couple of his men over to investigate it.

He reached out and inspected my PCD. Without hesitation, he handed it back to me. "I'm Major Warren. We are with the SG2 3rd Battalion regiment. What happened to your PCD, son? Where is your CCD uniform insignia?"

The major was a crusty middle-aged man. I could tell he wasn't willing to take any crap. I replied courteously, "My PCD was damaged in a KEM detonation as I was escaping from the 4UB6 surveillance facility. I removed my insignia as a precaution. I am trying to get back to SG2. I'm hoping it's only about seventy kilometers north of here."

One of the men returned and whispered in the major's ear. "How did you come to be in possession of this vehicle and the weapons inside?" the major asked. I was nervous about saying too much about my escape from 4UB6 or the battle with the Carnivore bounty hunters. I decided I had to at least explain how I'd gotten the vehicle. "I stole it from a group of bounty hunters who were attacking unarmed refugees."

The major looked at me skeptically. "And just how did you manage to accomplish that, all by yourself?"

I briefly explained about the fight with the Carnivores and that the refugees provided me with food and shelter for assisting them. I said when we parted ways, I took the truck north and they headed south. I fabricated the distances to the locations of the events and numerous other details. The major spoke with a soldier who walked up and showed him something on a display.

The major turned to me. "This vehicle belongs to a known DRM affiliated outfit. You may have picked the wrong side when you engaged them. They probably would have helped you out. They might have given you a lift to New City, for a little reward."

"Given the damage your drone just inflicted on this truck, I'm not sure teaming up with its former owners would have been advisable," I said. "Besides, at the time, I wasn't in a position to verify affiliations. The men I killed were intent on kidnapping children and raping three women and a young girl. I wasn't going to let that happen. I didn't have time to verify they were fugitives from New City before I helped them."

I showed the major the insignia I had ripped off my jacket. "It was only a handful of men, women, and children. Interdicting defectors is not why I'm in the DZ. Getting back to New City is my only priority now. Frankly, helping those people was the right thing to do. I make no apologies for it. As for any other details about the incident at the surveillance facility, I am afraid I can only debrief my CCD superiors. I would be grateful if you could arrange passage to get me back inside the city. As I said, I have sensitive intelligence on the 4UB6 incident and the battle that took place."

The major gave me a questioning look. "The reports of the 4UB6 attack said there were no survivors of the original operations detail— military or civilian. There are no active beacons."

I nodded. "I'm the only survivor. The GS planned their attack so they could ambush the forces sent to retake the facility. This is all I am willing to say about what happened down there. It was a classified CCD mission."

The major scoffed. "Don't give me any 'classified mission' bullshit. Who do you think provides security for those missions? You're probably the luckiest SOB I have ever met, to have made it this far."

He checked the time on his display. "If you want an escort, you will have to come with us. I realize the DRM engages some of this vagrant trash out here as bounty hunters from time to time, but my orders are to kill or capture any human inhabitants or hostiles we encounter, all the way to the crossroads and east toward the escarpment. We are supposed to camp overnight at a SL2DZ08 checkpoint; we won't be back inside the walls for three days."

"Please, can you at least let them know you found Mark Verigratu so they can inform my wife I am still alive," I pleaded.

"Give me a minute to report this to my superiors at SG2 battalion command. I'll find out what they want us to do with the 'lone' survivor from the 4UB6 operation." The major headed back to the lead transport.

He returned a few minutes later. "Apparently the CCD wants you back in one piece, as soon as possible. I have orders to turn around and take you directly to SG2. It's too dangerous to have you flown out of here with all of the hostile activity, even in this part of the DZ. You can ride with me."

The major nodded to one of his captains. "Mount up and turn this convoy around. It looks like we will be having dinner at the battalion mess." I was relieved my ordeal was over. As it turned out, we had to back down the road for three kilometers before finding a place to turn around.

* * * *

Our operations team was supposed to have been back by Friday, mid-afternoon. This meant I was only a few hours late, thanks to my encounter with the NCSF patrol. Sadly, the rest of my team would never be coming back.

When we arrived at the New City Sanctuary Gate 2, I was greeted by two well-dressed CCD junior executives who escorted me to a private executive jet. From there, I was flown directly to the NCGD. This was the first time I had flown anywhere. I was amazed at the aircraft's rapid vertical takeoff. I assumed this was Director Pythorael's private jet. On the way, I showered in a well-appointed cabin, was provided with fresh clothes, and had my injury treated. I was even given a temporary PCD and a CCD security tag.

An hour after take-off from SG2, the sleek craft touched down in a smooth vertical landing at the executive sky port next to CCD headquarters. Apparently there were no restrictions on supersonic flight for Pythorael. I was quickly led from there to the director's conference lounge on the executive floor of CCD headquarters, where I was told to wait. I remembered I had a weekend celebration to attend at the Citadel, but hoped my ordeal would give me ample excuse just to skip the event. All I wanted to do was go home.

Director Pythorael arrived about fifteen minutes later. He greeted me with a congratulatory handshake and a cordial smile. "Mark, I am so pleased you managed to escape the horrible business in the DZ. It's a shame about Merrick; he will be dearly missed, and the others as well."

He said, "I know you are probably exhausted. However, the Archon still insists you attend the festivities this weekend. For your benefit, he has arranged for some extremely comfortable quarters for you at the Citadel manor. You can have a private dinner of your choosing. I promise, no one will disturb you and you can rest. He would also like to meet with you. You will be provided with appropriate clothing and I've had your wife informed about your return. You may, of course, contact her without worrying that you'll be disturbed. I'll even send my plane to pick her up, so she can join you."

I was stunned at the hospitality being afforded me. I was also suspicious; this was the same man who had me drugged and interrogated a few days ago. "Thank you, director ..."

He held up his hand to stop me. "Please, call me Dalen. Once again, accept my apology for the way you have been treated recently. I hope we can put the matter behind us."

"Well, Dalen, while I appreciate the offer, I am not in the mood for a celebration. I just barely escaped with my life. I am emotionally and physically exhausted and traumatized, not to mention injured. I am not sure I can transition from being a suspect to a fugitive in hostile territory to a pampered guest at the Citadel. After my ordeal, I'd rather go home and forget the whole experience."

"Frankly, I must insist, for your own sake," he said.

"I want to spend time with my wife ... alone!"

Pythorael wrinkled his brow in thought. "After you are debriefed first thing Monday morning, you can take the rest of the week to recuperate. Besides, I already said you could take some time off."

The last thing I wanted to do was spend the weekend at the Citadel, regardless of the luxury afforded me. "I don't care whether I meet the Archon!" I threw my electronic security tag on the side table beside my chair. "I quit! Over the last ten days, I've been strip searched, interrogated twice, probed and dosed with Phencol twice, and my home has been ransacked. I barely escaped death numerous times over the last three days. I've seen my team members killed or led to their deaths. I'm done. If this is what it's like to work for the CCD, I'd rather not work at all. Frankly, I don't need this job."

"The debriefing on Monday will be an official debriefing, not an interrogation," Pythorael insisted. "We only wish to gain additional details and insight into those matters you appropriately withheld from the NCSF. Mark, even if you resign, you are still going to have to be interviewed about what happened at 4UB6. You can either sit for the interview now or have a pleasant weekend first."

I shook my head. "Then interview me now. I'm done."

Pythorael appeared apprehensive. "You don't understand. You must go. No one turns down a request from the Archon, especially one as simple as this."

"Are you going to arrest me if I walk out?"

"He probably only wants to confirm my assessment that you're innocent. This security breach has him on edge. He may even honor you for your miraculous escape. As for your resignation, think about it over the next week. If you still want to resign by a week from Monday, I will respect your decision."

I shook my head. "I don't know why you care. You treated me like a criminal last week. Now you're pleading with me to stay? I don't get it."

"You're a talented operative. What happened was unfortunate. I will personally contact your wife and ask her to join you here for the weekend. You must go."

I was still determined to resign, but I agreed. "I'll contact her myself. I'll let her know I'll be home on Monday and we'll make our own plans."

Pythorael looked satisfied. "Very good, a limousine is waiting for you downstairs to take you to the Citadel. I'll see you tomorrow. Maybe you can regale me with some unofficial details of your ordeal, if you're up to it." He called for someone to escort me out. "By the way, you might be interested to know that Jerome Haley has been released from custody. He is only being admonished for his inappropriate downgrade of a C3SD. It turned out to be irrelevant since the targets had already escaped the SJ before the directive was actually submitted to his office for further action."

* * * *

After I left, Rogan entered Pythorael's office. "You know the Archon will have the ēlan begin her investigation of Mr. Verigratu."

"I almost feel sympathy for the man," Pythorael said. "She's the most arrogant, pompous bitch I've ever met, and I've been around a long time. I'm sure he'll hate her, as anyone would."

"Don't underestimate her," Rogan said. "Keep your spybots close; she may very well sweep him off his feet. If so, he may deflower the Archon's princess before the weekend is concluded."

Pythorael laughed. "I wish him luck flipping *her*. Devan is convinced she's been a practicing lesbian since she was an adolescent, which officially makes her still a maiden, according to his bullshit mystical requirements."

"Still, she's beautiful, and most New City ēlans aren't too particular over gender."

"The man is a peasant," Pythorael scoffed. "But if he does bed her, he won't survive to see his lovely wife again. Devan will be so angry that his obsession is damaged that he'll do away with both of them. That would be the end of the K15 program for good and solve this twenty-year-old problem. I could only hope."

CHAPTER 23

THE CLARION AND THE CAUSE

It was a relatively short ride to the Archon's Citadel from the CCD HQ. I was overwhelmed at its grandeur. The Citadel was a stunning palace, surrounded by immaculate gardens and beautiful landscaping. For people such as myself, who had never seen the place, it was overwhelming, even at night. Both the house and the gardens were spectacularly lit. I'd never imagined it could be this magnificent.

I was provided with my own suite of rooms, along with a personal butler. I was also offered a private dinner with a choice of several succulent entrees and a fine selection of the best wines. After dinner, I contacted Ari. We talked pleasantly for a while, but I avoided disclosing the details of my experiences in the DZ.

My room had a large balcony overlooking a garden, which appeared to be spring-like, although it was early fall, with colorful flowers and foliage lit up with bright lights. There were magnificent fountains and astonishingly intricate water features. Although my own penthouse was nothing to look down on; the closet here was as large as my living room. The huge bathroom had a gilded marble bath with countless unique features. The place upended one's conception of true luxury. This was certainly a palace fit for a king. I also couldn't help notice how similar it was to the luxurious accommodations afforded the unfortunate "subject one" whose lascivious videos I had watched. I wondered if she was here.

This next morning, I awoke around eight. At nine o'clock I was escorted to a spectacular banquet room filled with well-appointed tables laid out for the weekend's guests. There was a full breakfast buffet with everything anyone could possibly desire for the first meal of the day. I filled my plate, then looked for a seat near the rear of the hall, by the side doors that opened out to a terrace that ran the length of the hall.

That's when I noticed her. Wow! Apart from Ari, she was the most stunning young woman I'd ever seen. She looked at me and smiled, then turned away. There was something very familiar about her.

She was elegantly dressed for a casual breakfast, even one at the Citadel. She was adorned with exquisite jewelry that matched the intricately woven royal blue and gold of her attire. Her beautiful blond, loose curly hair was pulled up and perfectly coiffed. No girl I had ever seen looked like her. As well dressed as the women here were, none held a candle to her. I knew she was someone important. I could hardly take my eyes off her.

When I stopped gawking, I located a seat at one of the smaller tables, where no one was seated. Before I could sit down this entrancing beauty was standing beside me. "You must be Marcus Vincent Verigratu," she said in a distinctive aristocratic tenor.

I was speechless. I finally managed, "Just Mark, yes, and you are?"

She held out her hand. "Allow me to introduce myself. My name is Tabitha, Tabitha Norean."

I should have guessed, because I knew who ēlan Tabitha Norean was, even though I didn't keep up with New City nobility. I didn't recall ever seeing her image, but vaguely recognized her. Everyone in New City knew of her family. At the age of twenty, she was credited with orchestrating the successful implementation the latest version of LEOH. She was the main reason for this weekend's celebration. I should have hated her because of who she was. Yet she was so striking, such thoughts didn't occur to me, even if she was a notorious collaborator, not to mention Zack's infamous spider. I thought it odd that he wanted to meet her before he died.

Meeting her in person was intimidating. I wasn't sure if she intimidated me more because of who she was, or due to her exquisite beauty, which overwhelmed me. I had never even spoken with anyone within the sphere of this girl's family. "So, you are the guest of honor today?" I gestured with my hand. "It's a pleasure to meet you, ēlan. I've heard quite a bit about you and your achievements."

Tabitha shrugged off the compliment. "Just call me Tabitha. Yes, it's not every day a human is fantastically honored for pleasing the world's most tyrannical megalomaniac from another planet." Tabitha smiled at me and laughed. I managed a chuckle, uncertain how to respond. Her laugh was amazingly similar to Ari's. Even the way she smiled reminded me of Ari. I found myself comparing them.

Ari's beautiful brunette hair and gorgeous brown eyes were a direct contrast to Tabitha's loosely curled blond hair and bright blue eyes. Ari wore hardly any makeup; she didn't need any. This girl was made up like a fairytale princess. It wasn't gaudy; it was flawless. She wore an elegant sapphire and diamond tiara with a matching choker similarly festooned with jewels. Ari dressed well, but nothing like Tabitha. Ari wore little jewelry. This girl was ornamented with a fortunes' worth of diamonds, pearls, and precious gems. Besides rings and bracelets, she wore diamonds on her ankles and she had ribbons of sapphires and diamonds bedecking her slender upper arms. It wasn't over the top, it was just right for her. I was mesmerized.

I was silently contemplating my comparisons when Tabitha said, "Do you mind if I join you? There's no formality at breakfast, so I don't have to be seated at the head table with the aliens."

I didn't quite know how to react to her repeated alien references. I wasn't certain what they were, but I thought her comments that the Archon and his retinue were aliens was amusing. I felt guilty, probably because I was attracted to Tabitha. I nodded. "Be my guest." I realized it wasn't just her looks which made me think of Ari. It was also her mannerisms; the way she gestured, smiled, and laughed.

"I'd rather be anywhere than here in their lair," Tabitha said.

For an instant, she looked up toward the lights in the room. I froze with shock, seeing her in profile. She was a few years older now. Yet, even with her hair pulled up and makeup on, I knew why she looked familiar. I was looking at "subject one" and I realized only now how much her face kind of reminded me of Ari.

Granted, she was much better dressed. In fact, she *was* dressed, unlike in her candid performances. I hadn't seen a close-up image of the girl's face in the videos. Yet there was no doubt that this was the same girl. I was shocked and embarrassed for her and felt guilty for having looked at them. It was as if I had violated her perfect image. She had been drugged and hypnotized to perform for some bizarre purpose, probably without her knowledge. She had been abused and exploited. I felt sorry for her. I was ashamed for her. And I was ashamed of myself for knowing about it and for having kept a copy.

"What's wrong?" Tabitha said. "Are you off in another world? I'm sorry I mentioned aliens." I wasn't sure how to react, so I kept silent and smiled.

"There was considerable conversation around the Archon's dinner table last night about you," she said. "It's not every day one gets to meet the sole survivor of a failed CCD operation into the DZ. I was pleased to hear you would be joining us today. Since you missed dinner last night, I didn't have a chance to meet you then. I hope you don't mind if I impose upon you this morning. We have much to discuss." Tabitha declined a cup of coffee from a waiter, which I accepted.

"What do you mean, we have much to discuss?" I said, confused.

"I've reviewed your profile," she said matter-of-factly.

I wondered why an ēlan who was the head of the L2 development project had read my profile, and why she was even talking to me. If she only knew what I had recently viewed of her profile. I stared at Tabitha, waiting for her to continue. "Okay … I assume you're going to tell me why you reviewed my profile." She gave me a shush signal.

Moments later, a poached egg and grapefruit juice was brought to the table for her. A few guests came by. Tabitha introduced me to them; she seemed to know everyone. After each one walked away, she explained who they were. A female couple approached and asked if they could join us. Tabitha said, "No! We're catching up; *he* is an old boyfriend!" As they walked away, she shuddered. "Blah-ick, I can't stand those two fish lickers. That tall ēlan is four years older than me. At the Academy, she called me Tabithspla... I... shouldn't mention that."

Tabitha discreetly placed a small silk pouch on the table. When no one else appeared interested in us, she subtly indicated the pouch. "Don't mind my little bag. It will keep us from being overheard and scramble the relay of any spybots, but you know about those."

She gently tugged at her left earring. "If I keep this on, they will detect the localized interference, and by 'they' I mean just about anything here. For security purposes, the Archon's citadels are covered with surveillance and detection devices which far exceed those in any normal environment."

If you only knew, I thought.

After a few minutes, we finished eating. I started to ask Tabitha a question as I placed my napkin next to my plate. A server immediately appeared to clear our plates. Another one refilled my coffee. Tabitha waived them away, after saying something, then tugged at her earring again. "Don't say anything confidential unless I nod and touch my left earring." I could tell she was turning the device on the table on and off, so only bits our conversation would be picked up.

Tabitha got right to the point. "You have them all stumped, my friend," she said. "They don't know what to do with you. I, on the other hand, know all about you. There is no need to put up any kind of pretense with me, about what you've been up to ... since a week ago last Thursday, around this exact time."

I kept quiet since Tabitha hadn't given me a signal to respond. She, on the other hand, continued without missing a beat. "They are not supposed to be surveilling us, but I've learned it's best not to trust these aliens, or whatever they are, especially here. I'm talking about the Archon and his inner circle of oddly named cronies, which always end with an el, al, il, or something. This includes that snake Rogan, whose actual name is Larens Aroganceal and Talen Place who is really Tal Complaceal. They pretentiously call each other lord and prince and other nonsense. I'm supposed to befriend you for the Archon."

I just sat there blinking stupidly while admiring her.

"You are going to meet him, and he will attempt to read you. Let me warn you, he is a highly adept clarion. He can also be a total doofus. It means he can look beyond what you are saying and figure out what you are unwilling to say. Not the doofus part, the clarion part. That pointy-headed reptile Pythorael is the same. He is far more devious than the Archon is intelligent."

Tabitha spoke so fast I could hardly keep up. She gave the signal indicating I could respond. "What do you mean you are supposed to befriend me, and what is a clarion?"

Tabitha laughed. After saying something off topic, she replied, "I told you, it's just a skill, consider it to be like Phencol without the sickening side effects." She abruptly stood and asked me to accompany her. She smoothly picked up the tiny pouch from the table and secreted it away. I walked with her out to the wide terrace. Its two stairways, on either side of the terrace, led down to a different garden than the one my room overlooked.

Tabitha affectionately took me by the arm. This was too close for comfort. She said, "It's best we keep moving while we talk. This way our PCDs won't synchronize immediately, nor will LEOH register the temporary interference from my little device on any nearby surveillance collection nodes. You should ask me the obvious question: Why am I being asked to 'befriend,' or rather spy on you? Don't be nervous, I'm not going to try to seduce you."

"That possibility did occur to me."

"I know you're married. I'd hate to break up a happy marriage."

I shook my head. "I'm not referring to being seduced. Why would the Archon send someone like you to spy on someone like me? Why are you even talking to me? You're the Norean ēlan and in charge L2. That's beyond absurd."

Tabitha giggled. "My thoughts precisely; spying is such a profane, lowlife profession. Yet here I am. I've been reduced to the mundane reality of becoming a secret agent for a madman who isn't human. He thinks my talents will be useful in discovering what I already know about you, or perhaps more. I guess I'm more of a double agent, or a triple agent, since I'm conducting espionage on two aliens and you. Then there's the odious system I built, which I also must confront. I have such a difficult life."

"I imagine you have it rough," I said. "Do they think you will have more success than the Ministry at getting me to admit I've done something subversive and betray my supposed co-conspirators … to you of all people? My wife's great-grandfather referred to you as a spider; he said LEOH is your web." I laughed, incredulous. "What a ridiculous plan. Were I involved in anything, and I'm not, I wouldn't tell you. This is the most flawed infiltration scheme ever concocted."

Tabitha laughed. "Exactly; it's crazy. I won't dignify the spider comment. You should never tell a clarion something like that. We tend to explore tangents relentlessly.

"Anyway, am I right?" she continued. "They, of course, would know you would be suspicious of me. Thus, even if I tried to further convince you I'd like to help you, by pretending to keep our conversation quiet, to find out what you stole, who helped you steal it, and to whom you intend to give it, then maybe you would trust me. Then again, not a chance. They aren't that stupid. This is a much subtler game. I would, of course, have to convince you I can help—or, I could seduce you."

"Why would I need your help?" I said, ignoring the seduction comment.

Tabitha barged on. "To do this, I would, necessarily, have to prove it to you. In other words, they expect me to help you and pretend I am in league with you, regardless of whether I actually am. There you have it. You have no reason to trust me. I fully expect you not to trust me. On the other hand, it's in your best interest to do so, in case I am someone you can trust, which I am. Besides, you must trust me, since I can save your life. I'll help you if you will trust me. I already know everything about you, anyway, trust me. Did I use the word 'trust' far too many times? I could have said that a little more coherently. I think you get the point. And yes, I am a spider, but I'm not trying to catch bugs. Rather, I intend to catch two snakes in my web. I was only kidding about seducing you."

I was befuddled. Yet what this strange girl had said oddly made sense. "That's almost exactly what Zack said. I think he used the term serpent, not snake. Strangely enough, he said he likes spiders for this reason, and wants to meet you. This keeps getting weirder."

Tabitha looked at me curiously. "Wow, something else you shouldn't tell to a clarion. You're a horrible spy. You just admitted everything and didn't realize it. Besides, I've already met Zachariah Waters. I'm curious about him."

"I'm not a spy," I objected. "Wait—you've met Zack? Anyway, the rest of whatever you said makes no sense. I've admitted nothing. It was interesting talking with you. I don't think anyone has ever been spied on in such a useless, fascinating way."

"What I said made perfect sense! I met Zachariah when I was a little girl," Tabitha said. "He was strange. I like him now, perhaps because of the spider comment. I didn't like him then, but now my mind is on overload with what you've told me."

Tabitha laughed even harder. She had a bizarre sense of humor and was good at amusing herself. Her complex, yet oddly friendly personality bordered on manic insanity.

Tabitha said, "I realize this exercise may seem pointless, perhaps even confusing, but you know how precisely correct I am. I hope you don't lie to your cute wife so much. When you think about it, it's puzzling to be confronted by someone who knows more about what you're up to than you do yourself. I have no need to interrogate you or attempt to entrap you into saying anything. You will play this game with me because your life, our lives, and the lives of everyone you know—or don't know—for that matter, depend on it. Let's approach this a different way. Good grief, I need to come up with a better expression. I'm starting to hate any phrase with the words 'game' and 'play' together. This is not a game at all."

Tabatha stopped at the edge of a tiny pond that was filled with beautifully colored fish. She turned to me. "You can dispense with the denials, Mark. They know you were the one who used ghosted access codes and an MDC to sneak classified data out of the NCGD. What were you thinking trying to download so much data so quickly? I bet a cute girl distracted you and made you forget you were running a dozen formulations simultaneously on a hyper-speed tri-con VTH splitter? They've searched your apartment three times and found nothing. Not to mention that you avoided succumbing to two chemical interrogations. Do you keep an antidote you can self-administer? That's very dangerous; you could kill yourself. Before you respond, let me tell you what else I know."

As we walked around the pond, Tabitha took the next five minutes to catalogue exactly what data I had stolen. She summarized everything stored in my secreted vault, much of which I was not aware. She even assumed I had a hidden vault. Thankfully, she didn't mention the embarrassing information I had about her I was aware of, that she hopefully wasn't.

Tabitha even speculated that Zack or my wife were the real culprits behind my espionage. We walked back toward the terrace. I was silent, refusing to admit to anything.

Tabitha relentlessly continued, "It's not often a thief is confronted with the exact details of what he stole, the means by which he stole it, and the evidence to prove it, then still deny it. But it doesn't matter. My clarification is, you have a gullible discernment and you've admitted your crimes to people you should not have. They suspect you had help getting out of the DZ09, probably by the same people they believe you are working with, the ones who helped you steal the data. I think it's far less complex than this for you."

"You talk so fast you are seriously giving me a painful headache," I said.

"Hmph ... Mark, there are far too many coincidences and discrepancies in your genetic profile to make this appear to be a conspiracy you are managing. It also goes way too far back for you to be the mastermind behind it. Yet I should warn you, when they do discover who you are, they will not hesitate to kill you."

"What is gullible discernment and why would you know anything about my genetic profile?"

Tabitha stopped. She looked me in the eyes. "Waters, that *is* your real last name. Your father was adopted, even though your grandfather changed his name. He was the son of Zachariah Water's brother. It's kind of creepy and weird that you recently married your great-grandfather's brother's eighteen-year-old great-granddaughter. You're like a third of her life older than her. You must really like younger girls who are related to you since you started dating her when she was sixteen. What girl gets married at eighteen? Did you impregnate your own cousin? I have the whole matter sorted out. I don't need your confession. The good news for you is, the Ministry doesn't know anything about this, and neither does the Archon. I mean, they know you married little Ariel. They just don't know your incestuous family connection to her and Zachariah Waters. By the way, when I say little, I'm not referring to her breasts, just her super young age ... at the time you started dating. It's shameful, really. Although, she did look well endowed, even at sixteen."

Before I could protest, Tabitha said, "They don't know for absolute certain you stole the data, nor do they know exactly what you stole. They only know that numerous payloads requiring a maximum SADEX score were downloaded. I have already proved to you that I do know all this. Just as I traced the ghosted access codes to the VTH you used, the port at your desk, and the exact time you logged in and out that day. Would you like me to tell you the codes you used?" She rolled one off by memory, including the hexadecimal passkey. "Have I left anything out about which you would like to elaborate?"

"What you just said about Ari is outrageous and unjustified ..." I started to argue.

"The pedophile part or incest part? Tabitha said. "What I don't quite understand yet is why or how there are so many ghosted access infiltrations into the system to keep you and your wife's identities secret, and those of many others as well. It may take some time for me to sort it out. I read extremely fast. I also never forget anything, which is not always good. Unfortunately, my brain doesn't have a delete function. I wish it did, so I could delete the memories of my ... never mind."

I listened in stunned silence. *Who is this crazy girl?*

Tabitha wasn't finished. "Don't get me wrong, they suspected you were the culprit until I stopped them. Now, I'm in charge of investigating you! They were reformulating all the matrixes related to the coincidences of your association with Zachariah Waters. I hope to meet him again one day, especially because of the spider comment, and your wife. Mostly, for the last few days, I have been looking forward to meeting you. What matters is this: You can confide in me, Mark."

We had arrived back at the stairs leading up to the terrace. I remained silent, unable to grasp everything she had said.

Tabitha continued, "You must be curious as to how I discovered what I know. Let's just say, I found a way to see what both LEOH and the Ministry can't see. I can rationalize the irrational, while I sort out both logical and illogical considerations. Obscure truth is my specialty."

"You've nothing to say?" Tabitha said when I didn't respond. She continued, "The other morning, Dalen Pythorael came to my house. He is likewise seeking his own advantage against the Archon. Pythorael wants to thwart the Archon's plans. He's confident I won't betray him; so confident, in fact, he believes I will ultimately help him. One might say I am between two rocks, as this situation concerns my dealings with these two snakes. At the same time, I am playing with fire in my role of trying to pry the organizational secrets of New City's enemies from you. I swear if someone calls it a game, I am going to damage something. For good reason, the director believes I will betray the Archon in order to genuinely help him and help you. After all, they know I know, and they know, whoever stole their secrets, also knows what the Archon is up to. But who cares, what everyone in the whole world should be freaked out about is the fact they are actual aliens in clone bodies, maybe even cyborgs. That alone should be enough for you to believe I would never betray you to either of them. I don't choose aliens over humans."

"Sure, you only develop the systems to allow them to control us," I retorted. "Otherwise, I see absolutely no conflict of interest in your declaration of sides, not to mention, you're a Norean ēlan."

"You're a simpleton! Don't you realize a sword has two edges?"

"Unless it has only one," I said. "You should try a different analogy."

"That was an implied metaphor and you ruined it! I may start to dislike you."

I needed to rest after listening to Tabitha. She talked so fast her words were like a relentless torrent of information pouring out of her mouth. Yet how could I deny what she was saying, when she was right about everything, at least the part I could understand. I asked the most stupid question I could come up with in response to everything Tabitha said: "Do you really believe they are aliens?"

She looked at me quizzically. "Really, that's it? Have you looked at the data you stole? Oh my God, what human would think of those things and plan all that? Humans don't live very long. If they did, they certainly wouldn't look the same age today as they did a hundred years ago."

"I don't know what stolen data you're talking about."

Tabitha glared at me with an expression of shocked certainty. She was like a mother who'd caught her child with one hand in the cookie jar as he tried to deny it with a crumb-caked mouth and a cookie in his other hand.

"Mark, seriously, you have to come to terms with this. You are starting to exhibit disturbing signs of a pathological inability to recognize reality." She waved her hands in my face and put her hands over her lips. "Were you hypnotized? Did that old fart hypnotize you? Did he tell you you're related to him and you married your own cousin? He sent her after you, didn't he? He sent his own great-granddaughter to seduce her cousin, so you would impregnant her and then he hypnotized you.

Maybe *she* hypnotized you. Is she a witch? Does she smolder when she gets wet, play with potions or crystals, and exhibit mystical powers?"

I looked at Tabitha indignantly. "She's a distant cousin and no, she's not a witch. She's the most beautiful, wonderful, kind person I know and she … I think it's time for me to leave."

Tabitha grabbed me. "Aha! I am telling you, you can't trust me, even though you can. I am the key to destroy the means by which I was able to discover what I know. Don't tell me you haven't considered how you could destroy LEOH yourself? You are probably regretting ever coming to work for the Ministry. Yet you know you have a job to do, and fortunately for you, I am the means to do what you can't possibly do without me." She said this with absolute confidence.

I thought I should give up trying to deny anything to this scary girl. Yet instead of boldly asking for Tabitha's help as I had with the ATO, I said, "I'm not sure if talking with you is more difficult than what I've been through recently, but it's a close call."

Tabitha pouted. She said, "What do you think you can do without me? I told you I'm choosing sides. Since no one has ever been on my side, I might as well help you, even though you are clearly an insane liar. Nobody can lie while under Phencol, except you did. That's a true gift, unless you had an antidote. Still, how did you get it out of the NCGD? I probably don't want to know where you put it. If old Zack told you Ariel is your cousin, then he told you everything else. After what he said to me when I was a little girl, I have to meet him again. I don't want to freak you out, but are her breasts real? I have a legitimate reason for asking."

"I think I am well past the point of being freaked out," I said.

"Mark, I am trying to help you. I can defeat these beings. These aliens are a strange crowd. They also have a dark secret. I've not yet fully clarified it, other than I am certain they sense they are running out of time. Pythorael mentioned something written in an ancient paradox; something which drives them. The good news is, for you, me, and in fact, all humans, they are helpless without us. There are very few of them. All they really have in their arsenal to control humanity is LEOH and other stupid humans. Now I control LEOH! 'Élan Tabitha controls LEOH'—run for your lives!"

She paused. "At least, I control it except for the static code sequence algorithm, which ... anyway, I will control it entirely once I figure out a way to deal with that little puzzle and the Archon's implant. This just proves how helpless they are. They need technology—and people like me. They are helpless and thus totally screwed!"

There was a long pause in Tabitha's ranting monologue as we circled back around the pond. We walked in silence until we once again reached the stairs. We walked up to the terrace level to the double doors that led inside. Tabitha sighed as she studied my reaction, then smiled at me. I stared at our reflection in the doors' glass panels. I was once again amazed at how beautiful this strange and terrifyingly insightful young woman was. I turned to her. "Tabitha, if you only knew what I've been through in the last week ... I need to think about things."

Tabitha replied, "You'd probably like to get out of New City and leave all this intrigue behind you. Am I right?" We walked inside to stroll around the gallery.

I was exasperated. "I see there's no point lying to you. Until now, I'd never heard of a clarion, and I still don't know what it is. You are one intimidating, scary girl. It's also freaking me out that you remind me of Ari." I let my emotions pour out. "Yes, I want nothing more than to get out of New City with Ari. I don't know how you know what you know, but if you truly understood me, you'd know I'm caught up in something I never wanted to be involved in."

"I think I've proved that you can't lie to me," Tabitha said. "It's funny that I remind you of your wife. Apart from her obvious chest enhancement ..."

"Look, I'm tired, and over the last three days I've seen more people die than I'd ever imagined or want to see again. The worst part is that I killed most of them. I did it to help people on their way to a new place to live, away from New City. They were being rescued by an organization I know nothing about and with which I have nothing to do. If they could help me and Ari get out of this city, I'd jump at the chance. If I could help them, I would. I don't know how to contact them or how they infiltrate the system to help people. I wish I'd never gotten involved in this. At the same time, I can't ignore what I know now."

"Wow, you really don't know what to never reveal to a clarion, and you're a terrible spy," Tabitha said. "I know exactly how they get into the system. They do it the same way you got behind the T-Alpha SADEX firewall."

"*I'm* a terrible spy?" I said. "You're the one supposed to be spying on me. It took you one minute to admit it. Then you downloaded my family tree and told me what I did and and how I did it. What's left of any edifice of subterfuge between us is an exposed smoldering ruin in your mind."

"Fair point. It actually took me nine minutes. Give me some credit. Also, you've no idea what's in my mind concerning weird things about you."

We continued to walk around one of the many galleries filled with priceless sculpture and artwork. I started to notice occult symbols and esoteric emblems everywhere. It was like a museum of shrines shrouded with mysterious pictographs intended to enlighten or reveal secret, hidden knowledge. Tabitha was strangely silent. She too seemed to be studying the ubiquitous inscriptions, signs, and pictures we passed.

I broke the silence. "I don't know anything about you. I have no reason to trust you. When you said I have gullible discernment, what did you mean?"

Tabitha laughed. "A clarion is trained to determine the logical outcomes, as well as the causal conditions necessary for a given set of facts and circumstances to be true. Mark, no one can do what you've done and escape a telemetry facility overrun by hostile forces without having received help. Help is not given freely by New City's enemies unless something is offered in return."

"And your point?" I said.

"When the one in need of help is perceived to be an enemy, what he offers in return must be substantial, even if it's intangible. The 4UB6 facility was not overrun by a force of hostile guerrillas intent on destroying it. It had to be destroyed from the inside. Only a highly skilled, sophisticated organization that knows about New City's security access could break in. I assume you must have convinced those people you could help them, in return for them helping you escape. You were therefore both gullible and discerning in those to whom you confided your theft, or convinced them you had something in common. Maybe they had the technology you used to steal data from LEOH and you recognized it. I could disclose more of my clarification to you, but that's the gist of it."

I raised my eyebrows in bewildered admiration. I rubbed my hands down the length of my face, then over my lips. "How do you know I received any help at all? I haven't told anyone how I made it out of there."

"Everybody on your team died except you. Do you really think I believe you managed to get away by yourself? I assume you encountered the people who broke into that station and *they* didn't kill your team. Was one of them a pretty girl? I figured they helped you because you wanted to help them. Maybe you thought of them as the enemy of your enemy."

"You are truly a scary, smart person," I said.

"How pretty was the girl?" she said. "This organization must have the same type of ghosted access codes you used. At some point, assuming you decide you can trust me, even though you shouldn't, despite the fact that you can, you will have to tell me everything. We don't have much time left. You have to meet the Archon soon. I have to ... I have things to do a girl needs to do."

"Can I walk you to wherever you need to go?"

"I just need to know if you trust me enough to allow me to help you."

"I will give it my full consideration. But how do you learn to become a clarion?" I said when we arrived at the lift.

Tabitha smiled. "I think it's natural. You may even be one. Officially, one can only call themselves a clarion with a certification from the Clarion Academy of Adept Sciences." She paused. "I never received a certificate from the school. I was 'graduated' after I moved on to study molecular formulation. There was sort of an incident or a thousand, so

I left school at fifteen, before I was officially initiated. It's a total load of mystical hogwash anyway."

"An incident or a thousand, what does that mean?"

"Way too many! It's a six-year program, although my experience was considerably abbreviated. Mostly kids from wealthy families attend. They also take a few peasants who qualify. Only about one in a thousand applicants are accepted. They teach a bunch of numinous mumbo jumbo. That's where I was introduced to my 'gift' and, unfortunately, a few other things a twelve-year-old girl shouldn't … at least at that age. The place is obsessed with … anyway, I left after three years. Let's say it's a haven for creepy girls and other perverts. They hypnotize kids and give them hallucinogenic drugs to make them … do things. They also have secret initiations. Kids have to swear not to reveal them. If I talk about it, I have to kill people."

"You don't have to talk about it," I said.

"I had a friend there, for a while," Tabitha confided. "He said he stayed as long he did to protect me. Nevertheless, I learned the basics of the art. Over the years, I developed and honed most of the skills and acuity necessary to apply it, absent the esoteric, creepy, predator aspects. I graduated because I scored exceptionally high on the senior aptitude test. My father made certain his little ēlan could say she was a graduate of the vaunted Clarion Academy, since his ēlar, my brother Stanley, is such low achieving wanker. He even flunked out of a school for rich nerf-heads."

"It must have been horrifying for a girl," I said sympathetically. I wondered what this might have to do with her "subject one" experience and the Archon's obsession with her.

Tabitha said, "Underneath the façade of this wholesome city is a mania for abusing children with mind experiments, drugs, and bizarre mystical arts. It's sick. You should look more closely at the data you stole, Mark. You will see things that will shock you!"

No shit … if you only knew.

There were tears in her eyes. "You have no idea what it was like growing up as a Norean. Your father would have never made you go through rituals or swear oaths to aliens when you were a child. Mine did! My mother ignored me my entire life. I have no one in this world, except myself, Julian, my valet, and one other person. I know he loves me and he doesn't ..." Tabitha stopped and composed herself. "I don't know if he loves me. He said he did. I hope he does, but he still treats me like a little girl."

We walked up the wide stairs leading to my suite. We stopped when we reached the second level. "I'm supposed to introduce you to the Archon a half hour before the luncheon banquet," Tabitha said. "Be very careful when you talk to him or Pythorael. Trust neither of them and don't look directly into their eyes for long or they can hypnotize you." Tabitha hugged me, then lightly kissed me on the lips. As she walked away, I wondered if this was something ēlans normally did with people they'd just met.

* * * *

Back in my room, I went over my conversation with Tabitha. I wondered how Zack would react to these revelations: *Oh, I met the spider. She has a bizarre personality and talks faster than I can think. By the way, she figured out, on her own, our entire family history, everything I stole, and how I did it. Did I mention she was ordered to spy on me by the Archon, and she's insanely brilliant? Don't worry, she said I can't trust her, then said I should trust her, anyway. As a side note, your formulations captured three years of highly classified videos of her while she was hypnotized and naked.* I couldn't tell Zack about that.

Then there was that fact that Tabitha reminded me of Ari ... the way she talked and her facial expressions. Unrelated people can look alike, but not accompanied by identical mannerisms, the way they laugh, their smile, and their voice inflections. When I say Tabitha talked like Ari ... if Ari talked ten times faster than normal and added a huge dose of aristocratic arrogance, as well as being an annoying right about everything. Come to think of it, Ari is usually right about everything.

* * * *

While I waited in my room, I turned on the New City News Service—and saw a shocking story. That morning, one criminal fugitive had been killed and another captured in a pre-dawn raid a couple of hundred kilometers south of SG2. Kirk Daniels and Gilliard McCaughey were named as allegedly wanted in connection with a corruption scandal. They'd been smuggled out of the city by bribing military officials. Kirk and Gil's faces were displayed side by side. Most of the story was fabricated. I knew the NCNS wouldn't mention Bob, or anyone else in the ATO, if they'd captured them. I felt panicky. Bob knew everything about Zack, me, and probably Ari.

I was about to head downstairs to meet Tabitha in the hall when my new PCD pinged. It was Ari. I authorized the voice dialogue. She was distraught; she had just heard from Zack's doctor. He had been taken to the medical center in Park Central after his nurse discovered him face down on the floor. She said she was taking the next FRS home. Could I join her? Ari knew I was at the Citadel. "I have one thing I must do here before I leave," I said. "I'll meet you there as soon as I can."

Ari was crying. "What do you have to do?"

"I have a meeting with the Archon in a few minutes. Afterward, I'll make my excuses and leave. I promise I'll be on the next FRS to Park Central. You are not going to believe what I've been through and who I just met …"

CHAPTER 24

THE ARCHON

Tabitha greeted me with another quick kiss on the lips, as if this was normal. I imagined cold viruses must spread rampantly among the nobility if this was their standard greeting. She looked more stunning than before. She had changed clothes, although I couldn't imagine why she'd needed to. She escorted me through a labyrinth of wide halls and doors to an immense circular library lined with three floors of books.

We didn't speak, as she had given me a shush signal. Within moments of our arrival, a door opened on the opposite side of the room. The Archon emerged with two attendants, who immediately turned and exited. In person, he looked like most of the images I recalled. An extraordinarily handsome man with dark hair and strikingly sharp features, he had intense grayish-blue eyes that seemed to stare right through one.

He spoke as he approached. "Please have a seat Mr. Verigratu, or may I call you Mark?" He shook my hand and gestured to one of the large leather upholstered chairs. "I understand you met the talented ēlan, Tabitha Norean. I hope you two had an opportunity to get acquainted?"

"Yes, we had breakfast together. It's an honor to meet you," I said in an obligatory fashion.

He replied, "Please, call me Devan, that's what ēlan Norean, or rather, Tabitha calls me, or something insulting. At least she does when she is annoyed with me, which is often." He smiled at Tabitha. It was obvious he was genuinely fond of her. Yet his mistreatment of her made me hate him. Then, of course, there were all the horrific things he was doing and planned to do to humanity. He sounded so suave and sure of himself. It made me feel sick to be around him.

A bit of small talk consumed a few minutes. I was beginning to think this was going to be a meet-and-greet with the leader of the world, no less. I kept glancing over at Tabitha, trying to avoid direct eye contact with the Archon for more than a second or two, based on her advice. I wanted to get out of there to meet Ari and visit Zack. I was terrified at the thought of him dying and leaving us to fend for ourselves with everything he had gotten us wrapped up in. It was a selfish thought. It dawned on me I was hardly paying attention to what the Archon was saying.

He was speaking directly to me and had noticed I wasn't listening. He cleared his throat loudly. "As I was just saying, I am shocked at what happened in the DZ this week. The loss of Merrick Taylor and your operations team is a tragedy. I am anxious to learn how you managed to escape—and how you made your way back to New City alone."

I gave him my somewhat truncated version of the events in the DZ. He peppered me with questions, especially about the fugitives I encountered, but didn't mention their capture.

After I finished my explanation he said, "I didn't want to make your acquaintance merely to discuss your recent adventures in the DZ. I also have some concerns about your entanglements with Ministry security. I have a few questions I would like to ask you about the matter of this data theft, to set my mind at ease ..."

* * * *

Twenty minutes later, as he watched Mark leave, the Archon turned to Tabitha, who was staring at him angrily. Once the door to the library closed, he said, "I am sure you would like to hear my assessment before you divulge your own calculations. In any case, you will need to convince him it's in his best interest to come work for me."

Tabitha raised her eyebrows. "Of course, Devan, however, if you wish to hear a snippet of my assessment first, I'm more than willing to give it. I would hate to taint your insights with my own clarification. Here's a highlight: You're an idiot! A classic cartoon character comes to mind. I thought I was running this investigation. You were supposed to read him, not interrogate him in front of me. Then you offer him a job? After what he's been through on his DZ trip to hell and his tender treatment at the hands of Rogan, obviously, offering him a job is completely sane. After the way you questioned him, I'm sure he'd love it, despite the fact he told you, NO! At least you let him leave so he could go home to see his wife and to be with her great-grandfather, who probably just dropped dead."

He sat back and smiled. "Besides your biting insults, that's what I like about you: You think you might have an influence on my own assessment. You freely admit it. You're not even smug about it. You simply believe you're always right."

"You sabotaged my investigation before it got started," Tabitha complained.

The Archon ignored her comment. "I will say, you either managed to coach him this morning in such a way as to mirror your clarifications perfectly, or your prior assessment was uncannily accurate. I think Mr. Verigratu has no reason to trust you in either case, nor would he be able to be so readily coached on the questions I posed to him. Perhaps his empathy for those defectors is understandable. I do regret he no longer has any ambition to serve in the prestigious CCD because he believes he has been harshly mistreated. He is clearly not a man given over to excessive ambition. I am not sure he can be trusted as such men have a tendency toward subversive ideology."

The Archon lit a cigar and puffed at it repeatedly. "There is another possibility. He could be lying about some matters without being entirely deceptive, and truthful about many things without disclosing anything useful. I think it unlikely he is being used or blindly being assisted by someone. I need to know if he is, in fact, in possession of the stolen data.

What does he intend to do with it? If he has the data and doesn't know it, he must be a fool."

"You could have tortured him with that cigar, Blofeld. I'm ready to spill my guts now, or my breakfast."

The Archon chuckled, "As you said, no one at his level should be able to pull this off. And no novice operative could manipulate our interrogations—with or without Phencol. Yet I find it disingenuous of you to speculate that he may be a victim of extraordinary circumstances. You're too talented for this to be your conclusion. Was there anything in his answers just now that give you cause to change your original clarification?"

Tabitha tried to keep from coughing as the Archon's cigar smoke wafted in her direction. "I was hoping to talk with him more than during breakfast. I thought I was supposed to befriend him, not interrogate him. Now you've have made it appear that I was trying to assess his guilt or innocence. Is this all you intended for me to do to infiltrate his conspiracy? If you still believe there is one to be infiltrated this strategy has been shredded. What little trust I may have garnered with him is now in tatters. Besides, I would have to meet this Zachariah Waters, if he hasn't died." She sniffed at her clothes, "I'm going to have to have Julian wash my hair and I need to change my clothes again. I smell like a hookah lounge."

The Archon sneered at her. "Did you read Mark at all or was I the only one in the room?"

Tabitha shot back, "Look, Inspector Clouseau, your ridiculous job offer did not convince him he's no longer a suspect. You should not have had this interview. This attempt to ingratiate yourself to him by offering him a position in the NCIC was worse than your plan to have me, an élan in charge of the L2 development, befriend him here at snoop central. Obviously, there's nothing for him to be suspicious about any of this, provided he's a complete idiot."

The Archon began to laugh. "I convinced him that I believe he is innocent."

Tabitha raised her eyebrows. "No, you didn't! A vampire doesn't invite people to his spooky castle to convince someone he is not going … on second thought, maybe they do. Anyway, he doesn't trust *us*. Tell me, Devan, what did you expect to achieve from this interview?"

The Archon replied, "I am not ignorant that you would try to gain his trust by convincing him you are willing to help him, even while he is under suspicion. This would naturally imply you told him you were there to befriend him for the purpose of spying on him on my behalf, and you are willing to betray my trust."

Tabitha smiled at her ability to confound the Archon. "I already told you I would!" she said. "He would have suspected this is precisely what I'd do, if this were the case. I must prove to them I'm your worst enemy. If you want me to bring them to you, they must be certain I am willing to join their cause at my own peril."

The Archon suddenly doubted his own clarity. "Your initial assessment was less forthcoming than this. Is there something you aren't telling me?"

Tabitha nodded. "Yes! You're like a blind dog in a meat house when it comes to intelligence. I won't disclose every detail of my methods to accomplish your ends. Oh, and as for Pythorael, he is trying to intimidate me to work against you."

The Archon studied Tabitha momentarily. "I will deal with Pythorael."

"I mention him because we need to establish broader protocols for exactly what is covered under the umbrella of this investigation," Tabitha said. "I can't have Pythorael and his dirt diggers undermining me by running parallel investigations on me, anyone named Waters, or anyone related to Zach Waters or Mark Verigratu. I insist on a quarantine on all official directives with these names, so they will be transferred to your jurisdiction. Then they'll be officially assigned to me. I don't want them under the CCD or the Ministry, including the GIA, until my investigation is complete. This is highly sensitive. All Ministry divisions need to be kept out of this."

"Agreed. Draft the investigation protocol and I'll authorize it," the Archon said. "Having said that, you are not going to be running the entire Ministry as an adjunct to this investigation. And the name Waters is associated with Class 1 dissidents. You cannot permanently have jurisdiction over it."

Tabitha coughed. "I'm going to throw up on you, Baby Herman, if you don't stop smoking that turd! Devan, you have a serious problem. Your Ministry director is working against you. He has disclosed things to me in an attempt to make me uncomfortable around you, as if what you are smoking wasn't enough. He is trying to drive a wedge between us."

The Archon said solemnly, "My dear, you are the key to my own legacy of immortality. You may have been born to be an ēlan of New City, yet I will ultimately transform you into the most powerful queen the world has ever witnessed. There are prophecies about you which must be fulfilled. The glories you can conceive of now and the gifts you think you have now will pale in comparison to what you will become with me. You were promised to me."

Tabitha choked as the Archon stared at her intently. "I don't care if I was promised to you. Consider the promise broken! Only I can promise me to anyone. You have chosen the wrong girl to bestow your gifts upon. Everyone pretends your kind are merely exceptional men. I have my own theories about what you are and what you are able to offer. Unless you tell me everything, do not promise me anything."

"I am a man with a body of flesh and blood. You are a beautiful woman," the Archon said.

Tabitha scoffed. "I'm not one of your courtiers or ladies vying for your affection. I'm certainly not some arranged bride who is awed by you. Let's keep our relationship entirely professional!"

The Archon continued to study her. Tabitha said, "Look, Yosemite Sam, stop blowing up my investigation. Give me free reign with Mark Verigratu. Keep Pythorael and his Ministry hounds off my back by authorizing the investigation protocol! If there is something here, I will uncover it. If Mark or Zachariah Waters have a connection to any organization, I will discover it. If there is a city hidden somewhere in the vastness of the DZ, I will find it. Continue to grant me whatever I need to succeed. Don't interfere, as this could cause me to fail. Also: No more meetings with my target!"

CHAPTER 25

THE CONNECTION

The light in Bob's face was blinding, and he was beginning to feel the effects of the drug that had been administered to him. His head was spinning and all he could consider was his own shame. He had failed to take his own life, just as every Tracer was obligated to under oath.

There were two new men in the room; they hadn't been there during his initial questioning. He sputtered, coughed, and started to feel nauseated. His chest wound ached. A cool rag was used to wipe his face. Finally, he was allowed a long drink of cool water. They had not tortured him yet, but he was certain it was only a matter of time before they resorted to it, if only for the mere pleasure of it. The effects of the potent truth serum once again started to overtake his mind.

One of the new men sat down opposite him. "Are you able to understand me?"

Bob nodded yes.

Pythorael continued, "What is your real name, including your surname?"

Bob struggled against the drug controlling his mind. "My name is... Jonas Peres," he lied.

Pythorael glared at him. "What is your father's name?

Again, Bob was finding it nearly impossible to resist the drug, but he managed to. "His name is Tony."

"What's the name of your organization?"

Bob's resistance was slipping away. He felt compelled to answer, to tell the man whatever he wanted to know. After all, he had no reason to resist. He blearily conceded, "We call ourselves Tracers or ATO."

Pythorael grimaced. "Where were you taking the dissidents we recovered?"

"I was taking them to Cardwide, then to Tidewater."

"Where were they being taken from there?"

Bob answered honestly, "The next leg in the south, where the dead river runs into the sea, is where they go from Tidewater. That's not my job. I only get them to Tidewater."

Pythorael learned forward. "Where were they going to take them from Tidewater?"

"I don't know. They don't tell me anything."

Although the captive was clearly under the effects of the truth drug, Pythorael could sense the man's high resistance to it. He ordered the attendant to increase the dosage. Bob hardly felt the sting of the second needle.

Minutes later, Pythorael continued his questioning. "I want to ask you about the man who helped you at the transit camp the day you were attacked. Did he tell you his name?"

Bob had to concentrate because his head was spinning. "He said his name was Mark something. I was wounded. I don't remember anything about the attack."

"Tell me how he became involved with your party?" Pythorael insisted.

"He just showed up," Bob said. "They told me afterward that he managed to kill the bounty hunters who tracked us a day out from Silver."

"Is he connected to your organization?"

Bob shook his head, becoming more disoriented, "No, he'd never heard of us before ..."

"He claims your group helped him return to New City. Why?"

Bob laughed deliriously. "That's a stupid question. He saved our lives, while risking his own. Of course, we helped him. People do this sort of thing for each other."

"Did he tell you how he managed to escape from the 4UB6 telemetry station? If so, what did he tell you? Did anyone help him?"

"Yes, he encountered two people from our organization. They helped him escape, just before it was destroyed by the GS. I told him he was lucky they didn't kill him," Bob replied.

"What else did he say? What were their names?

Bob was beginning to feel sick. He started to convulse. The attendant cautioned, "Director, we cannot continue if he becomes unconscious due to an overdose. We may have administered too much."

Pythorael demanded, "Answer the question!"

Bob stuttered, "He told me he threatened them and forced them to help him."

"Tell me their real names."

"Kalina Savadnetski and Boris something," Bob said. "I think it is Jovanos or Joranos.

"What is their role in your organization?"

Bob shook his head. "He's a tech. She runs transit operations in the DZ."

More questions revealed Bob knew little about ATO technological capabilities.

Pythorael focused on another line of questioning. "Is there anyone inside New City who provides your organization with intelligence or technology, or who has helped your organization in the past?"

"Sure, there are lots of people. I don't deal with any of them. It's not my job."

"Do you know any of their names?"

Bob began to struggle; he became agitated. "I can't ... They don't use real names."

"Try to remember a name!" Pythorael shouted. "Give me a name!"

Bob felt extremely sick. "Wasser, there was a man named Jack Wasser, a long time ago." His head began to pound, his eyes grew dim, and he lost consciousness.

The medical attendant intervened. "He was struggling to resist the effects. I strongly recommend allowing him regain consciousness on his own, rather than administering the counter meds to awaken him. Otherwise he may go into cardiac arrest. His heart rate is already erratic."

Pythorael turned toward Rogan, who had been standing beside him. He spoke softly. "I want to question him again first thing tomorrow morning. Have a utilization matrix ran on all the names he just mentioned; Jack Wasser, Kalina, and Boris whatever, as well as Jonas and Tony Peres. Prepare an updated matrix on his responses."

The two men strode out of the interrogation room. They headed down the passage to the elevator that would take them back to the main level from the CCD's primary detention center. Pythorael turned to Rogan. "Anything interesting from our other subject?"

Rogan sighed. "So far, everything checks out with the story Verigratu gave the NCSF. We need to debrief him on the details of the 4UB6 incident. He didn't tell the NCSF much."

Pythorael stopped a few feet from the elevator. "It seems the Archon and his ēlan have decided to intervene. All we have is her less than adequate summary from the Archon's interview with him at the Citadel. We have no access to him until further notice. We can't even run a utilization matrix on him. All directives on him have been quarantined."

Rogan stepped forward and pushed the key on the lift. "Just an observation, the name Wasser is German for water. Do you think Jack Wasser could be an alias for Zack Waters? I'm not sure how he could have kept this information hidden from us, if he knew. Yet, something seemed to come over him during your last line of questioning. He was fighting against revealing actual names."

"Did you get anything useful out of any of the others?" Pythorael said.

"The girl is useless. She was sent to a juvenile institute. The mother and the boy are not much help, either. They're awaiting transfer to permanent detention or a labor colony. NCSF forces are still in pursuit of at least four, maybe five, others who eluded capture."

"This is the first ATO we've captured alive in a decade; I want to get something from him besides a few names," Pythorael said.

Rogan responded, "What about the latest captive we caught inside the walls this morning near Sanctuary Gate 2? I had him delivered to our nearby clandestine facility in the Highlands as you requested. I don't understand what you intend we do with him."

Pythorael grimaced. "Don't concern yourself about him right now. I'm keeping any record of his capture and our facility off the grid for a reason. It's only for a contingency plan that I'm considering. The dossier we're building on him may prove useful."

Pythorael's PCD indicated an incoming message from his executive assistant. "Yes, what is it?"

"Ēlan Tabitha Norean is waiting in your private lounge. I assumed you would wish to speak with her directly. Shall I tell her you are expected back in a few minutes or send her away? She was most insistent that you meet with her."

"Tell the ēlan I am finishing up my afternoon appointment and will be there directly. Oh, and please tell the GIA director to contact me immediately."

The voice replied, "Of course. But you do realize Janice is at the Citadel today, as are all the division heads, except for yourself and Director Rogan? The Archon has not dispatched a message, yet I wouldn't be surprised if he hasn't noticed your absence."

Pythorael snapped, "I have a Ministry to run. I don't have time for his festivities."

* * * *

Pythorael entered his office through his private elevator. He sat down behind his desk just as Janice Corupreal contacted him. "Director Pythorael, I thought we had plans to meet next week to go over your priorities concerning the GIA. I don't have anything prepared at the moment."

Pythorael cut her off. "That's not why I'm contacting you. I had one of your operatives run an off-the-grid DNA analysis on a person of interest to the Ministry, ēlan Tabitha Norean."

"Let me look at our unreleased notes on your request concerning our guest of honor this weekend," said Janice. "With this implementation going on, I'm behind on everything."

A moment later she continued, "Dalen, her genetic profile has been quarantined by LEOH. Apparently she knows we are looking into her; it was her authorization that quarantined it. Yet according to the analysis we were able to complete, her latest sample was taken eight years ago while she was at the Clarion Academy."

"Is there anything unexpected in the results?" asked Pythorael.

"She indeed has the enhanced ATK15 sequence, which is an aberration. She is clearly an enhanced natural clarion. Most clarions have only two or three indicators. She has all five. We also confirmed that she's the biological daughter of the Noreans. As far as we could tell her index is clean, no apparent corruption."

Pythorael said, "I need to know whether someone could have tampered with her profile more recently. I'm not referring to the mess that happened eighteen years ago."

"I'm not aware of any recent index corruption. I would say, if her sample came back clean, and especially if it indicates the proper lineage expectations, its uncorrupted. That is, assuming our profile sample is hers. If you need to verify this, your only course of action would be to have her re-sequenced with an updated sample. We could run it, then make an offline analysis, but we are locked out of her current profile."

Pythoreal nodded thoughtfully. "It seems the Norean heiress is, in fact, her father's daughter. Yet, something about this troubles me. That's all for now."

* * * *

A few minutes later, Pythoreal entered the lounge in his CCD executive suite where Tabitha sat drinking tea and watching the NCNS on the room's large display. "Tabitha, I wasn't expecting to meet with you again so soon. I hope this is not about something which could wait until Monday to discuss. Shouldn't you be at the Citadel, enjoying the festivities?"

Pythoreal sat down across from her.

"I don't enjoy festivities to celebrate the further subjugation of humanity. Also, this may be our last opportunity to talk before I'm fully engaged in my investigation of Mr. Verigratu, which will include spending time with him and his family. After the ridiculous ball this evening I'll be leaving the NCGD to pursue my target."

Pythorael seemed amused. "I'm sure your covert intrusion into his world will be greeted with delight, especially by Mark's young wife. Eighteen-year-old girls can be so understanding. Especially when it comes to rich, beautiful, slightly older ēlans showing up in pursuit of their husbands."

Tabitha sighed. "I'm not pursuing her husband for anything unto-ward. Based on what I've seen of Mark's wife, she has nothing to be concerned about.

"By the way, I assume you've noticed; the Ministry no longer has *any* jurisdiction over the stolen data incident. You are not going to run a concurrent investigation and we aren't collaborating. This also includes your peripheral inquiries, including those you're conducting on me. I know you've had people snooping around my profile, including my GIA matrix. That's off limits for you as well.

"I don't know exactly what you're up to, Dalen, but I'm here to tell you to stay out of all of it. You will be informed should I discover anything significant that may be of interest to the Ministry."

Dalen looked at Tabitha contemplatively. "It is quite ironic; you're telling the head of the NCMIA to back off an investigation of one our own operatives, for a matter of the utmost importance to the Ministry."

Tabitha nodded, as if she understood. "He's decided to resign. Even so, he *was* one of your operatives, until Devan decided to appoint him to work for him at the NCIC. I thought I should tell you before you had the chance to find out from the intelligence gathered by one your spybots, or from the Archon himself."

Pythorael intentionally ignored the mention of his bots. "I was informed a short time ago that my interrogation, or rather, my scheduled debriefing with Mark on Monday, would no longer be necessary, thanks to you. However, no mention was made of his appointment to an NCIC staff position. That is surprising, given the amount of suspicion he is under. I assume you are here to enlighten me on this mystery," Pythorael said, pouring himself a cup of tea.

Tabitha replied, "Devan is being ridiculous, as usual. At my home, you alluded to the fact you wanted me to help you oppose him. I'm here to extend you an offer, to make certain *you* help *me*."

Pythorael eyed her suspiciously, "I didn't think you were interested in joining my efforts to undermine the Archon's more outrageous ambitions. Is this why you rushed here to see me?"

Tabitha laughed. "Oh, I'm not joining your conspiracy. You will join mine. You can rest assured Devan will be paying close attention to your interrogation of the recent captives from the Dead Zone," Tabitha said. "Very close indeed."

She finished her tea. "After all, it's not every day you manage to capture a genuine Waters. By the way, your credentials are now cleared for T2 Alpha X for LEOH II."

"What do you mean, I captured a genuine Waters?"

Tabitha grew irritated. "I will tell you my secrets if you tell me yours. This is a quid pro quo. You must first answer my questions. Your prisoner could expose this entire mystery."

Pythorael nodded. "I'll try to be accommodating."

Tabitha said, "First, what does Devan really want with me? He made some off-the-wall claim about making me a powerful queen. He said I was the key to the 'legacy of his immortality.' You said I'm just the key. What does this mean, exactly? I also want to know what you and your kind are and where you came from. I want the truth. Then I'll tell you about the man in your custody."

Pythoreal paced uncomfortably, gathering his thoughts. "I assume your father never told you who you really are and the reason you were created? He paid a lot of money to have you engineered to perfection for the Archon. Have you not considered why you were kept isolated at Interlochen for the last three years? I recently uncovered the Archon's confidential communications with your father. As you say, my spybots can even infiltrate his private security perimeter. You were sold like a commodity to him before you were even born."

"Perfection? Hmph, he obviously missed something that most girls have considerably more of than me." Tabitha fumed. "But I'm not stupid. I know my father promised me to him, but that doesn't answer my questions."

"You really *don't* want to know the answer to those questions," said Pythorael. "It is your family, and others like them, that have made the Archon's plans achievable. You are the heiress to a great fortune because of the complicity of the Norean family. People like you maintain the Archon's power. This is the way it has always been. We've always been around this world. It's just we're a bit closer now to those we rule over."

Tabitha said, "Where have you been 'around'? So far you haven't told me anything useful."

"You wouldn't believe me if I told you, so what's the point?" Pythorael said. "Let's just say, we have been in charge of this world for quite a long time."

Tabitha scoffed, "You may in charge now, but once this stolen classified data is disseminated, it's the rest of humanity who will rise up to destroy your kind. The complicity of people like my family will no longer benefit you. Tell me what you are and where you came from and what does Devan really want with me?"

Pythorael countered, "It's your complicity which most concerns me. All I can say is, we are not born like you. We now exist in bodies which are no different than yours. Yet the immortality the Archon desires with you extends well beyond your flesh. This, you can't possibly understand. Your clarion pontifications could not come close to understanding what you are to him."

Tabitha was quick to respond. "Whatever he desires with me he will never have. How does one come to possess so much power over this world, yet at the same time appear to have become so powerless? You are dependent on unstable and fragile technology which you didn't create. And now the Archon is dependent on a someone as fragile as me for his immortality? I don't just sense that you have lost something; I sense your inability to find what you seek, and what you seek is to discover how to regain what you've lost. Am I right?"

Grinning with satisfaction, the director looked dismissively at Tabitha. "The Archon believes in the ancient prophecies from the age of myth and magic that pre-date enlightened minds. Those powers are confined in the darkness of the past, especially since the Final War. He thinks he can possess what you have if you give yourself to him. You also must have the blood of your father, who gave you to him. You should avoid him, especially on your birthday. October 31st is a date of arcane convergence when you will be three sevens. For your own sake, you should be as far away from the Citadel as possible."

Tabitha said with acid in her voice, "He just wants to have sex with me, and that will never happen."

"He's not interested in you for that purpose. The Archon wants to bond with you because he wants to possess your hidden name. He thinks you will give him ethereal power and offspring. He has done this in ages past. However, this time, the offspring he wants from you will preserve his longevity."

Tabitha held up her hand. "That's enough! I am not having sex with him or marrying him. I'm sure as hell not going to become his concubine or queen or have his children. He is foul, old, disgusting, and a liar. He is also weak if he truly needs someone like me for his ... longevity. It's more like the longevity of his alien pecker. And what in the hell is a hidden name? That doesn't even make sense."

Tabitha continued her tirade. "I would never want to live forever in a world governed by him. I was not born to serve the Archon, no matter what my father promised him. His ideal world of having humanity integrated with him is a nightmare, not a utopia. I've seen enough about the Optimus Directive to understand his objectives. I assume your objectives are the same."

Pythorael raised his eyebrows in astonishment at Tabitha's impertinence. "I hope you haven't spoken to the Archon in this manner. You should be more careful before you speak."

"He's trying to destroy humanity. Idiots like my father are helping him."

"Of course, and what you've just completed building for him, will ultimately finish this task," Pythoreal said. "I'm starting to like you, Tabitha. You are not far from the truth. Yet I deal in knowledge. I must be honest with you. You can't possibly understand the truth. You don't have the requisite connection to its source. As a Norean you are as doomed as I am if the Archon succeeds. There is no hope for anyone of your pedigree. In this respect you are just like me, but you have no idea what you were genetically engineered to be."

Tabitha said mockingly, "I will tell you what I don't accept. It's the lie my father believes about your kind. You're as much of a liar as he is. No one is measured by their pedigree or lineage. How can you say that I can't possibly understand the truth? All this about what he wants with me on my birthday is insane. None of it makes sense. You're just trying to get me to join your conspiracy."

Pythorael grinned. "You must look outside this world for the answers. Unfortunately, this door is not open to someone like you. You don't have the ability to connect with anything beyond your own intellect. Those who do are considered by the Archon to be enemies of New City. It is my job to hunt them down and your job to engineer the most efficient means to find them. You have done this admirably and efficiently, if what I hear of L2 is as capable as the Archon says it is. If I told you I don't agree with his objectives and together we could oppose him, perhaps you would change your attitude toward me. You can help me fix the mistake you made when you completed the development of L2 for him."

A look of anger crossed Tabitha's face, then she sighed with frustration. "You don't need to remind me of my mistakes. I will correct them myself! I want the truth about your kind. Should I consider you aliens, cyborgs, vampires, or possessed clones? Giving me nothing but riddles and saying I can't understand the truth will make things worse for you. If you want to know about your captive Waters, you must tell me everything."

Pythoreal sighed and rubbed his forehead. "I thought you said you wanted me to help you. Do you really just want the truth now, and no more? You ask the impossible. You cannot possibly discern what is written. It's in a language you can't comprehend. It is not a human language. I cannot tell you more. You know far too much already, more than enough to put your life at risk. As I said before, you are playing a dangerous game with me. Even so, I did tell you a great deal. You simply choose not to accept it."

"Stop trying to intimidate me with your stupid 'dangerous game' threats." Tabitha stood up. "Let me know when you're ready to be more forthcoming." She started to storm out. Pythorael stared at her with an expression of panic.

He leapt after her. "Tabitha, wait! Seriously, I need to know what you mean about me having a Waters in custody. In return, I will give you a clue about what is written. It will give you the answers you seek about who we are. It is a contraband book—the most illegal one of all. But you cannot understand it without having a connection to something beyond this world, which is impossible for you. Yet only this source will allow you to discern its secrets."

Tabitha pursed her lips. "I don't believe you. Are you saying some harmless illegal book contains the truth about your kind?"

Pythorael paced nervously. "If it were harmless, it wouldn't be banned. In fact, if the Archon knew I revealed this to you, he would likely try to obliterate me."

Tabitha narrowed her eyes. "What is this contraband book called?"

Pythorael sidestepped the question. "It's not just the words on the pages," he said. "A spirit dwells within the words. Unless you are connected to this spirit you cannot comprehend the words. But this spirit can never dwell in a child born a Norean. It could be dangerous for you. Someone like you has little hope of grasping it. How you came to possess what is supposedly hidden within you is a mystery to me. I don't know how that quack Dylanis discovered you, or if he really did engineer the fabric of such an alluring name into your DNA. Yet even if you do have a powerful ethereal connection this will not help you decipher the secrets of a book you can never understand. The House of Norean belongs to Devan Elaniel and thus, so do you!"

Tabitha shook her head. "How could Dylanis engineer my name? I don't know what that means. My father has countless contraband books and I've read them all. Most are worthless. Besides, if people can't understand it, why is it banned? Why should the Archon care if anyone reads it?"

Pythorael said dryly, "You've made my point precisely. Trust me, it's not someone like you he is concerned about—it's those we hunt. If they are blind to who they are in what has been written, they will be blind to the knowledge of how to defeat him. Faith is a powerful force in the hands of someone armed with the truth. It is an extremely potent weapon, but not for you. You are already condemned for being a Norean. For this alone, you *must* tell me how you know one of my captives is a descendant of David Waters."

Tabitha paused. She had worked her distraction well enough. All she had really wanted was to make Pythorael think she was bargaining with him. She decided to give him what she had wanted him to know in the first place. "Your prisoner Bob's real name is Ryan Waters, specifically Robert Ryan Waters, or plain old Bob. He has previously gone by the name Ryan."

Pythorael shook his head, mystified. "How could you possibly know this?"

Before Tabitha turned to walk away, she said, "Here is your quid pro quo, which is about as clear and honest as the answers you gave me. I have my sources. The how is, I'm far better than you at figuring out what is right before your eyes but not always visible. When you personally sign an authorization to murder a man's family, their names do not die when one or more of his children live."

Pythorael shouted at Tabitha as she left: "What is that supposed to mean? This doesn't tell me anything except the man's name is Robert Ryan Waters! Tabitha!"

"Touché! Neither did you tell me everything I wanted to know."

Pythorael carefully placed Tabitha's teacup in a plastic bag. He now had his updated genetic sample.

* * * *

Robert Ryan Waters. Tabitha thought about what she had just revealed to Pythorael as she returned to the Citadel. *I hope giving up your name is going to be worth the risk.* Tabitha assumed she didn't have a single ally in this struggle. She had no idea how wrong she was. Yet she was determined to get the answers to all her questions.

* * * *

In her dreams, Ariel saw Tabitha coming as the cracks in the shattered sea of glass of her reflection grew more distinct and ominous. She knew that, whoever Tabitha was, she was dangerous and would bring a raging storm upon the world. Everything about to occur would happen with speed and finality.

* * * *

I didn't realize how sorry I would become, knowing the sordid truth of Tabitha's abuse. I had kept the evidence like a personal possession.

I started to obsess over this beautiful ēlan. As irritating and arrogant as she was, I began to fantasize about her, for reasons I didn't fully comprehend. Yet sometimes, what is wrong can be used to make something right, or better yet, complete what isn't whole. It would ultimately become part of the tapestry of who Ariel Waters truly is and the mystery behind her own alluring hidden name. Zack had used me to capture his venomous spider, but in truth his spider had already captured me.

CHAPTER 26

THE WATERS

When I arrived back at our apartment, I knew Ari was at the medical center with Zack. I told her I would be along shortly. I didn't mention there was something I couldn't get out of my mind that I had to resolve. My apartment had obviously been searched again while I was in the DZ. Tabitha had, in fact, told me they had searched it three times. Even so, the safe room containing the stolen data remained undiscovered.

I located the data cube with the videos of Tabitha. I was looking for just one image of her, at a certain angle, when she was the same age as Ari. I didn't need to confirm Tabitha Norean was "subject one." I expanded the images of her face, until I found the right one. *This is insane!* The eighteen-year-old Tabitha looked identical to Ari, except for the color of her eyes, her loosely curled blond hair, and lighter complexion. They could be identical twins. Even their eyebrows were the same shape, as I compared their images side by side.

I tried to brush off the notion that this was anything more than an incredibly strange coincidence. I had been seeing Tabitha's face in my mind since our meeting in the Citadel. I couldn't shake how much she reminded me of Ari. I guess elegant clothes, a fancy hairstyle, two plus years and makeup can make you miss the obvious. The twenty-year-old Tabitha, with her hair up and makeup, may not have been entirely convincing. The close-up image of eighteen-year-old Tabitha was. The only discernable differences in their appearance were superficial.

I cropped the close-up of the younger Tabitha's face and saved it on my PCD. I had to show Ari this image to see if she recognized the striking resemblance to her own likeness. I wondered if Zack was aware his spider looked exactly like his great-granddaughter. I recall Zack saying if I met her, I would never forget her. *Did he already know?* Bob had claimed Ari was a clone with two identical sisters. *That isn't possible,* I thought dismissively. *Or is it? Ari or Zack would have told me if she was a freaking clone; but could the Norean ēlan be one? No way!*

* * * *

Ari and I were able to spend the remainder of the weekend together. We spent several hours at the medical center with Zack on Saturday and again on Sunday. He was recovering well from what turned out to have been a mild heart attack.

I was sure I was still being traced, so I was careful not to tell Ari about my experiences. Remaining silent was driving me crazy. Yet we'd agreed not to discuss anything of importance until Zack was home the next day.

Ari and I slept late on Monday morning, then enjoyed a pleasant brunch. Afterward, I pinged an SDPV to take us to Zack's. While we waited, I decided to get some use out of Zack's walnut. After activating it I said, "I've been dying to tell you what's happened to me and who I met at the Citadel. I wanted you to know before we sit down with Zack. Something strange is going on. I have an uneasy feeling that it's all connected. I also have something I need to show you ..."

"Mark, first, I need to tell you something," Ari said. "You know about my dreams and visions. Usually they're confusing. I've seen parts of this dream before, but over the last seven nights it's recurred—in full."

"I was going to mention the dream you had before I went to the DZ came true," I said. "I was in a battle and I ran away. A child did lead me, sort of. As a result, I met people who are connected to Zack in some way. It's all crazy. Then I met this girl at the Citadel who ..."

"Mark, I have to tell you first!"

I threw up my hands and nodded.

"In my dream I'm above this mirror," she said. "It's more like a sea of glass. I see my reflection, and it shatters, and my reflection changes, so it isn't really me anymore. The person in the image captures you; she takes you away from me. A storm surrounds her—and all of us. I know the dream means she's almost here. I'm afraid for you. She's dangerous."

I laughed. "Who is dangerous? I've been in danger in the DZ and ever since I carried out the data theft for Zack." I became serious. "You knew about all of this and never told me. I've done what he needed me to do at the Ministry and I am out of it. I even met his crazy spider. That's why I need to show you ..."

Ari shook her head. "No, this is different! The girl in my reflection is going to take you by the hand to lead you where you don't—or shouldn't—want to go. Whoever she is, she's bringing a storm, especially upon you. It's so confusing. She's not who you think she is, or there is more than one of her. I don't fully understand it."

I said, "What does this stormy reflection of yours look like when it changes?"

Ari shook her head. "You wouldn't believe me if I told you. It's different each time, but most of the time it looks like me with blond hair and blue eyes. I know that sounds crazy. And I didn't dream this because I want to become a blond, if that's what you're thinking."

I was stunned. "No, I wasn't thinking that at all." I was alerted that our SDPV was about to pull up outside. "We'll talk about this with Zack. I have something I really need to show you, and it might help explain this reflection in your dream." I hurriedly put the walnut back in the saferoom and took the MDC to deliver to Zack.

* * * *

That was a worthless meeting, Tabitha grumbled after leaving Jerome Haley's house in North Park. She had setup the meeting the day before.

He'd asked to meet at his house, instead of his office. This gave Tabitha some hope that he might be forthcoming with her. It turned out he was very cautious; unwilling to say much at all. He was obviously still a little nervous after his release from being incarcerated.

She checked the time; she was thirty minutes away from Park Central. She was traveling at high speed in her private luxury SDPV in the designated fast lane reserved for "privileged" travelers.

Tabitha was determined to talk with Zachariah Waters that day. Things had been way too weird since she'd returned to the Southern Jurisdiction. It had started with the bizarre earthquake and perfectly cracked mirror in her bathroom. Things had gotten even stranger when she started looking into Mark and the Waters family. Tabitha hated inexplicable coincidences. Everything in her world was predictable; calculable like an equation. Algorithms produced a certain result when applied to a given set of inputs.

Due to her investigation initiated by the Archon, Tabitha had now been issued a class T-Alpha Prime security clearance. She could officially override any integrated coded entrance or security monitoring station. She could go anywhere unchallenged. She had extraordinary authority, to essentially do anything, and her movements and activities were completely shielded from monitoring by LEOH.

* * * *

Tabitha checked her tracking application. Mark and Ari had left his apartment. She knew Zachariah was back from the hospital, and they were apparently taking a SDPV to his home. There would be no way for her to confront Mark before he arrived. She thought, *Now is as good a time as any to pay the old man a visit, and they'll all be there together.*

She smiled as she admired herself in the backseat mirror. *I look pretty cute.* Tabitha had studiously converted herself into a regular New City girl. She wore little jewelry, certainly no silly tiara, and just a few casual accessories. She even wore her hair down. Her loose blond curls

cascaded over her shoulders, down her back and to just above her chest.
She grimaced as she considered her breasts. *Maybe longer hair will help
hide these tiny things.*

She knew being dressed like this would scandalize her prudish
personal valet. Julian was always so particular about how Tabitha
dressed. If she had so much as a hair out of place, the woman would fix
her. God forbid, if her eyebrows weren't perfectly plucked or an earring
broke. It was as if Tabitha was always being cleaned and ornamented
for display. Even so, she loved Julian, since she was the only one who'd
ever cared for Tabitha.

She checked the tracking again. Sure enough, Mark had arrived.
He was on the seventh floor of the upscale apartment building at the
residence of Zachariah Waters, former deputy director of the CCD. She
shook her head in astonishment. The man was bold enough to use his
real last name, since anyone with the last name Waters was immediately a suspect. She laughed at the apparent incompetence of Dalen
Pythorael and the NCMIA.

She pondered what her investigation had revealed thus far and how
these ghosted access codes had been used over the years. It was time
get some answers as to what Zachariah Waters was really up to.

* * * *

Tabitha approached the front entrance of the apartment building,
called Beacon Place. As she entered, there was second set of doors with
a standard integrated security console, which required activation from
an ID sensor.

Tabitha's security authorization automatically released the inner
door. It opened instantly; she barely broke stride. As Tabitha approached
the elevator, she transmitted Zack's apartment number to the lift, which
took her to the seventh floor.

* * * *

After we arrived at Zack's apartment, Ari and his attending physician helped Zack get settled. I waited in the den of what was now Ari's former home. Once Zack was situated, she joined me. We snuggled and kissed, almost like we were still dating.

"Does this still seem like your home?" I said.

"Of course; this will always be my home. I mean, your place is still more yours than ours. I live out of a travel bag when I'm there."

"I want so show you an image," I said. "Tell me what you think. I pulled out my display. Before I could activate it and bring up the image of Tabitha, the door com buzzed.

"Who could that be?" Ari said. "I don't think Zack's expecting anyone."

Tabitha pressed the com again. A few moments later Ari's face appeared on door display so Tabitha could see it.

"Yes, who is it?"

Tabitha knew Ari's face. She responded, "This is Tabitha, Tabitha Norean. Your husband, Mark, knows who I am. May I come in?" The display went blank. Tabitha contemplated barging in. She decided that would be too rude. She was about to press the com button again when the door opened.

I stood in the doorway in front of Tabitha; Ari stood just behind me to one side. Tabitha looked markedly different from our first meeting. Her blond curls flowed around her face and neck and she was much more casually dressed. She had on less makeup and wore only a simple necklace and a couple of rings. I caught my breath. A blond image of Ari was standing in front of me.

"Tabitha? What are you doing here?" I said more calmly than I felt.

"Aren't you going to invite me in?"

I gestured for her to enter. "This is Ari, my wife," I said. "Ari, this is Tabitha ... Norean. I was thankful that Tabitha didn't kiss me as she had at the Citadel.

"I know who she is," Ari said, stepping forward. "And she just said her name. Please come in."

Tabitha reached out a hand. Ari took it reluctantly. She was clearly confused by the arrival of this mysterious young woman who happened to look like her. "Can I offer you something?" Ari asked.

Tabitha shook her head. "No, thank you. It's a pleasure to meet you. It's nice to see you again, Mark. I hope you had a pleasant weekend." Tabitha turned to Ari. "How is your great-grandfather doing?"

Ari frowned. "He's better now, thank you," she said.

Tabitha stood in the foyer, as if waiting for something. "I suppose Mark told you about our conversation, and how we met two days ago?"

Ari stared over at me.

I blushed, then hurriedly led them into the den.

Tabitha looked around the well-furnished apartment. "So this is where Zachariah Waters lives. He probably doesn't remember meeting me. It was a such an odd thing to say to a little girl."

Tabitha barreled on in her usual way. "Mark told me that you were coming home to be with your great-grandfather, because of um … what happened. Is he able to get around yet?"

Ari stiffened at Tabitha's repeated references to Zack as her great-grandfather. "No, not yet."

Tabitha nodded, sympathetically. "I would like to meet him again, when he has recovered." Tabitha placed the small bag she'd had at the Citadel on the end of the low table.

Ari whispered in my ear, "It's her. She's the one from my dreams."

"I was about to show you an image of her, but I guess that's not necessary now," I said in a low voice.

"I can read lips. What dream? Don't say things like that to a clarion," Tabitha said. "Why would you show her an image of me?"

"Look," I said, "you came here. We haven't been here five minutes, then you happen to show up. Tell us why you're here."

Tabitha was immediately annoying. "You've been here fourteen minutes to be exact. I'm sorry to intrude on you uninvited. Actually, I'm not sorry. This is extremely important. I hope I can speak freely in front of your wife, Mark. Have you had a chance to tell her everything?"

I pursed my lips and said, with a tinge of anger, "I haven't had a chance to talk freely with my wife."

"Is there no dead space in your apartment?" Tabitha asked. "Then I suppose you haven't told her how you encountered your great-uncle, or rather his son, in the DZ."

I scoffed, "What are you talking about? Tabitha, I don't mean to be rude, but you need to slow down, or leave. This is not a good time for you to be here."

Tabitha didn't flinch. "Have you forgotten our conversation already? I thought we had come to some understanding about what I already know. You can dispense with the pretense."

Just then, a well-coifed woman of about fifty appeared from the hallway. "I'm sorry; I wasn't aware you had company," she said to Ari. "Zack is awake and he's doing fine. You can go in and spend time with him. I need to run down to the medical center for an hour or two."

Tabitha extended her hand to the doctor. "You must be Dr. Ellen Cavanaugh. It's a pleasure to meet you. I'm Tabitha, Tabitha Norean. I spoke with your brother yesterday. Jerome is an exceptionally nice man, although not very forthcoming and ..."

I interrupted. "I'm sure Doctor Cavanaugh needs to be on her way."

Confused, Ellen smiled. "I should be back in a couple of hours. It was nice to meet you."

As the doctor left, I turned to Tabitha. "I don't know what you're up to, but you need to stop!"

Ari said, "What do you mean Mark encountered his great-uncle's son in the DZ? What would Zack know about you? I'd like to know why you're here."

"I was just trying to be friendly," Tabitha said. "Is the doctor in on it? I would have thought the half-sister of Zachariah Water's former colleague at the Ministry would have tipped them off that he hasn't always been as sick as he pretends to be. I guess familial associations aren't as well identified in the security profiles of certain individuals as they should be."

Ari said, "Mark, why is this rude girl here? Please tell me what's going on. What I really want to know is, why does Tabitha Norean look like me? This is disturbing."

"You're the one who just told me you dreamed of ..." I started to say.

Tabitha cut me off. "This rude girl, as you put it, is here to help both of you and possibly save your lives. I need some answers and I need to speak with Zachariah Waters. May I call him Zack? I'd prefer to speak with him now! The doctor said you can go in and see him. He can provide the answer to your question to both of us."

Ari and I stared at each other in shock. Tabitha raised her voice again, "Look, you two, do I need to spell it out any more clearly? I'm on your side."

Ari objected, "He just had a heart attack. You are so rude!"

The three of us turned our heads as a gravelly voice spoke from the hallway, "All of you, come into my study. It's time I told you *everything*." We did as Zack instructed. We sat down in four leather chairs arrayed around a small round table. Zack poured a cup of hot tea from a tea service. He offered it to Tabitha, then offered tea to me and Ari.

Zack turned to Tabitha. "Hello Tabitha. I'm not sure you remember me. We met when you were a little girl. I knew your father. It's been a long time. You look so much ..."

Tabitha said sharply, "I didn't come here to discuss my childhood. I came for answers!"

Zack seemed confused. "All right, what is your question, then? There's no need to be rude."

"My apologies, Zack, it is nice to meet you again as well. Now, why has my genetic profile been accessed repeatedly by those ghosted access codes? Who is doing this?"

Zack was momentarily surprised. "I'll explain everything. How did you discover that?"

I cut in. "So you're saying you followed me here so you could ask Zack about your profile? I thought you were supposed to be spying ..."

Tabitha said, "That's only one question I have, but it's the key to understanding more than a few highly improbable coincidences. Isn't that right, Zack?"

"It's actually dangerous for us all to be here together," Zack said. "Even so, I thought this introduction would be far more deadly for me and certainly more difficult for us all."

Tabitha said, "Don't push it! Devan wants his stolen data back and he wants me to expose your organization. He will kill all of you when he finds out. He sent me here to entrap you."

Tabitha leaned in toward Zack. She pointed to Ari. "They will figure it out! L2 will discover everything if I don't stop it. They won't need my help. Who is she? Who is Ariel to me and who am I to her? We aren't related. I have access and I know how to run a formulation on a genetics profile. I double checked it! Even though she has larger ... anyway, why does she look like me?"

"Zack, what's going on?" Ari pleaded. "Why do you know her? This is frightening me."

Tabitha said, "Everything leads back to you, Zack. Everything! I want to know what is going on with you and the moons in your orbit, like Jerome Haley. Who are you people?"

Zack gently patted the air to calm Tabitha. "OK, let me think about where to begin. Tabitha, I assume you realize you were the result of a genetic cognitive trait enhancement project called K15."

Tabitha nodded. "Of course. That's why I am so famous among the tediously scientific types."

Zack pressed on. "The woman you know as your mother, the woman who gave birth to you, is not your biological mother. The same is true of your father. You are genetically more closely related to Mark or me than to them. You are infinitely more closely related to Ari, who is technically your identical twin sister. The reasons you look different, in addition to being a different age, is complicated." Ari gasped, and I grabbed her hand. Initially, this revelation didn't startle Tabitha. She seemed to be processing this incredible fact as if it was just another data point.

"You are as much a genetic dissident as the rest of your family in this room," Zack added.

Tabitha's mouth gaped open in disbelief. "I know you people are genetic dissidents, but I can't be related to you! I've had multiple utilization matrixes ran on my DNA profile over the years. I'm a curiosity. They wanted to know what makes me tick. Private research companies paid my father for my profile. Any dissident markers would have been flagged. I would be dead or in prison if I were a genetic dissident. This is impossible."

Zack shook his head. "Your profile comes up clean, but not because it is. It is clean because the utilization output says it is. It also makes certain you're a Norean, not a Waters."

Ari and Tabitha stared at each other in astonishment. I was equally flabbergasted.

Zack said, "Tabitha, you and Ari are clones. In addition to your augmented mental acuity traits, there were a few additional cosmetic alterations. In your case, this was done so you more closely resemble the Noreans. If you colored your hair like Ari's you would look identical. There is no question that each of you strongly favors your stunningly beautiful mother."

"Is that why she has larger breasts?" Tabitha asked, as if this were relevant.

"Seriously? I said. "You find out you and Ari are sisters and breasts concern you?"

Zack said, "You two would have probably grown up together, but Kim Norean had a condition which prevented her from carrying another child. Ari was only partially modified as a control on the K15 trait, but Lara, your mother, refused to allow Ari's cosmetic traits to be modified in the same way as yours."

"Then how did I end up as a Norean? Tabitha demanded. "You have no idea how horrible it has been growing up in that family."

"Right, growing up in the richest family in the world must have totally sucked," I said.

Tabitha glared at me. "I know my private valet and steward better than I know my own mother! My brother molested me, and my father neglected me. It would hardly call the Noreans a close family!"

Zack replied, "Being raised as a Norean was part of your destiny."

Tabitha was in tears, "What destiny? My father pledged me to the Archon when I was a child. Actually, it was more of a pre-arranged hookup ... that asshole!"

Ari pleaded with Zack, "Why didn't you tell me about this? You know I always dreamed about having a sister. You kept this from me my entire life. I feel betrayed. It's like you lied to me."

"Ari, please, let me explain," Zack said. "I couldn't tell you about Tabitha. It would have put her at risk if they discovered who you were. It was best for both of you if you didn't know the truth."

He continued, "The Noreans were not a family Dr. Dylanis could refuse. He made certain they qualified for the K15 program. It was then that Dylanis approached Lara, his research assistant. He asked her and Neil to be tested. They were able to produce a single, uniquely viable embryo. I assume he intended to give both the clones of this embryo to the Noreans, without their knowledge or Lara's. According to Lara they always kept the original embryo in order to validate the DNA sequence for each clone It is a very complex process apparently."

I interjected, "Are there other girls? Does Ari have other sisters?"

Zack shook his head. "I didn't know about Ari at first," he said resignedly. "It wasn't until Ari was born that Lara told me what Dylanis had done. I realized that Tabitha would eventually be profiled as a genetic dissident. Tabitha's genetic profile was elaborately fabricated by Dylanis. The only proof of her true genetics remained in the biological samples in his lab. Yet the problem of future samples being discovered remained. Tabitha was already two years old. There was little I could do about it."

"Apparently, you managed to do something, and those access codes are part of it," Tabitha said. "Who is using those codes to access my profile?"

"I devised a plan to permanently hide each of you," Zack continued. "At least, it was my hope at the time it was permanent. A gifted algorithm developer wrote a process which has kept you from being discovered, countless times. He was able to install it in the GIA compiler using one of those ghosted access codes. This algorithm uses the codes to alter the index output on your DNA sequence anytime a utilization runs on your profile. Tabitha, this brilliant man spent almost six months, nonstop, working on the sequence index modifier just to protect you. Thankfully, it also protected Ari and all of us."

"This whole thing with Mark, the data theft and everything, was some kind of elaborate scheme to lure me here," Tabitha said, astonished. "You thought L2 would expose those ghosted access codes and all of us ... and it will eventually. Had I rebuilt the security platform as I intended it would have already."

"She has an annoying ability to figure things out, Zack," I said

Zack shook his head sadly. "Tabitha, many people have given their lives to protect you and Ari, including your actual mother and father. I made the fatal mistake of convincing Lara and Neil to go to the lab early one morning to replace Tabitha's biological samples with the Noreans' failed fertilization material. They were also going to destroy any potentially incriminating documentation. Unbeknownst to me, Dylanis had arranged for some thug to destroy the lab. He was under investigation at the time for several unrelated fraudulent activities."

"I don't want to hear any more of this!" Tabitha cried.

"You need to know," Zack said in a somber tone. "Lara and Neil died to protect you and Ari. Within a day of the incident, Dylanis, his little girl, and his wife were killed in a horrendous attack on his home. It was never fully investigated. Everything about the K15 project was quarantined. It wasn't merely classified; it was deleted. Santos told me Pythorael wanted everything obliterated, not just covered up. I have always been afraid he wanted you and Ari killed."

Tabitha managed to regain her composure. "Is this why you spoke to me? We met at my parent's home on Lake Carmel. You said to me, *There are many bad people in this world; you can overcome them. You have gifts from God no one else has; never forget this. People will tell you technology endowed you with your gifts. In truth, only God holds the stars in his hand.* Do you remember telling me this? I was eight years old. It was such an odd thing to say to a little girl."

Zack handed Tabitha a tattered book. "Tabitha, you are not a clarion because of your skill or training. Rather, you are gifted beyond almost every other person because God created you this way, not Dylanis. God speaks through this book. His name is a curse to them and to this city they created. They hate him without reason. His spirit is in the words written in it. His spirit is also in you. You only have to accept what is freely given to us all." Zack pointed straight up.

I couldn't believe Zack was going down this road.

Tabitha smirked. "I know who you are talking about and I know his name. It doesn't offend me. I just don't believe in religious myths. It's all been debunked. My father has one of these. I've tried to read it and didn't understand it. It doesn't make sense."

Zack said, "The Archon understands it. His doom is prophesied in this book!"

Tabitha seethed with anger. "That slithering snake Pythorael told me the same thing ... well, not exactly. He said I am doomed because I'm a Norean. It's a load of crap, anyway. This book was outlawed for a reason. I want nothing to do with it or with any religious myths."

Zack raised a hand up to stop Tabitha. "No matter what you believe, the Archon and Pythorael are deathly afraid of what is written in this book. The part which concerns them the most doesn't read like a linear story. Rather, it reads like a complex tapestry, which for them is slowly unraveling."

Tabitha looked at Zack. "What are they? Pythorael said a contraband book would tell me. I assume he was talking about that one."

Zack handed Tabitha a small data drive. "Here, download this. It's a digitized version, besides, this one is for my own personal use." Reluctantly, Tabitha took the drive and inserted it into her external PCD interface to archive the book. After placing his book in his desk drawer, Zack sat back down. "One might say he and his kind have been cast out of the heavenly realms, into the physical realm of the earth."

Tabitha stared at him blankly.

I added, "Zack believes the Archon is the devil."

Tabitha laughed. "So, the Archon is supposedly the devil, and the rest of them are what, demons? That's crazy. Devan is an imbecile. I outwit him as easily as breathing. The stories about the devil are about how ruthless, smart, evil, and powerful he is. Devan is only powerful because stupid people like the Noreans help him."

Zack shook his head. "You should be careful. He *is* powerful, but he is trapped in a human body. All those characterizations of a mythical beast with horns are just that. He was an angel of light, the son of the dawn. The name Lucifer means morning star. He was a being of immense beauty, intellect, and power. He and his fallen angels with him are consummate liars and deceivers. He desires to be worshipped as God and to become God. But we have a true savior and he is also written of in this book that you think is a myth."

Tabitha looked over at me. She said, suggestively, "Yeah, I know something else he desires, which he isn't going to get." She turned to Zack. "He will stop at nothing to recover that stolen data. He also thinks you people can lead him to this ATO that is infiltrating LEOH, and to their hidden city."

Zack demurred. "I've never mentioned the name ATO to anyone."

I raised my hand like a schoolboy. I was about to interrupt when Tabitha cut me off and treated me like one. "Mark, you can tell everyone about your adventures with the ATO when I'm finished."

She continued, "Trust me, Devan is not powerful and there are not many of these beings. If people stood up to them, we could kill them all. Their experimentation with children and this so-called Optimus Project has something to do with the fact that they are dying. Many people, like my father, think they're immortal and have the power to grant people eternal life. That's a lie! They are aliens who occupy the body of humans. They might be vampires or cyborgs, but they're certainly not devils or real humans. They may be a hundred years old, but that's because they probably keep coming back in new symbiont clone bodies once they grow too old."

"Tabitha, they are all fallen angels and very dangerous," Zack said.

"If I tell you something, please don't laugh," Tabitha responded. "I know they are weak because Devan said *I* am the key to his 'legacy of immortality.' Pythorael says Devan wants to … he wants to impregnate me on my birthday. I'm supposed to become his concubine or something. Pythorael said I have something Devan wants and there won't be anything left of me once he takes it. He wants my hidden name. It sounds crazy, but he's obsessed with it." She shuddered. "The thought of him grosses me out. That's absolutely not going to happen. I'm not having sex with an alien."

If she only knew how obsessed he really was, she would be shocked, I thought.

Zack raised his eyebrows. He didn't scoff at the possibility. He said, "That may well have been the purpose of the K15 project. The idea of creating the ideal hosts for their offspring is not out of the realm of possibility. Believe it or not, it's happened before. I was always concerned Ari was at risk because of that project. I never believed it was only for genetic enhancement. The High Echelon wouldn't fund a project like K15 to improve humanity. They don't want to improve humanity. They want to destroy humanity and become an immortal race of godlike beings. They use people because they don't have the power to create. They can only steal what they want. Although I am not sure why Pythorael opposed K15."

"Pythorael mentioned something like this happened before," Tabitha said.

Ari turned to Tabitha. "I studied the history of ATK15 enhancement project, in preparation for my placement exams. It suggests there is a certain gene sequence for synaptic fortitude commonly found among those with natural clarion abilities. It was one of several resequencing projects sponsored by the High Echelon, GIA, and the NCIC to …"

Tabitha cut Ari off. "Thank you for the textbook summary. I bet you got that test question spot on. I know what the K15 project was meant to achieve. *I* am what it achieved. What does he really want with me? I also know they are trying to purge something out of humanity by hunting down Class 3 dissidents. Then, there's their experimentation on children."

Ari said, "I had a vision about you, Tabitha. I don't know exactly what you are planning to do, but once it begins no one can stop it. The fact that you work for the Archon and you're the daughter of the wealthiest man in New City is not why I fear you. What I saw will lead to destruction; people are going to die. You are going to endanger all of us, and yourself. I saw you bring a storm upon this world. It can't be stopped once it's unleashed. I saw you take Mark to …"

Tabitha said angrily, "Vision update, sister! I'm not the daughter of the wealthiest man! I've also already unleashed something which will destroy us all. Everyone in the world should fear what I've created. I didn't improve it, I perfected it. I just turned on a system capable of destroying humanity. L2 will make it possible for the Archon to accomplish his every horrifying objective. They're building a mechanized army. L2 will control everything, and they won't need people to kill people."

She broke down in tears. "I've got to fix this. I have to stop what I unleashed. I created something which can't be stopped unless I stop it. He can't destroy or control the world without LEOH and he can't control LEOH without me. I intend to take it from him. He thinks he can control me, but his fantasy about me will never happen!"

Tabitha collected herself. "Before I walked through the door, I thought I was alone, the only one who knew what is going on. Don't take away my hope by saying I'm going to destroy everything. I'm going to save everyone; I have to gain control of L2 to save everyone! I came here to help you and to warn you. I came to save your life. I told Mark I have chosen which side I am on. Your plan succeeded Zack. You somehow lured me here, and now I am here. Isn't this what you wanted?"

I knew the Archon was in control of Tabitha in ways of which she was unaware. Yet I was too much of a coward to say anything. I asked, "What do you think he will do if he discovers you're Ari's identical twin and a genetic dissident?"

Tabitha looked down at her chest and over at Ari's. "I wouldn't say we are identical. Are those original and real, or did you get an upgrade after the fact?"

Ari ignored this. "What did you mean about Mark meeting his great-uncle's son in the DZ?"

Zack looked confused. "I would like to know the answer to that myself." He turned to Tabitha. "Tabitha, you are Norean because God placed you there to oppose the Archon and LEOH. This is exactly why you were created, and for so much more which you can't imagine."

Tabitha scoffed, "Apparently, I'm either created to destroy him or to become his knocked-up, skanky girlfriend. Also, either I finish LEOH to destroy humanity, or I take it away from him. It's a tough call. Don't put too much pressure on me. Mark, tell them about your great-uncle's son while I decide."

Everyone looked at me. I shrugged. "I have no idea what she's talking about. I don't know anything about meeting my great-uncle's son."

Tabitha replied, still focused on Ari, "I'll tell you in a minute. First, I want to know if Dylanis endowed you or unendowed me. Is that a real word? This is criminally unfair. If we really are identical clones, it's intentional malpractice."

I switched my attention to Zack. "Zack, are you sure we can really trust her? There are things about her you don't know."

Zack nodded as Tabitha blurted out, "What things? Don't say things like that to a clarion. I'm your wife's sister now! I'm here because of you, Mark! I discovered what you did the day after I left the Citadel at Interlochen. Am I the only one who sees how crazy these coincidences are? This is like seeing the future. I have a sister now and a new family, although I'm pretty sure something went horribly wrong in the cloning process. I should file a lawsuit to get to the bottom of it. Maybe this tragedy can be reversed without breast implants."

Ari burst out laughing.

I said, "Zack, there's something important you need to know."

"Did you just change the subject?" Tabitha whined.

I pulled out the MDC. "Zack, before Tabitha came, I was hoping to tell you what happened to me in the DZ. I also want to give this MDC back to you."

"Is that the device you used to steal the data?" Tabitha said. "May I see it?" Zack nodded, and I handed it over. She popped out the MDC core to study it, like she knew her way around it. "It's hard to believe you downloaded so much on this thing so quickly. Do you have a backup? These old prototypes aren't very stable. I could copy it onto my PCD."

Zack said, "You may as well, as long as you think it's safe for you to do so."

Tabitha shrugged. "Since I'm already a genetic dissident, having a backup of stolen classified data I already know about won't make me less of a target. Besides, this old thing can be easily discovered and mine can't. How did you get it out of the NCGD? Oh my God, please don't tell me this was in your elferdinky." She set it down, like it was contaminated.

"No, I swallowed it ... what's an elferdinky?"

Tabitha shuddered. "Mark, everyone knows it's where that leads ... eventually."

Ari just about rolled over laughing, and put her hand over her face.

Zack said calmly, "I hope we can disseminate the relevant portions of what's on this device as soon as possible. This is something you could probably help us accomplish."

Tabitha considered this. "I'm not sure you realize what you pulled down with this thing. It's not like I could just lower the SADEX score on these records to public content. You got it all."

Ari said, still laughing, "Can we please get to the part about Mark's great-uncle's son?"

I replied, "I need to tell Zack something first, which may be more important right now. While I was in the DZ last week I encountered some refugees along with a guide from this ATO organization. I heard on the NCNS some of them were captured."

Tabitha started to say something, but I cut her off. "This ATO guide I met, Bob, knew about you. That's probably not good if he's among those captured. They didn't and wouldn't mention him. He said to tell you Jonas Peres sends his regards. I know it was stupid to tell him anything. I never imagined he'd be captured. He knew who you are. I never mentioned your name but he knows you. Not only that, he told me you had three great-granddaughters and that Ari is a clone, with two identical sisters!"

"You knew about this all weekend and didn't tell me?" Ari said.

"Ari, Bob said this was dangerous information. We didn't have a dead space, apart from that worthless walnut, which lasts only a couple of minutes. We also agreed not discuss anything until we came here."

Zack looked at the three of us. "That walnut is not worthless. It got me out of some sticky situations in the past. As far as I know, Ari and Tabitha are the only other members of my side of the family. I know I told you before that Ari was the only one, but this time I'm telling you the truth. You said the man you encountered used the name Jonas Peres?"

"He said it was an old alias and you would recognize that name," I said. Then Tabitha started to speak up, but Zack cut her off.

"Mark, this is serious," he said. "What did you tell him? He could have. ... They are going to be questioning these people for days. You should never have told him anything."

"I know, I know," I said. "I'm not a professional spy, you know. I met two other ATO at the 4UB6 station. I may have told them a few things as well."

"You're a horrible spy and have no idea how to talk to a clarion," Tabitha put in.

"Zack, the ATO people I met at 4UB6 had one of these," I said, picking up the MDC. "I told Bob that I married the great-granddaughter of the man who likely gave them this device. I never mentioned your name. He knew who you were. The news only referred to the two men, Kirk and Gil, and one of them was killed. I wouldn't dare run a formulation on their capture to find out anything else."

Zack said to Tabitha. "How in blazes did you know this man is related to Mark?"

Tabitha yawned as she poured more tea. "I could use a strong cup of coffee. Can I say something now, without my interruptions being interrupted?"

"By all means," Zack said.

Tabitha sat up. "I'm sorry to have to tell you this. Ryan Waters was captured. Director Pythorael knows who he is, at least now he does, since I'm the one who told Dalen his real name."

Zack buried his hands in his head. "Why would you do that? How would you even know?"

Tabitha shrugged. "It was a calculated risk."

"A calculated risk? A calculated risk for what purpose?"

Tabitha held up both hands. "Look, they have one of your ... our ... relatives in custody. They've already interrogated him under Phencol. He's going to tell them everything eventually, if they don't kill him first. Now Pythorael knows he has a genuine Waters in his custody. What he doesn't know is, as soon as he adds this information to the security directive, LEOH will automatically quarantine it and transfer his capture matrix and incarceration order to me. Besides, I thought I would help you get him out ... as an addendum to my diabolical plan to take over L2 and then the world."

This girl is so strange and scary, I thought. She might be serious.

"They have one other man, Kirk Daniels, held with him in the CCD primary detention facility," Tabitha added. "They also have Daniels' wife and children. The girl is being held not far from here."

Zack became animated. "How on earth did you discover his real name?"

I turned to Zack, "Please don't ask her that. She already figured out our entire family tree and …"

Tabitha said, "I know Jonas and Peres were Anthony's other two children. When you put the two names together it makes a fine alias, don't you think? He told them that was his real name. They terminated his interrogation because they overdosed him on Phencol and almost killed him. He's still sick as a dog, so the Ministry can't talk to him right now. Once Pythorael adds this little fact about his name to the SD only I can talk to him. It's all part of my awesome plan."

I had forgotten about these names. Yet somehow Tabitha had connected it all.

Zack was red in the face. "This is terrible. Mark discloses things he should never have to people he doesn't know. Then, for some unfathomable reason, you give Pythorael Ryan's real name. I thought you all were smarter than this. This family is an open book. You can't get anyone out of CCD detention. It's impossible."

Tabitha insisted, "I agree, Mark is a terrible spy, but what I did was brilliant, and not for some unfathomable reason. Besides, I bet I can get him out. You'll see. I don't know how, exactly, but we can come up with a plan. I don't do anything without exceptional reasons."

Zack started pacing. "There is no way to get a prisoner out of a CCD detention facility."

Tabitha shrugged. "Not if they're under my jurisdiction. I could probably just order his release."

"You can't do that. He's a Waters," Zack insisted. "You would be implicated."

"Fair point," Tabitha responded. "Nevertheless, I'm very good at getting away with stuff."

"Where's the girl?" I asked. "You said she's not far from here."

Tabitha studied her display. "She's at a detention school for juvenile girls in the Carrington district, fifteen kilometers from here. She'll be fine. They're not going to kill her. She's of no value to them."

Ari spoke up. "She will probably be sold into prostitution or worse. That's her value to them."

Tabitha said, "Sometimes entire families are sent into the labor allocation system. God only knows what might happen to a young girl in one of those places. She's probably lucky."

Ari was adamant. "Lucky? Even though it's illegal for these children to be trafficked, the system is corrupt. You could probably do something to get her out."

Tabitha objected. "It's not wise, given the amount of scrutiny which could result. I don't think we want to expose ourselves by trying to rescue some little girl."

I agreed with Ari. "The girl's name is Tina. She is twelve years old. When I realized what was about to happen her, I decided help those people. That little girl's bravery was what emboldened me to help save them. Seriously, Ari even predicted it in a dream. It's no coincidence that she's close by."

Tabitha turned to me. "OK, but I guess you only care about this girl. What about the rest of the girls in there, and everywhere else in New City? Helping one girl is not going to make a difference to them."

Tabitha looked at Ari. "We might need a miracle to pull this off. Rescuing little damsels in distress is not what I'm good at, nor what I had in mind. If I got sentimental over every child caught up in a life-threatening situation, I could not function. However, since we could probably get away with rescuing this one, I will do it for you, little sister."

"And rescuing men from CCD detentions centers *is,* apparently, what you're good at?" I said.

Ari didn't know the first thing about Tina. Yet she'd always had a genuine soft spot for others, especially children. She hugged Tabitha, then kissed her cheek. I think my wife was beginning to warm up to her strange new, older twin sister.

"By the way," Tabitha said, "Ryan's sister Peres isn't dead. I know where she is. She is actually married and has a five-year-old little girl."

Zack took Tabitha's hand and kissed it. "I am anxious to hear about that. I'm so glad you're finally here. I been wanting to tell you your whole life how much I've always loved you. We are your family and we all love you."

This realization hit Tabitha hard. She broke down in tears. The Noreans never loved her, and she had never had anyone close to her. She had a whole new family, and she wasn't alone anymore. She thought about the boy from school, who was now a man, and cried even harder.

CHAPTER 27

A COMPILATION OF COINCIDENCES

As it turned out, among Tabitha's many talents was being a consummate strategist. She quickly devised a brilliant scheme to obtain custody of Tina. It was a scenario that would make the most brazen and creative con artist envious.

Tabatha decided it would be amusing to identify the most notorious person among a host of potential guardians. In the process, she intended to implicate the individual in the illegal abduction of Tina Daniels from the Carrington Columns School for Girls, ages eight to sixteen. There was apparently significant demand, for ninety-pound twelve-year-old girls with light brown or dirty blond hair and hazel eyes. I was sickened by the specificity of it.

Fortunately, Tabitha's formulation activities were essentially off the grid. It was relatively easy for her to make a few connections to identify the school administrator most likely to be involved in child trafficking. She then identified a person at the NCSS that such administrators had worked with before. By virtue of this person's agency, she found someone who had brokered "adoptions" of at least a dozen similar young girls for a woman living in the Marshall district.

She deliberately chose as the prospective adoptive parent someone with numerous quashed security directives against her for suspected child prostitution offenses, none of which had been fully resolved. When I say this was relatively easy for Tabitha, I mean that it would have taken any normal human a week to do what she did in a couple of hours. Ari and I hardly helped, except to throw out a couple of suggestions.

Zack allowed Tabitha the exclusive use of one of the ghosted access codes to discover the PCD passcodes for those she intended to implicate. Once she'd obtained those, she created a complete trail of communications, including initiating the transfers of funds between the various parties involved, which mirrored similar incident SD matrixes.

She also drafted official digital documents, so that when Ari arrived at the Carrington school later that evening, Tina would be handed over to her as a duly authorized representative of the NCSS. The ruse was, Ari would be acting as a co-perpetrator, with the express authorization of the school's deputy administrator in charge of custody transfers and adoption releases.

Tabitha adeptly reprogrammed an older, unregistered PCD device of Zack's and removed any matrix index references to its serial number. With this new PCD Ari was now a different person, with the identity of a legitimate NCSS official. She was also someone no one at the school would be able to recognize.

It took almost as long to create an identity and suitable disguise for Ari as it did for Tabitha to complete everything else. Ari had to at least look like the woman she was impersonating. In a world where facial recognition was the norm, we all knew it would be possible for a security directive to be initiated against Ari should someone run a utilization on any facial scans picked up on the school's monitors. Even so, Tabitha planned to temporarily deactivate them when Ari arrived in a public SPDV. She also planned to scramble the SPDV's registration index, in case it was picked up during the process. Although I tried to dissuade Ari from doing this, she insisted she could.

Zack admired and approved of the plan. He said he hoped we could come up with an equally well-orchestrated plan to get Ryan and Kirk out of detention. Watching how Tabitha worked, I realized she didn't miss much when it came to immensely complicated details.

Ari was brave and played her role perfectly. Tabitha knew who was on duty at the school. Yet she must have missed some part of the usual transaction, which almost resulted in disaster.

The evening administrator didn't question the official documents. A sad and quiet Tina was promptly delivered to Ari in the administrator's office, with virtually nothing in her possession. She was wearing a ragged school uniform. Ari offered Tina no explanation as she took the girl's hand and prepared to leave.

The administrator stopped her. "Excuse me, Miss, one thing before you go. I'm assuming I will receive my usual fee for this? I really must insist."

Ari turned. "I don't handle that. May I ask what your usual fee is?" The administrator wrote a number on a scrap of paper. She handed it to Ari without saying a word. Without a moment's hesitation, Ari said, "Check your account, Mrs. Aberdeen. I believe the 1,500 NCCUs are in your account."

Tabitha, who had been listening in on the conversation, initiated a transfer to the woman's account after doing some quick research. Unfortunately, she had to make the transfer from her own private account, because she didn't have time to reestablish the ghosted key connection. She would have to clean this up later. Tabitha hoped the quarantine on her own activities would override any potential security directive.

Moments later, the administrator checked her PCD. She seemed satisfied; the funds had arrived in her account. "Thank you, Ms. Daughtry. I hope Tina enjoys her new family."

Ari wanted to strangle the pompous woman. "I'm sure she will do well."

Instead of returning to Zack's apartment, the SDPV took Ari and Tina a few kilometers away. It dropped them at a busy shopping and restaurant complex, where they went inside a shop to wait. Tina kept asking Ari questions: *Where were they going? Could she see her mother?* Ari tried to quiet her and said nothing revealing. Minutes later, a limo SDPV pulled up with Tabitha inside.

It was important that Tabitha to do this to keep Tina and Ari shielded from active surveillance. The two got into the vehicle. As soon as they did, Tabitha and Ari hugged each other. They turned to Tina, who stared at them intently, still wondering what was going on.

Tina said, "Are you two sisters? You look alike."

Ari and Tabitha laughed. Ari answered, "So much for my disguise. My name is Ariel and yes, this is my sister, Tabitha. Everyone calls me Ari. Tabitha came up with the plan to rescue you. We hope to reunite you with the rest of your family. You'll stay with us until then."

Tina said to Tabitha, "You remind me of somebody I met when we were leaving the city. Do you play checkers? She was really weird and funny, but super good at playing checkers, and I'd thought I was pretty good."

"No, but I can teach you how to play chess," Tabitha said.

"She beat me at that too, in about one minute," Tina sulked.

When the trio returned to Zack's apartment and Tina saw me, she could hardly believe it. Tabitha gave her a warm smile. "Mark sent us to rescue you. It's become an obsession of his."

The Noreans owned a house in the scenic Highlands district situated in the sparsely populated mountainous region of the Southern Jurisdiction. This district bordered Sanctuary Gate 2, and was located about 275 kilometers from Zack's Park Central apartment. It was not their primary residence and was one of a dozen homes that belonged to Tabitha's family. She insisted it would be a safe place to hide Tina until we could figure out what to do next. With no full-time caretaker in residence during the fall, the place was empty.

After some discussion, it was decided Ari would accompany Tina to the house and stay with her. I reluctantly agreed. After packing some food and supplies for the girls, Tabitha sent them off to the Highlands in her private SPDV. She synchronized her vehicle with her own PCD so it would automatically open the gates in and around the secure, exclusive enclave where the house was located. I was a nervous wreck until ten o'clock in the evening when I was assured they had arrived safely.

Now I could fully participate in Zack and Tabitha's plan to rescue Kirk and Ryan. I didn't want to seem too pessimistic, but I thought it would be next to impossible. Tabitha didn't think in terms of impossible. She even infected Zack with her zealous overconfidence. She approached the most insurmountable problems as if they were mathematical equations. To her, if you solved all the variables and the formula worked, the solution was a forgone conclusion. As Tabitha and Zack worked out a plan, I could hear her say "see, easy peasy" or "boop" at intervals. At some point, however, I fell asleep.

CHAPTER 28

THE DUNGEON MASTER

Tabitha nudged me to wake me up. She spoke quietly, although no one could overhear us in her private SDPV. "We're at the Citadel. The Archon is expecting us. Mark, it's critical you go ahead with this. If you remain employed by the Ministry, Pythorael and Rogan have internal procedures I can't control. But as soon as Devan orders you to be put under the jurisdiction of the NCIC, you'll be assigned a different credential level. NCIC access supersedes even the CCD security protocols. There will only be a short period of time while you're still under the Ministry's jurisdiction. Have you gone over what we discussed about joining the NCIC staff?"

I nodded my head. "I think so. I can't help but think we are playing right into his hands. Are you sure this is necessary? I was adamant about my decision not to stay with the Ministry or work for him at the NCIC. I don't know what he's up to, but you should realize he's still convinced I'm involved with the data theft."

Tabitha glared at me. "Trust me, this is going to be necessary in the long run. Just answer his questions and follow my lead if necessary."

Her vehicle pulled up in front of the Citadel's massive gate. It was waved through immediately as her credentials were transmitted. The vehicle slowly wound its way up the drive, through the palace grounds. A uniformed man at the front entrance escorted us inside.

As the Archon entered the room where Tabitha and I were waiting, he bade us remain seated and came over to shake my hand. He kissed the back of Tabitha's hand affectionately. "I suppose I have you to thank for this, ēlan? Mark, I was delighted when Tabitha told me you wished to accept my offer to work for us at the NCIC. She told me you had been brooding over this for three days. I'm glad you decided this was the right choice, given everything that's happened to you. But I thought you said you wanted to spend time with your wife for a few days."

I glanced at Tabitha. "I want to get this decision off my chest. I still intend to spend a few days with my wife. Frankly, more than anything I want to remove myself from the Ministry's extra surveillance and the threat of my home being ransacked again. Tabitha has invited me, or rather offered my wife and me, the use of one her family's private homes in the Highlands for a few days. This will give us an opportunity to get away from the Park Central district for the remainder of my brief sabbatical."

The Archon hesitated for a second. "Well, there's nothing I can do about their extra surveillance in the short term. However, once you are fully under the directorate of the NCIC, there are very different security protocols for IC members and their staff. I am personally convinced you had nothing to do with this theft. I told directors Rogan and Pythorael as much. What really made you come to this decision? You seemed determined not to accept my offer."

"Mostly, I don't want to work for Dalen Pythorael, for personal reasons."

"I understand," Devan said. "Even so, working for the CCD is a prestigious job."

"Before I came to work for the Ministry, I thought people respected it as the premier security agency in the city. I have since discovered the Ministry is not well liked or trusted. I assumed I would be investigating criminals. Instead I'm compiling dossiers on people who complain too much about their neighborhood amenities. Despite Director Pythorael's attempts to dissuade me, I would, nevertheless, still resign my position at the CCD. Working for the NCIC is a unique opportunity. I decided I would be crazy not to accept this position. I hope you haven't changed your mind because of these recent allegations."

Tabitha glared at me like I was pushing it a little too far.

The Archon smiled. "My offer still stands. I was going to have to make my excuses for next Monday. Something has come up and I must leave for the Central Jurisdiction later today. I should return by the middle of next week if things go well, although I may have to travel to the Eastern Jurisdiction for a few days to deal with another matter before I return. This will give you a full week to rest up from your ordeal. I can't do much about the Ministry in the meantime. We'll get everything sorted out when I return."

The Archon glanced over at Tabitha knowingly. He wasn't about to disclose that he had now assigned all investigations of me exclusively to her. "Pythorael won't take any action against you without my express authority. He is still hounding me to debrief you on your recent activities in the DZ, especially after the capture of some of the fugitives you encountered there. But since he is also a member of the NCIC council he has also been summoned to the Central Jurisdiction."

Tabitha said, "I could establish Mark's credentials whenever you are ready to authorize them. I'm still technically the administrator of L2. Only you can authorize the creation of a TA2E security clearance, the lowest level NCIC staff designation. There will be no need to immediately authorize his access to the primary NCIC system sectors. You can make this determination later. This will at least give him legitimate immunity from NCMIA oversight in the meantime. It's only a suggestion."

The Archon thought about this. "Send me the AR. I'll consider approving it. Mark, if you would excuse us, I'd like to have a private word with Tabitha, if you don't mind."

That made me more than a little uncomfortable. "Of course, and again, I appreciate this opportunity to be of service to the NCIC, in whatever capacity you believe is beneficial." Within seconds, a servant appeared to escort me outside, leaving Tabitha alone with the Archon.

* * * *

The Archon turned to Tabitha. "From your report this morning, I noted you haven't discovered anything useful about our stolen data. You obviously haven't infiltrated this group of conspirators or gained their confidence. It was disappointing and you didn't elaborate. Tell me about your clarifications on Zachariah Waters."

Tabitha glared at the Archon. "What are you doing, sending him out of here like that? Having this impromptu meeting with me will only make Mark suspicious. Sometimes you can be a complete nitwit, Wile E. Coyote. Are you trying to derail everything I'm doing? I'm just getting started. As far as Zack is concerned, there isn't much to tell. He returned from the hospital yesterday."

The Archon ignored Tabitha's insult. "Was it really Mark's idea to accept my offer?"

Tabitha grinned. "He doesn't trust me, but I have made my negative feelings about New City, you, and Dalen Pythorael quite clear. He has to believe he is no longer a suspect."

"Do you have any clarification about a conspiracy?"

Tabitha said, "Despite Mark's relationship to Ari, he is relatively unconnected to Zack. Evidence proves he only met him right before he came to work for the Ministry. Mark doesn't fit the profile of a subversive. Nevertheless, he does hate the Ministry because of his mistreatment. As to the whereabouts of your stolen data and the contraband device, I've seen no evidence of it yet. Also, there is no evidence Mark is part of an active cell of this ATO organization, or any other. As for Zack, I've hardly had an opportunity to prove myself useful. I need more time."

"All this sounds speculative; it's unworthy of your talents," the Archon said.

Tabitha responded, "This could all be misdirection orchestrated at the highest levels of the Ministry or perhaps some fantastically sophisticated conspiracy to point us to the wrong suspects. Zack Waters and

Mark Verigratu would be perfect targets, precisely because of their coincidental relationship. There is another culprit higher up in the IC hierarchy who may be orchestrating events behind the scenes. The coincidences are too incredible to be ignored, yet they also appear to be too obvious."

The Archon smirked. "I know what you keep implying, ēlan. I don't think Dalen Pythorael would create a fake scenario to frame someone. He would have no motivation to do such a thing."

"Perhaps it was someone outside the Ministry? Look, I realize either Mark and Zack Waters did it, or someone made it look like they did."

The Archon shook his head in frustration. "I feel no more certain about this than before I assigned this investigation to you. You should join Mark and his wife at your parents' house in the Highlands. Consider having Zack brought along to convalesce. I'm sure it is large enough for all of you to be comfortable." He added, "In the meantime, we can have Zack's apartment thoroughly searched, without his knowledge, for anything incriminating."

Tabitha objected. "Stop trying to run this investigation. If you start sending in your gorillas to search Zack's apartment, you will screw up any possibility of my gaining their confidence."

The Archon fumed. "I want results! You haven't exactly delivered any."

"Two meetings with Mark, that's all I've had, and one with Zack. What did you expect? At least I've dressed the part for this covert operation." She gestured to her casual new look. "Seriously Devan, if they are involved in anything, it will be far bigger than what they openly discuss around the dinner table. This is going to take more time. Besides, I've already proposed that Zack join Ari and Mark in the Highlands."

"What was the pretense for your visit?"

"My pretense is not your concern," Tabitha said. "You are incompetent at handling intelligence assets. I brought Mark here to fix your last terrible mistake. Now I'm going to have repair this. You need to stay out of it. And keep your snickering Muttley Magoo, Prideil, out of it as well, Dr. Claw."

"You are fortunate I adore you or I wouldn't tolerate your childish insults," he said mildly.

"I wouldn't insult you if you would let me do this my way! Stop trying to second guess me! How am I supposed to infiltrate them and convince them I'm working against you? You can't call private confabs like this, Cobra Commander."

"Very well," the Archon said. "There is another matter I need you to look into." Pulling up his display, he said, "Have you read the interrogation reports on the captured ATO, Robert Ryan Waters, and the other prisoner, Kirk Daniels? This matter was just transferred to my authority. It has now been transferred to you, under the L2 protocol we established for your investigation. Dalen is not going to be happy about authority for his captives being transferred to your special investigation umbrella. Especially since this is the first Class 1 dissident we've captured in years, and the man is an ATO operative. L2 correlated them together."

Tabitha hesitated. "It correlated them? I hadn't noticed," she lied, smugly. "Why do you ask?"

The Archon seemed puzzled. "Does it not interest you that we seem to have captured an actual descendant of David Waters? Don't get me wrong, I was thrilled we finally captured one of these ATO scoundrels. What troubles me is that there is nothing in the directive matrix that indicates how this information came to the attention of the CCD. His name was clearly a detail Pythorael added later. This is, in fact, what triggered it to be moved out from under his authority. I want you to find out exactly where this information originated. Prideil has no idea where Pythorael got it. He said Dalen was evasive, unwilling to divulge his source, but it couldn't be Verigratu."

Tabitha tried to look unphased by this revelation. "That is very odd."

"Here is the way I see it," Devan said. "Mark Verigratu may have nothing to do with the data theft, however, he is directly implicated by his proximity to the event as the source of the intrusion. He may have nothing to do with the ATO infiltration of the DZ 4UB6 facility, yet once again he is present as the event takes place. Then, the ATO assists Mark in his escape from the DZ. Mark then encounters a group of escaped dissidents our forces later recapture in the DZ, and their ATO guide just happens to be a descendant of David Waters."

"Mark is not the mastermind behind any of this, Devan."

"I know, but he married Zachariah Waters great-granddaughter. Waters was at the Ministry when these rogue access codes were created. We know they were utilized to steal the classified data and they've been used to infiltrate LEOH's security directive matrix for decades. We know Zack had a hand in the R&D projects which developed the technology used to capture and store the stolen data. He is also friends with the current deputy director of the CCD, who formerly reported to him. This is the same man implicated in the inappropriate downgrade of the very GIA security directives issued for these captured fugitives. There are too many connections to ignore."

"Didn't I just say these coincidences are too incredible to be ignored, and yet appear to be too obvious? You're slipping, Dick Tracy. I didn't need a recapitulation of what I already know," Tabitha quipped.

"What do you think of this, when you line up all of these circumstances?"

Tabitha responded coolly, "I see one other person who may be at the center of it all, who is trying to cover up his own conspiracy. Coincidences may make Mark appear to be involved. Yet, there has to be at least some tangible evidence. I don't even know if they have the stolen data."

"I don't want to hear any more about your suspicions of Dalen Pythorael! And there is one other matter. Apparently, the young daughter of one of the prisoners was released under suspicious circumstances. We are, of course, investigating the matter. It would be incredible if this shadowy organization has the capacity to infiltrate and bypass our security so easily as to have rescued one of our captives, albeit an immaterial one. I want you to run a diagnostic on it.

"Something is going on here that has me on edge. Yet, I have more important matters to attend to for now. I will expect a comprehensive update by Tuesday, at the latest. In the meantime, the HESF will be at your disposal."

Tabitha was aghast. "Hold on, Adolph. I'm still trying to finesse this, not arrange for an assault from your jackbooted HESF. Hunting escaped captives is *not* my responsibility, but I'll look into it.

"Can I say one more thing about Dalen? Did you know the director quarantined the investigation into the K15 debacle and the death of Dr. Dylanis eighteen years ago? The only witnesses to what happened are all dead, except for Pythorael and Lawrence Rogan. Only a very intrusive bot could be used to completely scrub something like this out of the system. I may be fortunate to be alive. I think he wanted to destroy the project and its results, including me!"

The Archon seemed disturbed. "What made you investigate the K15 project?"

Tabitha shrugged. "I'm investigating all the events surrounding the creation of the ghosted access codes. In the process, I discovered several vague, tangential references to former Deputy Director Nicholas Santos and his involvement in the K15 incidents. He's also dead. I knew, of course, I was a product of this research, so I decided to investigate. Everything has been scrubbed. It's all gone."

Bewildered, the Archon said, "Why would he have wanted to destroy the K15 project? Your father warned me of your tendency to chase rabbits down holes. Stay focused on your assignment."

Tabitha replied, "My father is not someone whose judgment I would trust. He put Stanley in charge of Castle Point. That was like putting Caligula in charge of a day care center. Need I say more? Pythorael is afraid of your plans for me. It seems to me he was deathly afraid of someone like me being born. This is my clarification, after thinking about what he told me. He is going to try to take over this jurisdiction and kill me. I've told you, he indicated as much to me in his attempt to coerce me into joining his conspiracy. Pythorael is treacherous; he can't be trusted."

"I told you I will deal with Pythorael!" the Archon insisted. "I need you to stay focused."

Tabitha stood up. "I see how it is with you ... whatever you are. I'm just another of your little pawns in a game. If you want what's between my legs or whatever else you desire, you are never going to get there unless you deal with Pythorael," Tabitha said with finality. "Mark Verigratu, Zack Waters, subversive organizations, stolen data, and genetic dissidents are not what you should be worried about. Dalen Pythorael is." She walked out briskly.

Tabitha thought as she left, *I can't believe I just offered myself to that monster for the sake of discrediting Pythorael. Yet, if Devan wants me bad enough, maybe this will motivate him to deal with that slithering CCD director. Then I'll have free reign to deal with Devan.*

* * * *

Mythrael entered the room from the door opposite the one Tabitha exited. Elaniel turned to him as he entered. "So, Lord Mythrael, what are your thoughts?"

Mythrael hissed, "Surely, you do not intend to put up with this impudent girl any longer. She is of no benefit. You know she has met secretly on more than one occasion with that dialectic schemer, Pythorael. Who knows what she is concocting with this Verigratu boy? She has managed to cloak her activities completely, even from the High Echelon. She has far too much power over your systems and sensitive projects. You should allow me to have my way with her. I'll teach her respect."

Elaniel hissed back, "She is a Norean and belongs to me."

"I'll crush the insolence out of her. Then you can still have her for your ritual."

Elaniel countered, "She will serve my purpose at the right time. She is like the one before, yet far more powerful. I know when someone has the gift. She doesn't realize it, nor does she understand she is connected to me. It was prophesied, one of the descendants of that little miracle worker would be given to me. I need only one. I made her."

Mythrael laughed. "Do you really believe you actually conjured a descendant of that infamous young maiden? Such a hidden name is not so easily fabricated, even by genetic manipulation. I don't care what that blathering old crone promised you. Less than half of what she has ever predicted has come true. Ever! You and your myths. Perhaps that tree-bending triangulator Pythorael is right. What if you're wrong about this girl?"

"The girl ultimately had thousands of descendants. The ATK15 sequence has even found its way into our own most noble families. Ēlan Norean is proof of that," Elaniel said with certainty.

Mythrael walked to the large window that overlooked a courtyard. He said menacingly, "What if she's not who you think she is? For once, I agree with Prideil. He says Pythorael is having her re-sequenced offline to make certain she's even a Norean. Something has made him suspicious of her."

Devan snapped, "If any of you touch her, you will face my wrath."

"Do you believe that Pythorael tried to have her killed?" Mythrael asked. "Is it possible he knows the real reason you created this little ēlan K15 female?"

Devan replied, "There would be no reason for him to be concerned with the girls engineered in the K15 project. He knows what they were intended to be used for. But I am curious if he has knowledge of my plans for the Inner Circle and the High Echelon."

"I assume, if your merger is successful, you will keep your agreement with myself and Baalen Arianael. But I'm beginning to have doubts you will succeed, considering how spiteful your precious ēlan is. She was insulting you by calling you those names. It sounded disrespectful; it is deserving of death. She has obviously studied historical villains who have been defeated and is recklessly mocking you. That's what I suspect, considering my friend Adolph's name was mentioned. I'm sure the others are equally diabolical."

"Who isn't deserving of death to you?" The Archon laughed. "Those others were pre-war classic cartoon villains. She's just being Tabitha. She has no idea how much she is under my control. I can ignore her spiteful, petty insults. Everything will go according to plan. Your dungeons will be filled when the time comes."

CHAPTER 29

SLEIGHT OF HAND

After Tabitha and I left the Archon's Citadel, she filled me in on their private conversation on the way to the Norean estate. I was more suspicious of her than ever. Her uncanny skill at effortlessly discovering information supposedly hidden from the eyes of the Ministry made me nervous. Then there was the fact that she'd developed the latest version of New City's technological monstrosity. Yet here I was, about to put my life in the hands of this strange, terrifyingly brilliant girl.

I was astonished when I saw the Norean's main residence. Granted, it is not as magnificent as the Archon's Citadel palace. Even so, the Norean estate in the NCGD is an incredible palace itself, surrounded by lush gardens. It even had its own immaculately maintained golf course. I had never seen a private home this magnificent. As I walked inside, I gaped at the grand foyer and the high glass domed ceiling. It was all literally breathtaking. Yet it didn't occur to her that I would be amazed by her home or by all the servants at her beck and call.

Tabitha and I were sitting across from one another in plush lounge chairs in a rather large den. This was one of the cozier rooms in her house. After she caught me staring at her for the tenth time, she glared at me. I had to confess. "I'm sorry I keep staring at you. I just can't believe the moment we met I didn't recognize your resemblance to Ari. I did sort of, but now it's so obvious to me you are sisters. And it's amazing to watch how fast you work. Do you always use four displays?"

She ignored me. Finally, she said, "Enough! Do you want me to strip naked so you can see if I have the same birth marks? Stop staring like a hungry wolf."

I was embarrassed. "Do you actually have any? Birthmarks, I mean? Ari does; one on her tush."

Tabitha glared at me. "Ēlans do not have birthmarks! You are starting to remind me of my creepy brother, who always looked at me like a predator!"

"That's hardly fair. It's just that I think you're beautiful, and you remind me of Ari." *I have enough images to find your birthmarks.*

Tabitha huffed, "I need to concentrate. Go find something useless to do."

"That's just it," I said. "I'm not sure what's supposed to happen next. You're sitting there doing all this work, while I don't know what's going on."

Tabitha groaned. "I didn't make you sleep through most of the planning for this. For now, we have to wait for the bearer token to be issued, authorized, and validated."

"What's a bearer token? What am I supposed to do?"

Tabitha took a deep breath. "Go have a beer! We've had a change of plans. The Archon and his entourage will soon be leaving for the Central Jurisdiction. We need to wait until he is well on his way before *we* do anything. Pythorael and Rogan will be attending this meeting, as well."

"I'm not following. How will you know this?"

Tabitha rolled her eyes at me. "Do you really need to ask? I'll know."

We had gone over few details of the rescue plan she and Zack had decided upon overnight. Since I'd slept most of the way to the NCGD, I missed an opportunity to be fully briefed. It was still all pretty vague to me. Apparently, it was also still a work in process in Tabitha's mind, which consisted of numerous fragments and potential improvisations.

Tabitha finally gave me a brief, ultra-fast, rapid-fire download of the details of the plan. What little I could swallow seemed way too complicated. I became increasingly nervous. Yet Tabitha remained calm and confident. It was as if once she put her mind to something, she didn't imagine the possibility of failure. This was true, regardless of whether she had all the details worked out.

I kept waiting for more, but Tabitha's single tidal wave was all I was going to get. After that, we talked about anything except the plan. Tabitha was a fascinating individual. Yet she seriously gave me a headache when she went off on tangents and weaved together multiple topics. Although she looked like Ari, spending time with Ari was like a pleasant walk in the park. Spending time with Tabitha was like running a marathon.

We watched silly classic cartoons on the ED for a while; they were her favorite thing to watch. Then Tabitha started working furiously again. After a few minutes, I said, "Tabitha, all I have heard so far about this plan are a mishmash of vague details covering a rough outline which sounds like it could get us killed. Real people capable of pulling this kind of stunt off would plan it for weeks or months. You and Zack came up with this plan in a few hours. Unless you tell me exactly what's going on … I have to say, it's not going to happen."

Tabitha looked shocked and disappointed. "You can't back out now. It's happening; the messages have already been sent. The bearer token has dropped."

A minute later, Tabitha's SPDV pulled up at the front door. Tabitha smiled. "It's back! Time to go." Unbeknownst to me, after we were dropped off, she had sent her vehicle on an errand, perhaps to disguise her whereabouts and movements. We went outside and hopped inside the vehicle. The autopilot drove it into their spacious garage. Tabitha said, "Wait here for a minute."

"What was the point of us getting in at the front door, only to drive to the garage?"

She ignored me. Minutes later, she returned with a small bag. She then made us change vehicles. This next vehicle was even more luxurious than the first. Tabitha patched into Jerome Haley's PCD. "Jerome, this is Tabitha Norean. Our man is Chase Carrabin from the D14 HE detention facility. The encoded bearer token was delivered."

There was a pause on the other end, as Jerome waited for confirmation that his communication was not being intercepted. "The line is secure. Go ahead, please."

Tabitha rolled her eyes. "Of course, it's secure. Have you secured the Cat 9?"

Jerome responded, "It is on the way to Delvos. I missed the first part. What did you say?

Tabitha said, "Perfect! The transfer orders are on a certified encoded bearer token. You will be receiving a visit from an HESF officer with a prisoner transfer request for five prisoners to the High Echelon detention facility D14. Their transport is programmed with the credentials of the D14 associate commandant, Chase Carrabin, authorized by the encoded bearer token. It's programmed to deliver the prisoners to the prescribed coordinates."

There was silence on the line. Jerome asked, "How did you manage to get an HE bearer token encoded, issued, and delivered to the D14 commandant so quickly?"

Tabitha yawned. "It's the orders it contains that were the hard part. I assume the bearer token was dropped to the courier according to standard procedures, like any other token you guys use for stuff like this. I don't know how it got there. Just validate the orders to indicate your receipt of the token. Zack is the one who told me how this works ... sort of. His memory was a little fuzzy."

Jerome said, "This is an extremely rare way of doing things. Zack has been out of circulation for a while. I didn't even know those things were still used."

Hearing this made me uncomfortable.

The transfer request arrived at Jerome's office an hour later. The authorization was in impeccable order. He validated it exactly as he would have had this been a real transfer order issued by the office of the Archon himself.

While we waited, Tabitha explained the process. I realized she was rattling off Zack's word-for-word explanation to her about how bearer tokens worked.

She said, "According to Zack, when transfer orders are issued under such conditions, they are transmitted via a coin-like device, only to the receiving facility. There is no electronic corresponding transfer authorization sent to the holding facility. The encrypted device is then required to be hand delivered to the highest-ranking executive on station, in this case, Jerome. The token is verified by a confirmation scan to validate the authenticity of the device's transfer orders. It is then hand delivered to the holding facility commandant, who is charged with carrying out the orders to release the prisoners into the custody of those holding the now verified and validated token. While this method of prisoner transfer authorization is infrequently used, it is still recognized as a standard operating procedure in the rare circumstances where the High Echelon intends to intervene to take charge of high-profile detainees. Boop!" (The "boop" part was Tabitha's.)

The problem was, this kind of transfer hadn't been used for over a decade. Tabitha added other detainees to the orders as a distraction. They would be recaptured.

When the transfer orders arrived, Jerome entered the encryption code for the validated orders into his Ministry issued PCD. He transmitted it to the detention facility, according to procedure. This would alert the shift commander on duty that a High Echelon transfer was being initiated. All other confirmation procedures were subordinate once the token device was scanned and verified at the facility. Jerome strode to Commander Delvos' office. He used his access code, which Tabitha had stolen, to open Devlos' parcel delivery locker, where the Cat 9 had been delivered.

We drove to a secluded place. I had no idea where we were. At some point, Jerome arrived. He handed over a large package and then a smaller one, which he withdrew from his jacket pocket. It felt like we were doing a drug deal in the middle of nowhere. Without a word, he hopped back in his SDPV and headed to his home outside of the district.

Tabitha and I sped away in the opposite direction, toward the center of the NCGD, only to turn off on a side road. This led to a large agricultural processing and distribution facility. We stopped on the side of the road and waited. I looked at Tabitha questioningly. She said, "The prisoner transport will pass by on the main road in five minutes. I guess it's time I told you the rest of the details."

I snorted. "We're going to end up in a detention center doing this."

Tabitha pulled a weapon of sorts from the large package Jerome had just handed us. "This is an anesthetizer dart gun. The glass cartridges contain small vials of an odorless knockout gas. It will render anyone who breathes it unconscious for about forty minutes. It only has to break within two meters of someone; then they're out cold in seconds. This other package contains about a dozen doses of Catenine, or Cat 9. This, of course, is a short-term memory blocking serum."

"Is the Cat 9 for us? So we can forget what a terrible plan this is once we're caught?"

"We won't get caught. With your attitude, it's hard to believe you actually killed guys in the DZ, with a real gun."

"I would like to have a real gun to do this."

"Mark, you know guns are illegal. Besides, there are only six guards."

"Right, that makes complete sense. We don't want to break the law or anything."

Our SPDV suddenly took off at top speed, heading south on the NGCD's main highway. We traveled for half an hour, then turned onto a road and headed east along a wooded area surrounded by large farming operations. We eventually arrived at our destination, an older two-story office building. Our SDPV entered through the gates, which opened automatically. We were driven to an underground loading zone at the back of the facility. An automated door admitted us. As our vehicle entered, the lights came on inside the oversize area. We drove to the farthest loading platform and stopped. Tabitha turned off the lights. "I just wanted to make sure that when we make our move against the transport guards, we have plenty of light."

"What do you mean, make our move? What about the six heavily armed, and might I add, well trained, High Echelon security force personnel on that transport? I don't mean to be a pessimist, but neither of us are qualified, much less trained for this kind of operation. Then there is that other one small consideration. We don't have a real weapon!"

Tabitha looked at me incredulously. "Mark, you killed, how many men in the DZ by yourself? Now, you're worried about a handful of prison guards? Stop being a coward."

"I killed them with bullets, and I had a rocket launcher! Did you miss my point about us not having a real weapon?" I protested. "I also had the drop on them. Those morons were about as well trained as bears in the woods, with names like Snakeskull, Nachodip and Weasel."

Tabitha smirked. "And you didn't have a tranquilizer thingy either. You killed poor Nachodip ... augh?"

"Yep, it was a tough call. He was going to rape a child. By the way, I had a real gun with real bullets. They have a tranquilizing effect. Did I mention I also had a rocket launcher?"

* * * *

The prisoner transfer had apparently gone off without a hitch. The unsuspecting guards and prisoners boarded the transport thinking they were being driven by the pre-programmed vehicle back to the D14 HE permanent detention facility. But instead of driving west, the transport headed south, then east, about seventy kilometers toward the New City North Park district. Before it reached the North Park district gate, the pre-programmed transport was diverted onto a side road, which took them to an abandoned research facility operated by the Integration Science Division.

The facility had been mothballed for nearly ten years. It was now used to store surplus equipment once used in the development of earlier PCD prototype devices.

There was no need for guards at the facility since it was sensory controlled. It was also well within the heavily guarded NCGD security zone. Tabitha, however, was able to take over access to all the security controls at the facility and activate the entrance gates to the complex. She had the transport drive to the underground loading zone area where she and I were waiting on them ... armed with our tranquilizer thingy.

"I think they are going to be suspicious. They will be ready for anything, once they realize they haven't arrived at their intended destination," I said, my nerves on edge.

Tabitha motioned toward the nearest pylon. "Just stand ready behind that pylon over there. When the vehicle stops, sneak up to the back of the transport. When the rear door opens, fire at least one gas dart into the back. Within seconds, no one inside will be able to move, much less offer any resistance. There shouldn't be any problems. It's almost here. It will stop ten meters directly in front of that pylon. Don't miss! I'll wait for you to move forward before turning on the lights."

"What if they don't open the door? They could also call for support," I said.

Tabitha looked at me like I was speaking a different language. "They can't, there's no com node here and it's underground. Also, why do you think I chose this location? They traveled the precise distance to their own facility. They won't question it. Oh, I almost forgot, you need to put this on." Tabitha handed me a scarf and a cap.

"Seriously, this is the best you could come up with as a disguise? What am I supposed to do with this? This wouldn't stop a facial recognition sensor. Besides, it sucks ... pink and purple and with a yellow cap?"

"It's either that or the butterfly scarf. I'm pretty sure you wouldn't like the other hat, either. Sorry I didn't have a more manly fashion ensemble or a closet full of rubber face masks and assault gear. This will do; just wrap it around your face to cover your mouth. It's mostly to keep any latent tranquilizer gas from knocking you out. I'll delete the indexes for the surveillance feeds. Don't worry, no one will see you wearing a cute girly scarf. Get moving, hurry!"

"Well, why didn't you say so? I'm confident these are of sufficient quality to prevent harmful gas molecules from permeating them. Did they actually teach you about the properties of gases in molecular chemistry at the Clarion Academy, or was it all just about hypnotic potions?"

Tabitha pointed toward the pylon with gritted teeth. "Shut it, or I'll give you a potent concoction."

I scurried behind the pylon, as I was instructed by *General* Norean. She remained behind at her command post beside her vehicle, looking far too prissy and well dressed for someone trying to facilitate a prisoner escape. I don't think she had any rugged clothes, or at least none for something like this. I started laughing at her in the butterfly scarf and her bright green hat, which was actually velvet, with a ruffled fringe. We both looked ridiculous.

"I'm not sure you are wearing the right amount of jewelry for something like this," I shouted, once I was in position. "Also, who does something like this in a vehicle that costs more than most people make in three years? We really should have discussed the scarf part of the plan. Come to think of it, who does something like this ever, especially without actual weapons?"

Tabitha shouted back, "You're lucky I brought the scarves. That's what I ran back inside to get."

"Wow, there was a tactical breakdown in your meticulous plan? You can manage a fake High Echelon credentialed bearer token, but you ran back inside for these things?"

"It's your fault! If you hadn't been snoring and drooling on the couch, obviously dreaming of Ari while Zack and I made plans, I would have thought of everything."

"That's unfair. How do you know I was dreaming of Ari?" I said, embarrassed.

"Some things are hard not to notice. Get ready, here they come," she said.

Moments later, on cue, the transport vehicle stopped. I crept close to the rear of the vehicle. I crouched low, so no one inside who might be looking out the back windows would see me in the tail lights. The garage lights came on. After a few seconds, the back door opened. I fired the gas cartridge through the door, then rushed back behind the pylon to avoid the gas. Unfortunately, one of the guards scrambled out with his weapon at the ready. A second one quickly followed. So much for immediately disabling the guards.

I heard loud coughing from inside the vehicle, as the broken glass cartridge released the anesthetizing gas. The two guards facing me were temporarily blinded by the bright underground lights. One of them saw Tabitha, who was foolishly standing in the open, about fifteen meters away beside her SDPV. He raised his weapon at her and yelled for her to freeze. As she attempted to duck behind the vehicle, a round went off from his weapon. Tabitha squealed in pain. I started to panic, afraid she might be mortally wounded. Now there were two very alert and heavily armed guards standing outside the transport. This wasn't going according to plan.

I loaded another cartridge, then jumped out from behind the concrete pylon. I shot toward the ground, between the two guards, who were starting to spread out. The cartridge ricocheted off the ground. Little gas was released near them as the cartridge skittered away.

I took cover again behind the pylon. One of the guards, clearly unaffected, raised his weapon and headed in my direction. The other guard wasn't so lucky, as a puff of gas had escaped near him. He called out to his friend with a panicked plea for help, then collapsed. I peeked around. The second guard had turned to look back at his friend. I rushed toward him to tackle him to the ground. I hit him so hard, his weapon flew out of his hands, but he quickly recovered.

He was much larger than me, and threw me off him. He swung his fist at me and missed. A second punch hit me squarely in the jaw, knocking me back. He punched me two more times. I was getting the crap beat out of me. It became a desperate struggle to see which of us could reach the guard's weapon first; I was clearly losing.

I saw Tabitha out of the corner of my eye. She rushed forward and picked up one of the discarded weapons. She yelled, "Stop right now!" and pointed it at both of us, as we were entangled. The guard's hand was a few centimeters from the other weapon. We froze as Tabitha said, "Move, or you won't have a head."

Tabitha was bleeding from her left arm, near her shoulder, where the bullet had grazed her. The man released me. He stood up and stepped back, then lunged toward Tabitha and tried to grab her weapon. As quick as a cat, she stepped aside and grabbed his arm with her free hand. She sent him sprawling forward, giving him a swift kick in the back that put him face down on the ground. He managed to scramble to his feet. He stood up to go after her again. Tabitha did a quick turn then aimed another powerful kick at his face, which sent him flying over backward. Flat on his back, he lay on the ground motionless.

A moment later he sat up looking dazed and confused, with Tabitha pointing the weapon at his head. "Do you want to try that again?" she said. He looked at her in disbelief.

Tabitha, in what was perhaps a rare moment of ignorance, may not have realized the weapons might be encoded independently to each guard. But I don't think she really needed it. The guard held up his hands. I told her to move away from him. Both of us backed up about ten meters from him. I fired the last of the tranquilizing cartridges. It shattered on impact with his chest, releasing the gas. Seconds later, he lay unconscious. We moved even farther away as we waited for the gas to dissipate, in hopes that we wouldn't render ourselves unconscious.

My senses became foggy. This underground loading area was not well-ventilated. Much of the gas lingered in the air. Although it only had an effective concentration range of about three meters, it was extremely potent. Any latent gas in the air could partially impair someone, even well beyond this range. Tabitha and I walked back to her vehicle.

She produced two syringes from her bag and injected both of us. "This is to keep the gas from affecting us. I thought about dosing us before, but the effects can be harmful so I ..." she trailed off, about to pass out. "We should have brought gas masks and real weapons. We have tons of awesome weapons, a whole arsenal," she mumbled. Our scarves were on the ground, several meters away.

"You have real weapons and didn't think it would be a good idea to bring at least one? Are you going to blame my sleeping on the couch for that?"

I was starting to feel dizzy. Seconds later, we both passed out, collapsing on the ground beside each other. When I woke up, I looked at my PCD. At least ten minutes had passed. Tabitha was still unconscious. I attempted to rouse her. I thought she was dead or dying because of her injury or perhaps the injection, but she was still breathing and didn't appear to be bleeding too badly. After five minutes, she opened her eyes. "How long was I out?"

"About fifteen minutes. Either whatever you gave us knocked us out or it finally woke us up. I'm not sure which. I feel like I've been through another chemical interrogation."

She got to her feet. "We need to get out of here!" Tabitha looked wobbly, as if she might faint again. She started entering something into her PCD.

"Are you hurt bad?" I moved toward her, but she held up her hand to stop me.

"I'll be all right, the round just grazed my arm," she said.

"What about all this blood evidence? There could also be blood on that ballistic round. They'll know that a weapon was discharged. They might locate the bullet. They'll know you were here."

"Forget it. They won't know anything took place here," she said calmly.

We waited a few more minutes to allow our heads to clear. Once Tabitha recovered, she hacked into the guards' internal PCDs. She deleted footage of the last few minutes. "We wouldn't want embarrassing footage of your butt getting kicked to be circulated," she teased.

"What about the video of you rendering us unconscious, along with our awesome scarf and hat protection? They fell off at just the right time to make a splendid final highlight shot for this event. You should save a copy of any video feeds for stupid criminal bloopers."

"You weren't supposed to shoot tranquilizer gas out here," she said. "That was dangerous."

"Well, since the guards weren't supposed to be out here, and I didn't have a real gun, I decided to ignore that reasonable precaution, which you never mentioned."

"Fair point, still, you were the one who knocked us out," Tabitha said. "I totally saved us. Otherwise you would still be having another Ari dream, probably about her huge boobs."

"Apparently you dream about them, or at least talk about them, way more than I do," I said. "Besides, they're not even that big. Well, I guess compared to ..."

"Shut it!"

We made sure the gas was fully dissipated before we hauled Ryan and Kirk out of the transport and the two guards into it. They were all still asleep, along with the decoy prisoners. We then gave them all a Cat 9 injection, including Kirk and Ryan. In the event they were later recaptured, we didn't want them to remember anything about their rescue.

Tabitha had the prisoner transport programmed to drive to an isolated location several kilometers to the west, on the way to the NCGD corridor gate in the direction of the D14 High Echelon detention facility. We waited in the garage for about a half hour until the other decoy SDPV arrived. We were only about fifteen minutes behind schedule, thanks to our little nap.

This second SPDV was programmed to pick up two high-ranking female executives at a house in one of the upscale neighborhoods within the government district. At least, that's what the vehicle's log register would indicate. The plan was for this vehicle to take the two prisoners, once they were hidden in the trunk, to Jerome's married sister's old condo, where he would meet them. The unit was currently unoccupied. A new tenant was not expected to be moved in until the following month. The apartment was located outside the NCGD, in the North Park district, not far from where Jerome lived.

As we watched the SDPV drive away with Kirk and Ryan, presumably unconscious in the trunk, Tabitha and I gave each other a high five. We hugged and laughed at our success. Really, it was entirely Tabitha's success. I had had no idea at the time how intricate the plan had been. I was there primarily to botch up the last step. Even so, I was elated, because we'd lived through it and nobody died. I preferred this plan to what I'd dealt with in the DZ. I guessed it had been best that I didn't have a real weapon after all.

However, we hadn't worked out the details for what to do with Kirk and Ryan after the rescue. They would have to remain at the improvised safehouse until arrangements could be made to have them reunited with rest of Kirk's family and the ATO. This was a problem we could solve later. For all intents and purposes, the escape plan was a superb success.

Tabitha told me she still had work to do to cover up the trail of events. She also needed medical attention, although her injury didn't require emergency services.

As Tabitha's vehicle drove us back to her house, I used a first aid kit we found in the prisoner transport to doctor her injury as best I could. There was an auto suturing device, which I used to stitch up her wound. She squealed with pain as I not so expertly sutured her laceration. Between yelps, Tabitha started to tell me about a few matters I had not considered. For the next few hours, she said she had to be at the L2 server complex near the Citadel.

We arrived back at her house pretty late. Tabitha went upstairs to change her clothes, then she rejoined me in the den. It was obvious she was about to head out again. This girl had amazing stamina for someone who had had only three hours of sleep the night before.

"This involved a genuine Waters, so there's going to be an extensive investigation into it," Tabitha said as she checked her display. "Soon the CCD detention commandant will realize the prisoner transfer was a fabrication. According to protocol, he should notify Director Pythorael, who is presently half a world away in the Central Jurisdiction. I had a few archived messages sent to the Archon hours earlier in response to certain security issues I discovered. He will think I've already been at the L2 server complex investigating the technical security breaches leading to the escape. See, easy peasy."

"Yeah, it's just like ... Boop!" I said, smiling.

"L2 will eventually lock down all the data patterns to build a directive matrix for an investigation. The good news is, it should automatically be assigned to me to investigate, because I gave Pythorael Ryan's name. Brilliant, right?"

I was in awe of what Tabitha had accomplished. "I don't understand why you have to go to the server complex, considering you achieved all this without being there," I said.

"In part, it's to complete my alibi. It's also much easier to execute the cleanup from there, so it won't leave external systems trails. Sit tight. Watch more classic cartoons."

"Wait!" I exclaimed. "I just want to say that you are amazing. I don't know how you orchestrated this whole thing. You're brilliant and you're beautiful. You didn't need me. All I did was screw up the only part of this plan that failed. Then you kicked the crap out of that huge guard who was twice as big as me and three times bigger than you."

Tabitha held up her hand. "Mark, we aren't out of the woods. This is going to make things interesting. When I get back, I need to talk to you about something extremely important. I hope I've started to earn your trust. Between L2, Pythorael, and the Archon, I feel like I'm fighting three monsters—and I created one of them. So in a way, I'm fighting myself. Mark, I can't live with what I've done. You don't understand what L2 can do, especially if the next two phases are completed. I should have done more to stop it when I had the chance. I'm a fool and a coward. I have to fix what I've done; I have to make amends for it."

"Tabitha, there is one thing of which I am certain. You are the bravest person I've ever met. The Archon would have found someone else to do what you did. Maybe it would have taken longer. You can't blame yourself for his intentions."

She started to cry. "I solved the one problem they couldn't. Actually, I solved several. L2 is far more powerful than LEOH. It can learn quickly. It can program itself faster and actively manage complex decision-making processes on a much greater scale. It just hasn't been fully activated to be integrated with. … I read the testing transcript results from the Optimus Project. Mark, it can make people do things. I know what he plans to do with it. Ultimately, he wants to control people by himself and kill the rest of us. It's terrifying and its real and *I'm* guilty. I built what can kill billions of people!"

"Billions? In the stolen data I saw a reference to the population of New City being two nearly billion people, Are there really that many people? That doesn't seem right. What does he want to control people to do?"

"Yes, there are billions, and nearly eight hundred million of them are slaves. And how would I know what he wants to control people to do? I'm not a freaking alien. He can hypnotize people. This is like him doing it to a billion people at the same time."

Tabitha was genuinely sad. I reached out to embrace her to comfort her. She shrank back. I held up my hands. "I was just going to give you a hug," I said, "nothing else." The next thing I knew she was passionately kissing me. I kissed her in return as we embraced, then I pushed her away.

"I can't betray Ari."

Tabitha stepped back. She wiped away her tears. "I'm sorry. I shouldn't have done that." She turned and walked out without saying another word.

I thought, *I have to tell her about what I found in the classified records. She deserves to know what the Archon was doing to her for the last three years. She has to know. I don't want to humiliate her. What if she breaks down? Maybe I shouldn't. I don't even know how to tell Ari or Zack. I need to get rid of it and pretend I never saw it,* I reasoned. *I can't tell her. She would die with embarrassment, or she would kill me after I tell her.*

Then I thought about how she had kicked the snot out of the huge guard while she was wounded. *Normal girls can't do that. Tabitha is not a normal girl!*

CHAPTER 30

THE LOYAL OPPOSITION

Onboard Pythorael's executive jet on the way to Central Jurisdiction Pythorael and Rogan were discussing their plans. Rogan grumbled, "This meeting is a colossal waste of time. We have spent lavishly on them. They possess the land between the Nile and the Euphrates. We've turned it into a true paradise on earth. We are on the verge of completing the most spectacular temple ever conceived. Everything is in accordance with the specifications of their crazy old prophet. Some people can just never be truly satisfied, no matter what you do for them."

"I doubt less than 5 percent of them have even a drop of Jewish blood in their veins," Pythorael scoffed. "Even so, since the Final War they have certainly been enjoying the fruits of their alliance with Elaniel. I warned Elaniel about this. The true reason for this uprising, at least according to the intelligence I have, is that there are factions among them who don't believe what is happening is in accordance with what is written. At least, not to their satisfaction. They are trying to amend the protocols. Even so, I think persuing this delusion is only going to serve to imbalance the scales."

"The protocols aren't prophecy," Rogan blurted out. "They are fictitious guidelines for the implementation of their Zionist vision for the world. We were never obligated to follow them."

Pythorael retorted, "Not those protocols, you fool. I'm referring to those which established the Central Jurisdiction, its governance, and boundaries. The last thing the Archon wants is an armed insurrection in his Garden of Eden. It doesn't matter if it's the best money can buy or by far the largest expenditure among all jurisdictions. He can't overcome the religious issues with these people."

* * * *

Within two hours of their arrival, the New Accord Sanhedrin (NAS) and the Council of Seventy had congregated in a spectacular underground meeting hall excavated beneath the temple mount. As the factions assembled, the meeting was called to order by the Central Jurisdiction's regional governor, Rutherford Van Degen, head of the Ashkenazi faction.

The governor introduced Devan Elaniel. As Elaniel stepped to the podium from behind the dais, a loud murmur arose from the crowd. Pythorael, Rogan, and Complaceal sat near the front, in seats reserved for the council, while most of the NAS sat in the rear of the hall. A wide gap separated either side of the assembly hall to allow for pageantry, the grand entrance of dignitaries and nobles, or other ritualistic displays. Only the governor and the Archon took seats on the dais.

As the Archon rose to speak, the restless crowd quieted. "Let me begin by saying to each of you, as highly regarded and special members of this body, that everyone will have his or her opportunity to be heard. This assembly is only the first of numerous meetings in the coming days, many of which will be held in a much less formal, more comfortable setting. To inaugurate this series of talks, it was agreed by all parties that we should convene here, underneath our magnificent temple. It is even now nearing the final stages of completion."

A man shouted, "Blasphemy!" He was forcibly removed from the assembly.

Elaniel remained calm; his demeanor did not change. "Remember, each of you once swore a blood oath to New City and to me, its ruler, as one of your fellow brothers. This is the last phase of an ancient and historic struggle to bring about the glorious rebirth and vindication of Jerusalem. Everything we have done is so that all that is written about this city and this people will come to pass, whether you are secular or religious.

"From the time of the declaration of the decree to rebuild this city, to the first stone of the foundation of this temple, it has been less than sixty-three years," Elaniel proclaimed. "Yet our struggle has been ongoing for millennia. We have been firm in our agreement that we would endeavor to fulfill the dream that has been handed down to us from the learned elders of ages past. All your enemies have been swept from before you. They have been trampled under your feet. There is no more war or threat of war from any nation or province. We have subdued the nations of the world. We have brought them together under one government and under the power of one city. This city! This nation!

"Make no mistake, the Central Jurisdiction of New City will soon have a new name, as the Israel of God," Elaniel declared. "The whole world will be its kingdom and dominion. Regardless of whether you believe the ancient laws should be fully reestablished, we are, nevertheless, building a glorious capital for New City here. All people will soon look to this temple for spiritual fulfillment, enlightenment, hope, and to the one God for humankind."

Thunderous applause was heard throughout the cavernous hall. The Archon raised his arms to quiet the crowd. "Now, as we near the completion of this temple, our temple, God's temple, we are confronted with the not-so-quiet discontent of those who desire more. They grumble, despite how the deserts bloom and the construction of this new Jerusalem rises from the ashes of war. They grumble, despite this glorious edifice to our accomplishments and our victory over our struggles through the ages. I ask you, who can say God is not with us? Even as I speak, I can declare to you the riches of the world are overflowing into the coffers of this jurisdiction in fulfillment of all that is written about this holy city."

There were more shouts of adoration and praise. Yet many sat stone faced and silent.

The Archon continued, "I was not negligent, nor did I ever forsake our agreement. Israel will rule the world. I promise you, all nations will come to this place to worship. They will henceforth bring gifts and offerings to this temple. Did you not know, your forefathers also worshipped a pantheon of gods in this very chamber? Read your own prophets. They will tell you the truth of what was done in this place. Some of you grumble because we have not done enough to acknowledge these old gods. Some of you grumble because we have not done enough to follow the God of Abraham. But our great cause, whose seed has formed in you, has given birth to a new people of Israel, who are the kings of the earth, for you to rule over the nations."

The Archon looked out over the crowd with a grave expression. "No other people have ever been so favored. I am certain we can reason together over the next few days to come to terms over our petty disagreements. I trust we have far more uniting us, as the glory of Israel is what makes us one.

"I have a few minutes for questions. Then we shall dine together in the new royal banquet hall. It's my understanding the chefs have prepared a magnificent dinner, in accordance with all proper customs."

Many in the crowed once again cheered and shouted.

A short old man of about seventy years of age stood up and introduced himself as a rabbi of the orthodox faction. "I will not trouble you presently with our entire list of grievances. There are irreconcilable differences between those of us who adhere to the orthodox traditions and those elitists, like yourself, on the council, who are steeped in this blasphemous Kabbalistic mysticism and the occult. Those I represent would like to ask you plainly, who you claim to be. There are more rumors about you than there could possibly be truth."

People jeered and shouted, "Insolent fool!"

Undeterred, the rabbi continued, "There are rumors that you intend to proclaim yourself to be the messiah, to bring about the restoration of the kingdom. Others claim you will proclaim yourself to be king. Still others say there is another yet to come. We have both doubts and reservations about you and your longevity. We have waited over three score years for an answer."

The Archon stood still, as if waiting for inspiration. He answered, "First, with respect to your initial comment about myself and some of my fellow devotees as being involved in the occult: Let us wait and see if we cannot, for the most part, remain in agreement about what is truly important. We will discuss matters of the practice of religion, and of faith and doctrine, in a respectful way, later. It is my firm belief that we should allow each person to decide for himself based on the dictates of his conscience."

A mixed chorus of voices started shouting and arguing.

The Archon shouted over them, "I must remind you, the last temple, which was destroyed by the Romans on this site in the first century of the first common era, was dedicated by Herod. You all know he was a man of questionable faith. His views ranged from religious tolerance to paganism, and he was of dubious Jewish pedigree and practice. Nevertheless, he created a glorious masterpiece. He dedicated it to God and the Jewish people. It was accepted and worshipped in by even the strictest pharisaical and religious sects. Now we have a greater temple. The advantage is, it is we who rule the world, instead of it being ruled over by pagan Romans."

The old rabbi shook his head. "There is only one God, one law, and one true religion."

Elaniel said, "I claim nothing beyond what I am entitled to claim. At present, the only position I claim is Archon and the ruler of New City. I intend to give you all you deserve and desire. Yet I must remind you, everything which has taken place, and all which is still yet to come, is by the providence of God. Your traditions and scrolls do not make a complete record of what is written about this question. Neither does your understanding encompass all which must take place. As for now, I intend to remain only to my appointed office."

This back and forth went on for another half hour or so, with the Archon fielding questions from various factions. Finally, there was one last question from the governor himself. "Tell us, Lord Archon, about rumors we have heard, that there are still pockets of those who claim to be Christians and other religious sects roaming freely in the uncontrolled territories, especially near the Southern Jurisdiction. We were led to believe over three decades ago that this menace would soon be eradicated, and there would no longer be any threat from other sects. What do you have to say about this? Are the rumors true?"

The Archon shook his head. He hid his embarrassed frustration at the question. "We have eradicated all Christian and Islamic factions. It is true, there are still pockets of insurgents located in what we call the Dead Zones outside the city walls around various jurisdictions. I would hardly describe these insurgents as religious. More likely they are bandits, and simply prefer not to live in the society we have created for them. I believe you are misinformed. This is a relatively minor security issue, kept well in hand by our various Ministry divisions."

* * * *

Pythorael and Rogan watched these proceedings with disinterest. Then they simultaneously received an alert concerning a potential security breach at the CCD primary detention facility in the SJ, where the fugitives Kirk Daniels and Ryan Waters were being held.

Several prisoners, including Waters and Daniels, had been released under questionable pretense. The commandant of the detention facility requested a direct conference line with the director immediately, to receive instructions on how to proceed with efforts to reacquire the prisoners. The commandant demanded verification that the transfer was initiated pursuant to a jurisdictional change for the prisoners, from the CCD to the High Echelon, by order of the Archon.

It was not clear if the Archon was aware of the situation. Pythorael sent him a message asking for an urgent and private meeting. Moments later, while delegates were still filing out of the meeting hall, the Archon, Prideil, Pythorael, Complaceal, and Rogan gathered in a private room in one of the temple's underground chambers.

Pythorael got right to the point. "Apparently, our Class 1 dissident prisoner and ATO operative, along with the other man we captured in the DZ, have escaped. Someone with a High Echelon security credential issued a prisoner transfer order. The detainees were removed from the CCD detention facility about two hours ago, along with three other unrelated prisoner transfers."

"Why should I give a damn about this at the moment?" the Archon snapped.

"Pythorael elaborated. "The duty chief indicated the credentials overrode all CCD protocols, because they were issued with a High Echelon bearer token, pursuant to a change of oversight authority. I've not had a chance to review all the details."

The Archon shrugged. "This is obviously because the jurisdiction over these prisoners has been transferred to me. I am sure removing them from the CCD detention facility is not unusual."

"How was jurisdiction over these prisoners transferred to you?" Pythorael said.

The Archon held up a finger for Pythorael to wait as he checked his messages. There was string of communications from ēlan Tabitha. The first had arrived four hours earlier.

It read: "Received a validation security alert on L2 system ... apparent breach into bearer token credentialing subroutine ... not familiar with this ... still checking on what is compromised."

One hour later he had received another message: "Running a diagnostic on questionable release of the Daniels girl ... plugged into CCD detainee control system. A pending bearer token transfer is active ... set to authorize transfer of several prisoners ... preliminary indications are false NCSS credentials used to obtain release of the Daniels girl ... still researching ... should I redirect efforts to investigate CCD matter further?"

An hour later, another message from Tabitha: "Received notification from CCD detention control module … confirming suspected false prisoner transfer involving the two recent DZ detainees and three others is directly related to bearer token credentialing breach … unauthorized ghosted access codes used in both incidents involving the Daniels girl and false prisoner transfer credentials … should I investigate? Time is critical … please advise."

With her last communication Tabitha attached a thoroughly detailed analysis of what she had discovered so far about each of these events.

After scanning Tabitha's communications and analysis, the Archon was furious. "Apparently, another ghosted access code was used to access the HE credentials platform. Shortly thereafter, a bearer token was issued to initiate a phony prisoner transfer to override the CCD detainee controls for our two DZ fugitives. My L2 project director is now expanding her investigation to include this matter."

Pythorael said, "Expand what investigation? How could she know this? I only received a communication from the detention center commandant ten minutes ago. I can't even remember the last time a credentialed bearer token was used for a prisoner transfer."

The Archon took a seat at a small conference table in the room. "You know very well that she's investigating the initial data breach and the situation involving Mark Verigratu. I also asked her to run a diagnostic analysis on the circumstances surrounding the release of the Daniels girl from a facility two days ago. The latest communication I received from her was time stamped almost two hours ago; she alerted me about this incident four hours ago."

Pythorael glanced around, clearly frustrated. "While I can't explain why it took so long for the commandant to notify me, I don't understand how or why she is even involved in this."

Pythorael added, "The CCD is already looking into the release of the Daniels girl. I read the latest case directives. There is a communication trail a mile long. We've already detained three people involved. I wouldn't say the case is closed, because we haven't located the girl yet.

We believe we have the people involved. This kind of kidnapping scheme routinely happens at these institutions. I see no reason to involve the ēlan in this or in any CCD detainee matters, especially one involving the two other fugitives."

The Archon crossed his arms. "If you haven't been notified yet, know that these captured fugitives are no longer under your jurisdiction."

"I realize that. Why would authority over these prisoners be transferred to you? There is no reason for this, under any circumstances," Pythorael said.

The Archon glared at him. "It's because you're an incompetent fool. All security directives related to these access code infiltrations, Mark Verigratu, and Zachariah Waters are under my authority. This means they are now under the authority of ēlan Tabitha, who is personally assisting me in these investigations. This includes any matters related to these fugitives, who, by virtue of your findings, are connected in any way to anyone with the last name Waters. Clearly, she is always four steps ahead of you, or in this case, four hours."

"That's absurd," Pythorael sputtered. "She's an arrogant rich brat who can't investigate anything."

"Apparently, she is far more aware of what's going on right under the nose of the Ministry than you are, director," the Archon said. "She knows the NCSS credentials used to obtain the release of the Daniels girl were likely counterfeit. I am thus convinced she should take charge of this and triage all of the LEOH security directives on these events."

Prideil shook his head in disgust. "She is as untrustworthy as it gets. For all we know she orchestrated this escape. She has access to everything. If anyone could have created false credentials or a fake bearer token it would be her. She could be in league with Mark Verigratu and Zack Waters. You can't put this girl in charge of investigating anything related to this."

The Archon snapped at Prideil, "The perpetrator used ghosted access codes to infiltrate the system, you imbecile. Yet, let me get this straight. You suspect the ēlan for this? Only two weeks ago it was she who was furious because she was never informed about the existence of these codes. It was she who pointed out the far-reaching implications of this systemic control failure. She was the one who repeatedly argued against migrating the security and credential platform from LI to L2. She was the one who complained that L2 was prematurely rushed, contrary to her express and repeated recommendations to rebuild the entire security platform."

The Archon gazed at Prideil as he leaned forward and pointed to Pythorael. "Let me remind you Nathan; it was your true liege, Pythorael, who is solely responsible for the creation of these codes and their subsequent proliferation when the ēlan was a toddler. Am I supposed to suspect her in the creation and spread of these access codes when she was unable to read and drinking from a sippy cup? Am I supposed to believe she smuggled the necessary stolen technology out of a Ministry R&D facility before she was born in order to carry out this theft?

"Ēlan Tabitha has only met Mr. Verigratu twice and Zack Waters once. She met Mark for the first time well after the initial data breach and after he returned from the DZ. She has also been living in my Citadel at Interlochen for the last three years. She wasn't in the Southern Jurisdiction when the data was stolen. Am I supposed to believe she was in league with them when this happened? She is investigating them and trying to infiltrate them for me!"

The Archon continued to fume. He turned to Pythorael. "I am convinced our entire system is at risk, but not because of her involvement. Rather, it is because I failed to follow her explicit and insightful recommendations. It was your failure to inform her of the very risk we face. You are the one to blame for this situation, Dalen!"

Pythorael was clearly embarrassed by this sharp rebuke. "Lord Archon, may I point out ..."

"No, you may not point out anything! Do not presume to tell me whom I should trust when it is clear your Ministry has been bamboozled for years by an organization responsible for turning our security apparatus into a leaking sieve. May *I* point out, this organization is also capable of physically infiltrating our supposedly secure surveillance stations in the DZ. They have been doing so for years. Did you even read the report the ēlan prepared on what Mark Verigratu encountered at the 4UB6 facility?"

"For all we know, Verigratu conspired with those who breached 4UB6," Pythorael retorted.

The Archon continued to rant. "Do not tell me Mark was in cahoots with them. He was assigned to that project by Merrick Taylor. Let's go over the other evidence against Mark Verigratu, shall we? He's married to the great-granddaughter of a sickly, ninety-three-year-old former deputy director of the CCD, who he meets one day before he interviews for a job at the Ministry. That's it! He is cleared by no less than two chemical interrogations, including one conducted by you. Nothing was found at his apartment, despite it being searched three times. My own L2 project lead has found no evidence of a conspiracy involving him. I recognize a scapegoat when I see one. I can also see a treasonous fool who tries to frame someone to avoid taking responsibility for his own incompetence and treachery. And don't get me started on the GIA profile matrix corruption over the years."

The Archon slammed his fist on the table. "All this is due to your utter incompetence, Dalen, or perhaps your purposeful intent! I should have listened to ēlan Tabitha when she suspected you were conspiring against me from the outset."

Pythorael tried to calm the Archon. "I understand your lack of confidence in me and the Ministry. I admit some responsibility for this. I made a serious error in judgment years ago in the matter of creation of these access codes. But ēlan Tabitha is now the only one capable of masking her own movements and identity, with the credentials you authorized for her. She has wormed her way into your confidence and blinded you. You fail to see how dangerous she has become."

"Are you referring to how dangerous you thought ēlan Tabitha would become when you attempted to have her murdered before she was born? Are you talking about how dangerous you thought the K15 project was when you had the evidence of its destruction purged from the system and covered up? Perhaps you are talking about how dangerous she is to you now, because she has exposed what an incompetent, treacherous, treasonous, lying scoundrel you are. Perhaps you are talking about how dangerous she would be when she discovered how you used the ghosted access keys to create spybots to cover up your deeds and your spying activities against me and other members of the NCIC. Perhaps you are mainly concerned, despite all of your efforts, that I still intend to carry out my plans with her."

The Archon stood up to leave. "I am placing Tabitha in charge of all of this above the NCIC. You will not observe or interfere with her any further on this. It surprises me that you lack an understanding of what is taking place here, Lord Pythorael."

Pythorael was appalled at the Archon's words. "I am merely concerned with your blind obsession with her. She may rather become the one who destroys you—and all of us. I beg you to reconsider this course of action. Allow me to regain control over LEOH. What if she isn't a true Norean? At the very least, you should have a carmelineal read her. Prideil is too weak and you are not as skilled in this practice since you are now weakened in this sphere."

Elaniel's wrath intensified. "Your perceived freedom to profess your opinions to me comes at the peril of being obliterated." With a flourish of the tip of a finger, he caused Pythorael to rise in the air, half a meter from the floor, then slammed him hard against the wall of the chamber. He pinned him there; it was as if a hidden hand were grasping Pythorael's throat and squeezing it. "So, you believe my powers are weak? I can crush you as easily as I can obliterate you. Each day, I become increasingly more powerful as I turn what is written to my favor."

Pythorael dropped to the floor, grasping at his throat and struggling for air. As he staggered to his feet, he saw the door to the chamber shut as Devan Elaniel left. In exasperation, he looked at Complaceal, Rogan, and Prideil. They were all shaken. He rubbed his throat and said with a raspy voice, "I didn't realize he retained so much control over the craft.

I fear my overconfidence in believing I could persuade Tabitha Norean to work for me has resulted in her turning him against me. I think it is time that we get rid of her—permanently."

* * * *

Back at the hotel, in Pythorael's luxurious suite, he convened a meeting with his co-conspirators. His mind worked quickly. "My spybots have informed me the ēlan will soon be traveling to her family's home in the Highlands district. She is continuing her so-called 'investigation' of Mark Verigratu and Zachariah Waters."

"Obviously, he isn't yet convinced of their innocence," said Prideil.

"Exactly," said Dalen. "The recent captive we are holding at our clandestine facility provides us with a unique opportunity to rid ourselves of the ēlan and her influence over the Archon. At the same time, we may be able to successfully infiltrate the ATO organization by using the identity of our prisoner."

Rogan was confused. "Do you really believe she had something to do with this escape?"

"It doesn't matter whether she had anything to do with it."

Rogan shook his head in bewilderment. "Jack Wasser may not be Zachariah Waters."

Pythorael said, "I know Zach Waters is dirty and so is Mark Verigratu. I also believe ēlan Tabitha has switched sides and is helping them, if for no other reason than to spite me. They are all likely in league with the ATO. I realize this is a hasty plan. However, if successful, this will end this annoying K15 loose end for good."

"What makes you confident she is conspiring with these people?" Prideil said.

Pythorael erupted. "How do you think she stole jurisdiction over these prisoners and convinced a remote HESF detention facility that a bearer token drop for a prisoner transfer was legitimate? She gave me Robert Ryan Waters' name, fool! She wrote the damn protocol. She knew that when I updated the matrix for this it would automatically transfer oversight of these prisoners to her, via the Archon. I don't know how she knew, but she did. My guess is Mark Verigratu must have given her the man's real name. He met the man in the DZ! And yet, I can't be certain Mark was the source, because the girl also stole my authority to interview him. He's the sole survivor of a failed CCD operation where a Ministry facility was infiltrated and destroyed, yet I'm barred from debriefing him. Treacherous bitch!"

Pythorael turned to Complaceal. "It is time for you to pay a visit to Valen, our old companion in Rome. I am going to have our carmelineal released. I contemplated this the moment we captured the ATO mercenary, Nick Chancery. It is why I had him transferred to our black ops station in the Highlands."

"This could work, but you are taking a huge risk," Rogan warned him.

Pythorael replied, "The one whose oath I possess can do far more than become our eyes and ears. That ēlan's deviousness will be no match for a carmelineal's cunning and skill."

Prideil cautioned Pythorael, "As one who was among their number at one time, I think you are making a grave mistake by releasing this man. There is a risk in doing this that cannot be overlooked. He will use his powers of possession. You know the prohibitions against this. Although he is bound by an oath of obedience to you, no oath can prevent him from exercising this power. Their kind also have a connection to the Archon that could prove equally dangerous. This girl isn't enough of a threat to risk releasing such a creature. What if she is receiving help by our true enemies from another sphere?"

Pythorael contemplated this as he stood before his three companions. "She is not receiving any help from *them*. I would know. She is doing this on her own. Even so, the Archon is obviously blind to her disloyalty. She believes she can resist him when the time comes. I doubt she is even aware of how he has conditioned her. With her power, he plans to transit the ethereal spheres again to control all of us. On the other hand, should she overcome him, she could take his powers in this sphere from him."

"Valen will not hesitate to kill her if so ordered," Complaceal said. "If she truly is what Elaniel believes she is, she will be more vulnerable to a carmelineal than she will be to Elaniel. They can sense other humans who have connections to the higher spheres."

That vulnerability works both ways," Prideil warned them. "Don't forget, I was overcome by one with this kind of power; that's how I ended up in the pit."

CHAPTER 31

THE AWAKENING

Tabitha's decision to incriminate Dalen Pythorael by convincing the Archon that he was working against him was only part of her strategy to divide them and isolate the Ministry. She realized she was about to bring the Archon's wrath down on Pythorael. She knew this, even as she transmitted the carefully redacted transcripts of their private conversations. The Archon would now know what Pythorael had told her about his plans for her. She was convinced the man had attempted to murder her before she was born. She added her conclusions about what a deadly nemesis he was.

She contemplated the reasons Pythorael was so terrified of her existence. Her clarion insight was not, in this instance, revealing. The bizarre ritual he claimed the Archon wanted to undertake with her on her upcoming birthday made her increasingly uncomfortable. Unfortunately, she had no idea of the extent to which Devan Elaniel had conditioned her and controlled her.

As she prepared to leave the L2 server complex she decided to check the trace on Pythorael's private plane. She wanted to find out if he was returning to the SJ to deal with the prisoner escape. Her curiosity was aroused when she saw where the plane had been. This might be something the Archon would be interested to know. She included this in her last updated com to him.

Tabitha knew Mark was probably up by now, and would be anxious to leave. She gathered her things and headed back to the house. She wanted to make certain they left before her parents returned from one of their homes in the Western Jurisdiction. She hadn't slept in a day, and she was in intense pain from her wound.

On the way she began to cry, but not because of the pain. She was heartbroken and lonely, and she felt guilty for everything she'd done. She pulled up the latest results from an algorithm that she kept continuously running—and noticed an astonishing result. She doublechecked her findings and realized something extraordinary. If what she'd seen was true, she was caught up in something beyond what any ordinary circumstance could explain. It was as if her entire life had been leading to this moment. Perhaps Zack was right—she had been born as an ēlan in the House of Norean for a time such as this.

* * * *

I had done what Zack wanted. I had stolen classified data that would expose the Archon's plans. In the process, I'd inadvertently lured his venomous spider to him. Zack knew this strange, clever girl was the key to overthrowing the Archon, as well as to revealing his secret plans to the world. But Zack didn't know his spider was caught up in her own inescapable web, as was I. He only knew it was up to Ari to save Tabitha from herself and convince her of who she truly was.

I contemplated how this alluring ēlan had turned out to be my wife's twin. Everything had come together from Zack's interpretation of Ari's dreams. I knew one thing was certain: Ari was terrified of Tabitha and of what she was about to do. She had a vision into the future that included enormous death and destruction.

I remembered what Ari told me about her dream of a shattered reflection just before she met Tabitha: *She is going to take you by the hand, to lead you where you don't want to go or shouldn't. Whoever she is, she's bringing a storm, especially upon you. She's not who you think she is, or there may be more than one of her.*

I kept thinking about what Bob, or rather, Ryan Waters, had told me. Ari had another sister. I was certain of it, even if Zack wasn't aware of her. There was another girl identical to Ari and Tabitha somewhere in New City. I also knew we had to find her, and quickly, and so did Ari. It was her dream, to find them all.

To be continued ...

I hope you enjoyed this book. Would you do me a favor?

Like all authors, I rely on online reviews to encourage future sales. Your opinion is invaluable. Would you take a few moments now to share your assessment of my book at the review site of your choice? Your opinion will help the book marketplace become more transparent and useful to all.

Thank you very much!

Made in United States
North Haven, CT
03 January 2022

14173896R00214